PYRAMID

SCHEME

BAEN BOOKS by DAVE FREER & ERIC FLINT
Rats, Bats & Vats
Pyramid Scheme

BAEN BOOKS by ERIC FLINT
Mother of Demons
1632
The Philosophical Strangler

The Belisarius series, with David Drake:
An Oblique Approach
In the Heart of Darkness
Destiny's Shield
Fortune's Stroke
The Tide of Victory

The Federation of the Hub series,
by James H. Schmitz, edited by Eric Flint:
Telzey Amberdon
T'nT: Telzey & Trigger
Trigger & Friends
The Hub: Dangerous Territory
Agent of Vega & Other Stories (forthcoming)

BAEN BOOKS by DAVE FREER
The Forlorn

PYRAMID

SCHEME

DAVE FREER
ERIC FLINT

PYRAMID SCHEME

This is a work of fiction. All the characters and events portrayed in this book are fictional, and any resemblance to real people or incidents is purely coincidental.

A Baen Books Original

Baen Publishing Enterprises
P.O. Box 1403
Riverdale, NY 10471
www.baen.com

ISBN: 0-671-31839-X

Cover art by Bob Eggleton
Interior maps by Randy Asplund

First printing, October 2001

Library of Congress Cataloging-in-Publication Data

Freer, Dave.
  Pyramid scheme / by Dave Freer & Eric Flint.
    p. cm.
  "A Baen Books original—T.p. verso.
  ISBN 0-671-31839-X
  1. Human–alien encounters—Fiction. 2. Chicago (Ill.)—Fiction.
  3. Mythology—Fiction. 4. Pyramids—Fiction. I. Flint, Eric. II. Title.

PS3556.R3935 P9 2001
813'.54—dc21   2001035798

Distributed by Simon & Schuster
1230 Avenue of the Americas
New York, NY 10020

Production by Windhaven Press, Auburn, NH
Printed in the United States of America

10   9   8   7   6   5   4   3   2   1

To L. Sprague de Camp and Fletcher Pratt,
who are gone;
And to Zachary, who just arrived.

When 'Omer smote 'is bloomin' lyre,
He'd 'eard men sing by land an' sea;
An' what he thought he might require,
'E went an' took—

Rudyard Kipling,
Introduction to the *Barrack-Room Ballads*
in "The Seven Seas"

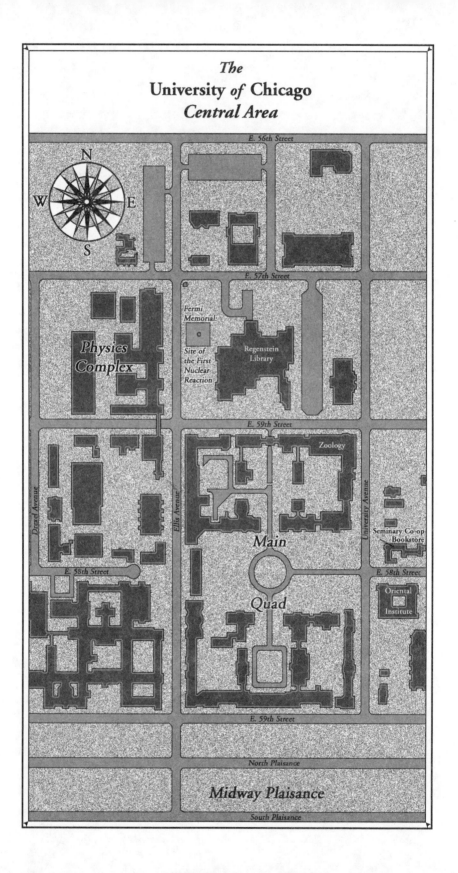

The
University *of* Chicago
Central Area

E. 56th Street

N
W — E
S

E. 57th Street

Fermi Memorial:

Physics Complex

Site of the First Nuclear Reaction

Regenstein Library

E. 59th Street

Zoology

Drexel Avenue

Ellis Avenue

University Avenue

Main

Seminary Co-op Bookstore

E. 58th Street

E. 58th Street

Quad

Oriental Institute

E. 59th Street

North Plaisance

Midway Plaisance

South Plaisance

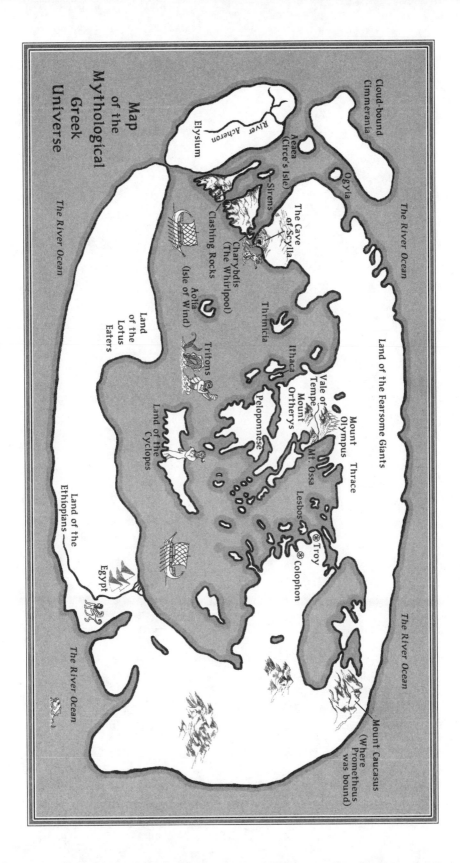

Map
of the
Mythological
Greek
Universe

Cloud-bound
Cimmeriania

River Acheron

Elysium

Aeaea
(Circe's Isle)

Ogygia

Sirens

The Cave
of Scylla

Charybdis
(The Whirlpool)

Clashing Rocks

Aeolia
(Isle of Wind)

Thrinicia

Tritons

Land
of the
Lotus
Eaters

The River Ocean

Land of the Fearsome Giants

Ithaca

Vale of
Tempe

Mount
Olympus

Mount
Ortherys

Mt. Ossa

Peloponnese

Thrace

Lesbos

Troy

Colophon

Land
of the
Cyclopes

Land of the
Ethiopians

Egypt

The River Ocean

Mount Caucasus
(Where
Prometheus
was bound)

The River Ocean

The River Ocean

PROLOGUE

The new NESOT (Near Earth Space Object Tracking) satellite paid dividends less than three months after its launch. The computerized system spat a data stream on the incoming object to NORAD. It did this for any detected object which would enter the Earth's atmosphere.

The level of NORAD tracking which dealt with objects that should burn up on atmospheric entry was computerized. An alarm sequence was triggered by any anomaly. Twenty-three seconds after it took over from NESOT, the alarm sounded.

Brigadier General Durham looked over the shoulder of the warrant officer at the screen display. He took a deep breath. *Chicago!*

He took another deep breath. The procedures were laid down. It had been something of a joke. But the NESOT data showed that it wasn't a joke. Not *at all* funny, in reality. This was incoming from deep space. And it was decelerating. Falling objects don't naturally do that.

Incoming. Incoming and *alien*.

While on its final approach, the American Airlines flight inbound from New York abruptly lost radio and radar contact

1

for fifteen seconds with Chicago O'Hare's Tower Approach Control. The explosive reactions of the pilot were mild compared to those at Chicago Air Traffic Control. And those in turn were mild compared to the reaction at Cheyenne Mountain.

They'd lost the object. And they'd lost all radio contact with Chicago. Fortunately the fiber-optic link between Cheyenne Mountain and Chicago Air Traffic Control remained functional.

Air traffic controllers are renowned for their imperturbability. The senior ATC on the other end of the line managed a perfectly controlled level voice—that could have etched steel.

"NORAD? Ah! *Right.* Are you folks doing something we need to know about? Because we just nearly lost a fully loaded heavy." Despite the angry tinge underlying her voice, the controller wasn't actually snarling. Not quite. NORAD and Air Traffic Control centers worked closely together and were generally on good terms.

Brigadier General Durham was able to reassure himself that whatever had happened, it hadn't included destroying Chicago. But he was quite unable to reassure the woman on the other end of the line that it wouldn't happen again. NORAD had no more idea than she did what had caused the temporary radio blackout.

"I've already got two companies from the 101st on their way from Fort Campbell. They're only four hundred miles away and can get there in their own Blackhawks. But I want the entire 82nd mobilized and ready to go. That's going to require—"

"Goddamn it, Fred," snarled the National Security Council's representative, Tom Harkness. "According to your own satellite data, the object has an estimated maximum diameter of four to six feet. This isn't *Independence Day*, for Christ's sake, or *War of the Worlds.*"

Harkness rubbed the sleep from his eyes, scowling fiercely. Clearly enough, he had *not* appreciated being awakened from a sound sleep for this—this—

Harkness' lip curled into a slight sneer. The expression had a well-practiced air about it. "*If* the thing isn't some kind of prank in the first place—and I'm smelling *hoax* here."

An idle thought flashed through General Brasno's mind. *Takes one to know one.* But he restrained himself manfully. Harkness was continuing to speak.

"So I can't see telling the President at this point that he should send in more than a token force of paratroopers. Mainly just to reassure any agitated local officials that the government is on its toes."

General Brasno had dealt with Harkness before. Unfortunately. He sometimes thought the NSC official's conception of reality was that it was a spin created by a public relations campaign. Presumably for the sake of creating an audience.

"If it *is* real—*if,* I say—then it's bound to be a *friendly* first contact, not an attack." Harkness pointed a dramatic finger and wagged it in his best professorial manner. "You can't cram an invasion force into something that size. And we don't want to *start* a goddamn war—or trigger off a major panic."

General Brasno folded his arms across his chest. "You don't scramble friendly communications either. *That* is a pathfinder. Either a pathfinder or a Von Neumann-type machine, capable of replication. Which means one machine is all you need for a geometric progression of invaders. If that thing shows any sign of replication we need to have adequate personnel to deal with it."

Harkness shook his head stubbornly. "You do *not* have authorization at the moment to do anything more than send in those two companies from the 101st." The NSC man glanced at his watch. "And now I've got to catch a plane, in order to get a first hand look at this so-called 'UFO.'"

As soon as he was gone, General Brasno was on the phone to the commander of the 82nd Airborne. "George? It's me again. They won't agree to sending you in yet. But I want you ready to go at a moment's notice."

He hung up the phone and scowled at one of his aides. "Pity those poor bastards in the 101st, if anything goes wrong. Two companies!"

PART I

—as the blasts
of loosened tempest, such the tumult seemed!

—The Bhagavadgita

1

░░░░░░░

NO BORROWER MAY REMOVE
MORE THAN THREE BOOKS.

The silence was all a fussy librarian could have wished for. It was 2:29 A.M. and the second floor of the Regenstein Library was deserted and dark . . . except for the prowling flashlight.

They had said that the noise came from here. . . .

The security guard thought it was probably nothing. There'd been no external alarms—just some "weird noise" the two cleaning women claimed to have heard coming from somewhere in the general bookstacks in the west wing.

The guard rounded the corner, and halted in his tracks. Shredded books lay scattered around the bizarre-looking object. The surrounding shelves hadn't just been knocked down. The force of the thing's arrival had crumpled the metal shelving as if they had been made of aluminum foil. He started to turn away . . .

From the apex of the five-sided black pyramid, a beam of violet light engulfed him. Briefly. Then there was no one there to engulf.

The Krim device expanded, covering some of the debris generated by its arrival. It was nearly sixty yards off target, but the probe

7

was not concerned. That was a perfectly acceptable margin of error for a journey through a wormhole, across 2740 light-years.

The apex of the pyramid was now almost against the ceiling. Yet the object couldn't have been very heavy. The crumpled paper it rested on was scarcely dented.

"There's no sign of the entry control officer," came the voice of the University of Chicago policeman, crackling over the radio. "Except a plate of gyros on his desk. The cleaning women say he went up to the second floor quite a while ago. Probably nothing to get excited about."

Lieutenant Solms scowled and exchanged glances with the dispatcher. Then spoke into the radio: "Stavros, you *always* think it's 'nothing to get excited about.' Do your job, dammit. You've got Hawkins for backup."

The dispatcher rolled her eyes. *Backup,* her lips mouthed, exuding silent sarcasm. Solms' own lips quirked appreciatively. The University of Chicago police lieutenant was the watch commander. Of all the officers under his command, those were the two he often found himself wishing fervently would take an early retirement. A *very* early retirement.

"Go see what's up," Solms ordered into the phone. "And report back as soon as you can."

Solms straightened and sighed. "I'd better go down there myself. What the hell, the Regenstein Library's only a block away. I'll just walk it."

He headed for the door. "Stavros is probably right, but—"

The dispatcher snorted. "Those two clowns could screw up buttering bread."

The U of C police cruiser was parked in front of the Regenstein. Neither Stavros nor Hawkins was in it. Solms marched through the front entrance and looked around. The wide and open ground level was well lit. Everything seemed perfectly normal, except for the abandoned entry control desk. The two cleaning women had apparently left.

Solms headed for the stairs on the left leading up to the stacks.

When he got to the landing, he spotted a flashlight lying on the floor. It was the same type of flashlight he was holding himself.

Belonged to Stavros or Hawkins. He turned his head and looked down the stairs. His eyes ranged over the ground floor, most of which was open to his gaze, searching for a body anywhere.

Nothing. *Like one of them dropped it while they were running— but if that's the case, where are they now?*

He shifted the flashlight to his left hand and drew his gun. Then, slowly and carefully, finished the climb to the second floor and started searching through the maze of stacks.

Solms showed that he hadn't forgotten what he'd learned as a regular street cop, when he saw the pyramid. Something about that black thing said: *your next step on your way to somewhere else could be much farther than you want to go.*

Then, when he got outside and reached Stavros and Hawkins' cruiser, he showed his political smarts too. Had he still been on the city of Chicago's own police force, of course, he would have called in for backup right away. And he still had every intention of doing so—*after* he notified the university's own officials.

Solms was savvy about how things worked, officially . . . and unofficially. He'd seen the University of Chicago Police as a good career, and after he transferred from the CPD he discovered he had a sharp nose for campus politics. Whatever that thing was, the University administration would be furious if they didn't get word of it first.

The Chicago Police Department routinely monitored radio calls made by the U of C police. Solms got out of the cruiser and went back into the library. Leaning over the entry control desk, he snagged the phone and called the dispatcher.

"Marilyn, get me Professor Miguel Tremelo on the line. Patch it through to here. There's something screwy in the Regenstein. Then I want some backup—and ask the CPD to send a few cruisers too. But don't do it until *after* I talk with Tremelo and give you the okay."

Miggy Tremelo was still more of a scientist than an administrator. Once he'd had a thirty second look at the object, his training and instincts came to the fore. "Just keep everyone out, Lieutenant," he said, achieving an evenness of tone that amazed even himself. "I need to make a call. I'll go across to my office in High Energy Physics."

"You can phone from here, Professor," Lieutenant Solms offered.

"It's more convenient from my office," Tremelo lied transparently. "It isn't going to take me five minutes to get over there."

He walked off with a speed that belied both his calm tone and his age. Professor Tremelo was a widower, and he had time on his quick walk to the lab to feel a moment's gladness that his wife Jenny wasn't around to see the havoc wreaked in the bookstacks. Jenny had been the head librarian of the Regenstein, and had taken bibliophilia to the point of near-obsession.

By the time the university president's Lexus got there, the Regenstein's grounds were swarming with cops—both university and regular CPD varieties—and six excited physicists were trying to manhandle a portable industrial X-ray unit up the Regenstein's entryway. The Chicago officers were fussing about "disturbing evidence," and Tremelo was attempting to explain that X-rays wouldn't disturb anything. They were getting a little heated about it. Meanwhile, Lieutenant Solms' university cops had brought some yellow police line and carefully cordoned off the area.

O'Ryan had already spoken on the phone to his friend the mayor, and his face was very pale. Very pale indeed. Finding Mayor Caithorne wide awake at four in the morning had been alarming. Finding out *why* had been even more so.

The university president hadn't gotten to his position without being able to exhibit forcefulness when necessary. Before too long, he had reassured the police that no evidence would be destroyed *but* that they really needed to let Professor Tremelo and his physicists proceed.

"The FBI will be here in a few minutes. Now, listen. I've just been speaking to the mayor. The Pentagon is already onto this. That *thing* is some kind of satellite. Or something. And it isn't one of ours. Obviously they want this kept out of the media for as long as possible. It's a national security matter already."

Solms nodded. "We've got the area secured. But I have a problem, sir. Two of my officers are missing. And so is a security guard. We need to get forensics in here ASAP. And we'd better call the bomb squad as well, in case that thing is dangerous."

The university president fought down an anxiety-driven angry response, reminding himself firmly that Solms was just a good cop doing his job. Then, in a carefully controlled voice, O'Ryan said: "I suggest you wait until the FBI get here. Apparently they're already on their way. After all, they might just have run away or be absent from their posts for a few minutes . . . *mightn't they?*"

Solms looked stubborn. "Stavros and Hawkins are useless slobs, sir. But police crime-scene procedures have to be followed in something like this, or we're treading on a very fine legal line." Two of the regular Chicago officers echoed their agreement.

The president looked at his watch. He sighed. "Lieutenant, the federal government will have some men to take it out of here before first light anyway. Then your investigation can proceed as normal."

Lieutenant Solms' father was a builder by trade. As a result Solms knew something about bricks and mortar. And if they could get that thing out of the building without knocking down a few walls, he was a Dutchman's maiden aunt.

2

॰॒॒॒॒॒॰

A BIBLIOPHILE'S PROGRESS.

At the same time that Dr. Jerry Lukacs was looking blearily into the mirror in his cluttered apartment in Hyde Park, a party was boarding a military aircraft in Washington. The NSC had dispatched Tom Harkness to go to Chicago and inspect the "object."

Washington had been through mild panic, and had now slipped into skepticism. The magic word was spreading—*hoax*—and since Harkness had done more of the spreading than anyone, he got tagged for the assignment.

He strode aboard the aircraft with confidence. And why not? Tom Harkness hadn't climbed this far up the NSC ladder by not finding exactly what he'd been told to find. . . .

Not one of the team of hangers-on and Pentagon desk jockeys boarding with Harkness had ever allowed themselves to look like Jerry Lukacs. Not even first thing in the morning. Jerry tugged at the almost-goatee on his chin. He must buy some razor blades again. Really must. He didn't even notice the disordered bush of hair. If he had noticed it, he'd have chuckled and said "medusoid" and left it at that. Jerry was

13

possibly the most unsartorially elegant person in the entire universe.

He dressed his scrawny body by guess, and with some difficulty. He was trying to read at the time—Jerry was usually trying to read at *any* time—and the clothes kept getting in the way of the book. It was only with great reluctance, and great haste, that he tore his eyes away from the print from time to time to finish his vestmental chore.

Finally, he was clad in clean jeans, unmatched socks, a shirt and a windbreaker. The prerequisites of not being arrested for public indecency being fulfilled, he wandered into the kitchen for a cup of black coffee and a bowl of cornflakes. He was still reading as he went. But, since he was familiar with the layout of his apartment, he did manage to avoid bumping into corners. Or, at least, to turn head-on collisions into glancing encounters.

Once in the kitchen, alas, he discovered that there was almost no coffee left. And, while there was a full box of cereal, there wasn't more than half a cup of milk left in the carton. Jerry was as absentminded about grocery shopping as he was about getting dressed.

He peered peevishly at the note pinned to the refrigerator door with a small magnet. *Must buy more milk. Really must. Coffee too. Razor blades.*

Jerry sighed. Then, steeling himself to necessity, he set the book down on the counter—carefully marking his place with a fork— and set to work. Fortunately, long experience had inured him to such hardships. He rather fancied himself a kitchen survivalist, in point of fact.

Old coffee grounds with a spoon full of new coffee on top will work, after all. And this wasn't the first time he'd turned insufficient milk into impromptu skim milk by simply adding water to his cereal. As he ate his breakfast, the reopened book propped against the laid-flat cereal box, Jerry even congratulated himself on improving the healthfulness of his diet.

On the flight from Washington, Tom Harkness complained about not having real cream for his coffee.

✧   ✧   ✧

Jerry Lukacs headed out for the Oriental Institute. Most people had long been at work already, but, well, he was pretty near nocturnal.

His progress was slow, of course, since he was still reading the book. Fortunately, with the honed skills of a rabid reader, Jerry had an almost instinctive sense for when he was approaching an intersection. A quick glance was enough to check the traffic light. Green, he marched across, still reading. Red, he waited. If he was lucky, and someone else was also waiting at the corner, he didn't even have to glance up to see when the light changed. He just started walking whenever he sensed the person next to him go into motion.

As usual, therefore, he missed the scenery of the University of Chicago's rather charming environs. As one of America's older universities, the U of C had grown up inside a city rather than on a set-aside campus. Except for the central quad adjoining the Oriental Institute, the university's grounds were intermixed with the city's Hyde Park neighborhood. The end result was a kind of cosmopolitan pastiche of staid old college buildings and far less staid commercial establishments.

But Jerry, this day as on most, didn't notice any of it. He also, of course, failed to notice the unusual number of police vehicles cruising the area. He was far too preoccupied with his dissection of *this idiot thesis!* advanced by Professor Kilmer concerning the origins of the sphinx mythology prevalent throughout the ancient eastern Mediterranean.

The Oriental Institute was only two blocks away from the Regenstein Library. By the time Jerry reached the steps leading up into the Institute, the population density of police vehicles resembled an ant hill. But Jerry was oblivious to it all.

As Jerry Lukacs walked through the entrance to the Oriental Institute, Lamont Jackson opened up his toolbox, down in the air handler room of the same building. It was a noisy place, buried in the middle of the large edifice. Lamont was one of the university's mechanical repairmen. He was usually the one sent to the Institute whenever a job needed to be done. He was the acknowledged expert on all aspects of maintenance in that particular building.

To a large degree, the reputation was due to Lamont's general level of skill. But Lamont also engaged in shameless self-promotion whenever repair work needed to be done at the Institute. Lamont was fond of working in that building, for a variety of reasons. For one thing, over the years he had found himself becoming fascinated with the work they did there. In his own eclectic way, the maintenance mechanic had developed a level of knowledge concerning ancient history and mythology which would have astonished the academics who worked at the Oriental Institute.

Well, except one—Jerry Lukacs. Which was the second reason Lamont was looking forward to the day's work. The absent-minded Dr. Lukacs, Lamont had discovered, was not given in the least to putting on professorial airs when talking with a mere repairman. The visiting professor seemed to find nothing odd in Lamont's interest. The fact that a man with no better than a high school diploma should be both informed and curious about mythology didn't seem to strike Dr. Lukacs as odd. He seemed to assume everyone would know the Gilgamesh legend and the tales of Homer. Well, he obviously wasn't born and raised in Chicago's south side! And the professor shared Lamont's own enthusiasm for that lowest of all literary art forms: the pun. Later that day, Lamont would wander up to Dr. Lukacs' office on the third floor. They'd enjoy a few minutes' worth of punstery. Since their last exchange, Lamont had thought up several new word-plays. Ancient names and terminology gave you a lot of scope.

For the most part, however, Lamont enjoyed working in the Oriental Institute's air handler room for another reason. He could play music—to which he was even more devoted than puns—and play it loudly. The air handler room was isolated from everything else, as well as being noisy in its own right. So nobody could hear the music and complain.

Lamont had always found that Tina Turner and a nice collection of jazz improved any work environment immensely. So, pulling out his tools, he began his day's labor with a willing spirit. Five minutes later he was oblivious to the outside world. The demands of the job itself, and the loudness of the air handler room, isolated him. So did Miles Davis' *Sketches of Spain*, played at a respectable level.

Dr. Elizabeth De Beer, sitting at her desk in the nearby building which headquartered the University of Chicago's biologists, was also completely oblivious to the rest of the world. The cause, in her case, was grief.

It was a quiet kind of grief. More in the way of melancholy than anguish. Liz had long known that her marriage was gasping its last breath. So the final gasp, coming over a restaurant table the night before, had come as no surprise. Nor could she even say it came with any real regrets.

Still . . .

She remembered a day once, in her native South Africa, when she had worn a wedding gown instead of the utilitarian work clothes she was wearing now. The sun had shone so brightly that day, it seemed.

So, at least, she remembered. True, it was not a memory she particularly trusted. Looking back now, she could easily see how foolish she had been to think that a marriage with such a self-centered man as Nick would ever work.

Still . . .

She remembered another day, and was oblivious to the present one.

3

◨◪◪◪◪◪◻

ANYONE CAUSING A DISTURBANCE WITHIN THE LIBRARY WILL BE ASKED TO LEAVE.

Ten hours after its arrival, the object just sat there. True, the team of scientists (which had now grown to seventeen) found the manner of its sitting there very impressive.

Harkness, who had just arrived, did not. You'd have thought that this bunch of supposedly high-powered scientists could have come up with something better. That black pyramid wouldn't fool anyone with common sense, least of all him.

Harkness' lip curled. What fools these so-called scientific experts *always* turned out to be. Fancy being suckered by what was an obvious hoax. The thing didn't even *do* anything. Well, their asses would flame out, when the "UFO" proved to be a fake.

Harkness turned to study his prey: Professor Tremelo. One of Harkness' assistants was busy with background security checks right now. Harkness didn't like Tremelo's attitude. Not one damn bit.

He decided to turn on the pressure. But first—

He turned to the Chicago police officer who had attached

19

himself to Harkness' group. A classical ass-kisser by the name of Lieutenant John Salinas. Harkness recognized the type perfectly.

"John, I can't abide this crap." He waggled the packet of powdered creamer and tossed it into a nearby wastebasket. "See if you can find me some real cream somewhere, would you? I can't think clearly with my mouth tasting like mud."

It was a staged performance—Tom Harkness would have cheerfully stirred turpentine into his coffee if that was the preference of his own superiors—but it helped to establish control. Nodding eagerly, Salinas took off at a half trot.

Harkness turned to the swarming scientists, fiddling with their electronic toys. "Tremelo!" he said loudly. "Come over here. We need to talk." The tone said that it wasn't going to be a nice talk.

Those who knew Miggy Tremelo well would have been running for cover. Academics are easygoing about titles—among their peers. Chairs of departments are small tin gods within their own firmament. And generally speaking they stick within that firmament, believing all else to be of lesser virtue. This former head of High Energy Physics, otherwise known as HEP, was one step worse. He was a big platinum god. As a consultant for certain very secret Department of Defense projects at Nellis proving grounds, he was a big platinum god with the Pentagon too. As it happened, he had a higher security clearance than Tom Harkness. And he was *totally* unused to a lack of respect.

"That's *Professor* Tremelo to you, whatever-your-name-is." The professor didn't let the fact that his pajama jacket was sticking out of the top of his lab coat stop him from giving the NSC representative a glare that had withered many a bumptious colleague.

It nearly made Harkness' piggy little eyes pop out of their sockets. "Now see here, Tremelo! You don't take that tone with me . . . "

Lieutenant Salinas was returning to the scene, triumphantly carrying packets of real creamer he'd found in a refrigerator in an adjoining lab, when he heard Professor Tremelo erupt like a volcano. Salinas was still an entire corridor's length away, but the verbal imitation of Mount St. Helens stopped him in his tracks. The tall gray-haired physicist had one of those piercing voices which, when raised in anger, can carry for an incredible distance.

"*God grant me patience, you mindless idiot!* What do you mean—A FAKE? If I ever had a student as stupid as you, Harkness, I'd flunk them all the way back to the second grade. *No* substance absorbs all energy. That material is harder than diamond, it *absorbs* laser with no effect, it—"

The violet discharge from the apex of the pyramid cut the diatribe short. Tom Harkness got his wish. The device had finally done something. It made Harkness disappear.

Professor Tremelo found himself leaning over empty air.

Lieutenant Salinas would have described the next few seconds as being full of screaming and running, if he hadn't been too busy to notice. He was busy both screaming and running. Well, nearly everybody was. He found out later that one of the remaining FBI agents stood his ground emptying nine-millimeter rounds ineffectually at the pyramid before fleeing. The rest of them didn't waste that much time.

Three of the NSC team had vanished, including Tom Harkness. Two of the six FBI agents had disappeared too. So had one of the scientists . . . as abruptly as a promised Christmas bonus.

It was just as well that all the survivors ran like hell. A few seconds later the pyramid expanded once again. It didn't just topple bookcases, it sent entire stacks sailing like so many missiles.

Miggy Tremelo knew that slowing down to look back was plain foolishness. But he had to. Therefore he saw the ceiling above the pyramid shatter explosively as the object trebled in size and drove right through it.

"RUUUUN!" he yelled.

That bellow saved a good many lives.

The floor did not succeed in resisting the pyramid's sudden expansion either. When the debris finally stopped falling, the black pyramid was now resting on the ground floor. It emerged from the cloud of dust, amid the tumult of falling masonry. Oddly, no dust clung to the sides of the pyramid. It gleamed as slick as new-cut metal. An academic confetti of thousands of volumes fluttered gently down amid the bedlam of crashing shelving and shouting people.

When it was all over, the interior of the library's west wing was a gutted ruin.

In his visiting professor's office on the Oriental Institute's third floor, Jerry Lukacs was supremely unaware of all this. Actually, in his ardent pursuit of the genii-sphinx linkage in the disparate mythologies of the Near East, Jerry was as near to being absent from this world as you can be—outside of a coma or death.

In the air handler room two floors below, Lamont Jackson was now enjoying some Coltrane. His only concern was whether he could reasonably milk the job long enough to spend the whole day at the Institute. It was a cheerful sort of concern. Lamont's skill at overstating the difficulties of a job was not much less than his skill at the actual repair work itself.

No sweat, he told himself. *Think I'll play Thelonious Monk next.*

In her office, less than two blocks away, Liz De Beer finally began shaking off her sorrow. Yesterday was yesterday, she reminded herself firmly, and today is today. Besides, she had work to do.

4

I DON'T THINK SO . . .

Major Gervase pointed at the map stuck up on the wall. "Radio is being intermittently interrupted again, so we'll be using telephone linkage as much as possible. The SITREPS coming in are confused as hell." His lips quirked slightly. "As you might expect, given the—ah—unusual situation."

Sergeant Anibal Cruz swallowed. He was the leader of first squad, second platoon, B company, so part of his mind had paid close attention to the details of evac zones, aid stations, LZs. Another part of his mind was still shrieking: *Aliens?* He glanced to the northwest, as if he could see the pyramid and the wreckage inside the Regenstein Library almost half a mile away. Then, he forced himself to concentrate on the major's words.

"To summarize," Gervase was saying, "we have two mission objectives here. Firstly, the MPs will assist with the setting up of a perimeter cordon. You will be liaising with Chicago Police Department, who are here in—ah—force." A little gesture was enough to indicate the hundreds of policemen who were now swarming the University of Chicago and its immediate environs.

Gervase frowned at the MPs. "You are *not* responsible for evacuating the area. Let the police deal with any civilians. I want

23

to remind everyone that under the Posse Comitatus Act, soldiers of the United States Army are not permitted—"

As the major continued with his summary of the legal complexities involved, the officers and NCOs of the two companies under Gervase's command listened attentively. None more so than Sergeant Cruz. There was still, of course, a bit of an air of unreality about the whole thing. The heavily wood-paneled room exuded an aura of sedate, staid, scholarly decorum—quite out of keeping with the soldiers and military hardware which had piled into it.

But the major himself quite obviously took the situation dead seriously. And his men were in the habit of taking him the same way.

"Okay," Gervase concluded. "Captain Marcus will continue your detailed briefing. Follow him."

After the MPs had moved off, the major turned back to the map. "We'll be setting up a staging area for the troops which are coming in just south of us. Here"—he pointed to a spot on the map—"in Midway Plaisance. But, at least for the moment, HQ will remain here in Ida Noyes Hall."

He gave the assembled officers and NCOs a hard look. "Let me state something clearly. We are *not* going to assault this thing. The Pentagon just wants accurate and reliable SITREPS for the moment. *That is all.* Unless aliens emerge from the device. Then— *if* fired upon—we may return fire. But *only* then. Is that understood?"

The center of the University of Chicago—with live ammunition. *Aliens!!!* Cruz swallowed. His sensei had been right. You can *never* train for everything.

A tall red-headed corporal standing nearby grimaced. Tapped his head. Cruz scowled faintly. That McKenna kid was heading for trouble. Mind you, it looked like they all were. . . .

The major was now talking about containment. *Containment!* Cruz was a bit of a science fiction fan. If David Drake and David Weber were anything to go by, that thing might be beyond the ability of two paratrooper companies to handle. Still, there were more troops on the way. According to the major, backup from the 82nd would start arriving in forty minutes. After ten years, Cruz knew what that meant. On time, possibly; late, probably.

Liz De Beer looked out from the window of her office in the Department of Ecology and Evolution. They were running around like mad ants down there, swarming in front of the huge library across the street. She shook her head. She'd been in America for less than two months and she was still confused half of the time. There were just too many people. It was even worse than Jo'burg.

Looking out at the lanes of milling vehicles, almost all of them police cars and paddy wagons, she finally reached her decision. She was going home. Well, back to Cape Town anyway. Screw this post doc. She'd only come here because of Nick, and that was all over now.

A helicopter came over, low and fast. Military. Jeez. Maybe something really was going on after all. She shrugged and turned away from the window. It would probably turn into a storm in a teacup. Americans seemed to count as "disasters" what people in Third World countries regarded as daily life.

If the visiting South African biologist had continued to watch, she'd have seen what happened when the helicopter flew into the pyramid's selection-perimeter zone. That would have changed Liz De Beer's mind about the seriousness of the incident.

Cruz, taking up position with his squad behind a large ornamental wrought iron gate, *did* see. The pyramid itself, still buried somewhere inside the Regenstein, wasn't visible from their vantage point. But a sudden violet flare seemed to reach through the wall of the library and intersect the body of the Blackhawk.

It didn't disintegrate the helicopter. It *did* cut the engines.

It also "disappeared" two of the soldiers inside the helicopter, including the copilot. Reacting frantically to the Master Caution Light—practically *every* light on the warning panels was on—the pilot lowered the nose steeply to avoid stalling and flattened the blades. Forty feet from the ground, he yanked on the collective to make the blades bite and slow the descent.

Watching from the ground, Cruz knew nothing about what was happening inside the helicopter. But he did understand that the pilot was trying to bring it down by autorotation—and Anibal knew as well that "autorotation" is a euphemism for *controlled crash.*

He was hollering for a medic before the helicopter hit the ground in a crumpled mess straddling the pavement and the street. Men spilled out like fury, running for cover. The pilot, his face a bloody mask, staggered out clinging to someone's shoulder.

Sergeant Cruz exhaled. He hadn't even realized he'd been holding his breath. *Aliens!*

He tried to console himself with the thought that the helicopter hadn't actually been *disintegrated* or anything. The thought did not cheer him up very much.

5

IT LOOKS FISHY TO ME.

To a younger son of a farmer, the army had seemed like a pretty good option. Hell. It had seemed like the *only* option at the time. A short stint and then college. Shepherding these two along to Major Gervase, Corporal Jim McKenna began to seriously wonder about other options. The tall civilian named Professor Tremelo seemed okay, even if he was dressed in what seemed to be his pajamas and a lab coat. Hell, he'd been herding the police officer along. The guy was supposed to be a lieutenant, for Christ's sake. The heavyset cop had been acting like a kid with a wet diaper when the professor had called them.

That hail had nearly gotten them shot. The paratroopers were more than a little jumpy after what had happened to the chopper. Fortunately, Sergeant Cruz had steady nerves and quick reactions, so he'd kept his men from opening fire. McKenna was more than a little jumpy himself, truth to tell. Seeing two crewmen disappear in a violet flash wasn't something they prepared you for in jump school.

Major Gervase was on the telephone in the command post when Corporal McKenna came in with the two men he was escorting.

"Yes, sir," the major was saying. "You can reassure the President that whatever the thing is doing, nothing has come out of it—yet. And the alien object is still just a single item. No sign of any more being built. I've got scouts within thirty-five meters of it."

The major raised his eyes to heaven as the distant questioner held forth. "Yes, sir. As I've already said, sir. Distance and cover seem to make no difference at all within a radius of about five hundred meters. We lost a man standing behind a building which separated him from the object. All I can say is that if any victim is touching another, sir, it seems to mean they both go."

He paused again. "Yes, sir. The area is being evacuated. Yes, sir. I am aware of the Posse Comitatus regulations." The major eyed the police lieutenant McKenna had shepherded into the room. "We've established liaison with the Chicago police. The colonel will be here within the next few minutes, sir." McKenna could hear a loud voice droning from the telephone in Gervase's hand. "Yes, sir." *Drone, drone, drone.*

A soldier came hurrying in. The major eyed the out-of-breath runner with relief. "I'm sorry, sir." He interrupted the flow. "A runner has just come in from one of the outposts. I must deal with the matter immediately, sir."

The major put the phone down and turned to the panting runner. "Well?"

"Sergeant Roberts sent me, sir. Reporters, sir. Two of them must have sneaked through the cordon. The pyramid got the one. We've got the other. She's, uh, flipped. Sir."

A wry smile tweaked the major's mouth. "The thing doesn't respect the accredited press much, huh? Tell Peters to detail an escort and ship her off to the aid station."

The police lieutenant cleared his throat and puffed out his chest. "Major, I'm Lieutenant John Salinas. Are you in overall command here? I was the last man in touch with Mr. Harkness. I feel obliged to make a personal report to the National Security Council in order—"

"You've arrived too late. I've just been speaking to the NSA himself," said the major sourly. He did not sound as if he had considered it an honor. He peered at the policeman's name plate. "Lieutenant Salinas, is it? I am in charge of this operation until Colonel McNamara gets here. Which," said the major, looking at his watch, "should be in less than ten minutes. In the meantime, I need a responsible Chicago police official to liaise with. Under federal law, U.S. troops cannot—"

The doors to the room were thrust open violently. Two soldiers with a burden burst in. "It's the copilot of the Blackhawk!" exclaimed one of them. "He just fell out of the sky, Major. Just dropped out of *nothing* almost on top of us!"

Gervase cocked his head. "Marrano! Get the aid station. We need a medic!"

Jim McKenna reacted fast. He was already trying CPR before the major got out from behind his desk. Tremelo was kneeling next to the injured copilot. The physics professor wasn't trying to render medical assistance. Instead he was examining the man as if he were a valuable microscope specimen.

"Get this civilian out of here!" roared Gervase. "Unless he's a doctor?"

Tremelo stood up and looked down at the stocky major. "I was leading the research team into the alien artifact," he said, quietly and calmly. "I don't think I should go anywhere until I've been debriefed. Also you may need me if the pyramid starts doing something new. I'm on the presidential science advisory council. I also have a top secret security clearance."

"Stay," the major snapped. "Just keep out of the way, while we try to keep him alive."

The medics arrived at a run and relieved McKenna. But it was too late for the pilot.

McKenna stood up. His knee was blood-wet. "It's no use," he said grimly. The medic, who was feeling for a throat pulse on the cooling body, nodded.

Tremelo looked at the body. "Did he fall onto anything sharp?"

One of the paratroopers who'd brought him in looked startled. "No, sir. He landed on a grassy area in the quad, as a matter of fact."

The scientist rolled the dead man over onto his stomach. The broken legs turned at sickeningly odd angles. The flight suit was blood-soaked. The physicist calmly pointed to a narrow cut in the fabric. "Something stabbed him. I *thought* the blood was coming from somewhere other than his legs."

Cutting away the flight suit revealed a wide, nasty wound. Somebody or something had stabbed the pilot in the back—and not with a stiletto, either.

"Major!" one of the men manning the field telephones shouted. "The forward OP. They've got another one back, sir!"

The medics left hastily with one of the major's runners.

"I need to see this too, Major," said Tremelo.

Gervase glanced at McKenna. "Take him there, Corporal."

So McKenna escorted the tall scientist along after the running medic. Tremelo walked briskly and calmly, making no effort to look for cover. "The alien artifact appears to detect humans even if they're out of line of sight. It doesn't take *some* of those in line of sight. I'm pretty sure that if it wants you, Corporal, it'll take you."

McKenna knew that the guy was crazy then. He sounded deeply disappointed that it hadn't taken him.

This time it was an Air Force officer that Jim McKenna had never seen before. Tremelo obviously had. "Hmm. One of that ass Harkness' men."

If it hadn't been for the medics, it would have been one of Harkness' ex-men. It was a relatively hot dry autumn afternoon. The Air Force colonel was wet. Sopping wet. He was also trailing brown streamers of ribbony, leathery stuff. Water was pouring out of his clothing . . . and his lungs, as the paramedics "emptied" him out. A number of other things were also falling onto the paving stones.

Hopefully, most of them came from his clothing and not his lungs, because some of them were definitely fish. Silvery, flapping little things, about seven inches long. To McKenna, with the ichthyological knowledge of a farmboy, they looked like . . . fish. And a little thing with tentacles. All of the critters were very much alive.

The two medics worked fast. One kept up the artificial respiration. The other tied a tourniquet onto the remainder of the NSC man's leg. He then cut away the rest of the trouser leg, exposing a triple crescent of sluggishly bleeding wounds.

Jim McKenna's eyes went very wide. Whatever it was that had a mouth that big and teeth that size, he didn't want to meet it.

Tremelo calmly bent over, stuck a finger into the bloody water, and tasted it. "Salty. Sea water."

Then with perfect aplomb, the scientist picked up one of the fish, a piece of the brown ribbony stuff and then the little thing with the tentacles. He dropped them calmly into his pocket. "Okay, soldier. I've seen enough. Let's go." McKenna noticed the pocket dripped black liquid. The scientist either didn't notice or didn't care.

Sergeant Anibal Cruz watched them go. Then he turned to look at the man the paramedics were working on. Cruz flexed a burly forearm. He'd never seen a real shark bite before. But it sure looked like the pictures. And the little fish sure looked just like anchovies . . . he'd seen them whole and salted often enough. But these fish were just too big. So what the hell was going on?

6

⊡⌐⌐⌐⌐⊡

SO GET ME A FISHERMAN!

Back at the command post, McKenna saw that Colonel McNamara had arrived, along with a lot more men. It was very apparent that Lieutenant Salinas had been getting on his nerves already, in the way that a first-class ass-kisser can do to someone who neither wants nor appreciates the fawning attention.

"So the NSC wants us to find Mr. Harkness. He'll probably be returned dead—like the Blackhawk copilot," snapped the colonel. "The Regenstein is a heap of rubble. The area where you last saw him is full of pyramid."

"Colonel," interjected Tremolo. "He was certainly consumed by the pyramid. I saw that. If you like, I'll tell them they're wasting your time."

The colonel looked at the oddly attired professor. "Who the hell are you, mister?" The tone was less abrasive than the words.

"Professor Miguel Tremelo."

A wintry smile lit the colonel's face. "I've had the MPs out looking for you. I've got orders from on high to find you and get you here. The President wanted to know what the hell was going on and somebody gave him your name. We're supposed to render all possible assistance."

33

Tremelo smiled back. He stuck a hand in his pocket. And pulled out a fish and the thing with tentacles, which clung to his hand. "First assistance I want is a marine biologist. Preferably one who knows something about sharks."

"Sure. We've got some helicopters on standby, Professor. We'll take you wherever you need to go."

Tremelo shook his head. "No." He looked at Lieutenant Salinas, who was staring at Tremelo with an entirely new vision. "I need to stay near the artifact." The scientist turned slightly away from Salinas and McKenna saw the wink to Colonel McNamara. "I'm sure I could trust the lieutenant to fetch me a suitable man."

"You can count on me!" said Salinas crisply.

McKenna decided that if the opportunity ever arose, he'd never play poker with his colonel. "I'm sure he can," said the colonel, with near-perfect sincerity.

McKenna *wasn't* delighted when he found himself detailed to accompany the policeman to one of the university buildings on the north end of the quad, right across the street from the library. The MPs, assisting Chicago patrolmen and university policemen, were just in the throes of attempting to evacuate a building full of biologists. As librarians are to their books, so too are biologists to their animals, alive or in jars. McKenna would have been amused if the whole situation wasn't so tense.

As he and Salinas charged up the ramp leading to the entrance of the building, they passed two Chicago PD patrolmen. McKenna saw one of the men glance at Salinas, scowl, and whisper something to the other. McKenna wasn't positive, but he thought the cop had said: *Just what we need—Lootenant Zorro.*

He *was* sure he heard the riposte correctly. *Who was that masked asshole?*

The sign on the building announced it to be the location of the Department of Ecology and Evolution. Once inside, McKenna followed Salinas as the police lieutenant wandered through the corridors. It became clear almost immediately that Salinas hadn't the faintest idea whom he was looking for or where to find them.

McKenna shook his head. The Army prepares you as widely as possible, for as many things as possible. The idea is to make the training worse than the reality will be. It works pretty well. Mostly.

But the training schools had certainly left out *aliens landing in Central Chicago*, for one. For another—this one almost *did* have him laughing—they'd left out *how to prevent a little gray-haired five-foot-two-inch biddy from bullying a beefy six-foot-tall MP armed with an M16*. Corporal McKenna was almost sorry not to be able to stay and watch. She already had the soldier carrying a bag of fish. But Salinas hurried ahead, demanding to speak to the head of this facility.

There were two people in the department chair's office. One was a tiny, white-haired old gent, with bifocals. The other was a big woman somewhere in her early thirties. Despite her advanced years—practically "middle-aged," to the 21-year-old corporal—McKenna's interest was aroused. The woman was a bit hefty, but not fat. Very buxom. She wasn't really even that big— except compared to the old dude. It was just the square and solid way she stood. Five foot seven, he estimated. Hundred and forty pounds, give or take a few. Big shoulders for a girl. She needed those shoulders, in order to heft those big—

"You want to look at my teeth too, *troepie*?" She snapped. It wasn't an American accent. She sounded vaguely German or Dutch, which went with the blond hair, he supposed. She was very suntanned, though, which didn't fit his image of North Europeans.

"Now, now, Dr. De Beer," reproved the old man in a reedy voice. "Calm down. We'll sort all this out after the evacuation. I've just got some papers to get together and a few boxes of microslides . . . "

"I'm Lieutenant John Salinas. If you are the head of this department, I'm afraid we have been sent to co-opt you. The colonel— the *government*, I should say—wants a marine biologist."

The little man tilted his head forward to peer thoughtfully through the tops of his bifocals. "I'm a freshwater limnologist, young man. I have some knowledge of aquatic microfauna, and some small expertise with ostracods and various copepods. Has the city been overwhelmed by mutant plankton?"

This was obviously rather over Salinas' head. McKenna hadn't the faintest idea what the old guy was talking about either. The woman obviously found it funny, though.

Salinas frowned and tightened his heavy jaws. "We need an expert on shark attacks."

The little man gave a reedy, asthmatic chuckle. "Most of my work involves SEM—scanning electron microscopy. Are these really really *small* sharks? The bites are micrometers in diameter perhaps?" He shook his head. "No, gentlemen. I'd be quite willing to help you. But it doesn't sound as if you have any idea who you are looking for. Besides I've got responsibilities here. Go away." The old man continued to grub in his desk, ignoring the lieutenant.

Salinas stepped forward. "I am empowered to use force if necessary . . ."

"Oh, leave him alone!" the woman snapped. "I'll go with you. I'm a *marine* biologist. And I've worked on sharks."

Salinas stared at her. His thoughts were obvious. McKenna was tempted to stir the pot a bit more by whispering: "The colonel said a *man*, sir." But he managed to stifle the impulse easily enough. From the scowl on her face, he suspected the woman would belt him with that heavy bag she was carrying.

The moment passed. The female marine biologist brushed past Salinas and McKenna and began stalking down the corridor toward the entrance.

"Come on!" she barked. "Let's go and see what your problems are." She led the way, swinging her tatty leather shoulder bag like an offensive weapon.

7

HOLD THE ANCHOVIES.

The guy Liz squatted beside on the stretcher in the aid station was a mess. She thought he'd live, but . . . probably without a leg. And the other leg would carry some really impressive
scars. At the moment he wasn't conscious. Looking at that bite
she could only be glad for him.

"We found this bit of tooth, Dr. De Beer," said Tremelo, holding
an object out to her. "Imbedded in the bone and snapped off."

She wasn't surprised they'd found it. The tooth was the size
of a fifty-cent piece. Tricuspid. Cruelly sharp. She turned it over
in her hand. Hmmm. *Not* a fish tooth. She looked at the three
rows of tooth marks. Widely spaced. Equisized.

"Why are you so sure that this is a shark bite?" she asked.

The physics professor squatting next to her shrugged. "I'm not,
Dr. De Beer. I know the limits of my expertise. He was in salt
water and he had for company these, and several others. They
were all alive." He produced a mayonnaise jar. It now contained
his specimens.

"Call me Liz." She fished about inside the huge shoulder bag,
produced a pair of forceps, and started pulling out specimens.
"I'm not too hot on seaweeds. It looks like plain old Laminaria . . .

37

at a guess." She peered closely at it. "There is a colonial bryo-zoan growing here." She looked at the fish and the squid and smiled.

"What do you want to know about these? *Why* do you want to know?"

"The man disappeared in a violet flash. He reappeared in this state . . . Liz. I want any clues I can gather. Are these alien crea-tures?"

"Hmm. Right, Professor. Well, the fish is about as earthly as you can get. It's an engraulid. What you would call an anchovy. You say there were several of them?"

"About ten."

"And they were *all* this size?" She pointed to the seven-inch-long fish.

He nodded. "More or less."

Liz pulled a wry face. "Ah. Well, I don't know where on earth he's been—but there are several hundred million dollars worth of fishing fleets that would also love to know. That's a third-year-size class anchovy. I'll swear to that. I've seen too many thou-sands of anchovy not to know what they look like. But not usually of *that* size. That's unfished anchovy. I didn't think an unfished stock still existed. I didn't think one had for a couple of hun-dred years."

She pulled the little cuttlefish out of the jar. Liz liked cuttle-fish. Not as cute as Ockys, but still . . .

"I'm not familiar enough with these to swear to it, but I think this is *Sepia rondeleti*. Mediterranean species, if I'm not mis-taken. This is a big one, too. You should keep some of the water if you can. That could be diagnostic. The water from the Med is more saline than ordinary seawater. Besides, the plankton in it can tell you a lot. And I'd freeze these specimens if you have no other way of preserving them. Gut contents could be revealing."

She plopped the squid back, and wiped her forceps and her hands on her skirt. "I'd say that your man's been on Earth—or at least someplace with the same fauna. The probability of such familiar species being found off Earth, by mere chance, ranges from ridiculous to absurd."

Tremelo nodded. "And the bite?"

Liz pursed her lips and shook her head. "Now there you've got me. Except it *isn't* a shark bite. That tooth looks more like a seal tooth . . . "

"Excuse me, ma'am," said the doctor. "If you want any further examination you'll have to do it later. He's stabilized enough to be moved now. We want to get him into the hospital and get some whole blood into him."

The drowned and bitten man groaned . . . and began muttering. "S'ha' barsid Odisoos . . . " Then he opened his eyes and screamed, before lapsing back into a restless unconsciousness. The medics grabbed the stretcher and moved off to the waiting ambulance.

The professor stood up and thrust his hands into the pockets of his lab coat. Hastily he pulled one hand back out. It dripped black goo. "Well, I wish I understood what he tried to say? 'Barsid Odesoos' . . . ?"

"Uh." The heavyset, short, swarthy sergeant standing nearby spoke. "I can translate some of it, Professor Tremelo. He said it quite a lot. The first part is 'It's that bastard.' I don't know who 'Odesoos' is. I actually wrote down what he said, sir." The sergeant produced a little green notebook and turned it to a page covered in fine scrawl. Liz looked at it. It would have gotten the sergeant into fourth-year medicine instantly.

The professor looked at it too. Then, at the man's name tag. "Sergeant Cruz, you'd better read this to me. Or maybe you'd better come back to the command post and read it to me there."

The sergeant shrugged. "It didn't make a lot of sense to me, sir. He just said the same thing over and over again. And I have to get back to the OP, sir."

Tremelo cocked his head and smiled. "Get me your colonel on the line, Sergeant."

With Professor Tremolo, Liz, and Colonel McNamara peering over his shoulders, Sergeant Anibal Cruz pointed a thick forefinger at his pad. "Here's what it says. 'Twelve feet, six heads . . . six heads . . . six fucking heads.'"

His eyes avoided the female biologist. "I'm just quoting his exact words, sir. Ma'am. He said that a lot. And something about a sword. And what could be 'help' or 'yelp.' And that 'Odesoos' word. Oh, and here's 'black galley' and 'whirlpool.'"

Liz snorted. "I'd say you needed an historian more than a biologist. Swords and galleys! Fish we haven't found for at least a hundred years. Cuttlefish from the Med. Mind you, the six heads stuff doesn't make a whole lot of sense."

Professor Tremelo sighed. "None of it does. But there must be sense in it somewhere. And I think you're right—we do need an historian."

Salinas stepped forward. "Want me to get you one?" he asked unctuously.

The colonel nodded. "Won't do any harm, Lieutenant. It seems insane, but then so do the circumstances. Get us someone who is up on Mediterranean history. Who knows, it may produce something useful."

If Liz read his look right, the unsaid part of his statement was: *and it'll get you out of my hair.* But what the colonel actually said was: "Take the sergeant and Dr. De Beer with you, please. Perhaps they can tell the historian something first-hand."

That brown-noser Salinas obviously decided his exercise in "not being taken seriously" by the old geezer at the last place called for more men. Salinas demanded a squad this time around.

Jim McKenna grimaced. It was just his luck that Major Gervase should have seen him smile at the policeman's demand for "adequate personnel to ensure the success of his mission." A sense of humor was a necessity for an NCO. It was a pain in the ass in an officer.

Cruz was looking a little pissed too. McKenna found himself half hoping the obnoxious police lieutenant would *really* piss the sergeant off. Anibal Cruz had the forearms of a gorilla. He took weight training seriously, and had a brown belt in one of the martial arts.

McKenna was even more disgruntled when Cruz ordered all the men in the squad to bring their rucksacks. He understood the logic of the order. The headquarters building was soon going to be flooded with soldiers from the 82nd. At best, their rucks would get trampled. But he didn't much appreciate having to hoist the damn thing around.

Five minutes later, Jim's irritation with the police lieutenant deepened. Of course, thought McKenna sarcastically, you can always *rely* on a prick like Salinas. He knew *exactly* where they were going. Which was why the building he led them to, less than two blocks away, didn't say "History Department." It said "Seminary Co-operative Bookstore."

Cruz had the brains to ask a University of Chicago policeman directing traffic nearby. The man pointed across the street and suggested they try the Oriental Institute.

"Why not?" asked the female biologist, cheerfully shrugging her shoulders. "The Mediterranean's east of here, isn't it?"

She led the way, still swinging her bag like a deadly weapon.

8

⌐⌐⌐⌐⌐⌐

BETWEEN ORIENT AND ACCIDENT.

When Lamont Jackson finally put away his tools and left the air handler room, intending to pay his visit to Dr. Lukacs, he was surprised to see the Institute apparently empty. At least on the ground floor. The museum was open, and it normally had plenty of visitors.

When he wandered into the front entrance area, heading for the stairs leading to the floors above, moderate surprise turned into sharp apprehension. A half drunk cup of coffee sat on the counter of the Suq, the Oriental Institute's gift shop. The glass display case in the center was open, and a beautiful piece of onyx jewelry was lying on the counter.

Lamont wasn't stupid. The Institute wasn't "empty." It had been *evacuated*. He had no idea why, but there was only one place he was going—*out of here.*

Then, after dancing back and forth for a moment, he decided to postpone his own evacuation. Very briefly. It would only take him two minutes to grab his tools and the boombox from the air handler room. That coffee had already scummed over. They hadn't just left. No sense in running out on his personal possessions. Still, it was spooky . . .

43

✧   ✧   ✧

Hearing a voice calling out as he emerged from the air handler room, Lamont turned right and ran across Dr. Lukacs standing in front of the Assyrian Bull. As usual, the visiting professor looked vaguely puzzled. Lamont liked Jerry Lukacs, but he sometimes thought the professor only touched the real world now and again.

Lukacs smiled at him. "Hi. I'm relieved to see you. Where the hell has everyone gone?"

Just then they heard voices. Voices that sounded oddly loud in the strange silence. Lamont repressed a strong and irrational urge to look for somewhere to hide. There was no logic in it. They were just ordinary American voices. All except for one, and that was female.

"The place looks like it's been evacuated already, Lieutenant Salinas," said a male voice.

"Well, well, what a surprise. Shall we go on getting lost, and try somewhere else?" That was a woman's voice. Despite the foreign accent, Lamont recognized the tone. When his wife Marie spoke like that, it was time to start looking for cover.

The person who replied was obviously not as experienced. "We haven't been lost . . . "

Jerry cleared his throat. "In here!" he announced.

Lamont was glad that the decision had been taken away from him. Sighing with resignation, he set down the toolbox. No reason to keep lugging that heavy thing around for the moment.

Seconds later, when an armed and testy-looking group of soldiers piled in, he was less glad. Paratroopers, no less. Lamont recognized the insignia of the 101st. But it only took a few seconds for him to figure out that they were actually mad at the police officer in their midst.

"The United States government requires your services!" the policeman boomed. "We need an historian. Bring them along, men!"

Jerry blinked owlishly. "Er . . . I'm Professor Jerry Lukacs. I'm a mythographer, I work on comparative mythology."

Lamont chuckled. "And *I'm* the maintenance man. Is the government short of those *again?*"

Another two minutes, and the woman's going to tear that cop's head off his shoulders, thought Cruz. She wasn't American and sure as hell wasn't much on respect for pompous authority. Nor did she seem fazed in the least by the sight of soldiers in BDUs walking around a city with loaded weapons. She acted as if it was kind of normal. That was . . . odd.

Liz repressed a slight chuckle. This errand-boy policeman was a right royal pain in the backside. Arse-licking those above him and arse-kicking those below. His face, at being told the black guy—who looked the smarter of the two—was a mechanic, was quite a study. The other guy looked like a typical "nocturnal" arts major. Weedy. Slightly confused looking. The kind that always turned out to be at the top of some esoteric field of no use to man or beast.

More with the intent to irritate Salinas than in any real expectations of getting any worthwhile information, Liz introduced herself and began explaining. To her surprise the little man tensed like a terrier scenting rats when she got to mentioning what the survivor had actually said.

"He used the words: 'Black ship'?"

"No, sir," corrected the dark-skinned, powerful-looking soldier named Cruz. "Actually he said, 'black galley.'"

"Tell me what else he said. As much and as precisely as you can remember." The little guy was just about quivering.

The sergeant hauled out his notebook. "I wrote it down, sir."

"A man of intelligence, eh, Lamont?" The little mythographer's eyes were bright. "Read it, please. I just *may* be able to help you."

He listened in intent silence as Cruz read from his notebook. Then he shook his head.

Salinas snorted in disgust "Well, *ma'am,* now that you've wasted our time, we'd better get moving."

Jerry Lukacs cleared his throat. "Sorry. That headshake was— 'this is too unbelievable.'"

Liz looked at him grimly. "I've seen the evidence."

Lukacs' eyes were bright with excitement. "It's *got* to be Scylla. Somehow—somewhere—the myth must have a basis in truth."

Liz shook her head "Scylla? Look, I *saw* those bites. The biggest crab in the world couldn't have done that."

The mythographer looked puzzled. "Who said anything about crabs?"

It was her turn to look mystified. "I thought *you* just did. Swimming crabs. *Scylla.* A big one will take fingers off. But not *legs.*"

Salinas cleared his throat loudly. "It appears that all this is not getting us anywhere . . . "

The black mechanic chuckled. "Lieutenant Ra-Ra-Ra doesn't understand what you're getting at, Dr. Lukacs."

"Amon's got to think, Lamont." Jerry grinned.

Liz groaned. Die-hard punsters would make torturing language take precedence over matters of life and death. "Look you two, *I* don't understand, never mind this silly ass. And if you *don't* explain, Dr. Lukacs, I shall give you capital *pun*ishment by pulling your head off."

"Couldn't you just get that soldier"—Lamont pointed at McKenna—"to beat us up instead, ma'am? Then it'd just be corporal punishment."

The wild-haired academic groaned appreciatively. You could almost see his mind hunting links to "corporal."

By the look Salinas directed at Lamont, he did not enjoy this. *Not one damn bit!* He was plainly a humorless man. It looked as if there was only one thing he really hated more than being excluded from the joke—and that was being the butt of one. The big black guy had certainly pushed both sets of those buttons. The last time Liz had seen a look like that was when some Afrikaaner Weerstand Beweeging guys had found themselves in close contact with a visiting Nigerian professor. That had been ugly. She tensed. It was all sort of her fault. She had better try and move it all along. "Tell. Please."

The small mythographer assumed the posture of an orator. "Ahem, I quote: 'It is the home of Scylla, the creature with the dreadful bark. It is true that her *yelp* is no louder than a newborn pup's, but she is a horrible monster nevertheless, and one whom nobody could look at with delight, not even a god if he passed that way. She has *twelve feet*, all dangling in the air, and *six* long necks, each ending in a grisly head with *triple rows of teeth*, set thick and close, and darkly menacing death.' "

He relaxed his professorial stance. "It's from the 1946 Rieu translation of the *Odyssey*. Consider that the hero's name was Odysseus, that he was sailing what is described as a 'black ship' and that section of the *Odyssey* describes sailing between Scylla and the dreadful whirlpool, Charybdis. It all fits rather well, doesn't it?" The man smiled. He looked rather like a child who is showing you a puzzle that he's just put together and hopes you'll applaud.

It was apparent that Salinas was not going to cheer. "I've had enough! I'm putting both of you under arrest. We'll see how funny you are at the precinct!"

"Taking them to see Professor Tremelo would make more sense to me," Liz snapped.

Salinas' authoritarian instincts were now in full evidence. "If I need any further comments from you, *ma'am*, I'll ask for them. In the meantime, keep your mouth shut. This is a police matter now."

Lamont did not seem in the least intimidated. In fact, he laughed aloud. "I can't think what Silenius' donkey was called, Dr. Lukacs. But all this war talk *Mars* Lieutenant RaRaRa's complexion. It quite dis-*Troys* . . . "

And then it all happened very fast. Something in Salinas seemed to snap. He yanked out his pistol and grabbed Lamont. Something in Liz *did* snap. She grabbed the cop's wrist and shoved the gun upward. In what seemed like two seconds, she and Salinas and Lamont and Jerry Lukacs and Sergeant Cruz and Corporal McKenna and Privates Hooper and Dietz were all in contact with one another, shouting and wrestling.

The Krim device sensed a valuable one. Highly charged with emotion. A low personal credulity level. Perfect for the application of prukrin transfer. It responded.

PART II

It cracked and growled, and roared and howled,
Like noises in a swound!

—Samuel Taylor Coleridge,
"Rime of the Ancient Mariner"

9

IT'S ALL GREEK TO ME.

There was no moment of transition. One second there was a fight in the Oriental Institute, between polished glass cases and under modern track lighting. In the next moment there was searing sunlight. And the group tumbled onto the deck of a wooden ship, which was sliding down the front of the swell. The sea was wine-dark and laced with champagne bubbles, as the ram sliced through the wave.

Jerry had a fine view of the water. He'd nearly fallen over the front of the gunwale in landing, before pulling himself back from the drink. Then he almost wished that he hadn't.

The villainous-looking crewmen were rowing the wooden ship with frantic energy. Well, about forty of them were. The other ten or so were bearing down on the newcomers—armed either with bronze swords or with long spears in hand. There was something about the way they moved on the bucketing deck that, even to a landlubber like Jerry, said *old seamen*. The only thing that said it more was the stench. Jerry wasn't giving any odds that they were unfamiliar with the swords or spears either.

He glanced sideways. They were close to land. Worth swimming for . . . except that it was a sheer cliff that they were skimming next to. The gray wall looked almost polished. He looked the other way hastily, as the sailors advanced. What he saw made him swallow and wonder if he should grab an oar. The dark water was trailed with racing foam. No wonder the rowers were pulling frantically! Even from here he could hear the grumble of the white-lipped whirlpool. The air above it was hazed with a smoking mist. One way or another, this was going to be one mother of a wild, wild ride.

One of the advancing sword-swinging sailors shouted a recognizable word . . . "Odesoos."

Jerry Lukacs was, in many ways, the epitome of the absent-minded professor. And he was possibly the most frightened person on the ship. But camouflaged by the perpetually vague expression on his face was an acute mind. Quick, too. It took him barely seconds to work out where they were. Somehow they were between Scylla and Charybdis, on board Odysseus' vessel. One of the famous black ships.

The unknown holds terrors for the imaginative person. But knowing all about the terror that really *is* coming gives the imagination a focus. Jerry thought he knew *exactly* what came next—even if having read about it wasn't at all the same as actually being there.

Therefore he was the only one who was not giving his full attention to the advancing sailors. Instead he was looking ahead.

There, in the middle of the sheer, cloud-capped expanse of gray cliff, was a dark stain—the maw of Scylla's cave. And, if he understood the odd-sounding Greek correctly, then Odysseus was being wily again. The leader of the Achaean sailors was shouting: *"Herd them into the bow! The monster will take them!"*

It happened with such speed and casual brutality. Private Hooper was the closest to the advancing men. One of the scruffy-looking sailors stepped up to him and started yelling at him. Hooper was a big guy. He didn't take too kindly to being pushed and yelled at by someone at his armpit level. Not even on a strange boat with the pushee bellowing in some goddamn foreign language, with a pigsticker in his hand. So he pushed back.

Sergeant Anibal Cruz saw the sword blade come right through Hooper's back—in a fountain of blood. And then, abruptly, Hooper disappeared.

Cruz had grown up in a tough neighborhood. There'd always been some gang trouble, and Anibal had been familiar with violence since he was a kid. But that seaman took "natural-born killer" to a whole new level. That guy had stabbed Hooper just like a man might kick a stray dog.

But Cruz kept his cool. A few M16 rounds would change the bastards' cocksure attitude.

Lieutenant Salinas wasn't keeping *his* cool. "Shoot 'em!" he shouted, his voice shrill. "Shoot 'em all!" His pistol was still in his hand. He brought it up to a two-handed grip, stepped back a pace—and stumbled over an empty rower's bench and landed on his ass.

"Single shots!" ordered Cruz. "We're next to a whirlpool! We can't afford to hit the rowers!" He took a careful bead on the son of a bitch who'd so casually killed Hooper.

Then, from behind him, the little guy with the wild hair shouted, "Look out! *Scylla!*"

Cruz ignored him, still gauging the tactical situation. *Take the lead two with those big cheese cutters out. And then the one who had a spear ready to throw. Turn and check out what the guy was shouting about . . . What was that yowling noise, anyway?*

A thousand drills kept him calm. *"It don't mean nothin' . . . "*

He squeezed the trigger—and felt his stomach tie itself into a sick knot and his pulse start hammering.

When you've fired a rifle often—you know exactly how it should kick, sound and feel. It shouldn't—do what it had just done!

The "explosion," if you could even call it that, was piteous. The bullet plopped out and landed a few yards off. What could only be voices, tiny reedy little voices, issued from the muzzle. Anibal tried to swallow, his mouth suddenly dry. He risked a glance over his shoulder to see what the new problem was.

Facing up to *that*, with a badly designed club—which was all his M16 was now—nearly doubled his already racing pulse rate.

"Fix bayonets," Anibal croaked.

✧   ✧   ✧

The monster poured herself sinuously out of the dark cave. The black cave-mouth was perhaps forty feet above the water level. And the monster was going to reach them . . .

The six gleaming mottled necks weren't the worst part, thought Liz. They were like thigh-thick pythons with odd dangling clawed feet. But the heads! The heads were a terrible mixture between a woman and a shark—complete to the gill slits. Liz realized that the glisten on the scaly necks was water. The cave up there must be water-filled.

She also realized something more terrible still: the channel narrowed just here. Scylla's lair was perfectly positioned. The suck of Charybdis was now a furious roar of angry surf. The black ship barely moved, although the rowers stroked with frantic intensity. Actually, if they were moving anywhere, they were going backwards. Looking across, Liz realized she was looking straight into the terrible vortex. Such a volume of water was disappearing down the throat of the whirlpool that you could see the exposed rocks and sand . . . and even a few wildly flip-flopping fish.

This vessel would be lucky if it managed not to be sucked into that terrible hole. They certainly weren't going anywhere. Scylla could feed at her awful leisure. Her dreadful, high-pitched, puppy-in-fear yowling cut through even the wild sea-roar, echoing between the two cliffs.

Liz started to rummage hastily through her capacious shoulder bag. There was something for any emergency in there. The problem was always to find anything specific. Well, she could always just hit them with the bag. As usual, it weighed a ton. It seemed to accumulate junk faster than she could clean it out. Ah. Pepper spray!

McKenna looked briefly at the inoperative M16. No time to field-strip it now. He dropped it and grabbed a spare oar from between the rowers' benches. The damn thing was heavy. It would be like trying to fight people off with a telephone pole. Then the black guy yelled, "I'll be the rowlock! You swing it about."

It worked well. They could hold off the guys with the swords just as long as nobody threw a spear. Or the thing behind them didn't get them. Jim had risked one quick glance behind him . . . his mother was a fanatical conservationist. She'd even gotten him to like spiders, but snakes still freaked him out. Cruz and Dietz would just have to deal with that thing.

Jerry watched in horror as Scylla's heads swung lower and lower. One soldier tried what was presumably supposed to be a burst of automatic fire.

It didn't work quite the way he had intended. A wailing Greek tragic chorus issued from the rifle barrel. If Jerry understood it correctly, it was a lament for the death of several lesser earth-spirits killed by the next lump of lead while they'd been pushing this one out. The soldier peered in puzzlement at his weapon.

Always keep your attention on the enemy. . . .

Scylla obviously preferred prey that wasn't prepared for her. A head snaked down and seized the soldier. Kicking and shrieking, the paratrooper was ripped skywards.

The swarthy sergeant had grabbed an oar and swung it at Scylla's nearest head, smashing it sideways. He nearly rescued the other soldier—except that the man . . . just suddenly wasn't there any more.

Jerry realized that there was *one* way out of this nightmare. Die. Unfortunately, from what he'd been told, you got home dead too.

One of the Achaeans must have appeared tasty and distracted Scylla. She seized one of the sword-wielders next. The falling bronze Mycenaean blade nearly pinned Liz like a butterfly.

Liz grabbed it . . . just as, to Jerry's horror, a head dived at her. Maybe the monster thought a female would be easier prey. Liz sidestepped Scylla's lunge neatly. The head thudded into the deck planking. Hard. It didn't stop Scylla for an instant. The head turned upward and lunged. Somehow the biologist managed to trap it between her body and arm, and then throw her legs around it.

She'd tried to do to what a good fisherman would do to a *snoek*. Only this was more like a cross between a Great White

Shark and a python than a nasty-toothed predatory fish. It was also much bigger. Much, much bigger. And these teeth would make a big *snoek*'s needle-like teeth look like toothpicks. Her full-strength wrench hadn't been nearly enough to tear across the base of the gill arches. Instead, she was being lifted off the deck. The creature was shouting at her. Any moment now its slimy strength would overmaster her. She'd dropped her pepper spray. But she still clutched the overgrown cheese knife that the sailor had nearly pinioned her with. She shoved it into the gills and cut outwards, as she desperately pulled back on the nose.

You can snap a fish's neck if you sever the narrow piece of flesh where the gill openings nearly meet on the throat. On little fish it is surprisingly easy. With big fish, you struggle, but it is still possible. On really big fish it is virtually impossible unless you cut right through it. She'd cut it through. And fear lent her terrific strength. Truly desperate strength.

In a wild threshing and a spray of blood she was flung to the deck. Liz could have been badly hurt. But she hit Jerry, who'd been trying to grab her legs, and then crashed onto the hind end of the cowering Salinas.

The long neck swung about dementedly. The other heads withdrew slightly. Jerry, staggering to his feet, realized that they were lamenting. Well, most of them were.

"Poor Dindymene!" cried one, in tones of horror.

"How cruel and disrespectful!" said another one of the heads. It sounded as if the disrespect was what hurt most.

"She was always Mother's favorite, eh, Pleione?" said the head next to the dangling Dindymene, not sounding as if she missed her fellow Scylla-head much.

The biggest of the heads was plainly shocked. "You know Mother never played favorites, Enyo!"

"Did too!" Enyo snapped back. "And it serves Dindymene right, always trying to get the tenderest ones!"

"We must avenge her!" hissed one of the other heads. "We'll eat *all* of these."

"You just want to pick the fat ones, Phaedra. You got the last swordfish even though I spotted it first!" snarled another.

Dragon's teeth, thought Jerry. *If only I can get them to bicker . . .*

But he was no good at talking to ordinary people. Other academics were fine, but *these* were worse than bank managers. And it would have to be in ancient Greek too. He quailed at the idea, and then bit his lip. Somebody had to do something. And there was no one else . . .

He took a deep breath and shouted, "But, Enyo, how can I keep my promise to you, if you let them devour us. You promised! You'll never be human again . . . "

A head pulled back. "I never made any promises! Not to someone who can't even speak proper Greek!"

Jerry oozed puzzlement and sincerity. "But you agreed! 'The others have to go,' you said, and 'We cannot have one human body with many heads,' you said. 'Leave it to me,' you said. 'Especially Phaedra, she's a spiteful cat,' you said."

"You selfish little bitch!" The Phaedra-head snapped at the Enyo-head.

It went downhill from there. Fast.

Liz had staggered to her feet. She wasn't looking at the bickering, biting heads. She was looking at the sea. "Little guy, tell the sailors to start rowing like fury," she said, *sotto voce*. "The whirlpool has just stopped sucking."

"Row!" Jerry shouted in his best classical Greek. "Row for your lives!"

For a moment the Greeks looked at him. Then the armour-clad one on the stern said a word that was quite similar sounding. And in a hasty ragged chorus, oar blades bit water.

It took the squabbling heads some time to register.

"They're getting AWAAAY!" they snarled in chorus.

The oarsmen lashed the water to a foam. A head lunged furiously after them. Liz depressed the trigger on her little pepper-spray canister that she'd picked up from the deck. The effects were wholly unexpected. It should have sprayed an aerosol of eye-streaming, nose-and-throat-irritating gunk. But obviously, like the rifles, that would have failed to obey the rules of this strange universe. Instead they were all overpowered by the smell of fresh-cut onions . . . The essence of onions. About a thousand of them.

The head, streaming tears and spluttering, pulled back, hitting itself against the cliff wall in its haste to back off.

And from beside the far cliff Charybdis began to vomit back her water.

Looking back, Jerry saw an immense and ancient fig tree on the far cliff disappear into the whirl of upflung spray. He didn't see any more. He was too busy clinging to the gunwale. The oarsmen actually managed to get the black ship up on the plane on the first wave.

Jerry knew that he wasn't a great sailor. Within two minutes of riding out the waves from the erupting Charybdis, he proved that the whirlpool didn't have the proprietary rights on vomiting in this part of the world. He had Lamont, the police lieutenant and the tall soldier for company, too.

10

⌸⌸⌸⌸⌸⌸

TO HELL WITH THE CONNECTICUT YANKEE.

Ahead in the distance lay an island. Verdant and tranquil looking.

At the moment Jerry would have accepted *any* form of land. He just wanted off this ship. It was what the Greeks would have called a *pentekonter*. It was what a poor sailor called hell. Still—

That must be Thrinicia, Odysseus' next stop, according to Homer. Somehow Jerry was certain that it would be full of Helios' broad-browed cattle. Somehow he was certain that the weather would trap them there, and that, no matter what they did, the sailors would kill the cattle and feast on them. . . .

The hides would crawl, and even the roasted meat would groan and low. And then, the departing ship would be sunk.

The gentle breeze brought Achaean voices as well as Achaean rancid-oil-and-sweat bouquet to him. Classical Greek didn't sound quite like the linguistic theoreticians thought it would.

When he figured out what they were saying, it was even less appetizing than the stench. Odysseus was being cunning again. Jerry began to realize that Scylla and Charybdis might have been lesser evils compared to their present predicament.

" . . . The gods have sent us these fine barbarian slaves. They must be a sign. We are close to my principality on Ithaca. We must press on," said Odysseus. The oiliness in that voice said: *Do not buy this used car.*

The one being truculent must be . . . Eurylochus. He was certainly being insistent and not showing Odysseus a great deal of respect. Well, for all the self-praise in the *Odyssey*, Odysseus' men had always done pretty much what Odysseus claimed to have advised against. From what Jerry knew of the era, the crew were all minor noblemen, accustomed to doing as they saw fit, with Odysseus' control over them being tenuous at best. Raiding, piracy and slave-taking had always been part of their lives, and was taken for granted.

"We need rest and food and a decent chance to enjoy these slaves that the gods have surely provided for our pleasure. To Hades with Circe's predictions, Odysseus! She didn't tell us about the monster. Or if she did, then you didn't tell us about it. I want first turn on the yellow-haired peasant woman. And we're drawing lots for who gets the pretty red-haired boy. We know you, Odysseus. You want to get back to Ithaca to claim the whole lot as your share of the plunder."

The wind veered and Jerry had to stop his eavesdropping. But the snatch he'd overheard was enough to remind him that Mycenaean Greece was a good place to avoid. Mind you—that certainly wasn't the language of Mycenae they were speaking. It was classical Greek from later up the timeline, unless he was very much mistaken. But then this place was full of contradictions and impossibilities.

He forced his mind away from the attraction of playing with the puzzle. Whatever the answer, it didn't alter the fact that they had a very real problem here and now. He desperately wished that someone else would cope with it. But there was the language issue. He was the only one who could understand what was being said.

He turned to the woman. She'd been terrifyingly effective against Scylla. "Look, we've got to get away from these guys."

She picked something off her long, tanned calf and crushed it between short fingernails. Inspecting them, she pulled a face and said: "Yep. This smelly tub is crawling with damn fleas."

He took a deep breath. "Fleas may be the least of our problems. What do you know about ancient Greeks?"

She shrugged. "Not much. I'm a marine biologist, little guy. They were the source of western civilization. The founders of democracy. Can't be too bad, I suppose. Not compared to some of the other places back in time we could have landed up in."

Later he realized that he got the courage to continue principally from sheer irritation. She could skip the "little guy" stuff. He was as tall as she was. She just added an extra six inches of attitude. "One: We're not back in time . . . I don't think. These guys appear to be Mycenaeans or, as they called themselves, Achaeans—not Greeks, really. But they're speaking the language of a different people from later up the timeline. Two: Democracy happened much later. Anyway, it excluded women and slaves," he said grimly. "And you're both. At least as far as they're concerned."

She stared at him, silenced.

Lamont had been listening in. "Slaves. Oh, lord. Not me."

Liz shut her mouth with a snap. "Well, fuck me . . . "

"That's *just* what they intend to do, as soon as they get to land," said Jerry quietly. "And if I heard them right they're busy drawing lots for the corporal, too."

The expression on Jim McKenna's face was worth buying a video camera for.

"Instead of being gifts from the gods, can't we be messengers? I mean, if I remember correctly, Odysseus is a prince and a great general," said Salinas shakily, having emerged from under the rowing bench, but still looking green about the gills. "Explain to them the serious consequences of attempting to enslave Americans, Dr. Lukacs."

Liz snorted. "But I'm fair game. Listen, you spineless asshole: somehow I don't think they live in fear of air strikes. We don't have any modern weapons that work and they outnumber us ten to one." She went on rummaging through her bag. So far she'd found a Swiss army knife. It wasn't what it should be. It was rusty.

"I'll beat the living shit out of the first one of those little fucks to try anything!" McKenna was still red-faced. "They're half our size. And sure, our rifles are no use, but we've got bayonets. I've got my Gerber. And we're trained in unarmed combat. They're not."

Sergeant Cruz tensed his forearm muscles. "Corporal. If we've got to fight, we will. But we're soldiers. One-on-one, in a fair fight, we'd win. We're bigger than them and we're trained. But did you see how that guy killed Hooper? Like you would swat a fly. Get this: Those guys are goddamn killers. Even in Mogadishu they've got more respect for human life. And you can be damn sure they're not gonna stand back while we kill them off one at a time. Either they'll pack us, or, more likely, hold off and shoot us full of arrows or throw javelins at us."

Jerry nodded. "If you read between the lines, Odysseus' bunch were pretty much freebooters. And rather brutal. Actually, even in the *Iliad*—"

Liz interrupted his lecture on the realities of life in ancient Greece. "So, they're a load of scumbags. Tell me something that wasn't obvious. But what are we going to *do* about it, gentlemen? Fort up in the bow here, and try and hold them off with oars?"

Lamont shook his head. "Maybe Lieutenant RaRaRa has got something. Maybe we can talk our way out of this one, Jerry? Convince them that we're messengers from their gods or something. You know all their myths."

The mythographer shook his head. "Really, my field of expertise is the Middle East. But one thing is pretty well common knowledge: non-Hellenes were barbarians, one and all, even ones from more advanced cultures. Of course these people are not what we call 'Greeks.' They're the people the later Greeks or Hellenes displaced. However, the culture seems similar."

Liz snorted. "Yogurt's got more culture than this lot."

Jerry shook his head. "I don't think this was atypical. We tend to forget that life was pretty tough for ordinary people throughout most of human history. Power got respect. Pretty little else did." He looked at her speculatively. "Well. There is the sorceress option. Several foreign sorceresses got a fair bit of respect in Greek mythology."

She pulled a wry face. "I haven't turned anyone into a newt lately. Actually, I can't even do card tricks."

Lamont narrowed his eyes and looked at the marine biologist. "You don't happen to smoke, do you?"

"I'm trying to cut down," she said defensively. "It's hard to give up on ships where the whole crew smokes."

Jerry snapped his fingers. "Gotcha, Lamont! Connecticut Yankee in King Arthur's Court! Can you blow smoke rings?"

Liz looked puzzled. "Huh? Yes, of course."

"Well, Twain's hero convinced the guys back in Arthurian legend he was a wizard by smoking. Magic is simply something that you don't understand," said Jerry.

She snorted. "That'd make *men* magic, in my book. All right. Let's try it. It's a stupid idea, but at least it *is* an idea."

Liz fluffed the hair about her face into a wild blond cloud. The roots were going dark but Odysseus' crew probably wouldn't notice that. It didn't take much effort to "Medusa" her hair. It always went like that when the salt spray got into it. She concentrated on looking regal and mysterious as she and Jerry walked calmly between the rowers to Odysseus.

Nature designs some people to look honest and trustworthy. Odysseus' face was made for politics. It had plainly been a while since he'd bathed, and they were downwind of him. And his breath was something else again.

Liz willed herself to look imperious to the prince of Ithaca.

By the expression on Odysseus' face . . . it wasn't working.

Jerry began to speak. She wished like hell that she knew what he was saying.

"Noble Odysseus, our great sorceress Liz has performed an augury. If you land on the Island of Thrinicia you are surely doomed." Jerry tried to keep a quaver out of his Greek. If only someone else could do this . . .

"Just what I was saying to Eurylochus here!" The somewhat high-pitched voice didn't go with his princely bearing. Of all the lower forms of life Jerry had had the misfortune to have to deal with, bank managers just about topped his personal list. Jerry decided that Odysseus was natural-born bank manager material. It raised Jerry's blood pressure. That helped.

Eurylochus didn't place much faith in the pronouncement either. "Sorceress! If she's a sorceress then my penis is rabbit food! She's a peasant. Look at her skin. Even with the funny hair dye I know a peasant when I see one."

"Not as well as you do when you feel one," said Odysseus with an age-old gesture and a nasty chuckle.

"Time to start smoking," said Jerry, out of the corner of his mouth. Then he drew himself up and did his best attempt at a snap. It sounded pathetic to him. "My mistress will grow angry! We appeared on your ship by magic—"

The Greeks were laughing uncontrollably. "Your mistress . . . ho ho ho . . . " Odysseus slapped his thighs and guffawed some more.

With glowing ears Jerry realized that what he'd said was "the woman who is my master." An absolutely hilarious howler in these parts. It didn't help that she was suntanned as only peasant women were, and he was as pallid as their female aristocracy. Of course in a man that was not a desirable trait. Men in all the paintings are dark-haired and dark-skinned. The glow in his ears spread to his face as he realized that a pale-skinned man was truly the lowest form of life to these Greeks: a wimp.

Liz revived him with a long smoky exhalation.

The laughter had died away. Eurylochus backed off. . . .

Odysseus didn't. He watched as Liz trickled smoke out of her nostrils.

"She is very angry. When the smoke begins to come out of her nose, it is a sure sign. She will turn you into a . . . a . . . " What the hell was the Greek for "newt"?

Liz took a deep draw and blew smoke rings.

Odysseus smiled like a shark. "It's a trick, Eurylochus. She's no sorceress. She sucks the smoke from the smoldering stick, and then blows it out. I can do it too." And he snatched the cigarette out of her hand.

He sucked at it.

Hard.

✧　　✧　　✧

Liz had started smoking as a twelve-year-old, stealing her older brother's cigarettes. He, like many a young soldier of that time, had smoked only the strongest unfiltered cigarettes. You had to, to prove how tough you were. Filter tips were for weenies.

Liz had broken the habit—once. But when things went wrong she'd gone back to the same old smoking habits. In the U.S. she hadn't been able to find her brand. Bloody cheek. The adverts had had a cowboy! She still remembered her brother trying everything to get a match to strike against his boot.

Odysseus was a healthy Achaean with good strong lungs. He had sucked that smoke in hard and unprepared. . . .

It was a joy to watch.

He dissolved into paroxysms of violent coughing. Smoke erupted from virtually every orifice. Well, possibly not from under his sort of skirt thing. But she'd swear smoke came out of his ears.

Liz calmly reached down and took the fag from the limp hand of the doubled-up hero. Pah. He'd slimed it. She pinched off the damp bit and took another deep drag. She blew smoke into the goggle-eyed Odysseus' red face.

"Cigarettes may be harmful to your health. Want another drag, weenie?" she said coolly. Fortunately she didn't say it in ancient Greek.

"Well, all right. Maybe she is a sorceress after all," coughed Odysseus, waving the smoke away weakly. "No mere mortal could breathe the smoke of Hades like that."

"She says that if you touch the magic herbs of Persephone again she will turn you into a . . . frog," said Jerry grimly. "I am so pale because she turned me into a . . . goat for not obeying her orders quickly enough."

The Greeks regarded Liz with a bit of trepidation. Several of them edged away. But Odysseus looked suddenly *very* interested. "This turning people into goats . . . ask the sorceress if we could perhaps reach an agreement. I've a lot more serfs than I need, and a lot fewer goats. I asked Circe, but the nymph won't leave Aeaea. She says her magic only works there anyway. And goats are more valuable than pigs. Circe does pigs best. Tell the sorceress we could do business."

Jerry turned to Liz. "Look irritated and point at the island and draw your finger across your throat. Talk some gobbledygook."

Liz complied. Actually, she overdid it, demonstrating on the hapless Eurylochus. Unlike Jerry, she had no self-confidence problems. "This guy is a silly prat. I feel like kicking his balls in."

"The Sorceress Liz says, beware of your kinsman Eurylochus—he who suspected a trap of Circe, and would have you land on the Island of the Sun, Thrinicia. He will be the one to urge your comrades to slaughter the straight-horned cattle of the sun."

Odysseus was able to stick to a subject. Especially a subject he considered important. "About the goats . . . "

Liz had been staring at the horizon while Jerry warbled on. She'd spent a fair number of years going to sea in small boats. When the horizon went bumpy like that—it was time to run for port. Especially when the horizon got that gray haze about it. "Jerry. Tell this lot that I'm predicting a hell of a blow."

Jerry dug deep into his memories of the *Odyssey*. Had it been a wind from the north or the south that had kept them trapped on Thrinicia? "The Sorceress Liz says that the south wind and the storm are coming."

That was enough for the seamen. They'd been watching the drama. Now they too looked for weather cues. A low moan swept the ship. Well. They had just survived a whirlpool and a monster . . . Now a wind that would drive them back that way was rising. "Row for the island!" shouted someone. But the offshore breeze was already strengthening.

Odysseus was a son of a bitch with an obsession about goats, but he was no fool. Within minutes the ship was bearing northwest—quartering the storm, looking for a haven, any haven but the channel that housed Scylla and Charybdis.

Jerry didn't care that he'd successfully thwarted the myth. He was too busy being sick. Or trying to be. There was nothing left to come up.

11

GAMBLING WITH THE LAMBS.

The bay was a deep cookie-cutter bite out of the limestone cliff. Rimmed with a thin white-sand beach, the water inside it was blissfully still. To the south the sky was black, but here above the refuge the last of the sun still burnished the cliffs. Odysseus edged the black ship warily into the channel. Jerry remembered the Laestrygonians' slaughter of Odysseus' squadron. By the way Odysseus and his crew scanned the cliff that wasn't far from their minds either. But there was nothing more threatening to be seen than a silhouette of an umbrella pine clinging to the cliff edge.

"What happens now?" Lamont asked, looking warily at the scene.

Jerry shrugged. "Judging by other incidents mentioned in the Odyssey, they'll pull up on the beach, make a fire, eat and drink."

Liz scanned the cliff. "No water."

"Wine. Water in those days was stuff that killed you," said Jerry.

Cruz ground a fist into his palm. "That's when the trouble will start," he said grimly.

Jerry looked startled. "I thought we'd already dealt with that. I've convinced them that Liz—Dr. De Beer—is a sorceress."

The stocky sergeant looked at him. Shook his head. "Dr. Lukacs.

You know all about the history of these guys. And if you get a chance, I'd like you to fill the rest of us in. It might help. But I know troops. This bunch have as much discipline as a pack of wild dogs. That Odysseus guy has barely got them under control. Get them fed, rested, bored and with a few drinks in them—we've got trouble."

McKenna nodded. "Always works like that."

Jerry tugged his wispy beard. "That fits in with the myth, I'm afraid. Against the Cicones . . . "

"In the meanwhile, we're about to beach," Liz snapped. "Jump over and make yourselves useful pulling the boat up."

"Won't they kill us if we aren't all together in a defensive group?" asked Salinas warily.

Liz snorted derisively. "Not until the boat—I refuse to call this thing a ship—is pulled up. Believe me. The sergeant knows soldiers. I know seamen. Nobody is going to touch a hair on your little head until the work is over. Provided you put your back into it."

Salinas bridled. "You don't need to get smart, lady!" He swelled his chest. Alas, most of the swelling took place lower down. Salinas' belt groaned in protest.

"I'm an experienced police officer—we're talking about the tough side of Chicago, cookie—and I say—"

"We're not *in* Chicago, prat!" snarled Liz. She swelled her own chest. It was a far more impressive sight. "And if you're an example of a police officer, Chicago's crooks have got it easy. I'm not taking orders from you! And that's final!"

Salinas' glare bounced off Liz like a pebble off a steel plate. After a moment, he broke eye contact with her and looked to his fellow males for support.

No use. The contest of wills between her chest and his pot-belly was a rout. None of the other men so much as glanced at him.

His shoulders slumped. The belt sighed with relief.

That little sound finally tore Jerry's gaze away from Liz. Startled, he saw a tiny little figure—a leather sprite, perhaps—clambering out of the belt buckle and leaping to the deck. The sprite, casting an angry backward glance at Salinas, darted toward Lamont and vanished into one of his shoes. Lamont, still staring at Liz, never noticed. But, moments later, his feet shifted a little—as if the heavy work shoes had suddenly become lighter and more comfortable.

Up on the beach, the driftwood was stacked. It was also damp. So, after the encounters with Charybdis and running before the storm off Thrinicia, was the tinder. The grumbling from the Achaeans needed no translating.

Lamont nudged Jerry. "Time for a bit more of the sorceress spells. Fire-making, Dr. De Beer."

Liz looked uncomfortable. "I've got a lighter. It smells like mothballs, but it is working . . . but my fires always go out."

Jerry regarded her intently. "Mothballs . . . naphtha . . . Greek fire—something that was certainly known in ancient times . . . I think I'm beginning to get the 'rules' in this place. How are you on fires, Lamont? Or you Sergeant . . . Corporal . . . anybody except me?"

McKenna grinned. "I'll do it, sir. My brother and me, we spent half our time on the farm making fires. We also carry water-proof matches as part of our gear."

It was something of a shock to him to discover that his waterproof matches were about as useful and effective as his rifle had been. But Jim McKenna wasn't that easily stopped. "Just lend me the lighter. You wouldn't have a couple of sheets of paper in your bag, would you?"

"I think we should start calling that thing 'cornucopia,'" said Jerry.

"My ex-husband called it 'lethal weapon,'" said Liz pointedly. "Here, Corporal. And you get two pages of my diary, too."

"We'd better go easy on our modern stuff," cautioned Lamont. "We may need it later."

Liz shook her head. "We may need it just to get through tonight first. Come, Jerry. We'd better go and put on a show while the corporal does the work. We can do inventory later. Right now it is time for you to get inventive with your translations."

Liz put on a fine display of impromptu yodeling and turning and bowing while McKenna carefully built a little pyramid

of shaved splinters around the paper balls. Fortunately his pyro-
maniac youth didn't fail them. The Achaeans were suitably
impressed. Jerry obligingly didn't translate the gist of the admiring
comments about McKenna's body. If he'd understood what they
were saying, he'd never have knelt down to blow the fire.

Anibal Cruz stared at the firelight. The flames trailed green
from the salt in the driftwood, reflecting on the dark water of
the bay. The cliffs were a dark frame to a sky full of stars. Stars.
Stars shone down in countless numbers, in a sky as clear as a
virgin's conscience. The sheltered cove echoed with cheerful voices.
Yeah. Trouble for sure—even if the cheerful voices hadn't been
speaking ancient Greek. If all those clay things held wine . . .

The party of snatchees sat some distance from the fire, listening to the little guy with the wild hair. The—what did he call
himself?—*mythographer*. Anibal fished out a set of poker dice.
At least they hadn't changed into anything. The ration packs'
containers had . . . altered. Changed into paper-like stuff and bone
and leather . . . and broken. The mess in his rucksack really pissed
him off, besides making them short of food. Some of it had got
onto the set of pics he'd thrust in there. They weren't photographs from that trip to Vegas any more. They were paintings.
And in several cases, ruined paintings. But his dice were okay.
He hadn't been anywhere without them for ten years. Even had
them in Saudi. Over the years there'd even been some people
foolish enough to play with him.

He sighed. That lieutenant was going to cause shit. Salinas'
idea now was to try and buddy up to this Odysseus guy. Cruz
shook his head. Odysseus reminded Anibal of a street gang leader
he'd known as a kid. Deadly as a snake, and with a snake's utterly
pragmatic "ethics." Cozying up to someone like that was a sure
prescription for disaster.

"We seem to have been put into a Greek myth. The *Odyssey*,
to be specific. But there are several inconsistencies . . . "

"What I'm really interested in is not where we are, but how
we get back," snapped Salinas.

Jerry regarded him owlishly. "Well. One way would appear to

be to die, Lieutenant Salinas. I'm not sure how else. But, as I was explaining, the rules of this universe are different in certain respects. There may be ways to exploit this to our advantage— but first I've got to understand it. If monsters like Scylla exist, maybe other features of the myths do as well. Greek gods for instance."

"So we should try asking Zeus for a lift home?" Liz asked dryly, pronouncing it "Zee-us" instead of "Zoos."

"I'd go easy on the naming of names, Doctor," said Lamont quietly. "I think this weird place might have them really listening." He sighed heavily. "I wonder how my Marie is managing. . . ."

Jerry felt a pang of guilt. He was torn between a desire to get home safely, and the sheer thrill of this puzzle. He'd have said he was having the time of his life, if he hadn't been frightened out of his wits half the time. He didn't like being thrust into having to actually *do* things . . . but it had been something of a pleasant shock to discover that when he had to, he could.

But Lamont Jackson, Jerry knew, was a devoted family man. He just wanted to get home to his wife and children. Nobody but his academic colleagues would notice if Jerry Lukacs never came home.

Jerry's feelings of guilt deepened. In truth, he was immensely relieved that Lamont was there. First, because the man exuded a kind of practical competence. But, even more, because Lamont was a good guy to talk the ideas through with. As far as Jerry knew, the maintenance mechanic had no better than a high school education. But it was obvious, from the puns they exchanged, that Lamont was one of those people with a sharp mind that soaked things up like a sponge. Which, in this situation, was infinitely more useful than another hyper-educated professor. Jerry could talk to Lamont without sliding into automatic academese, and get ideas out without burying them under the passive tense and three uses of the verb "suggest" in every sentence.

He looked at the rest of the bunch, weighing them up. He dismissed Salinas instantly. If that pompous jackass had anything to offer, he'd be surprised. The South African Amazon seemed quick on the uptake, if as ignorant as a person could be about mythology or even history. She certainly had presence . . . as well as being pretty good-looking in a sort of outdoorsy way.

The two surviving soldiers . . . well. Muscles, he supposed. They seemed okay, though. The tall, handsome younger one that the Greeks fancied could make fires, if nothing else. And the squat gorilla of a sergeant, sitting tossing dice, seemed to have a lot of common sense.

The Achaeans weren't offering to share their wine or the meat they were roasting. The smell was enough to remind Jerry that his breakfast of cornflakes was a long, long way behind him.

Well, he'd had success so far. He decided to chance it again. He walked over to Odysseus. "The sorceress wishes to know: Where then is the famous hospitality of the Achaeans?"

Odysseus burped. "I was about to ask you about that! What sort of sorceress is it that doesn't even provide a few measly goats and maybe a fresh pig or two for the feast? We're as much her guests as she is ours. And she's got ample serfs."

Jerry blinked. One was inclined to forget that the Achaeans were rabid aristocrats. It was clearly shown in the *Odyssey*, and the *Iliad*—and the *Argonautica*, for that matter. But the modern eye glossed over it.

"We are not serfs or landless men!" he proclaimed, trying as best he could to put the tone of unthinking authority in his voice. "Even the least of us has great stocks of bronze and even wrought iron! We are on a holy quest, sent by magic by the gods themselves."

Speaking the language was pure murder. By the look on Odysseus' face, so was his accent. Or maybe it was the ridiculous suggestion that they were worth what the Greeks would consider a fortune.

Odysseus leaned back. The initial look of skepticism on his face was replaced by something Jerry took to be veiled interest. "A quest, is it? Any profit in it? Good looting?"

The mythographer reminded himself that, however romanticized "wily Odysseus" might have become in Homer's account, the ancient Achaean's reputation for cunning must have had *some* basis in fact. It wouldn't do to underestimate the man, even if he did have terrible halitosis and bear a closer resemblance to a Bronze Age gangster than a mythical hero.

Jerry tried to look wily himself. "No, no, none at all. Purely for the honor of the gods."

"Ah. Well, we could hardly refuse nobly born adventurers a bite or two," said Odysseus blandly.

The mutton they were determinedly chewing did not come under the heading of "tender." At this stage, Jerry didn't care. He was so ravenous he spared only a moment envying the cutlery advantage possessed by Liz and the paratroopers. She had a Swiss army knife. Cruz and McKenna had both nearly had fits to discover rust on their own knives. Still, it gave them something better than fingers to tear at the tough meat.

The Greeks were using their weapons for the same purpose. Seeing the casual ease with which Odysseus and his men handled the murderous-looking blades, Jerry reined in his hunger long enough to issue a low-voiced warning to the others.

"Go easy on the wine. Remember that this is the guy who got the Cyclops drunk and then put out his eye. He's half convinced we're rich and on a quest for some vast treasure with lots of loot. And for heaven's sake, Sergeant, Corporal, *don't* let on that you have lots of metal. You're carrying the equivalent of a million dollars in the company of a group of men who would murder you for a dime. At the moment they're not trying to kill us. Let's keep it that way. And pour a little of your wine on the flames as a libation. We're supposed to be religious types."

"I'm Episcopalian," protested Salinas.

"Somehow, Lieutenant, I knew that," Jerry said dryly. "High church, I imagine."

Sergeant Cruz stared at Salinas. From his appearance, Salinas had as much Mexican ancestry as Cruz did. Then, shaking his head, Cruz muttered: "I'm Catholic. More or less. And I got no problem with it at all." He leaned forward and splashed a dollop of wine onto the fire. "The stuff tastes like crap anyway."

Liz shook her head. "You Americans are strange. *I* think the wine's really not bad. Rather like a thin *soetes* from the Klein Karoo."

✦   ✦   ✦

Liz swirled what was left in her cup around for a moment. Odysseus, playing the role of expansive host to the hilt, had provided all of them with the capacious objects. *Very* capacious, she realized.

Then, leaning over, she poured it over the fire. "My own libation. And Jerry's right—Ody's being clever again."

Immediately, Odysseus arose and came over to Liz. A moment later, he was gabbling away at her. His tone of voice combined oiliness with insistence.

"He says it is disrespectful to the gods not to chug it," translated Jerry. "He also says he'll wager you have never tasted such mellow wine as the nymph, Circe, gave them. Bit sweet for my tastes, personally."

"He's obviously never tasted Domaine Danica '98 Zinfandel," Liz snorted. "But then maybe his tastes don't run to dry red."

She eyed Odysseus skeptically. Then asked abruptly: "What's he prepared to wager, d'you think?"

Jerry shrugged. "This is a bit out of my field. I worked on Assyro-Babylonian and Phoenician mythology. I only learned Greek because so much of the source material was in that language. Of course all the mythologies are intertwined, so you pick up a fair amount along the way. In Athens, if I recall correctly, they used to play for the favors of women. A game of tossing wine at a bowl."

Liz gave a wry smile. "I'd need a clothes peg if I lost. And what the hell would *I* want to win?"

Jerry shook his head. "I don't know. I suspect that you wouldn't be expected to bet."

Liz looked decidedly militant. "Ha. I'm going to have to shake their ideas up a bit. If we're going to be stuck in this environment, certain things are going to *have* to change. Like the frequency of their bathing, for starters. Well, I suppose I could bet for transportation or food."

Jerry shook his head warningly. "I wouldn't advise it. They might win . . . "

She raised her chin. "That's my lookout, isn't it? Hey, Sergeant! How good are you with those dice I saw you fiddling with?"

Anibal Cruz looked as innocent as a lamb. Melted butter would have solidified in his mouth. "I'm not really sure of the rules."

Liz gave a crooked grin. "I was *once* stupid enough to play strip poker with a guy who said that to me. Once. Save your tricks for these ... whatchacallem ... Achaeans. Come on, Jerry. Time to explain poker dice."

She took a closer look at Cruz. "Or should I say—liar dice? Are we going to lose, Sergeant?"

"Not fucking likely," muttered McKenna.

A brief flicker of white teeth showed in Cruz's swarthy countenance. "Like McKenna says, Doctor ... "

"Call me Liz. You're about to be gambling with my so-called virtue, after all. Don't you dare lose. I might survive his body but not his breath."

She looked at the open mouths of her companions. "You'll need some seed money too, won't you, Sergeant?" she said, evilly. "They seem pretty keen on the corporal's body. And you can throw in Salinas for good measure."

Jerry nodded. "The ancient Greeks weren't homophobic."

Salinas gaped. "Wha ... "

"Well, *Lieutenant, sir?*" demanded Liz. "Surely you wouldn't expect me to take a risk which you would not dare to?" The female biologist's grin was pure vixen.

Jim McKenna chuckled. "No sweat. We're safe enough, Lieutenant Salinas. Nobody in the battalion will play with Sergeant Cruz."

The sergeant raised an eyebrow. "Try to look a *little* worried, willya?"

"This is a really, really bad idea," interjected Lamont, frowning. "Gambling is a sure way to lose."

McKenna shook his head. "Take it from me, mister. This isn't gambling."

"Then you can put that chunky ring of yours up as seed money too," said Cruz.

Jim McKenna dug it out of his rucksack. "What else?"

"Not too much metal," said Jerry warningly. "It's too valuable."

"It's also changed into other stuff. Even my 'Leatherman' is rusty."

It was a bizarre scene in the flickering firelight. Three white oar blades did for a flat surface. Eager Achaeans surrounded the "table." Jerry should have remembered just how much of a passion gambling had been before television. Dice had been found in Egyptian tombs. They were mentioned frequently enough in Classical Greek literature. Poker was a new concept, however. Still, the Achaeans had picked up the rules of the game pretty quickly. They were just so silent and so intent on the fall of the dice. They even stopped breathing. Only the distant surf sound disturbed the hush. And when Odysseus won . . . jubilation. And that was just while they were playing for beach pebbles. Now that Jerry had suggested making the game a little more interesting, you could cut the tension with a knife. A blunt butter knife.

The dice fell with a clatter onto the three oar blades. In Jerry's ears the surf noises were overridden by the sound of his pulse. If something went wrong, they were in dire trouble. If that corporal ever found out just what Jerry had said he was offering to do for the whole crew, then he was dead. By the worried expression on the sergeant's face, it was a real possibility. Things weren't working the way they were supposed to. Odysseus was winning with monotonous regularity and increasing glee. All that was happening was that Cruz was picking up some phrases of ancient Greek.

Finally, they were for it. Nothing left—and Cruz, having occasionally taken small pots . . . A couple of pairs, facing down a trey . . . threw a flush. And then the tide turned. But Odysseus was hooked by now. Utterly, deeply, and completely hooked. Cruz let him win just enough to keep him in the game. Finally, when Cruz had won the ship, he said: "Double or nothing."

Jerry explained.

A dangerous-looking Odysseus glowered viciously at the sergeant. Their chances of making it through the night diminished. "I have no more to bet."

Jerry shrugged. "Take us where we want to go . . . and we'll call it quits."

Odysseus' eyes narrowed. "Very well. Or you are all mine to ransom."

Jerry was overly confident of Cruz's almost magical ability with the dice. "Sure."

Odysseus threw. A pair.

He threw again. Flush . . .

Jerry swallowed. Cruz shrugged. He reached out a hand to take the dice. Odysseus caught his wrist. "No. The dice fall as you wish them to. We don't trust you. Someone else must throw. Not the sorceress, or you, speaker of execrable Greek."

"That isn't what we agreed to!" said Jerry hotly, fear drying his mouth.

"Why should it be a problem?" said Odysseus smoothly. "Unlesss," he hissed . . . "he cheats!"

"*Cheat. Cheat. Cheat.*" It went around the watching circle, in a murmur. Each man who repeated it seemed to add a new degree of nastiness. And spoke the term more loudly.

Jerry swallowed. And he'd thought they were in trouble when it had just looked like they might lose! Swords were being drawn. Bronze gleamed evilly in the firelight. Jerry desperately tried to moisten his mouth.

"What's the problem?" asked Liz.

"They say we're cheating," he croaked.

"Oh, shit. We're in it deep," she said, as calmly as if they were discussing the weather. He noticed she was taking a firm grasp on that bag of hers.

"They want someone else to throw," Jerry said, looking at the others.

"Not me," said Lamont hastily, shaking his head violently. "I'm useless at games of chance. Got no luck. And I don't approve of gambling anyway."

"We want the Ethiopian," said Odysseus, who couldn't speak English, but wasn't blind either. He pointed at Lamont.

Jerry remembered that there'd been Ethiopians at the siege of Troy. Fighting on the Trojan side.

"I *can't* do this, Jerry. Talk us out of it!" pleaded Lamont.

Jerry looked at the Achaeans' faces in the firelight. "I don't think it's going to work, Lamont. Throw. At least losing's better than what we'll get for cheating."

In the firelight Jerry could see that Lamont's dark skin was beaded with sweat. He had a wine bowl in one hand and the dice in the other. "Oh, Jesus . . . "

Jerry shook his head. "Try Tyche. The Greek goddess of luck."

"Hell ... O Tyche. *Tyche.* I *can't* do this, Jerry. If I need luck, I've never got it. I never win."

"Throw and then run. Head for the water, while they watch the dice," said Cruz.

The Achaeans began to chant. "Throw, Ethiope! Throw! Throw!"

Lamont took a deep breath. Tossed the wine on to the fire. "TYCHE!" he cried ... the dice fell ...

Jerry turned to join the sprint.

And stopped dead.

Divine manifestations tend to do that to you.

Jerry didn't need the deadly silence behind him to know that the ancient Greek Lady Luck had intervened. That Lamont, the extremely reluctant gambler, had thrown a royal flush.

Tyche had compelling green eyes. She also had the kind of teasing smile that leads men into dire trouble. And she could speak English. Well, she was a goddess. Ordinary people don't come in neon glow.

"Well done," she cooed seductively. "I *love* this game. It will bring me many, many devotees. I can see it will bring me great power. I don't care what Zeus wants us to do to you. It pleases me to smile on you."

Lamont stammered. "But ... but ... I'm just not *lucky.* Never!"

She winked at him. "You are now. To Hades with stuffy old Zeus."

Jerry swallowed. "How come you can speak to us in our language?"

"I'm a *goddess*, dah-ling. I can speak to anyone I want."

"What are we doing here?" demanded Liz. "And how do we get home?"

Tyche shrugged broadly and lazily. The motion sent light rippling down her arms. "Even Zeus claims not to know. Magic, he says."

And with that, the goddess of luck departed. As was her way.

12

A TIME FOR PERSPIRATION.

The thin rosy fingers of dawn speared the morning sky and Jerry's eyelids. He groaned. He wasn't a morning person. This morning, doubly so. It had been an uncomfortable night on the foredeck of the black ship. He'd managed to convince Odysseus that there were religious reasons for them sleeping on the water—and that the Americans were incapable of stealing the ship. Their language difficulties were making an accomplished liar out of him. The goddess and the Achaean superstition helped.

Still, Odysseus wasn't that trusting. He'd insisted on putting an equal number of his men onto the afterdeck, once the ship had been relaunched. Both groups had been remarkably good at setting little booby traps to try and forestall any sneaky moves during the night. And they'd kept watch, especially after Jerry had recalled Diomedes and Odysseus' slaughter of the sleeping Thracians.

Unlike young McKenna, who still seemed to be laboring under the delusion that modern soldiering gave them the edge, Jerry knew that nearly every piece of nasty military thinking had been around for a long, long time. And whatever the Achaeans lost in physical size, they made up for in environmental and combat hardening. Every Achaean on this ship was a ten-year vet from a really nasty war.

In reality, of course, these Achaeans out of legend were not supermen either. Just, as Cruz put it, "killers." Jerry was getting to like the sergeant, even if he'd never gamble with him. He'd underrated both the man's intellect and perceptiveness.

It was obvious that Anibal Cruz didn't underrate the prowess of the Achaeans. And Jerry got the feeling that the sergeant was as tough as old boots. The others, Liz in particular, tended to underestimate them. He hoped that it wouldn't get them all killed.

Despite sheer exhaustion, Jerry hadn't slept much or well. The talk on "where the hell are we?" and "how do we get home?" had gone on in his head long after they'd all gone to bed—if you could call a piece of deck "bed."

There just were no easy answers. Only Lamont seemed to really understand Jerry's principal point: This place was achronous. The Mycenaean-age Achaeans shouldn't speak classical Greek. Mind you, there shouldn't be monsters or gods either.

It was the last one that really got to Jerry. The inner skeptic was severely troubled. He just didn't believe in ancient Greek gods. It was damned awkward that they seemed to believe in him. The more he thought about it the more convinced he became that this was somehow the product of advanced alien science. It was not just a step into the myths of yesteryear. But it was the *why* that really mystified him. Unfortunately—no matter what it was, it seemed to be real enough to kill them. And pain seemed real enough too. So did aches from sleeping on a hard wooden deck.

He drew from the last night's divine visitation all that he could: Tyche had said they got here by magic. Well, when it came to Greek mythological magic, your mind turned automatically to Circe. They'd decided on that the night before . . . only the idea didn't make him very comfortable. Like sleeping on the deck, or the knowledge that Odysseus was peculiarly ready to take them to see her. The only person who saw that as a good sign was that ass Salinas.

"Hi. You awake?" asked Liz

"No, I always sit up with my eyes open when I'm asleep," he

snapped, his irritation and courage fueled by a total absence of any chance of coffee.

"Ooh! Another one who doesn't like starting the day without caffeine," said Liz. Her voice was dry. The rest of her wasn't. She was down to a T-shirt and skirt. Wet. The wet clothing didn't leave much to Jerry's imagination. The early morning was still chilly, although the clear sky promised that it would be a scorcher later. The chill was having a marked effect on Liz's frontage.

"You've been swimming!" he stuttered.

"No, I just perspire profusely under your hot gaze."

"Well, perspiring is obviously no substitute for coffee either," he said, his dryness matching her earlier tone.

She acknowledged a hit with a small smile. "Yeah. Without coffee and a cigarette my day doesn't start. And I haven't had either. I've only got six smokes left in that packet. I'm saving them for emergencies."

"But why go swimming in your clothes?" he asked.

"If I took them off, I thought those bloody Achaeans might join me. I wanted to wash that monster's blood off properly and I wanted to get something for breakfast." She pointed to a pile of shells at her feet. "Clams. Big, beautiful clams. Hey—I can hardly believe that this is the Med. It is just so pristine."

Jerry's knowledge of seafood was at the eaten-it-when-paid-for-by-somebody-else level. That had been presented on a restaurant plate, not dripping and *au naturelle* on the deck of a pentekonter.

"How do we prepare them?" he asked warily.

She shrugged, scowled and shivered. "You're asking me? I can't cook!"

It was a relief to find *something* she couldn't do. "Can I offer you my jacket?" he said, offering the somewhat worse for wear windbreaker.

She smiled crookedly at him. Raised an eyebrow. "And deprive you of your view?"

Jerry had been *trying* not to stare. But there was something very compelling about that view. He felt himself blush to the roots of his hair. "Um . . . er . . . "

She chuckled. "I'd have taken it off if it wasn't for those goons.

Don't worry. I kept my coat dry. You can act the gentleman and hold your jacket up as a view-shield for the Achaeans."

Jerry decided his best move would have been to hold it in front of his own eyes.

13

WE WILL ROCK YOU.

The black ship picked her way along a coastline jagged with bays and sea-spearing headlands. Looking inland from the black headlands and white coves, Liz could see the land dancing a heat-hazed forest green. The sea was deep, clear and dark, with just a slight chop on it. Sometimes flying fish feathered away before the slicing ram. For a while dolphins surfed along the bow wave. To seaward, the skyline lay blue and limpid, unbroken by anything more solid than occasional twists of gulls hanging in skeins above distant fish shoals.

The close-up view was a lot less calming—grumbling Achaean sailors. And her translator was looking decidedly pale, and clinging to the gunwale. Liz never got sick, but the information Jerry had just given her was unsettling. . . .

For hors d'oeuvres, there had been his translation—given only reluctantly, due to her vehement insistence—of the chant the Achaeans had been using to time the oar strokes. A charming little ditty which reflected their cheery view of life.

Kill all the men!
Rape all th'women!

83

Sell all th'children!
Into sla-ve-reee!

Then, there was the main course.

The symplegades. The "wandering" or "clashing" rocks. And she, the sorceress, was supposed to steer them past them. "How can rocks move?" she demanded.

Jerry shook his head weakly. "How could you have half-serpent, half-fish, half-women monsters?"

"That's a half too many," she said, irritable because she didn't have an answer, and pedantic because of it.

"You know what I mean. The rules are different."

She shook her head. "I *don't* accept that. Underlying biological and physical principles have to apply . . . "

Jerry looked ahead. "Well, apply them to that," he said grimly, pointing.

They'd entered a long inlet. The water, far from becoming more still, was beginning to peak into little curls of foam. Applying her knowledge of oceanography, Liz realized they must have sailed over a high point somewhere back there. The big open-water rollers here were coming together; reinforcing each other, as peaks met peaks and troughs met troughs. And ahead, in a welter of thundering breakers, lay the wandering rocks. Enormous, sheer-faced, granitic-looking slabs. The gap they'd have to sail into was such a ravel of wild water that she wasn't surprised no ships passed through. It wasn't moving rocks—it was just really dangerous sea.

And then she saw it. A bird winging its way through the gap . . .

With a grumbling they could hear across a mile of water, the huge rocks slithered forward. The meeting was tumultuous. And then slowly the rocks moved apart again.

Liz stared openmouthed. "Oh—*shit!*"

Jerry nodded.

Odysseus gabbled something. He seemed oddly cheerful.

Jerry translated: "He's saying we'll have to head for Ithaca after all. No way to get through that."

"I think that would be wise," fawned Salinas.

Liz snorted. "We'll be slaves in a heartbeat. Nope. Let's just hold our position, while we think this one out. Tell him to tell them to stop rowing."

Jerry translated her reply. The broiled clams wanted to leave him. And they'd been truly delicious. That had been then. Even the thought of food was repugnant now.

Odysseus bellowed at his rowers.

And they yelled back.

Jerry swallowed, twice, before passing it on. "They say the wind is pushing the ship into the gap. It's pushing us forward faster than they can row."

"Get that sail down!!!" The order rang out in Greek and English almost simultaneously.

Liz peered at the sea. The foam lines suggested a current running counter to the wind. "Sea anchor. Have these idiots got one?"

Again, Jerry translated. It was soon obvious that neither Odysseus nor his men had any idea what the biologist was talking about.

"Ships in this day and age," Jerry explained, "rarely used any kind of anchor. They were usually beached at night."

Liz scowled ferociously. "Legendary fucking seamen, is it? 'Argonauts,' is it? Hah!" Her eyes began scouring the ship, looking for the wherewithal. "I'll show 'em some *magic* . . . "

Odysseus looked at the way the vessel was holding her position. Then at Liz. Speculatively. Very speculatively indeed.

"You say she can do goats as well as sea-magic?" he asked Jerry in a quiet voice. "You and I could make a bargain, you know. She'd be none the wiser." He looked meaningfully at the breaker line along the rocky shore. "Or I could toss you overboard. Then she wouldn't know where we were going, eh?"

Jerry looked uneasily at the towering "clashing" rocks. At the rock-toothed shoreline, which at least wasn't moving up and down. Being tossed overboard might be better than losing your insides overboard puking. Still, to survive the surf and ascend those cliffs afterwards . . .

"She'd put a curse on you," he said, with as confident a tone of voice as he could muster. Nonetheless he stepped away from the gunwale, to where Liz, Lamont, and Cruz were preparing little "boats," hastily whittled from a broken oar. Each of the finished ones had a long splinter mast and a paper sail.

Would it work? And what did she hope to achieve by it?

The answer, Liz was sure, lay in the timing. The wandering rocks had taken seconds to rush forward through the water. They'd groaned their way back considerably more slowly. If it was a mechanical process, then if they could time it right they should be able to sail through. The second bizarre possibility was that the rocks were alive and aware. Well, in this weird place anything was possible. Then the answer might be to tire them out. She tried to imagine what sort of creature the rocks might be. Siliceous? Calcareous? A filter-feeder of some sort, thriving on the detritus? She'd bet that it wasn't a biological niche that had a high requirement for intelligence.

The first of the little ships was launched. It rode, on a slightly less than even keel, toward the gap.

"I've lost it," said Liz, squinting into the water-reflected brightness.

Cruz shook his head. "I can't see it, either."

"There!" McKenna pointed. "Coming up on the crest. In the foam. It's just going into the gap."

"Time it," snapped Liz.

Luck and a ride with the wave enabled them to see the little model ship clearly.

It rode safely through.

"I suppose if they attacked little things like that they'd attack every bit of driftwood," mused Liz, looking down at the pile of miniature boats they'd prepared.

"Can't just be size," said Cruz analytically. "The rocks took out a bird."

She cocked her head at him. "What then? Movement? Or an intelligent decision? If it is movement, we should be able to just drift through. Except—"

She pursed her lips. "If we're wrong. The other problem is— besides taking a chance on being turned into jam—we're going to need Halitosis and Co. to keep rowing to give us headway to steer with. Or we'll just wind up on the rocks anyway."

The rolling and pitching was getting to Lamont. His face was beaded with sweat, and he stared very fixedly at the shoreline. But his brain was apparently working, as sharply as ever. "Wasn't Odysseus a legendary bowman?"

Jerry caught the point immediately. "Let's get him to try it with an arrow."

They edged in as close as they dared. Odysseus wasn't the only one who thought the idea was daft. The foam-crested waves seemed as high as the mast top to Jerry. From this close they could actually see the texture of the rocks. They looked like they'd had severe historical acne. The surface was pocked with a myriad of tiny holes.

"Looks more like a sponge than a rock," commented Cruz, as Odysseus loosed an arrow from his bow of ram's horn.

The spongy rocks remained impassive.

" 'Well, it is Ithaca then,' " Jerry translated the ensuing surly remark.

McKenna scowled. "Where's an F-16 with heat-seeking missiles when you need one?"

Liz snapped her fingers. "Heat-seeking! Of course. A dove is warm and moving. That's worth trying. Come on, Jerry. I've been told that if you don't think about seasickness, it gets better. Look at the corporal; he's much better today. Tell them I need some tinder."

Within two minutes, Liz had a piece of brushwood covered in olive oil and tied with a thong to one of her little boats. McKenna was summoned to do his fire lighting. It wasn't easy, but the brushwood burned.

So, unfortunately, did the little sail. However, it pushed the miniature boat far enough forward for it to surf a wave between the rocks. From the crest of one wave, they watched the smoke of the fire go between the rocks and then disappear in a welter of foam.

It didn't matter. Hot prey had been detected. From this close, the grumbling roar of the wandering rocks moving in on their prey was truly deafening. There was also little room for doubt that they were alive . . . and feeding. Long multi-branched ropelike arms ran between the two rocks in a complex network. The trapped water streamed through this and out of the holes on the rock faces.

"My god!" exclaimed Liz. "Those are not just two rocks—that whole thing is a mouth! Those rocks are just 'teeth' to help it filter-feed. That gives a whole new meaning to *Jaws*."

She wasn't horrified; she was just genuinely fascinated. She was also timing carefully. Part of her mind wondered how come watches still worked in this mythical world—when rifles didn't. The lighter worked also—but the lighter fuel had been trans-formed . . .

"Right. What I think we need to try are fire arrows," she said. "Get onto Ody and see if he knows what they are, Jerry."

Seven arrows. And, except for the one that had gone out, the rocks had attacked every one. But they were definitely slowing down.

Liz nodded. "Right. It's getting tired. One more, and as they start going back, it's out oars, and up sails, and the devil take the hindmost."

"Why don't we just keep peppering it with arrows until it's totally exhausted?" whined Salinas.

For an answer Liz pointed to the oar blades biting the water. "The tide is turning. It must be just about slack by now. The sea anchor is not holding us and the wind is pushing us closer, even with oarsmen backwatering. It's go at our own choosing now, or we'll be pushed into it anyway."

The flaming arrow arced upward against the cerulean sky. Even before it fell they were raising the sail. The coarse cordage cut at Jerry's hands, but he pulled with all his might. They all did. Even Salinas took a hand. The square sail with its emblazoned gorgon's head rose, bellied and filled, as the rocks crashed together. The great mouth began to open again. Odysseus' black ship was already surging forward, slicing through the water, with the rowers pulling as though their lives depended on it. "Row! You godsforsaken motherfuckers! ROW!" yelled Odysseus. He'd taken the steering oars himself, not entrusting this to anyone else.

There was a terrible scraping. The black ship shivered like a harp string and then leapt forward as they brushed across the sinewy "net" that drew the rocks together. Then they were in between them. The rocks were still moving apart, but the black ship had at least a hundred yards to cover. They surfed down the wave front, the oarsmen giving their utmost. The water was shallow and an azure blue here.

And then the grumbling of the rocks making their way inward began again. Jerry knew he was screaming. By the open mouths around him the others were too. But above the tumult there was no hearing it. Fifty yards . . . Thirty yards . . . Fifteen yards . . . And the sinewy net barred their way.

There was no way that the ship could be stopped before the net. They hit it full tilt with the ram. Oars snapped. The mast didn't, quite. It vibrated like a sapling before a gale. Nobody managed to stay upright. But before you could say "fiscal discipline," Cruz had grabbed his entrenching tool. "Hold my feet!" he yelled at McKenna.

The ram had nearly done the job. It had snapped the main sinew. Only a few minor ones remained. Even Cruz's strength and the entrenching tool would have been inadequate otherwise. He slashed away like a dervish as the crushing rocks came closer.

"Row!" yelled Odysseus.

Two of the Achaeans had come to help in the bow, and Jerry saw Eurylochus and an axe going over the side with Lamont clinging to one foot and an Achaean on the other.

With a shudder, the black ship slid forward. The rocks grated on the tail of the vessel, tearing half-inch-deep gouges. And then . . . they were free. Heading out for the open water. Jerry helped to haul Cruz inboard again, amid the laughter and the cheering.

"Why didn't you just give us a feather, Dr. Liz?" chuckled Cruz. "We could have tickled its tonsils on the way past." The stocky, wet sergeant was grinning from ear to ear.

"It's a good thing I was here, all I gotta say," growled Salinas.

Jerry gaped at them both, for very different reasons.

14

MEANWHILE, BACK AT THE RANCH.

The MP was finding this a revelation. Maybe it shouldn't be the cops when he got out. Maybe he should go into science. Professor Tremelo was questioning Private Cline in a fashion that police practice would not have allowed. The guy wasn't even a suspect. He was just a witness.

So far, in the process of extracting the tiniest details, Tremelo had stopped short of thumbscrews. Just short. And the professor and his team seemed to find nothing wrong with grilling people mercilessly.

Science was a lot weirder than the MP had realized, when his patrol had encountered the two soldiers who stumbled out of the Oriental Institute. The only ones who had escaped what, so far, was the alien pyramid's biggest disappearing act. Or *snatch,* as the troops were starting to call it.

These science guys were kind of . . . fanatically relentless. There was a sort of overwhelming assumption of what-we're-doing-is-*right* about them. These guys would walk into a no-go area and you'd assume they had a perfect right to be there just because they behaved as if they had.

The professor shook his head. "That's by far the biggest group yet—and we *still* have no idea why. Other than, once again, that they were all in physical contact with each other. That seems to be the pattern when more than one person is taken."

The tall physicist's dark eyes became a little unfocused. "And the fact that—so far—only two of them have come back dead. That's *really* atypical."

He turned to the MP. "Corporal, I want someone from the Oriental Institute. I need to know just who these two men you ran into were, besides a 'maintenance man' and someone who worked on 'comparative mythology.' And find out if there are any results from the comparison of the bite marks on Private Dietz and the earlier victim."

It was a bit odd being told what to do by a man whose turned-up pajama jacket collar stuck out of a lab coat, and who smelled faintly of fish. But somehow, just by the way the man calmly gave the orders, the MP obeyed unquestioningly. It must be part of the science thing. The MP resolved to look into this High Energy Physics stuff.

Miggy Tremelo was unaware of the sort of *third-degree-interrogation* image his team was building with the watching soldier. Not for a moment did it occur to him that the witness could possibly object to being cross-examined by five intent scientists.

So: they'd continuously questioned the man for more than an hour. So: every statement was ruthlessly shredded, and assumed to be false until corroborated. The grilling was similar, if milder, to that which a graduate student would have faced for their oral dissertation. And Tremelo wouldn't have minded if he'd been the witness. In fact, if anything, he was intensely jealous that he hadn't seen it. But it was true that he believed with a frightening intensity in the rightness of research.

Tremelo sat back. "Right. I think we want to try and establish physical and psychological profiles for these victims, as well as examining their background. We need a team on this. Eddie, you head it up. Phil, how's the gamma ray group getting on?"

One of the others shook his head and grimaced. "Simmons is squalling for more equipment."

"Well, get it for him, then!" Tremelo's eyes grew unfocused

again. "But I get the feeling that that avenue of research is going to lead nowhere. There's something about the way this damned thing selects its victims . . . "

He started pacing back and forth slowly, his hands shoved into the lab coat's pockets. "It *seems* haphazard, but I'm willing to bet it isn't. There's something—something—"

He stopped his pacing. "Especially *something* about the people in this latest group! Six of them still haven't come back. *Why?*"

He came to a decision and turned to one of his assistants. "First thing you do, Eddie, is track down the close relatives and friends of those six people. I want to talk to them, as soon as possible."

PART III

First witch: Where has thou been, sister?
Second witch: Killing swine.

—William Shakespeare, *Macbeth*

15

KILLING ME SOFTLY WITH THEIR SONG.

The black ship rode the gentle waves about a mile out to sea. The crew had shipped oars and only the helmsman was at work, using the steady breeze to carry them along the coastline. The cliffs had been left behind and now the coast was the white of sandy beaches and dunes topped with the gray-green of marram grasses.

The seasickness and accompanying nausea had gone and Jerry was wishing he had a horse to eat—or even a bowl of cornflakes. But at least the next stop was Aeaea, where Odysseus had promised to get them a good feasting with plenty of meat and sweet wine from Circe. Tastes had changed a tad from Homer's day, thought Jerry. What he was really craving was a peanut butter sandwich and a cup of coffee. It had been good of the paratroopers to share some of their rations which had survived the transition—but split six ways, and being conservative, it wasn't a lot.

On reflection, Odysseus was being very obliging. It made Jerry extremely suspicious. But he was so tired . . . he'd just rest a bit. They'd be safe for a while now, anyway.

✧　　✧　　✧

He awoke to find that the wind had dropped. The sea was glassy, and the only sound was the arrhythmic sound of oars. Odysseus' crew seemed to be struggling to row in time. No one was calling the stroke. Jerry concluded it was the silence that had woken him. The Achaeans were always talking, and if they rowed, they called the stroke. Now they rowed in silence. It had also become cool and the coastline was shrouded in a soft clinging mist. The sandy point and marram-clad dunes were gray and ghostly, even though Odysseus' ship lay barely a hundred yards off the shore.

"It's eerie, isn't it?" said Liz, from her post in the bow. "It's almost as if someone is singing in the distance."

It struck Jerry like a bucket of cold water. He was suddenly very wide awake. "*Sirens!*"

Only Lamont knew exactly what Jerry meant. But it didn't need much explaining. The singing was clearer now. And the Achaeans rowed stolidly on.

"The bastards have got beeswax in their ears!" snapped Jerry. The cunning Odysseus had hit on a novel way to get rid of his debts.

"Do we try to block our ears?" asked Lamont.

"I don't think it'll work. But I'll tie you to the mast." Jerry looked around for a rope.

"And then?" Liz asked sarcastically. "What's going to happen to you?"

Jerry shrugged. "It's my fault. I presume I'll jump overboard."

Cruz shook his head. "That Odysseus isn't going to untie us, Dr. Lukacs, no matter who does the tying. We might as well stay loose."

"And without you we haven't anyone who can speak Greek," pointed out Liz.

Lamont stared intently at Jerry. "Listen, didn't somebody else get past the sirens? I'm trying to remember."

"The Argonauts. Orpheus sang a song far sweeter than theirs. I can't carry a tune in a bucket, Lamont. And I've heard you 'singing.' Can anyone else sing?"

Lamont dived for his bundle and unearthed his precious boombox. "I don't think much of their voices so far. Let's see how they shape up against some *real* competition."

He pressed the play button and turned the volume up. Suddenly, Tina Turner's voice boomed across the still water. *"What's love got to do with it?"*

The mist seemed to waver. The melodious, but not top quality, club-standard singing was stilled, and replaced by a squawk.

"—but a second-hand emotion—"

It was a pretty good "I-am-a-bantam-and-have-just-laid-an-ostrich-egg" squawk. The sunlight suddenly cut through the mist, revealing a sandy marram meadow, flanked by three raised tumuli. The rank marram grew through the white bone piles that studded the meadow.

"What's love got to do—"

In the midst of this sat two very large birds—rather like overgrown penguins. They sported human heads. Female, to judge by the pale complexions and lack of beard. Hideous-looking things, really.

"—got to do with it—"

Expressions of surprise—then shock—then total outrage—and then rabid envy flighted across their gargoyle-ugly countenances.

Jerry wasn't looking at the legendary sirens that had lured sailors to their death with their sweet voices. He was looking at the boombox.

A golden nimbus clung about it. In the dancing shadows above the CD player you could see the singer. Tina Turner, her inimitable legs flashing and prancing, strutting her stuff. Big as life, and just as loud.

"That's not a CD," he said in a choked voice to Liz. "That's the real thing. It's . . . it's a summoning or something."

Liz laughed. "No wonder the sirens are outclassed! Real singing must be rare in these days. Nonexistent, I'd say. And will you look at those damn Achaeans!"

Not even the wax in their ears could keep Odysseus and his men from hearing Tina Turner. But judging from their bulging eyes, Jerry thought it was her legs which had them mesmerized.

Lamont, McKenna and Cruz didn't notice. They were too busy leaning over the gunwale, laughing as the plump sirens tossed their double flutes aside and waddled in haste towards the sea. They were flapping their wings frantically, but they were far too big to do more than short hops into the air. They plunged into the sea, swimming ducklike after the departing ship.

Lamont reached a hand behind him and clicked the golden voice off. "Let's give them a bit of rap, boys, whaddaya say?"

McKenna and Cruz grinned. A moment later, Lamont and the two soldiers were shuffling back and forth at the stern, doing an impromptu rap session.

"*Yo—bitch! I'm talking to you!*

"*Swim all you want! Flop all you want!*

"*Ain't getting none o' my—*"

Jerry found himself consumed by a deep longing for Bach's *Brandenburg Concertos*. Or Tina Turner. Anything.

16

᠎

THE ENCHANTED ISLE:
NO TRADESMEN OR HAWKERS.
BY ORDER: THE MANAGEMENT.

Naturally enough, Odysseus had understated the distance to
Aeaea. It was another cold, hard-decked night at sea before they
saw Circe's isle. Having to scrounge food made Jerry uncomfortable in the extreme. He was glad when a forested island loomed
out of the distance. It was green and pleasant looking in the
bright midmorning sunshine.

"Aeaea," said Odysseus, with all the air of a kindly gentleman
who is doing you an enormous favor. "It is a safe place with
kindly and hospitable people."

"We won't mention beeswax in people's ears, will we," said Jerry,
sarcastically. "We know about Circe, Odysseus." That was true
enough. What they weren't sure about was how to persuade her
to help them.

"What's he saying?" demanded Salinas.

After Jerry explained—and passed on his own misgivings
about Odysseus' intentions—Salinas shook his head. "Meaning
no disrespect, Dr. Lukacs, but I think you're taking much too
negative an attitude here. These men are soldiers and they

respect rank. And likewise we must respect rank. I've been doing my best to get onto good terms with Prince Odysseus. He's a powerful and influential man. We'd do well not to get on his bad side."

Jerry blinked. There was no point in arguing with this guy. "You should concentrate on learning some classical Greek. And I think you should watch Odysseus."

"Oh yes," said Salinas earnestly. "I'm planning to stick very close to him. Learn his ways, as it were."

Toady up to him, you mean, thought Jerry sourly, but held his tongue. Instead, abruptly, he muttered a phrase in Greek. Then repeated it, more slowly and aloud.

"That's the first classical Greek phrase you should learn, Lieutenant." He uttered the phrase again, this time slowly enough so that Salinas could follow. "What it means is: *you are my friend.*"

Salinas repeated it carefully, several times, until he thought he had it down. Nodding sagely all the while. "Yes! That's the very same phrase that Prince Odysseus has spoken to me. Several times, now. I was sure that's what it meant!"

Jerry turned hastily to look at the sea. "We'll be on the beach in a few minutes. I think we want to stick together. This could be a dangerous place."

"But I thought you said Prince Odysseus spent several months here?" asked Salinas.

"He did indeed. I meant it could be dangerous for us," said Jerry dryly.

Salinas scurried away. As soon as he left, Lamont approached.

"What did that son of a bitch want, Jerry?"

Jerry raised his eyes to heaven. "He's just telling us—again—how we ought to buddy up to Odysseus."

"Ha!"

"Exactly," said the mythographer.

It was obvious, from the minute they'd hauled the ship up on the tiny beach next to an even tinier stream, that Odysseus and his crew had plans. A party of five set off, then and there, to show them the way to Circe. The rest of the crew was left on the beach. Pretending not to snigger.

And it was Jerry, to his own irritation, who gave them the opening they were looking for.

The path next to the small stream became steep quite rapidly. The island was heavily treed and the gorge was in deep shade. It was the kind of place that would have been heaven for a leisurely ramble. It was pure hell in hot pursuit of wiry and fit Achaeans, especially when you aren't in particularly great shape. The sun had been searing outside the little gorge. Here the rocks were clad in velvety moss, and the trail was hung with ferns beaded with droplets from the tiny waterfalls. Beautiful. It was also as slippery as an expensive lawyer.

The place Jerry chose to lose his footing was about as bad a spot as possible. They'd climbed up a steep section, away from the stream, because the stream bed was choked with a couple of enormous boulders. They'd just got to the point where the path had leveled out slightly, and they were traversing in towards the stream above the boulders. Below the path the slope wasn't actually a cliff—because it was so thickly vegetated. It was still at about an eighty-degree angle.

The leaf-mould edge beneath Jerry's feet gave way. He had a brief moment of frantically grabbing handfuls of vegetation, and then the slope disappeared into a blur of snapping small trees and cascading plants. Then he felt a sharp pain in his leg and then . . . blessed oblivion.

He awoke against a soft and mammaceous cushion. It smelled slightly sweaty but somehow . . . feminine. He opened his eyes. Liz was peering down at him. It was her breast that he was cradled against. "Are you all right?" she asked.

Pain lanced up from the leg that rough hands were manipulating. "My leg."

"I don't think it's broken," said McKenna, squatting nearby. "Some nasty lacerations. I'm not so sure about your ankle."

Jerry moved it, warily. It was sore but it moved. He tried to stand up. His head was definitely still whirly.

"Stay still," said Liz gruffly. Jerry wondered if he'd cracked his skull. The tough cookie looked like she'd been crying.

Cruz and Lamont came up the slope. Lamont was severely

out of breath. Cruz wasn't. "Lost them, I'm afraid," he said grimly.

"Not"—pant—"a sign of them." Lamont looked at Jerry. "You okay, Dr. Lukacs?"

It was strange how the formalities slipped in again. Jerry blinked. "Fine, Lamont. Well. A bit sore and a bit dizzy. I think I hit my head."

"You're lucky to be alive," snapped Liz.

"Um. I'm sorry," Jerry apologized humbly.

She smiled. "S'all right. I don't think you were alive on purpose, somehow. Actually, I think Ody helped you on your way."

Jerry looked up at the slope that he'd obviously glissaded down. "Where is Odysseus?"

Liz shrugged. "Gapped it. Along with the lieutenant."

Jerry swallowed. His mouth tasted of blood. "They took Salinas?"

Cruz snorted and shook his head. "'Took him,' my ass. He scampered right after them, Doc."

"Chickened out on us," said Lamont grimly. "Wanted to stick to 'Prince Odysseus.'"

Jerry managed a weak grin. "He chickened out? What a *fowl* fellow."

Liz groaned. "The puns have started again. He *must* be feeling better."

Jerry felt a sudden sharp reluctance to move his head. The cushion was—splendid. *Duty calls.* He forced himself to sit erect. "Yes. I am."

"What do we do now?" asked McKenna.

Liz stood up. "Well, there's no sense in chasing after Odysseus. They know their way around here, and we don't. And I'll bet the ship isn't on the beach any more either. So: I'm going to have a bath. And I suggest you put that ankle into the stream. The water is pretty cold. That'll reduce the swelling a bit. I've got some soap in my bag and a couple of sachets of shampoo, if anyone else wants to wash."

"And then?" asked Lamont.

Liz shrugged. "And then we'll strap up that ankle and go looking for Circe, or something to eat. Whichever comes first."

When Liz had made up her mind on a course of action, you might as well follow it. It was too much like hard work not to. Besides . . . at least she *was* decisive.

As she walked away, Liz allowed the knot in her stomach to ease slightly.

She was scared, unhappy, and—worst of all—confused. She didn't like being out of her depth. But, as she'd learned the hard way on that first two-month stint as an observer on a Spanish vessel down in the Southern Ocean, you didn't let it show. And you didn't let yourself get upset. Get angry instead. This place was making her positively waspish. Ichneumonid wasp, to judge by the effect it was having on her waistline.

That thought led to another. She was sick of being filthy.

Besides, she decided, a bath always cleared her thoughts. She was starting to think like a stupid schoolgirl. Her idle attraction to McKenna was one thing. She'd always had a bit of a soft spot for tall, handsome men and had, now and then, indulged herself. Not that she'd had any intention at all of doing so, under these circumstances, because it would be sure to create problems. She had precious little respect for women, or men for that matter, who let lust overpower their brains. Still, she found Mac physically very attractive.

She pondered on that thought idly, for a moment. It was a product of her background, she supposed. Her former husband had been, physically anyway, very similar. It had taken her nearly two years to come to terms with the fact that, other than appreciating his body, she didn't really like the guy. And now she was behaving in her typical "can you dominate me?" fashion with this corporal. Fortunately he didn't even seem to understand the game, because she really had no interest in it herself.

But this *other* business, now. That was a different thing altogether. And, under the circumstances . . .

She snorted. *Sure to create problems? Say better: disaster.*

Fortunately, the water looked cold. Quite cold enough, she thought, to squelch silliness.

She walked about thirty yards downstream, just out of sight. There was a bath-shaped pool etched out of the sandstone, complete with a miniature waterfall shower. It looked like it was meant for her. She stripped off, took the little bar of traveling soap out of her bag, and jumped in. It was even colder than she'd expected.

The soap smelled odd. Still, it worked. The water was too cold to stay in. Freeze an improper thought solid, it would. She stood up and soaped.

And realized somebody was leering lasciviously at her.

Well—*something,* anyway. The lower half was very definitely goat, down to the cloven hooves and tangled black curly fur leggings. The protruding evidence suggested that it was as randy as one. It had devilish twisted goaty horns curling up out of the dark hair. The horns went well with the loose-lipped expression.

Liz reacted instinctively. The shoulder bag was lying on the far bank. She grabbed the strap and swung. She swung with all her strength and screamed bloody blue murder.

If she'd hit any harder the satyr would have had two extra Adam's apples. As it was, his flute went flying and he doubled over, lost his footing, and then fell into the pool. She leaped for the far bank, as running footsteps came pounding down from where she'd left the others.

As luck would have it, Cruz and McKenna were away higher up the slope, scouting. Lamont had been strapping up Jerry's ankle with a strip of shirt. He'd just finished this makeshift job, when Liz shrieked. He and Jerry both flew to the rescue. Well, tried to. Lamont, in his first three steps, peeled a section of moss off a rock and tumbled into a mess of washed-out roots. That left Jerry, hobbling and swearing, heading to the rescue in a sort of stumbling run.

Jerry was thus first on the scene. And quite a scene it was.

There, against a backdrop of wild violets, was Liz. Clad only in a few soapsuds, militantly swinging her shoulder bag.

She took a horrified look at him. Dropped her bag. Attempted to cover herself with inadequate hands, while stuttering and turning puce. And then, in desperation, as the others arrived, she jumped into the pool.

Unfortunately, it was still rather full of groaning and spluttering satyr. Having a hundred and forty-two pounds of embarrassed girl land on his *back* was not at all the reception the satyr had been planning on. With a squeal, he dragged himself out of the pool and hurtled his dripping way past Cruz and McKenna before bounding off into the woods.

"What are you staring at?" shrieked Liz.

Jerry tried to looked away. Failed miserably.

Outraged, Liz repeated the question. Pedantry came to his rescue.

"Well. You."

17

THIS LITTLE PIGGY WENT TO MARKET.

McKenna shrugged his shoulders. "Yeah. I thought it wouldn't be that hard to track them. I grew up on a farm, but it wasn't like this." He hefted the bayonet-tipped spear.

Jerry eyed the weapon a bit skeptically. After they'd lost Odysseus, the two paratroopers had taken the time to make themselves spears of sorts. What the paratroopers called the 550 cord in their rucks was no longer nylon parachute cord. It was . . . something else. But, whatever it was, it did an adequate job of binding their bayonets to longer shafts than their useless M16s provided. But Jerry was dubious that the bayonet-tipped former branches were going to be of much use in any real fracas.

Still—they were soldiers, and he wasn't. And, at the moment, he deeply envied their superb physical condition. Neither Cruz nor McKenna exhibited a trace of Jerry's own feeling of semi-exhaustion.

The path had led out to a tableland of mixed forest, oaks and beech trees, trackless and silent—except for the cicadas, who made up for the absence of other sounds in spades. The trouble was that it was all alike. Jerry had no idea any longer which direction

they'd even come from. His ankle was so damned sore and he
was really, really hungry as well as tired. They needed to take
some kind of action. Decisive action.

Liz hesitated. "I'm not much of a tracker. We always had track-
ers on the farm, and my brother learned a lot from them. But
I never really bothered. But there is a lot of game here."

Jim McKenna looked startled. "I haven't seen anything. I
thought you were a *marine* biologist."

"I've seen several buck, sign that looks like bushpigs and some
squirrels. And everybody grew up somewhere. I grew up near
Hoedspruit. Next to Kruger Park. On a game farm," she added.

"Where's that?"

"Northern Transvaal. They call it 'Northern Province' these
days." Nobody looked any the wiser. "South Africa." She looked
at them, clearly embarrassed. Particularly, she looked at Lamont.
"I never asked to get born there. And it *is* a democratic country these days."

Jerry suddenly understood why she insulted everybody except
Lamont. He hadn't really been aware of how she pussyfooted
around him—until this moment. Lamont was an even worse
punster than he was, but Jerry always took the rap from her.

"Look. I can't help where I come from. I've got several black
friends from university. I don't have a problem with it."

"Never said you did," said Lamont easily. "Come on. We've got
to get moving." He pushed forward into a mass of dogwood.

And found he was sharing it with a large animal. A large
animal that hadn't liked having its slumber disturbed. Broad-
spaced, angry little eyes peered shortsightedly at the intruder. The
black snout wrinkled and a short, angry grunt emerged. Liz was
just behind Lamont. She grabbed his shoulder and yelled:
"RUUUN!"

The boar was a monster. Not quite the black beast of Thessaly.
Not *quite*—but still very damn big. Cruz and McKenna and their
makeshift spears looked very small. Those tusks would gut a man
in a single jerk. Fortunately, the beast was obviously shortsighted.
It paused. Sniffed and then pawed earth.

"Don't be idiots!" yelled Liz, now trying to help the frantically hobbling Jerry. "Climb a tree!"

The boar decided on McKenna. A toothpick would have had more effect than the spear. It was ripped out of his hands. Only luck and fast reflexes saved his life. Cruz's attempt to throw his makeshift spear was not successful either. It stuck, briefly, in the flank of the boar before the pig turned again. Cruz pulled McKenna to his feet and they ran. Behind them the boar nosed the air, foam on its muzzle.

Cruz, moving like a quarterback on the charge, grabbed Jerry and continued to run. McKenna tried to do the same with Liz. She fended him off, nearly sending him to ground in front of the snorting piggy from hell.

Somehow, they scrambled up the oak tree just in time.

"You know," said Cruz, from the branch where he sat looking down at the boar, "you were right, Ms. South Africa. There *is* plenty of game here." The monster pig was rooting angrily around the dropped jackets, spears and M16s, but had as yet not found Lamont's precious boombox, thrust in a fork of the tree a few yards up.

Jerry felt his ankle. It had not enjoyed the walk up to here, and it had enjoyed the last run even less. "Yeah. Only trouble is that no one explained to the 'game' that we aren't the 'game.' "

Smoke was almost curling out of Liz's ears. She was nearly incandescently angry. "Listen to me, you two. You. Sergeant. And especially *you*, Corporal. If I say run, I mean fucking *run*."

"Sorry, *sir*," growled McKenna. "We make our own decisions." He inspected the slashed fabric of his trousers. The tusk had been *that* sharp and *that* close.

Her voice would have cut glass. "Listen, *Corporal*. I was dealing with meathead he-man parabats—those are our paratroopers—when you were still sitting on your mummy's knee. Get this straight. You're a soldier in the service of your country. Your job is to protect its interests and its citizens. And to do that, shit-for-brains, you have to stay *alive*. Wasting your life stupidly is not going to help anyone. We need you to keep Jerry and . . . and Lamont and even keep me alive."

She shook her head angrily. "I grew up on a farm adjoining

one of the largest wildlife reserves in Africa. I don't think I'm the great African hunter, but I know a fuck of a lot more about it than you could have learned on a couple of weeks' worth of survival course. I am *not* inclined to panic. I'm not going to tell you to do something just for fun. I'm not going to tell you how to fight men. That's your call. You say 'jump' then, and we'll jump. But when it comes down to dealing with wildlife or ships you're nothing but a goddamn *boot*. And I don't care how many 'training' sessions they sent you on. They were still *training*. This, *just in case you hadn't noticed*, isn't. We've got to work together or we'll all die."

She pointed at Jerry. "You've particularly got to look after him. Because, in case you haven't worked it out, Dr. Lukacs is the only one who knows this mythology stuff. If anyone can work out a way home, he can. Or don't you *want* to get back?"

The pig at the foot of the tree snorted.

"The pig seems to think you're right," said Lamont dryly.

McKenna shook his head. "Look, we were trying to provide you with cover to get away . . . "

"She's right, Mac," Cruz rumbled. "If that pig had taken you out, that would have left me to try and look after these guys. We've got to get our mindset into 'run first and fight when we haven't any damn choice.' It's different 'cause we're dealing with civilians."

"And if that pig had mauled you, we'd have been worse off," said Liz quietly. "Look, I lost my cool. But seriously, try listening to me, okay?"

McKenna took a deep breath. The pig stood on its hind legs and snorted at the tree. That helped to format his reply. "Yes, ma'am."

She grinned. It transformed her face, making her look like the kind of trouble she'd undoubtedly been at fifteen. Jailbait. "That's a *good* boy," she cooed.

The pig squinted up at her and snorted again. As if, again, it thought she was right.

Jerry took a deep breath. He hated telling anyone what to do. But somebody had to. "We need some sort of plan of campaign.

Circe's 'castle of dressed stone' is in here . . . somewhere. If I remember rightly, there was also a crag, but most of the island is low-lying. Odysseus caught sight of the smoke from her castle from the top of the crag."

"So we need to find the crag," said Cruz.

"Which is virtually impossible from down here in the forest," grumbled Liz.

"Well, maybe we could see it from the top of a tree," suggested McKenna.

Liz smiled nastily. "Up you go then, Corporal. We've got lots of time to kill until Mister Piggy loses interest in us after the little holes you made in his hide."

Salinas spoke his phrase of Classical Greek. Odysseus seemed . . . surprised. John Salinas said it again, smiling and patting his chest. The Achaeans seemed amazed. He was reassured. He felt sure that he'd made the right decision, although it would have been pleasant to have that long-haired translator around to confirm it.

At least the Achaeans knew where they were going. This forest was confusing. He was nearly exhausted when, at last, they came out in front of a fortresslike building of painstakingly fitted dry stone. It was set in a soft meadow—and guarded by wild beasts.

Salinas nearly turned and ran. That . . . that must be a wolf. And a leopard . . . And *lions*. They were coming forward. His bowels turned to jelly, as the creatures ran up to Odysseus. For a moment he was too terrified to even run. Then the prince cuffed them aside, and beckoned to Salinas. Warily, the police lieutenant followed as Odysseus pounded on the polished metal doors.

The doors were flung open. A woman with lustrous hip-length hair stood in the doorway. She looked anything but delighted to see them. John Salinas decided it was time to try his Greek phrase again. After all, they'd be glad to have him. He could show them such a lot.

He was quite right. She was obviously pleased. She sat him down on a settee and then brought him food and a bowl of wine.

It was a weird sort of porridge-like stuff, but he was starving. And the red wine, if sweet, was really nicer than the Cabernet Sauvignon he pretended to like for social purposes.

He made a bit of a pig of himself.

18

⊡⊡⊡⊡⊡⊡

ALIAS ALLIUM.

The view from the crag top proved that they were on an island. *Just like the Doc said it was*, thought Cruz. He was quietly but enormously relieved to find that the absentminded-looking professor had known what he was talking about—again. The tough sergeant was developing a genuine respect for Jerry Lukacs.

There was no sign of smoke to show where the home of this "Circe" was. All you could see was a lot of forest. It was an island all right, but not a small island. Maybe fifteen by twenty miles of island. Searching it was going to be next to impossible.

Among the rocks and out of the forest it was hot in the sun. Hot enough to make Anibal remember the stream—and just how far away it was . . . especially as that South African girl had pointed out those paw prints in the mud. The leather that their canteens had turned into made the water taste odd, but it was better than walking back.

The sergeant repressed a shudder. Lions! First that boar. And now *lions*. And if Doc Jerry was right there'd also be leopards and wolves. The little guy said that ancient Greece had them. Bears, too. And a whole lot of monsters on top of that, if all the mythical stuff were true.

He sighed softly. Ranger school had taught them every damn thing. How to live off the land. How to stalk. It had been physically and mentally demanding—more than surviving here had been, for the most part. It just somehow hadn't included wild boars *and* lions *and* legendary monsters at the same time, along with the other uncertainties of this place. It also hadn't included keeping untrained people alive.

Still, they were doing pretty well. Cruz knew that although he and Mac could move at twice the speed, they'd not have survived so far if it wasn't for the civilians. But they really needed something better than those spears if they were going to go on surviving. Fire was good for predators. It was also difficult to get going in a hurry. He resolved to look for a good dry branch full of twigs. It could be more useful than the M16s that they were lugging along. As far as he could work out, they were just dead weight. He decided to try burning some of whatever the stuff was that was in a cartridge now. That might be useful . . . more than some other things. Even being good at powerbreaking wasn't going to help in this wilderness.

He sighed again. He was a city kid, fer chrissake. You knew where you were, there, just like you did in the Army. And, sure, Ranger school had been tough. But it was *school.* You got out at the end of it. And you didn't have civilians to worry about.

Which led him into the other truly scary idea: They could be here forever. One of the most precious things that any soldier can take into battle is the knowledge that if he survives—he can go home. It wasn't true in this case. You only got shipped home if you got a bad case of "dead."

He looked across the forest again. Yeah. They were in deep shit. They were going to struggle just to survive the animals. Not to mention all of this "magic and gods" crap.

His eyes nearly bugged out. At first glance he'd thought they were horsemen. It was only at second glance he saw they really *were* horse-men. Centaurs. With bows. And they looked pissed.

Really pissed.

"Quick! Over the cliff!" shouted Cruz.

Liz had been musing, gazing over a panoply of forest greens that certainly was nothing like the modern Greece she'd visited in that long ago time with Nick. Her wandering thoughts—about just what impelled logic and hormones in the female of the species and why they seemed to work in diametrically opposite directions—was disturbed by a yell and the clatter of hooves. A second's glance was enough to tell her that Cruz had the right idea.

Alas, climbing down is never easy. It was touch and go on the lichenous rock. And then, when she reached the overhang—clutch and grow . . .

But that overhang was a blessing. The centaurs had showered a good few rocks down after them.

"It's a good thing they're half horses, not half goats," said Jerry, massaging his ankle with a grimace.

Liz smiled. "One thing we primates can do better than horses, and even goats, is climb. And run long distances too, for that matter."

"Run? I didn't think we could outrun those things," said Lamont, checking his homemade jacket-and-bandolier backpack, complete with his precious boombox.

"The size of their mouth and lungs is going to make suffi-cient respiration interesting," mused Liz. "They're probably much less efficient runners than a horse, at a guess. And humans can outrun horses, over a stretch."

"Well, I certainly couldn't outrun them. Not now—or ever," said Jerry. "Although I could *eat* a horse right now."

"That lot looked more ready to eat *us*," complained McKenna. "They just saw us and went on the hunt, no questions asked. Good thing they didn't catch us out on the flat."

Jerry chuckled. "True. So here we sit like a row of monkeys on a ledge instead."

Lamont smiled. "Me see-no-evil, you hear-no-evil and him speak-no-evil. Who are the last ones then, Jerry?"

"Well, the corporal is feel-no-evil, now that Odysseus is gone," said Liz, with a wry grin, "and in my case, I'm smoke-no-evil." She sighed. "I'm going up to have a look-see. Been no rocks or noise for a while now."

Feel-no-evil looked up. Listened carefully. "Yeah, but where do you want to go to, Liz?"

Smoke-no-evil stood up and felt for a handhold above the small overhang. "In search of dinner. If we go back down to the coast I can always catch something. Even up here we might be able to snare some small game."

"Yes, but what about the centaurs?" said Jerry.

She shrugged. "We'll just have to keep a lookout. If we get down to the beach again we can probably swim away from them. Although there are probably sharks and sea monsters and heaven knows what else in this water. It's that or sit here and starve. I've been meaning to go on a diet for a while, but this is a bit radical."

It went without saying that the only sign of the ship on the beach, when they finally found their way back there, was the keel mark on the sand.

Off to one side of the bay, there was a low cliff with steep and seaweedy rocks around its base. "Should be safe from centaurs along there," mused Cruz, looking at it.

Lamont nodded. "We'll have to see if we can find an overhang or a cave or something. You guys scout. Jerry needs to sit for a bit."

"I'm fine," said the mythographer.

"If you weren't sunburned, you'd be as pale as a ghost," said Liz grimly. "You look as if you're about to fall down."

McKenna nodded his agreement. "Yeah, Doc. Take a rest."

Jerry sat down on the sand. "Liz is as much a 'Doc' as I am."

McKenna grinned. "I think I'd rather call her 'Sir.'"

Liz threw the rock she'd been carrying at him.

"It smells and even looks like garlic," Jerry said doubtfully.

Liz nodded. "It's certainly a species of allium. And this is definitely fennel. I saw some sage back there, too. And there was lavender at the edge of the gorge."

"You certainly know your herbs," said Jerry, impressed.

She scowled fiercely. "My mother. She's kooky about all that herbal stuff. I have drunk more vile-tasting tisanes than I care to think about."

"Well, at least we can flavor anything we catch," he replied, pacifically. "And if the worst comes to the worst we can eat the herbs."

She pulled a face. "Yuck. I'll try my hand at fishing." The cornucopia-shoulderbag had yielded a spool of dental floss. The changes had probably altered its nature but it was still a fine strong line. She'd claimed a five-yard piece as her own, before offering the rest for future bird snares. There were no pins or safety pins, but the bag debris had yielded no less than seven paper clips of different sizes. Liz had been painstakingly trying to fashion hooks, when Lamont had come along. "Can I do it for you, Miz?"

She held it out to him. "Please call me Liz. Please." She smiled appealingly.

Lamont was not proof against the smile. "I'm a maintenance man . . . Liz. I'll turn those into hooks."

Liz smiled again. "I'm not handy. I'd be glad if you did."

Lamont picked up a rock. Looking at it, Jerry thought it had been beach sand not long ago in its geological history—assuming this weird place *had* a geological history.

"Going to be hell sharpening anything with this," grumbled Lamont. "I'll try to rub a hole through it."

"There are some good rocks back at the stream," said Jerry.

"Wait a minute," said Liz. "Do you really think you could make holes through this rock, Lamont?"

Lamont regarded the fist-sized but flattened piece in his hand. "I think so. Why, M . . . Liz?"

"I read every Gerald Durrell book ever written." She had a nostalgic smile on her face.

The two of them looked at her blankly. "Naturalist. Grew up in Greece. Well, for some of his childhood. And then he collected animals all over the world. Anyway, in the one book about South America he had described this thing called a . . . bolas."

Jerry nodded. "Ah. Yes. I know what you're talking about. Weights on a rope that are thrown to entangle things."

Liz pulled a wry face. "Well, my brother and I made one with ball sinkers. I killed a guinea fowl with it."

Lamont raised an eyebrow. "Liz, are sure your name isn't really 'Indiana Jones' or something?"

She looked embarrassed. "It was a tame one. And Dad nearly killed us. I cried."

Cruz and McKenna had gone off with the newly contrived bolas and, in case that didn't work, their spears. Lamont had just painstakingly constructed a hook . . . when Jim McKenna realized what he was doing and pulled out a sewing kit which also contained several hooks. But Liz had insisted on using Lamont's. She was fishing.

Gathering black mussels was all that Jerry was judged to be fit for. It was stationary if wet work. Lamont had first collected some firewood and then promoted himself to gulls'-nest-robber-in-chief on the low crag above their Robinson Crusoe beach-cave camp.

Jerry looked up to see Lamont in the act of discovering that Greek mythworld gulls were just as keen on having their eggs stolen as the ones back home. "Shit. It's just been *sick* all over me!" Jerry saw him snatch angrily at the gull. And catch it.

It all happened terribly fast. The ledge, about twenty feet off the beach, was made of the same soft sandstone as the bolas weights. Maybe a piece of it gave way. Maybe the gull pecking furiously at him caused him to lose his grip. Liz, fishing a few yards further out from Jerry on a rock point, and Jerry with a lap full of black mussels, saw Lamont plunge to the sand still clutching a large, angry gull. By a miracle he missed the projecting rocks. The gull's squawk even eclipsed Lamont's shriek.

They landed together in a flurry of squawks, yells and flapping wings. By the time Jerry and Liz got there, the gull had clumsily fluttered free. With a derisive final squawk and last vicious peck, it expressed its heartfelt opinion of all nest molesters. The piece of physical opinion landed with a white splat on the rock ten inches from Lamont's head.

Lamont sat up, amid their anxious entreaties. He waved a rueful handful of feathers. "I thought I had us a bird for dinner." He held out the other hand. In it was a mottled egg, miraculously intact. "All I got was the egg."

"Well, now we know which one comes first." Jerry waved his hand in front of his nose. "Phew. Fish!"

"Yeah. I think I need to wash. Jeeze, that thing made some holes in me."

"There's a nice deep spot next to where I was fishing." Liz cleared her throat, looking shamefaced. "Um. I think I've just lost the fishing line and that hook you made me, Lamont."

"And I've lost all those mussels I gathered." Jerry inspected the older man. He looked, miraculously, none the worse for the fall. "You've got all the luck. If it had been me, I'd have dashed my brains out."

"That might have stopped you punning for ten minutes," said Liz dryly.

Most of Jerry's mussels had indeed washed away. But, to their amazement, Liz's line was still visible. It was tangled around the seaweed on a wave-washed rock, a few yards off the shore. "I'll get it," said Lamont. "I need to wash this stuff off anyway."

It was not hard to get free, and Lamont did get his wash. He also got a fish.

"I don't believe it! I've got a fish! I've got a fish! I never catch fish!"

It was a monumentally ugly fish. Black and large-mouthed.

Liz snatched the line, allowing the fish back into the water. "Careful with that thing! It looks like sea catfish. Their spines are toxic." She led it through the water back to the shore, and dispatched it expertly with a piece of driftwood.

"Pity we can't eat it," said Lamont, admiring his catch from a good safe distance. "That's the only fish I've ever caught. Never had much luck fishing."

Liz looked puzzled. "They're nice eating. You've just got to avoid the spines."

They were so busy admiring the catch of the day, that they failed to notice the arrival of Hermes.

As Lamont later said, it was a pity—because it was worth watching.

The pictures of the winged, sandaled and helmeted messenger are well known. Only . . . well, as Liz later said—it was asking rather a lot of very small wings.

"Why are you not going to the castle of Circe?" demanded Hermes, messenger of the ancient Greek gods, while rubbing his jaw with both hands.

"How come you can speak English?" demanded Jerry in reply.

Hermes looked down his long nose at the mythographer. "Is it not written that 'the gods, after all, can do anything.' Come. I must give you the moly, the herb which will protect you from the goddess Circe, so the legend can be fulfilled."

"But what . . . "

"Enough talking. My jaw hurts from that cursed helmet." Hermes led the way to the forest margin where he pulled up an herb and handed it to Jerry. "This will protect you. It is called 'moly.' And when she offers her favors to you, you must not refuse. Now I must go. I am needed in Boeotia."

Hermes took up a stance as if running. The wings on the sandals began to flap furiously. So did those on the helmet. When they'd reached hummingbird speeds, Hermes took off and flew away rather like an oversized bumblebee.

Jerry stared at the herb in his hand. "There is something wrong with all this," he said quietly.

"You're telling me! There is no way that should be able to work. He's just too damn big for those wings."

"No. I mean with this." Jerry held out the herb.

"Looks like wormwood," said Liz, inspecting it.

"Well, it's supposed to be 'moly.' But that is supposed to have a black root and a milk-white flower. The authorities more or less agree it was some species of alliam."

"Allium," corrected Liz. "The onion family. Like that wild garlic."

Jerry cocked his head sideways. "So why did he get it wrong? And the instructions he gave me weren't complete."

"I thought he said you were to bed Circe," said Liz. Her smile was a little tight-lipped.

Jerry flushed. "Yes . . . That *is* what he is supposed to have said to Odysseus. But first he had to make her swear by the gods not to try any more tricks on him. Whatever is going on is trying to make the legend happen. And it's *cheating*. It wants Circe to bespell us."

✧   ✧   ✧

The Krim device had no teeth to grind in frustration, or it would have ground them. The humans must believe. Their legends must enmesh them. Yet these ones were filled with doubt. They must be killed. They must be removed from the Ur-legend dimension. But these once-human gods were amazingly intransigent. Just like this species. Obstinate and doubting.

19

GET A BIGGER HAMMER.

Miggy Tremelo blew desperately on his too-hot coffee. Caffeine he must have before he talked to anyone. He sipped cautiously, slurping off the top. Then he picked up the phone and called Colonel McNamara of the 82nd. "The men who were in the advance group. Are they being used today?"

There was a pause. "Yes. We've tried to redeploy them away from the snatch zone."

Tremelo took a deep breath. "Colonel, I want to ask you to undo that. Let me explain. The more I think about it the more convinced I become that the alien device is selecting people of a certain type. If they weren't selected yesterday they won't be selected today. I could be wrong; but the only way we'll ever know is to offer it the same choice."

There was a silence on the other end of the line. Then: "You're asking me to use my men as guinea pigs?"

Miggy saw no point in trying to deny it. "Yes. I'm afraid so."

There was another long silence. "Very well. But you'd better not be wrong."

"Pull them out the minute one disappears. Get them out of the five-hundred-meter perimeter."

125

"It's gone up to 673 meters," said McNamara grimly. "At least."

Tremelo sighed. "And the device has increased in size by steady incremental jumps. The whole west wing of the Regenstein has pretty much collapsed around it. Won't be long, at this rate, before the whole building is nothing but rubble." He ran fingers through his gray hair and then asked abruptly: "How did the satchel charges work out, by the way?"

There was another silence from the other end of the line. "You weren't supposed to know about that."

"I have infrasound and ultrasound monitoring teams on the site, Colonel, with the best equipment in the world. I could probably have listened to playbacks of the combat engineers' conversation. Besides, the NSA told me."

It was McNamara's turn to sigh. "We lost two men. Snatched from inside the tunnel. And the explosives had no effect at all on the pyramid. But you probably know that already."

"Yes. But I'd like a couple of my men to examine the debris and have access to information about the volume of the explosive. We can learn quite a lot from that."

"Be my guest. Of course, I'm not supposed to tell you we did this."

Tremelo chuckled. "I won't tell the NSA if you don't."

After he hung up the phone, Miggy stared at the mass of paper on his desk. It was the small hours of the morning and he'd been up since the small hours of the previous morning. His eyes kept refusing to focus. The U.S. government's mobilization was in full steam now. Midway had become a military base, for all practical purposes, and the streets of South-Central Chicago rumbled with Army vehicles.

And the new troops were losing about one man in ten the moment they crossed the invisible barrier which the troops were starting to call the "snatch zone." Most of the snatchees—87%—came back dead almost immediately. Which was just about the same "snatch" and casualty rate as that suffered by the initial group of paratroopers.

All except for that one group. They lost only two people, right at the beginning. Since then—all six of them are still unaccounted for.

He peered blearily at the paper sitting right in front of him. The leaden prose had OFFICIAL DOCUMENT stamped all over it.

IMMEDIATE

FM: CJCS WASHINGTON DC//
TO: USCINCJFCOM NORFOLK VA//
    USCINCSOC MACDILL AFB FL//
    USCINCSPACE FALCON AS CO//
    HQ NORAD CHEYENNE MT CO//
    USCINCTRANS SCOTT AFB IL//
    HQ ACC LANGLEY AFB VA//CC//
    HQ USFORSCOM FT MCPHERSON GA//

"And on and on," muttered Tremelo. "Christ, is there anyone they *didn't* mobilize?" He scanned through to the end of the list of recipients—USCINCPAC HONOLULU HI, for the love of God!—and got to the meat of the thing.

BT
SECRET   SECTION 01 OF 01
SUBJ: HASTY RECEIVER EXECUTE ORDER //
S E C R E T
OPER/HASTY RECEIVER//
MSGID/SYS.RRM//
REF A/DOC/NATIONAL SECURITY DIRECTIVE 346//
REF B/ORD/HASTY RECEIVER OPERATIONS ORDER//
REF C/LOI/JOINT OPERATIONS PLANNING AND EXE-
    CUTION SYSTEM (JOPES) LETTER OF INSTRUCTION
    (LOI)//
GENTEXT/IMMEDIATE EXECUTION OPERATIONS HASTY
    RECEIVER
1. (U) IAW NCA DIRECTION REF A, SECDEF ORDERS
    ALL ACTION ADDRESSEES TO BEGIN IMMEDIATE
    EXECUTION OF OPERATION HASTY RECEIVER.
    USCINCJFCOM IS DESIGNATED SUPPORTED CINC
    AND WILL ACTIVATE STANDING JTF. FALLING ANVIL
    PHENOMENON LOCATED WITHIN HYDE PARK

DISTRICT, CITY OF CHICAGO. UPON RECEIPT OF
THIS MESSAGE, ALL ILLINOIS NATIONAL GUARD
AND AIR NATIONAL GUARD UNITS ARE NATIONAL-
IZED UNDER THE COMBATANT COMMAND
(COCOM) OF USCINCJFCOM AND WILL ASSEMBLE
AT NORMAL DUTY LOCATIONS. IAW PUBLIC LAW
SUPPORTING REF A, POSSE COMITATUS RESTRIC-
TIONS ARE LIFTED WITHIN HASTY RECEIVER AREA
OF RESPONSIBILITY (AOR).

"Well, that's *something* useful, anyway," Tremelo growled. "At
least we won't have every damn soldier dancing around scared
to death he's violating the law by telling a civilian to get the lead
out. What few civilians are still left in the area."

2. (U) JTF/CC WILL GIVE CONSIDERATION TO LOCA-
   TION OF FALLING ANVIL PHENOMENON WITHIN
   CITY ENVIRONMENT IN TAILORING DEPLOYED
   HASTY RECEIVER FORCES. DETERMINATION OF C-DAY
   AND REQUIRED DELIVERY DATES (RDD) IS AT THE
   DISCRETION OF JTF/CC. JTF/CC WILL REPORT ON
   TAILORED FORCE PACKAGE AND C-DAY/
   DEPLOYMENT TIMING ASAP. IAW REFS B AND C,
   UPON IDENTIFICATION BY JTF/CC, TAILORED HASTY
   RECEIVER UNITS WILL PREPARE FOR IMMEDIATE
   DEPLOYMENT USING MOST EXPEDITIOUS MEANS.
   USTRANSCOM AND COMPONENTS WILL PROVIDE
   SUFFICIENT AIR MOBILITY AND RAIL ASSETS TO
   DEPLOY AND SUSTAIN HASTY RECEIVER FORCES.
   TRANSPORTATION PRIORITY IS 1B1, FORCES IN
   IMMINENT CONTACT WITH ENEMY. EXCEPT FOR
   AS DETAILED IN REF B, ANNEX D, LOGISTICAL SUP-
   PORT WILL REMAIN IN NORMAL SERVICE CHANNELS.
3. (S) STRATEGIC FORCES WILL MAINTAIN NORMAL
   READINESS AND REMAIN UNDER NCA OPER-
   ATIONAL CONTROL (OPCON). OPCON OF ALL
   TACTICAL AIR AND NAVAL FORCES WILL REMAIN
   UNDER USCINCJFCOM UNTIL OTHERWISE

DIRECTED BY SECDEF. INDIANA NATIONAL GUARD AND AIR NATIONAL GUARD WILL REMAIN UNDER STATE OPCON UNTIL OTHERWISE ADVISED.

4. (U) UPON DEPLOYMENT, JTF/CC IS RESPONSIBLE FOR THE FOLLOWING ACTIONS:

A. (S) USE ALL AVAILABLE EXPERTISE TO EVALUATE NATURE OF FALLING ANVIL PHENOMENON. ASSESS AND REPORT ON THREAT PRESENTED BY FALLING ANVIL PHENOMENON TO US NATIONAL INTERESTS, CITIZENS, AND PROPERTY.

B. (U) IAW REF B, ANNEX R, ESTABLISH CONTIGENCY OPERATIONS REPORTING PROCEDURES.

C. (S) PROVIDE RECOMMENDATION ON EXTENT OF HASTY RECEIVER AOR.

D. (U) ASSUME TACON OF LOCAL LAW ENFORCEMENT, STATE NATIONAL GUARD, AIR NATIONAL GUARD AND LOCAL COAST GUARD ASSETS WITHIN THE HASTY RECEIVER COMMAND AOR.

E. (U) IDENTIFY AERIAL PORT OF DEBARKATION(S), RAILHEAD(S), AND LINES OF ROAD MARCH REQUIRED FOR THE DEPLOYMENT OF HASTY RECEIVER FORCES.

F. (U) USE NATIONAL GUARD AND AIR NATIONAL GUARD ASSETS UNDER TACON TO IDENTIFY AND PREPARE SUITABLE LOCATIONS FOR RECEPTION, SUSTAINMENT, ORIENTATION AND INTEGRATION (RSO&I) OF DEPLOYING HASTY RECEIVER FORCES.

G. (U) IN KEEPING WITH PERCEIVED THREAT, USE DEPLOYED HASTY RECEIVER FORCES TO ESTABLISH DEFENSIVE PERIMETER AROUND FALLING ANVIL PHENOMENON.

H. (S) IN COOPERATION WITH FEMA, STATE, AND LOCAL AUTHORITIES, EVACUATE ALL CIVILIAN PERSONNEL FROM WITHIN THE HASTY RECEIVER AOR.

J. (S) IAW REF B, ANNEX C, PREPARE ALL UNITS
   UNDER TACON TO COUNTER OR NEUTRALIZE
   THREAT POSED BY FALLING ANVIL PHENOM-
   ENON.

5. (U) UNDER THE PROVISIONS OF REF A, ALL ACTION
   AND INFO ADDRESSEES ARE ADVISED TO ACTIVATE
   HASTY RECEIVER CRISIS ACTION TEAMS. RETRANS-
   MIT TO SUBORDINATE COMMANDS AS REQUIRED.
   FURTHER MESSAGE TRAFFIC TO FOLLOW AS SITU-
   ATION DEVELOPS. ENDTEXT//

SECRET

Tremelo laid the paper down. "All of which," he grumbled, "is
a lot of fancy official verbiage which translates: *get a bigger
hammer.*"

He lowered his head and ran fingers through his thinning gray
hair. "Ain't gonna work, fellas. I don't think there's a hammer
in the world big enough to crack this nut."

Tremelo was convinced, more and more with every passing
moment, that the key to unraveling the mystery of the alien
pyramid was subtlety, not brute force. Several things stood out
to him. The first was the peculiar selectivity of the pyramid—
towards those it snatched, and those who survived the snatching. The other was the obvious time dilation involved in the
snatching.

The dead were coming back, on average, about two hours after
having been snatched. Yet the physiologists said that the evidence
pointed to the victims having been gone at least twenty times
as long as the actual time. They'd first noticed it by the beard
growth on the "returned" soldiers. A man who vanished clean-
shaven, and came back sporting a two-day growth in a couple
of hours was quite an obvious clue to differential time rates.

They were obviously dealing with a level of technological
sophistication which could even manipulate space-time. So how
much chance was there that the application of force to the
pyramid was going to accomplish anything?

But what was particularly striking to Tremelo was that the victims usually seemed to have been killed in the most barbaric and primitive of ways. Miggy pushed back his hair. *That* was what was frightening *him*. Not the alien device itself, but the fact that no one knew what the hell it was doing . . . except expanding slowly. He took a pull at a cold cup of coffee.

What was worrying the military was that they seemed to be unable to do a pinprick's worth of damage to the device. Tremelo knew there were more combat engineers burrowing underneath it again. He hoped that the Pentagon would at least consult him before they tried anything extreme. His team, now working on one corner of the pyramid, had exhausted most conventional options already without having any effect on what Tremelo was certain was not a material at all.

Someone knocked. But Tremelo didn't hear them. He'd fallen asleep, his face against the paper he'd been reading.

PART IV

Of remedies of love she knew perchance,
For she could of that art the oldë dance.

—Geoffrey Chaucer,
The Canterbury Tales

20

MISLEADING MEDEA REPORTS.

McKenna looked like a pleased schoolboy as he jogged up to Jerry. "We've got us a buck. Cruz is just butchering—*oh, shit.*"

This time nobody had to tell anybody to run away and climb a tree. But it hardly mattered. A lion can be escaped by climbing a tree. But *this* thing—

Only the body of the creature was lionlike, tawny and immense. The sphinx also had wings. Huge wings. And the head and breasts of a woman—and the facial expression of a woman in an extremely bad temper.

Lamont happened to be in the nearest tree. She bellowed at him—in classical Greek.

"What walks on four legs in the morning, two at noon and three at night. And don't tell me you've heard it before! I am sick to *death* of humans telling me they've heard it before!"

Of course, Jerry was the only one who knew what she was saying. "Uh, Lamont . . . "

The sphinx swiveled her massive head. "Shut up, you! If I wanted *you* to answer, I'd have asked *you.* Any more interruptions and I'll eat all of you for cheating." She turned on Lamont again. "You don't know, do you? At last! It's throttling and gobbling time."

Lamont closed his eyes and dug through his eclectic collection of snippets of memory. Desperately. He knew what this monster was, and he even knew that it asked riddles. He could guess that he was being asked one, and he was pretty sure he knew which one it was. He even knew the answer to the damned thing!

What he didn't know was ancient Greek.

He cleared his throat. Twice. Then: "Er . . . Homo."

"What? *Erhomo?* No, sorry." The fact that the huge female face was actually rather attractive made the lip-smacking particularly horrible.

"I wonder what flavor you are, with that dark skin? Well, I guess all humans taste much the same." It began to advance towards him. "Besides, I've always had a fancy for exotic foods."

Lamont wracked his brains frantically. He realized now that he'd used the Latin term for "man." What was the Greek term?

The Anthropology Department.

"Anthropo!"

"What?" The sphinx paused her advance.

Jerry desperately drew an "S" in the air.

"*Anthropos!*" yelled Lamont.

The sphinx covered its head with its wings. Stamped its paws in frustration. The great talons ripped the soil like so many plows.

Lamont breathed deeply, knowing that he was off the hook. But his mind was still racing. "Hey, Jerry! Offer it a new riddle for its help."

Jerry tried. But the sphinx was apparently not even listening. It seemed lost in melancholia, muttering to itself.

"*Damned humans.* They've got nothing to do all day but gossip, gossip, gossip. So now everyone knows my riddle. It's not fair! Even in remote spots virtually next to Cimmuria they've heard." It began flapping its huge wings, while it ran across the meadow in giant bounds. Just when achieving flight seemed utterly impossible—it did.

Jerry wiped his brow. "Phew. I thought we'd had it that time."

"Well, it looked close," said Liz, climbing from her tree. "What the hell went on there?"

Jerry and Lamont explained, as they walked back with McKenna to the kill.

Liz shook her head. "We're going to have to learn some Greek, and some mythology. Soon."

McKenna looked up, his eyes caught by motion in the sky. "I think we just left it too late. What the hell is *that*?" He took a firmer grip on his bayonet-spear. A device which, judging from the look on his face, he didn't think was going to do him a whole lot of good.

The scales of the two dragons shimmered like polished bronze in the late afternoon sun. The dragons were more like the tasseled Chinese version than the European version, but they were still plainly dragons, even if they moved through the air like plump snakes. The chariot they towed was winged, however. The dragons and the chariot turned in the sky above. They were going to land virtually on top of them.

"Hide!" hissed McKenna. "Get into those bushes!"

The bushes felt pitifully inadequate. And, of course, they were thorny.

Anibal Cruz watched from behind a tree on the far side of the glade. Those flying monsters must be thirty-five feet long! He'd seen the others go to ground. But there was no way he could signal to them.

The woman who had been handling the reins got down from the chariot. For a moment, Cruz was just plain dazzled. A beautiful, patrician-featured face was framed by a cascade of long, dark ringlets. Her lustrous skin was a pale olive, and her . . .

He stopped right there. Fantastic figure, true—and so what? Those pets of hers were *dragons*. And even without them, she didn't look like the sort of woman who would respond well to any of Cruz's bar-room opening lines. He began to ease backwards ever so slowly.

✧   ✧   ✧

"That's Medea!" hissed Jerry.

"Who's she?" asked Liz in a whisper.

"The Sorceress of Colchis. She's one of the most evil, murderous and unpleasant characters in Greek myth. Chopped her brother up and tossed the pieces at her father to slow him down while he was pursuing her. Then, later, she murdered her husband's bride-to-be after Jason told her he was dumping her. Even killed her own two children to get revenge on him, before making her escape." He pointed a somewhat shaky finger. "In a chariot pulled by dragons."

The sorceress unharnessed the dragons. Someone stood up in the back of the chariot. It was a small boy of about six or seven.

"Mom? Are we at Aunt Circe's yet?" he asked, yawning and stretching.

"Not yet, dear," said Medea. "But the dragons need to eat."

The boy looked around curiously. "Can I get out and play?"

She smiled at him. "Just let the dragons check that it's safe first, Priones."

Another child stood up. A younger boy. "I need to wee, Mommy."

Among the things that Jerry could add to his growing zoological lore of the Mythworld was that mythological Greek dragons were very keen of nose and eye. It didn't take the dragons more than five seconds to spot Jerry and his companions as they tried to hide.

Very shortly thereafter, Jerry was able to add a few more items of information to his ever-expanding knowledge of mythology:

Greek dragons are very, very fast moving.

Their shimmering scales are diamond hard.

They were constrictor-like in their ability to hold prey. And . . .

They were toothless.

Which was something, Jerry realized as he gasped for breath inside a dragon's coils, that the dragon's mistress was *not*. Nor ever would be—even if you pulled out all of her even white teeth. The sleepy-looking young woman who had now also sat up in the back of the chariot was plainly gentler, if only in her demeanor. But they both looked more than a little angry. Far more.

✧   ✧   ✧

"Skulkers. Waiting in ambush! I told you he was scum, Glauce! And they're his own children, too!" The last part was said with an angry sob.

"How ever did he find us?!" The other girl wrung her hands. "Make them talk, Medea."

"They'll *talk* all right. Come on, Hellenes. Spit it out! How did Jason know where we were going? You're all dinner for Bitar and Smitar . . . but I'll let you choose in which order."

There was an outraged hiss and an equally outraged sniff. "We're not eating thi*f*s lot!" spittled the one dragon.

"You promi*f*sed u*f*s *f*something tender!" protested the other.

"*f*Soft and jui*f*sy, you *f*said." The red-tasseled one's eyes were reproachful and accusing.

"Ye*f*s! Ea*f*sy on the gum*f*s!" agreed its purple-tassled partner, with a display of sore-looking toothless gums. "Well cooked— you promi*f*sed u*f*s! " The voice sounded bitter—betrayed.

"Dige*f*stible, you *f*said!"

"Not the*f*se. They'll be too tough." The dragon with Jerry in its massive coils gave a squeeze that nearly cracked the mythographer's ribs.

"Far too tough, when we've got no teef," whined the other.

"I'm not a cook!" snapped Medea.

"You can *f*say *that* again," hissed the red-tasseled one.

"Oh, shut up," said Medea irritably. She turned away from the argument. "Now—you Hellenes. Answer me!"

Jerry had trouble breathing. "We're not Hellenes," he managed to squeeze out. There wasn't even much spare breath for that.

Not speaking good classical Greek can sometimes be good for your health.

"Loosen up a little bit there, Smitar." Medea frowned. "Then why were you waiting in ambush for us?"

The fierce-looking woman's chuckle was as fierce as her visage. "Nice to hear someone speak Greek even worse than I do! But if you're not Hellenes, then who are you?"

She still sounded suspicious, but no longer quite as homicidal. The difference was marginal, however. Jerry got the feeling that, with this beautiful but frightening woman, things could go downhill fast if he said something like "Colchian."

"We are Americans. We were stranded here by Hellene treachery. And we weren't waiting to ambush anyone. We were just on the way to fetch our dinner."

"Dinner! Did ʃsomeone ʃsay 'dinner'?" sprayed one of the dragons. "It'ʃs not maiden ʃstew by any off-chanʃs?" asked the other.

Medea paid the dragons no mind. "A likely story! You just happened to be hiding in the bushes on the exact spot where we landed. Ha! Tell me another one."

Exasperation took hold of Jerry. It was not wise, but on the other hand he had faced Scylla and Charybdis, the clashing rocks, sirens, a boar, centaurs and even a couple of Greek gods, not adequately spaced by sleep or even by his idea of decent meals. "Don't be so *stupid*. How would we know where to hide and wait? You could have landed anywhere. Besides, did you think that I was going to attack dragons without even a weapon? We saw you coming and hid away because we thought you were going to attack us!"

The dragon who had Jerry in its coils was examining him with eager interest, apparently oblivious to the mythographer's outrageous disrespect for Medea. "ʃSo what *are* you having for dinner?"

"ʃSure it'ʃs not maiden ʃstew?" enquired the other dragon, rather hopefully.

Suddenly, Medea emitted another chuckle. A much softer one than the first. "I like a man with a bit of fire," she admitted.

Oh great, thought Jerry. *As if I wasn't in enough trouble. All I need now is this world's most murderous sorceress taking a fancy to me.*

"If he'ʃs got a bit of fire can we cook them on it?" That seemed to be the dragon called Bitar, its voice plaintive.

"Oh, shut up!" snapped Medea. "Don't you two ever think of anything but your stomachs?"

The dragons stared at each other, wide-eyed.

"Not reʃsently," said Bitar.

"ʃShould we?" asked the other, wrinkling its scaly face.

Medea sighed. "I wish I hadn't given you the power of speech. Now what am I going do with this lot?"

"Mommy, I need to wee—*now*," whined the smallest boy, dancing from foot to foot.

Medea still seemed to be simmering a bit. She swiveled her head and glared at the child. "Be quiet! Or I'll expose you on a rock!"

The young woman in the chariot shook her head reproachfully. "Medea! That's not a nice thing to say, and you know it." Then, gently: "Just go around the back of the chariot, Neoptolmeus."

The dragons were more concerned with their captives' fate. "Brai*f*se them *f*slowly with onion*f*s," mused the one.

"What about *f*soup?" suggested the other.

"Ye*f*s! *f*Soup!"

Medea paid no attention to the dragons. "Where is this America place? Is it a distant island? And why are you the only one who has spoken?"

"Because I'm the only one who speaks any Greek." By her expression, that was a *good* thing to say.

"Ah! I can solve that." She walked back to the chariot, took a small clay vessel out of it and walked up to Cruz.

"Jerry." Cruz was plainly struggling just to breathe. "Huh . . . what's huh . . . she going to do?"

"Don't worry," said Jerry in his best attempt at reassurance. With luck Cruz wouldn't know that this was one of the most notorious poisoners in legend and myth . . . especially as she was smearing stuff onto his lips. Then she began smearing the same salve on his ears, chanting softly as she did so.

"Tastes . . . huh . . . shit."

She slapped him. Very hard. "How dare you say something like that about one of my potions?"

Cruz's eyes, already bulging, nearly popped out of his head. "I huh . . . understand . . . huh . . . you!"

"You'd better! And you'd better mend your manners. What's this 'Huh' you keep saying?"

"I can't, huh . . . breathe," gasped Cruz.

"Too bad," said Medea, shrugging. "Suffering may teach you some manners." She walked on to the others.

When she neared Liz, Medea's face darkened again with

anger. "Smitar! This is a *woman!* Let her go at once! How dare you?"

The dragon uncoiled Liz. "You never ſsaid," he muttered sulkily.

Liz was quick on the uptake. She volunteered her lips and ear. And vouched for the good character of her companions. And also said exactly the right thing. "No, I'm not married to any of them. And not going to be either. I've tried being married, but I left my husband."

"Why?" asked Medea, with obvious sympathy.

Liz shrugged. Then, thinking quickly, added an angry shake of her fist at the sky. "He started sniffing around a girl with lots of money. So I left him before he left me."

Medea hugged her. "Men!" she said. "What did I tell you, Glauce? They're all the same. Was he a Hellene?"

"Oh, Medea," said Glauce reprovingly. "Not *all* Hellenes are like Jason."

Liz shook her head. "No, he was Am—uh, Canadian," she lied hastily. "I really think these Americans are more honorable." She even managed to say it with a straight face. "Please, can you let them go? I swear they won't hurt anyone."

"You swear by all the gods? Not that I trust any of the gods but Hecuba and Helios. But I will admit that Hermes the giant killer said this was a good place to land."

Liz shot a glance at Jerry. "Yes. I swear."

"Very well. They can all go except that one who was rude about my potion. He can stay in the folds of Bitar for a while. The lout!"

Don't push it, thought Liz. "Well, can he at least have some air?"

Medea pursed her lips with thought. She considered Cruz. "I suppose so. He *is* going a bit purple."

"Hey! What'ſs for our dinner then?" exclaimed Smitar angrily, apparently forgetting that he'd complained that they were too tough.

"Yeſs! We need at *leaſt* one each!" The dragons were definitely on the fringes of rebellion.

Lamont came to the rescue. "We'll cook you dinner."

"Ooh! What'ſs on offer? Got any maiden ſstew?"

Lamont shook his head regretfully. "The last batch of maidens we got were all, ah, broken. But we've got venison."

"Don't like veni*f*son," said Bitar sulkily.

"Ye*f*s. Too chewy," agreed Smitar.

"Uh. Fish?" Lamont's eyes were a bit wide, as if he were trying to picture one fish divided by two dragons . . .

"Mussel soup?" offered Jerry.

"*f*Soup!" Bitar said eagerly.

"*f*Soup i*f*s good when you haven't got any teef. Medea can't cook," Smitar informed them all, sententiously.

Smitar sniffed. "Neither can Glauce."

"Typical king'*f*s daughter*f*s, if you a*f*sk me," said Bitar scathingly. "U*f*sed to *f*servants doing everything for them."

Don't ask about the teeth, thought Liz. *Just don't ask. Not yet. But whoever this woman is, she's okay. She's nice to her children.*

She gave the beautiful sorceress a quick glance. *Well . . . That really* wasn't *a nice thing to say to her kid. "Expose you on a rock!"* Suddenly, Liz found herself suppressing a manic laugh. *On the other hand, I bet those kids eat their vegetables without complaining!*

In the twilight, the waves curled about the dark rocks like phosphorescent lace. A dragon belched. "I'm *f*stuffed! Be*f*st meal we've had since Aeëte*f*s pulled our teeth for Ja*f*son to *f*sow."

"Ye*f*s," agreed the other. "Think I'm going to bur*f*st."

And so they should, thought Jerry, sipping some of Medea's wine. The dragons must have eaten ten gallons of mussel soup each. Fortunately, Medea had that enormous cauldron, and the mussels and wild onions were plentiful. Herbs and some wine from a *crater* of stuff that Medea had said was barely fit to drink, and hey-presto—happy dragons. Personally, Jerry thought the soup could have used some cream, but the dragons had liked it. Well, they'd also sampled everything else going.

He shook his head. From a disastrous start, it had actually turned into a pleasant evening. All they needed now was to find a way to stop Lamont from fishing. For a man who claimed he'd never caught a fish in his life the guy was an embarrassment. Even when he dropped an empty hook into a rock pool, he somehow caught an eel. Heh. It was definitely getting on Liz's nerves. She kept muttering something about "beginner's luck." But Jerry suspected that the goddess of luck's blessing had a more long-lasting effect on Lamont than he would have supposed.

More than anything else, the good relationship had been fostered by the two children. They'd been both trusting and inclined to questions which adults might have shied from. "Why is your hair such a funny color, lady?" demanded the younger child.

"I dyed it," replied Liz.

"Why? Did you want to look like a nereid?" asked the older boy.

Liz shrugged. "Because I thought it might make me look prettier."

Both children fell about in helpless laughter.

And then—wonder of wonders—the stolid Cruz turned into the kind of guy who liked playing "horse" and "merry-go-round" for kids.

The other thing that had been fairly priceless was the reaction of Medea and Glauce to the men cooking for them and serving them with food. It was known that men *could* cook—well, char meat—when they had to. But as it turned out it was the men of this party who could *really* cook.

Cruz's contribution had been particularly valued. Red mullet briefly marinated in some of Medea's olive oil, chopped fennel, and a little wine, and then encased in wild vine leaves and grilled. The sergeant seemed to be a cornucopia of surprises.

Also inspired had been Lamont's rosemary-twig-skewered venison liver. Pure chance had governed that one: "I want sticks that won't kill us and it's an herb, Jerry. It's got to be non-toxic." It had worked extremely well, especially basted with the hot sauce which McKenna had in his rucksack.

In each case, Jerry knew, it had been force of circumstance that had taught the men how to cook—but Medea seemed convinced that it was a general American trait.

"This island—America—where the men cook and wait on the women . . . is it the Land of the Giants?" she asked, peering up at the red-headed, six-foot-two paratrooper.

McKenna, very well oiled with wine by now, nodded eagerly. "And the Packers and the Jets and the Steelers and the—" Cruz belched. "Oakland Raiders." *Belch.* "My team."

21

PIGGING OUT WITH CIRCE.

Rosy-fingered dawn smeared the sky, outlining a solitary fisherman on rocks lapped by the full tide.

Jerry peered. "For Christ's sake, Lamont! Haven't you caught enough fish yet?"

Lamont shrugged. "Well, there's breakfast to provide for a fair number of people. And those dragons eat a lot."

"And you don't just like fishing?" Jerry grinned. "Don't expect me to swallow that *line*."

Lamont smiled back. "No, I don't like fishing. I like *catching* fish. I thought you'd have *hooked* onto that. Yesss! Another one!"

"It's only just dawn," grumbled Liz from the cave, "and you two are punning already. There ought to be a law against it."

Lamont looked at Jerry. "It's amazing how grumpy some people can be when they can't have any coffee first thing in the morning."

"Gah. Did you have to remind me?" Liz, tousle-haired and rumpled, emerged from behind the sleeping dragons. "I'll swear these things are twice as fat as they were yesterday. They look like little balloons. What are you up to?"

"I thought I'd get the fire ready for the great fisherma—"

The dragon-flatulent blast nearly shattered their eardrums. Cruz and McKenna appeared as if by magic—spears in hand, looking for a foe.

Liz waved a hand in front of her nose. "No naked lights or matches! Or it's your life!"

She moved hastily upwind. "Now I think I understand how they can fly. Talk about gasbags . . . "

Jerry grinned. "Good thing you weren't smoking!"

Liz raised her gentian eyes to heaven. "Something to be said for giving up. 'You won't accidentally set fire to dragon farts.' The born-again breathers will just *love* that."

Lamont found that the forest was a different place with an aerial escort flying overhead. He'd love to bring his girls here. Hell, it hurt seeing those kids of Medea's. That was one of the main reasons he'd been fishing. Well, he'd enjoyed the novelty of catching fish. But he *had* to get home. And if he pushed Jerry Lukacs hard enough, the man would come up with an answer. Jerry was good at putting pieces together. He'd spotted the achronology. He'd work out how to escape from whatever was trapping them in this terrifyingly real but unreal mythworld. He just had to be pushed. And he, Lamont Jackson, would do that pushing. He had a wife and children to get home to.

He spotted a pair of slitted eyes gleaming somewhere in the dark recesses of the forest. "Go ahead," he sneered. "Make my day." He jerked his thumb at the two huge dragons soaring above.

The eyes seemed to roll upward.

"Boo!" And they were gone.

Lamont's stride down the overgrown path turned into something of a jaunty little shuffle.

"*Yo—beast! I'm talking to you!*

"*Snarl all you want! Slobber away!*

"*Ain't getting none o' my—*"

Cruz leaned on his spear, his head tilted back. He spent a few seconds admiring the distant profile of Medea steering her dragons, her long dark hair streaming back. The sorceress was circling above them while they had a rest.

"Quite a woman, ain't she, Doc?"

Jerry was alarmed. "Uh—Anibal. That . . . ah, lady. Um. Legend appears to be wrong about several details. That's not surprising, of course, since it was a Greek legend and she was a foreigner. Still . . ." He paused.

How to explain this best? "She's, ah, not a woman you want to play around with. If you follow my drift. She takes commitment quite seriously. As in, ah, *dead* seriously."

The sergeant chuckled and felt his ribs. "Tell me about it!"

His smile widened a little, and he shrugged. "So what? I'm not really the man-about-town type, to tell you the truth. Although I'd appreciate it if you didn't spread that around the barracks if we ever get home. And there are advantages to a woman who doesn't let her man play around. It usually cuts both ways, you know?"

The smile faded a bit, and turned into something almost feral. "Sounds like she got a raw deal. Tell me about this 'Jason' guy, Doc. I might wind up meeting him one day."

By the way Sergeant Anibal Cruz was flexing his forearm muscles, Jerry suspected it might be a very unpleasant meeting. Short, though.

"Well, he was the leader of the Argonauts . . ."

They started to move off again, and Jerry, even with a stout stick, was finding the going tricky. "Look," he panted. "I'll tell you about it, when I'm not trying to—" *pant* "—keep up. Just . . . remember the story that I know . . . was told by her . . . enemies. She was supposed to have murdered her children before this . . . and they seem very alive to me. She's also supposed to have . . . killed Glauce . . . that girl who is with her, before this all happened . . ."

The dragons spiraled down onto Circe's castle of well-dressed stone, scattering animals. Jerry, tired but nervous, eyed it with extreme suspicion. The paratrooper's entrenching tool had made excavating the "moly"—well, the wild garlic they *thought* was the correct plant, reasonably easy. He resolved not to eat anything if he could possibly avoid it. Even the formidable Medea seemed a trifle wary about seeing Circe, and that, as far as Jerry was concerned, was enough to make anyone cautious.

The sounds coming from within were not those of a lady singing as she plied her loom. They were the raucous sounds of a bunch of good-time boys, deep into partying at what could not have been eleven in the morning.

Medea raised an eyebrow.

"Odysseus and his crew, I suspect," said Jerry grimly.

Medea pounded on the door.

A harassed-looking woman, with long and lustrous hair, opened the door. "Medea! Don't say you've brought the unspeakable Jason and his crew down on me as well! This is all just too much!"

"I've left Jason, Aunt Circe," Medea said quietly. "You were right about him."

Circe hugged her. "Oh, my dear. I never did like him. But your father won't have you back, you know. He was very upset about losing, and even more so about your half brother, Absyrtus."

"Absyrtus got exactly what he deserved!" said Medea fiercely.

"Yes, dear, I know. That's why I cancelled the blood debt. But your father didn't think so. Anyway, come in. Who are these people with you? The new boyfriend and his retainers?" Circe said dryly.

Medea sniffed. "Not hardly! These are your nephews, Priones and Neoptolmeus. And this is Glauce, daughter of Creon, King of Corinth. Jason of the golden fleas put me aside so that he could marry her."

Circe cocked her head and looked at the princess. "I take it you've got more sense than Medea? Wanted no part of that slob, ha. Good for you, girl."

Her eyes ranged over the others. "And these strangely attired ones? I have never seen cloth so fine—or dyed in such dull colors. But I wish you hadn't brought so many people, Medea dear. I have a house full of unwelcome guests already. I've gotten rid of them *twice*—and still they keep coming back! The nymphs can't keep up with the cooking, especially with the other demands . . . "

Medea smiled ravishingly. "Dear Aunt, *these* are *Americans*. The men love to cook and wait on the women." Her own eyes ranged over them, appraisingly. They lingered on Cruz, perhaps a bit longer than any of the others. "As for the rest, they seem well behaved."

Odysseus acted as if he were delighted to see them. "My friends! Come! Sit! Let Circe and her nymphs bring you bowls of pottage! Barley meal, good sheep's cheese and amber honey, all flavored with Pramnian wine!"

"Is this the same guy who promised to guide us and then ran off with Salinas?" asked Liz grimly.

Odysseus' mouth fell open. "How is it possible that you can speak our tongue now?"

Liz smiled nastily. "Magic, you bottom-feeding creep."

It was apparent that Odysseus, the noble son of Laertes, did not get such a description of himself very often. His hand was just falling to his sword hilt when Jerry added hastily: "And we had some help from Medea, the Sorceress of Colchis."

Odysseus' eyes flitted around, falling on the figure of Medea. Something about the woman apparently exuded *sorceress*, because Odysseus relinquished his grip on the sword instantly.

There were advantages, Jerry realized, to having a quick-witted man for an opponent. Even if he was completely treacherous, he was at least more likely to think things through before resorting to brute force.

"Besides," the mythographer added forcefully, "according to the wager, you and your ship belong to us until we arrive where we want to go. You know how the gods feel about oath-breakers, don't you?"

"That's not the story you told me, Odysseus!" said Circe sharply.

"But you said, 'Take us to Circe . . . ' My oath is fulfilled!" replied Odysseus, as righteously as he could manage. And, in the subtle fashion of a gangster, he set about displaying who held the balance of power here. "*Right, men?*"

Bitar pushed his head in through the doorway. He stuck out a long snaky tongue. "ʃSomebody pleaʃse come and fetch these fiʃsh. Theʃse animalʃs are trying to get into the chariot."

As a rabble silencer, Jerry reflected, there is *absolutely nothing* to beat a dragon.

Odysseus' eyes were flitting around again. "Well. Perhaps I misinterpreted our wager. But that was what was understood . . . "

"We brought you some fresh fish, Aunt," said Medea sweetly. "*Two* dragons are so expensive to feed."

Jerry shook his head and smiled sweetly. "*No* specific destination was mentioned, Odysseus. This is just part of the route—*not* where we're going."

Odysseus looked sour. Circe did not, especially once Liz took her turn at Odysseus baiting.

"We're so sorry our wager-slaves have trespassed on your hospitality, Ms. Circe. We'll see to it that that doesn't happen again. Outside, you lot! Fetch the fish and the bags. *Now*. Jump to it!"

She harried the laggards with her bag.

Bitar hissed supportively.

You get pretty good service that way, too.

"I don't know if I like this being on 'kitchen parade' much," said McKenna, looking at the scrubbed pots in the huge stone kitchen.

"Could be worse," rumbled Cruz. "I don't mind cooking. It's the washing up I don't like."

Jerry smiled quietly. "Hopefully, the nymphs will wash up for you. And cooking your own food around here is a really, really good idea. Remember that this Circe is the woman who fed certain herbal potions to people to turn them into savage animals."

"I get like that myself when I'm only given salad for supper," said Liz with a wicked smile. "What's for *lunch*, guys?"

Lamont seized a large wooden spoon. "Out of the kitchen, woman! Go and drink beer and watch the sport on the box."

Jerry, not having seen Circe and Medea enter, backed up the joke. "Yes. A woman should know her place. And that's not in the kitchen, Liz. Go on. You've got quite a lot of belching and lounging about to catch up on."

Circe's jaw dropped. Medea nodded with satisfaction. "I *told* you the men of this 'America' island are quite unlike other men, Aunt! They are strange beyond all belief. Come, Liz. They obviously get restive when women are in their kitchen. You can explain this 'box' we have to watch. Does it move if it is not watched? I'm already quite good at the belching part. We consider it unladylike, but customs differ."

Jim McKenna looked glumly at the mounds of vegetables and fresh fish. "If this ever gets back to the 101st . . . "

"First, we worry about getting us back," said Cruz.

McKenna sighed. "Yeah." Then he brightened slightly. "I bet I could make some kind of still with that pot."

"After lunch for the ladies," said Jerry. "What are we going to cook, guys?"

Lamont looked pensive. "A salad. Definitely."

In the outer chamber, Liz suddenly realized it had been a fine joke but now she was alone with the two sorceresses, without Jerry and his knowledge to turn to. It suddenly seemed a lot less funny. Their future could depend on what she said. And she'd never been much good at watching her tongue. Her nose got in the way.

Circe seemed well disposed, if still a trifle distant. They *had* gotten rid of a house full of unwelcome guests for her, after all. "What hospitality can I offer you, Liz?" she asked, shaking back her long hair. "Wine? A warm bath?"

"Oh! A bath, please! I can't wait to wash my hair."

Circe inspected the hair in question. "Indeed. But it appears very clean, if an odd color for these parts. In Colchis we saw traders and tribesmen from the far north with hair this color, sometimes."

Liz blushed. "It was a silly idea. I always wanted to be blond. It's really a mousy brown. It goes blondish when I'm in the sun a lot." She looked enviously at Circe's long dark tresses. "Maybe I should go black."

Medea giggled. "What about red?"

Both sorceresses found this almost irrepressibly funny.

Liz smiled. "Ah, I considered it. I've got a cousin who dyed hers green."

They gaped. "No! Really?"

Conversation proved easy. She was a bit taken aback to discover that she was going be bathed, and that the others were planning to stay and yack. But . . . well, when in ancient Greece . . . do as the ancient Greeks do.

Their response to the shampooing of her hair was first trepidation, and then, when they saw the results—delight. The only thing that tempered this delight was the discovery that Liz only had one more sachet—cunningly artificed out of thin leather. With real self-sacrifice she gave it to Circe. As a gesture to get she who was known as "Circe of the lovely tresses" on your side, it was inspired.

Liz got on well with doing things in the fashion of the locals, until it came to being anointed with olive oil. Well, that explained the smell from Odysseus' crew. If you oiled, sweated, but didn't bathe . . .

Her "I'm not rusty, thank you," provoked more mirth. She did, however, accept clean clothing with gratitude. She looked despairingly at her skirt and top. "Hard scrubbing . . . "

The others agreed. "I don't know if that fine weave will take it. Is it sprite-woven?"

"Ah—in a way. Machine sprites, they're called." She smiled. "I don't suppose you've got detergent?"

Both of the sorceresses looked doubtful. "No," said Circe at last. "Not if it's what I think it is . . . no. The animals don't do well here. The young ones all died last winter."

"It's soap." They looked equally blank. "What I gave the nymph to wash me with."

"We use certain cleansers, but none like that," said Circe.

Liz smiled. "We'll have to brave the kitchen. My mother couldn't teach me to cook, because she didn't. But she did teach me to make herb-scented soaps, because she did that for fun. We will need wood ash and some oil or lard."

Jerry had to admit that Lamont had been completely wasted as a maintenance man. Not only had he a gift for remembering things, but he also had a gift for presentation. A real gift. The combination of colors and shapes were pleasing to the eye. The platters were decorated with sprigs of fresh herbs.

The food was all also carefully scented with "moly." Just in case.

The salad—which was an ancient Greek version of tuna Niçoise, with a homemade mayonnaise—salt, crushed mustard seeds, two egg yolks, olive oil and a tablespoon of wine vinegar, with finely diced wild onion leaves. Set in a spiral of dandelion and young charlock leaves and olives, it looked almost too good to eat.

"How the hell did you know how to make mayo?" asked Jerry.

Lamont swatted away the tasting finger. "Didn't. Cruz did."

The burly sergeant looked a little uneasy. "My mother used to make it. It's nicer with lemon juice."

"Jerry. See if you can find some more of those golden goblets. We'll have to use them for dessert. Mac, go and find us some mint. That should be within your capability. Nuts and honey for a base. I'll beat this cream. What do you think it comes from? A goat?"

"Or a sheep," chuckled Jerry, setting out goblets.

Lamont snorted. "Well, if you don't tell Liz, I won't."

Cruz looked up from his crouton frying. "What in the hell are you doing now, Jerry?"

He grinned. "I got your goblets. Now I'm checking my roasting acorns."

"Why are you doing that?" asked McKenna, posing with a sprig of mint.

"WW Two coffee substitute," he said, hauling the smoldering acorns out of the fire.

McKenna shook his head. "Jeez. Caffeine-free too, I bet."

Jerry grinned. "I won't tell Liz if you don't."

"Me? If it improves 'Sir's' temper, I'll help you to roast the next lot," said McKenna.

"She's not so bad," said Jerry defensively.

McKenna snorted. "Compared to what? A drill sergeant?"

Circe wore a distinctly bemused expression. Mayonnaise was a hit. Some of the other food had been too bizarre, but this . . .

She turned to Liz. "Are you sure they're not under some kind of spell? If so, I would dearly love to learn it."

Liz swallowed. The mouthful of truly vile coffee substitute, with goats' milk and honey, at least stopped her from saying: *You, me and several hundred million other women.*

She fought down the impulse. "No," she said. "And unfortunately they're not all like this. But if you get them young enough they can be trained."

The mention of spells brought something to Jerry's mind. He felt rather guilty about it. It suddenly occurred to him that he hadn't seen John Salinas.

"Circe, you haven't seen any other people that wore clothes like us?"

"Barbarians, you mean? In leggings?"

"Uh. Yes."

"Indeed I have." Circe smiled. It was not a nice smile. "Two of them, in fact. They're in the pigsty. You can have the one, but not the other. He insulted me most dreadfully. A pig he is and a pig he stays."

Jerry had the dreadful feeling that a practical joke had gone way too far.

"Ah, did he say . . . " He cleared his throat, smiled apologetically, and repeated the phrase he had taught the police lieutenant.

"Yes, indeed!" Circe's teeth were showing. "Twice!"

Jerry looked *very* apologetic. "It's my fault. I taught him to say that. And I told him it meant 'I am your friend.' "

Circe's eyes narrowed. She picked up her wand. "Why?"

"Well, he was ass-kissing—I mean, being servile and obsequious to Odysseus, because he saw him as being the most powerful person around. So I, ah, played a practical joke on him. I thought he'd say it to Odysseus."

There was a silence. Then Medea and Circe burst into riotous laughter. After a moment, the rest began joining in, all staring in surprise at the red-faced academic.

"I'm really very sorry . . . " said Jerry in a small voice.

Circe continued to laugh. "Come." She rose, her shoulders still heaving. "Why not? Eventually I even felt sorry for Odysseus and his verminous crew. They behaved like ravening beasts and such they became." She shrugged. "It is the nature of the magic to make the beast reflect the inner man."

They went around to the pigsties. "Most of these are just ordinary pigs. I keep the transformed ones apart in this sty. They've got a regrettable tendency to become human again when slaughtered."

They were greeted with enthusiastic, frantic squeals from one of the two denizens of the sty. It was a small, blotchy Vietnamese pot-bellied miniature pig, weeping and snorting at them in almost equal quantities. The other, a large bristly hog, planted both feet in the trough and alternated between suspicious glances at them and angry, hasty mouthfuls.

Jerry bent over the small pig that was becoming quite asthmatic in its squeaking, snorting, and jumping up. "I'm sorry, Lieutenant. It was a stupid practical joke." The pig shook its head furiously and squeaked like an accordion on acid.

"I think," said Liz, "that he's trying to tell you he isn't Salinas." She turned to the larger, sleekly-fat, white porker. "Come, Lieutenant, let's make a man of you . . . such as you are. I'm sure you'll be ecstatic. We've got hardships, dangers and privations to face. Mortal peril. Companions to stand by. Women to defend . . . "

The large pig retreated into the far corner of the sty, where it stood with bared teeth. Pigs have quite awesome teeth.

"I'd say that Landrace is definitely our lieutenant," said McKenna, the only one of them that would know one pig breed from another. "And I'd also say he's very happy as a pig right now. He's in no danger. He can get both feet in the trough and he's bigger than all the other piggies around."

Circe nodded, while smearing salve onto the little pig, which was now mercifully still and quiet. "Besides, I've been using him to improve the quality of my broodstock."

The bristles of the little pig began to fall away. The person who stood up from the smelly mud of the sty was not unlike the piggy from whence he came. If Jerry recalled the Odyssey correctly, the pigs that became men again were supposed to be younger, handsomer and taller. The imagination boggled at what the previous version must have been like—if this was an improvement . . .

The plump gentleman with the very Gallic moustache and goatee stepped gingerly up to the gate. "*Mon dieu!* This is the most terrible affront of the dignity. *Un cochon!* Given," he shuddered, "acorns to eat. Only in America could this happen to one. In France we treat our visiting botanists with greater respect. The management of the University of Chicago will hear of this."

He bowed to Circe. "Thank you. I will not say *enchanté.*"

"What did he say?" Circe asked.

"He said 'thank you,'" said Liz, sparing the Frenchman a possible return to pigdom.

Circe looked him up and down. "You know, he was more attractive as a pig than as a man. He was quite cute as a pig. He was an excessively greedy guest. But at least he is polite."

The botanist turned to Liz. "*Mademoiselle.* You are conversant in the language of the lady, yes? Please tell her I am desperately hungry." He looked woefully at his hands and clothes. "Indeed, the only thing I desire more than dinner is a bath."

Jerry grinned. "You might get the bath. I could use one myself."

The Frenchman blinked. "Forgive me. My manners are most remiss. I have not introduced myself. I had despaired of finding anyone with whom I could converse in a civilized tongue." The slight hesitation which followed indicated some doubts as to the accuracy of that characterization of English. Then: "Permit me to introduce myself. I am *Professeur* Henri Lenoir, of the Sorbonne. Forgive me if I do not shake you by the hand, but until my hands are washed . . . "

22

YOU CAN GO TO HADES.

" . . . so," Jerry concluded, "we were hoping you could send us home."

Circe shook her head. "I am a sorceress, and a minor goddess. But my powers are small. I don't like to admit this, but Odysseus—a mere mortal!—overcame me on his first visit."

She took a deep breath. "But the part I find exceeding strange is the fact that to you *we* are creatures of legend. That you, Doc Jerry," she bowed respectfully, "have read of our deeds . . . even about things which we have not yet done. It is as peculiar as this feeling of . . . I feel I have done all this before."

Jerry had been unable to convince the aristocracy-bound mythfolk that "Doc" was not his hereditary title. He *had* been able to convince them he knew the details of the myths and legends. Some of that knowledge had nearly been bad for his health. Medea, the original victim of bad press, was still nearly incandescent.

How dare those Hellene bitches put the blame onto her? They'd cut up their *own* father and boiled him! And then said that she— Medea—had tricked them into doing it. Ha! The barefaced cheek of it! What kind of idiot would believe—

Halfway through her tirade, Jerry began muttering to himself. "Somebody—or something—is playing games with us. Using us. There are small inconsistencies . . . Medea is achronous with Odysseus . . . We also encountered the Theban sphinx. Something is wrong."

Circe overheard him and began nodding. "I was forewarned of your coming. Hermes came to tell me that barbarians who must die were coming." She seemed troubled.

Medea snorted. "Typical Greek gods! Hermes told me a 'safe place' to land. That nearly resulted in Bitar and Smitar eating them."

Lamont shook his head. "I don't understand it. Something brought us here. And now that same something is trying to eliminate us. And it has, at the very least, Hermes playing its games."

"Maybe it is sort of . . . destructive testing," said Cruz, flexing a forearm.

"Maybe. But let's be honest, it has picked some of the most appalling physical material, like me," said Jerry.

"Maybe it is the mind that it is wanting," said Lenoir, venturing his first comment.

"Salinas' mind? The man who is happy to be a pig? Or," said Liz, pointedly looking at Jim McKenna, who was winking at one of the attendant nymphs, "the mind of a randy paratrooper who can't keep his thoughts above his belt?"

Circe shook her head. "Whatever it is that is happening, it is a dark and evil thing. Yet if Hermes is involved you can bet the father of gods is in on it too. I think you should venture into the lands of Persephone, to the grim Halls of Hades, and consult the lost spirit of blind Teiresias the seer."

Jerry frowned. "Do you really think that'll help?"

Circe laughed her musical laugh. "Perhaps not. But it got rid of my last lot of troublesome guests, and sooner or later the dead know everything."

"So we sail a black ship into hell . . . " said Jerry.

Circe pulled a wry face. "I'll give you directions."

"Don't you mean: 'Don't think of lingering on shore for lack of a pilot'?"

"How did you know I was about to say that?"

"It's a direct quote," said Jerry grimly.

Whatever else Circe might do or not do, her curative magic was first-rate. Jerry could hardly believe that his ankle had been agonizingly painful. He tested it and turned to Medea, who was organizing the necessities for the trip. She seemed to be even more "organizingly inclined" than Liz.

"You really don't have to come along, Medea. We'll take Odysseus' ship. He's been there before."

Medea, as was her way, simply ignored the part of the statement she didn't want to hear. "Yes, we'll have to take the black ship. We won't all fit into the chariot, and anyway Bitar and Smitar need a rest."

"We'd better inform Odysseus and his merry men we're sailing a black ship into hell again," said Jerry, accepting the inevitable.

"Well, at least I've got something for the fleas this time," said Liz.

"What? And why have you been keeping it to yourself?" demanded virtually every modern, scratching instinctively.

"An herbal remedy of my mother's: wormwood, fleabane and rue, with added magic from Medea. Would you all like some? Every one of you looks as if you need it."

"And I'm going to try my hand at distilling. That son of a bitch Ody tries to get us smashed again, I'll spike his drinks for him," said McKenna.

"And I'm going to get a good night's sleep for a change," sighed Jerry. "Clean, full, safe, dry, and *not* on a ship."

The Krim device manipulated the prukrin threads of the Ur-universe's belief strands with skill. Already the reactivated long-moribund universe was nearly ready for the masters. And while the gods of this thread of Ur-universe were difficult to work with and unreliable in the extreme, it was also a valuable find. This species generated emotional intensities that the Krim would find delightful. The Ur-universes were intense and rich in the emotional flavors that the Krim relished. And it was all proceeding well. Krim-delighting rituals were being enacted faithfully . . .

Except for that one group! They were an irritation. A tear within the mantle of prukrin reality. Here they were, in a place rich in sorrows and misery and fear. And they were laughing! At ease! The masters would be furious. They would have to be eliminated, if they could not be turned to belief. Well. It would try using the darkness that lurked within this species' soul. It would tweak the legend. Human sacrifice was not unknown. Odysseus himself was believed to have insisted on the sacrifice of Iphigenia.

23

⌗⌗⌗⌗⌗⌗

CAM' YE O'ER FRA' FRANCE?

"We insist on seeing him!" demanded someone from the outer office, speaking accented English. An exaggerated version of the Queen's English, in fact.

Hunched over his desk, painfully working through another psychological assessment written in the specifically turgid jargon of that branch of academia, Miggy Tremelo found himself almost grinding his teeth. It was not the interruption in his train of thought which annoyed him. Truth to tell, that was a relief. Even by academic standards, Miggy found "psychologese" particularly aggravating. It was the inevitable—

His new secretary started booming her response. *Professor Tremelo is not to be disturbed; you have no appointment; procedures must be followed—*

Miggy *did* find himself grinding his teeth. If there was a more unlovely sound in the universe than that voice, he couldn't imagine what it might be. His new secretary, shoved upon him by the National Security Council because she apparently had a higher security clearance than God Almighty, reminded him of something out of the Grimm Brothers. A troll, composed of equal parts red tape, officiousness, petty self-satisfaction with the

163

exercise of petty power, and—last but not least—monumental stupidity.

As the row in the outer office continued, Miggy tried to block it out. But the noise was too loud.

Miggy sighed. He almost knew to the last word what the visitor would say next. *I'm-not-leaving-this-office-until-I-see-him!*

He snorted. *Fat chance, lady.* This much he granted: at least the troll kept unwanted visitors from bothering him. And Miggy couldn't think of a single person from England that he wanted to see at the moment.

Right on cue the woman made the predicted statement. Upper-class British accent. Shrill.

Suddenly a new voice entered the fray.

"Please, *Mevrou*," a man said, his voice pleading, gruff and heavily accented. A familiar accent. One Miggy had heard recently, listening to a female marine biologist. "We've come all the way from South Africa."

Miggy was on his feet and at the door in a moment. He yanked the door open, revealing the appointmentless visitors who had managed to get all the way through the security cordon. Actually, he was a bit amazed they had gotten that far. Looking at the big man and the blond, exquisitely coiffured and made-up woman, he realized it was probably easy enough for this couple. What the big guy couldn't simply bull through, she would arrogantly slice apart. The man looked grim, the woman angry.

Miggy smiled reassuringly at them. "Come in. Is your name De Beer? We've asked the South African Consulate to contact you."

The big man had a hat in his hand. A hat, in this day and age. He was twisting it. "Those *mamparas*, they're too busy worrying about cell phones and BMWs to do any work, *Myneer*. We tried to contact Liz when we saw the news on CNN. Got the first flight over here when we heard that she'd gone off to be with some of your military. I've come to take my daughter home, *Myneer*. I lost my son," the big man swallowed, "in our army. My daughter comes home. Get an American to do the job."

Miggy Tremelo took a deep breath. *Damn whichever incompetent deskwarmer had let him be the one to break it to them.* "I'm afraid, sir, that your daughter is missing."

The big South African went pale under his tan. He sat down abruptly in a chair in the outer office.

His blond wife was unfortunately not similarly affected. Her cultivated English accent did go to hell in a handbasket, though.

"Then you bleddy find her, you dumb American bastard. Trust Elizabet! Silly girl should have stayed at home and got married like I wanted her to." She glared down at her husband. "But no, Jan! *You* had to let her go to university. You encouraged her. You let her marry that American. This is all your fault, you hear me! Your fault!"

She went on. And on. The big guy just twisted his hat to ruination. His face was almost collapsing, in the way that a man who does not know how to cry wishes he did.

Well, that was no help, Miggy thought bleakly, about an hour later. Between the woman's outrage and the man's grief, neither of them had been able—or even willing, in the mother's case— to tell him anything about their daughter that he didn't already know.

Tremelo stared down at the psychological assessment report in front of him. This one claimed to be an assessment of Lamont Jackson.

"Assessment, my foot," muttered the physicist. "There's nothing here but the shell of a man, carefully constructed to deal with a none-too-friendly world. I need to know *him*."

Again, he sighed. Now that Mr. and Mrs. De Beer had finally showed up, Miggy had personally interviewed almost all of the close friends and relatives of that largest party of abducted people.

None of it had been very useful.

Jerry Lukacs had no immediate family left. A single child, his parents had died years earlier in an auto accident. He had a number of colleagues, many of whom considered themselves to be (and undoubtedly were) his "friends." But the friendship involved had been so curlicued with typical academic one-upsmanship-combined-with-qualifications that their accounts of Lukacs had been more useful as guides to *them* than he himself.

The young corporal's family had been large and helpful.

Helpful, at least, in their attitude. But—nothing. Just a tale of a young farm boy, ambitious in the way that such boys are. A nice kid, it seemed, if perhaps with more in the way of an "attitude" than most. But—nothing, really.

Cruz's family had been even larger, and less helpful. Not because they were hostile, but simply because they were heartbroken. The sergeant's father had died when he was only a boy, and Anibal Cruz had become the man of the family—a position he had apparently fulfilled very well indeed. Miggy winced, remembering a wizened grandmother weeping softly in one of the chairs in his office. Nothing.

Cruz's fellow soldiers had been a bit more informative. Slowly, under persistent questioning, a certain picture of Anibal Cruz had emerged. Miggy began to smile, remembering. The world-renowned physicist, born into a branch of Mexico City's elite and then transplanted to the United States in his infancy, suspected he would have enjoyed the company of another of Mexico's many offspring. Even though Cruz had been born and raised in an environment about as different from that of young Tremelo as could be imagined.

Thinking about Lieutenant Salinas, Miggy's incipient smile vanished. *Oh, well,* he thought philosophically, *such men can be found in every race, color and creed.* He snorted. *Nobody* seemed to have much use for John Salinas. Even his wife had been far more agitated over the fact that the life insurance company was demanding proof of death than her husband's actual fate.

That left only—

Bracing himself, he went back to the door to the outer office and opened it. The troll looked up from her desk.

"Sir?"

"Still no word from Mrs. Jackson?"

The troll's lips grew pinched. Well . . . the thin crevasse where lips were normally to be found on a human face vanished completely. She sniffed. Well . . . she uttered a sound through her nose which reminded Tremelo of—

He shied away from the thought hastily.

"In a matter of *speaking,* Professor Tremelo. The Jackson woman did call early this morning. But when I informed her that she was required to appear at your office in order to pursue the preliminary psychological assessment—"

Miggy stifled a combined groan and snarl of fury. The struggle was ferocious enough to cause him to miss the next few words.

"—could not *believe* her *insolence*. Can you imagine? Those *people*—!"

Even the troll realized she was treading on thin ice. "Well, in any event. You can be sure I informed her that under *no* circumstances would the United States government make good her so-called 'lost wages.' And of course when she—"

"*She's a waitress, you insufferable creature!*" bellowed Tremelo. The fact that the physicist rarely lost his temper was compensated, perhaps, by the volcanic results when he did. "*The United States government hiccups that much money for—for—*"

He clamped his jaws shut, stymied by his utter inability to think of *anything* the U.S. government spent so little money on.

The troll was ogling him, as pale as a sheet. Even she, apparently, had been intimidated by the famous Tremelo Tremor.

"She wanted her *tips* made good, too," squeaked the creature.

Tremelo's fury was instantaneously transformed into almost hysterical laughter.

"Good for her!" he managed to get out. After a moment, when he'd brought himself under control, he stood fully erect and pointed at the telephone. The long finger bore a close resemblance to a wizard's wand of wrath.

"You *will* call Mrs. Jackson. You *will* apologize for your rude conduct this morning. You *will*—"

Abruptly, he shook his head and advanced upon the telephone in question. "Never mind," he growled. "I wouldn't trust you to invite a crocodile to lunch. What is the number?"

The troll's thick fingers fluttered their way through the notes on her desk. Garbled explanations followed. It seemed Mrs. Jackson was rarely at home . . . children being taken care of by the grandmother . . . long hours at work . . . longer than ever, now that her husband had vanished . . .

Miggy sighed and began punching numbers into the telephone. "Information? I need the telephone number of the South Side Cafe, please."

❖   ❖   ❖

The telephone was answered on the third ring by a harried-sounding voice, rich with the accent of Chicago's south side. "South Side Cafe. Yeah, I'm Marie Jackson."

"Mrs. Jackson," said Miggy evenly, "this is Professor Tremelo. I just discovered that you were treated very rudely this morning. Please accept my sincere apologies."

For perhaps half a minute, Miggy listened to the voice on the other end. And a pungent half a minute it was, too. By the time the voice came to a halt, Tremelo was bestowing a wintry smile on the troll.

"I fully sympathize, Mrs. Jackson, and I can assure you that it won't happen again. Moreover, I will be more than glad to make good your lost income. But I really must speak to you as soon as possible. Would this afternoon be convenient? I can send someone to pick you up, if you need a ride."

Again, he listened to the voice. This time, for perhaps fifteen seconds.

"Excellent, Mrs. Jackson. I'll have someone there at two o'clock." A few more seconds of the voice. "Oh, you won't be able to miss them, ma'am. Look for some paratroopers in a Humvee."

A few more seconds. *Very* pungent, those.

Tremelo's smile grew positively arctic. "By all means. Be my guest."

He placed the telephone back on the receiver and walked back to his office. At the door, he paused and turned back upon the troll.

"I *do* suggest you not place any obstacles in the way of Mrs. Jackson, when she shows up here later today. Really I do."

He managed to keep a straight face. Even a solemn one. "Mrs. Jackson was quite precise. In a colorful sort of way. She says she'll either get the red carpet treatment when she arrives, or she'll make herself one. Ah, the source of the pigment will apparently involve, to use her expression, someone's new asshole."

He turned away. "Not mine."

PART V

To the hell dogs that couch beneath his throne,
cast that fair prey.

—Percy Bysshe Shelley,
"The Daemon of the World"

24

⊡⊐⊏⊐⊏⊐⊡

A GRAVE UNDERTAKING.

They sailed due south for Hades with a crew full of lamentations and hangovers, and a pair of sacrificial sheep. With a fair wind to carry them, they crossed the river of ocean and came at last to a bleak coastline shrouded in a swirling mist.

McKenna peered into the world of gray. "Jeez, I wish this stuff would blow away."

"It never does," said Jerry. "This is the frontier of the world. It's supposed to be beyond where the sun shines."

"So this is where the monkey puts his nuts!" said Liz. "They said it was a place where the sun don't shine." She was exceptionally moody today. One minute up, and the next snapping your head off. Jerry wished he could be sure why. But then he'd always found women to be slightly more confusing than calculus.

They sailed into a river mouth. On the low banks, groves of tall black poplars loomed out of the mist. It was a bleak place, enough to sink anyone's spirits. The talk dried up. The water was still and oily, covered in a network of floating willow-catkins. Unnaturally long and dark catkins. "The Acheron," said Odysseus.

171

"I go no further." There was a level of implacable grimness in that statement, which let them all know that they'd reached the edge of how far they could push him.

Medea took a deep breath. "Very well. Set us ashore. And then wait beside your black ship. I place this geas on you. Surely none of you will ever return to the lands where the sun shines, if you abandon us." She began chanting sonorously, flicking droplets of red wine from her fingers.

A low moan went up from the sailors.

"I think they might just be here when we get back," said Cruz.

"They have a reputation for being recidivists of the worst order," said Jerry, darkly.

Medea scowled. "Indeed. That's Hellenes for you."

The hull of the black ship grated on the coarse sand. Jerry and his companions helped to haul the ship up. Then they set out through the gloom between the black poplars towards the place where the River of Lamentation joined the River of Flaming Fire.

Henri was not terribly keen. He offered to remain at the ship as he particularly wanted to examine the black foliage of the plants. As a botanist . . .

"Typical frog-eater," said McKenna, dismissively. "Got no guts."

The cold mist was lightened by the apoplectic Henri's flaming red face. "How dare you, you insolent puppy? *How dare you?*" He stood on tiptoe to bristle his eyebrows at McKenna's chin. And then, pulling in his ample supply of guts, he turned. "I will lead. I will be your guide. For the honor of *la belle France!*"

Unfortunately, the drama of the occasion was immediately ruined. Charging ahead, Henri stepped unwarily into a muddy stream.

"Oh! *Merde!* My shoes! This place it is terrible! Oh my shoes, my shoes. The leather will be completely ruined! Oh, this is terrible. Even my socks they are muddy."

Jerry whispered to Lamont, under cover of the French footwear dirge, "I think we may just have found the River of Lamentation . . ."

But it must just have been a tributary of that rushing river. After that, the ground became rapidly steeper and more uneven and the lamentations grew in volume. And they weren't all coming from their French "guide."

Soon they stood beside the rushing torrent of weeping and wailing water and the gnashing of rocky teeth. "Where now?" yelled Cruz, above the anguished waters, struggling with the ram he was leading.

"Downstream," replied Jerry. "We're looking for where it meets the River of Flaming Fire."

Liz had apparently discovered a common thread between herself, Jerry, and Lamont—Monty Python. She nearly killed the other two with her next comment. She pointed to the river. "I think it's pining for the fjords."

25

⌷⌐⌐⌐⌐⌐⌐⌷

WE'VE ALL GOT TO MAKE SACRIFICES.

The place was one of smokes and steams. The weeping waters of the River of Lamentation rushed and fumed into a thundering waterfall, backlit by the River of Flaming Fire. The two rivers mixed in a tumult of green flames, shrieking and steaming around a dark monolith before cascading into the dark Acheron.

"Phew," complained Lamont. "This place stinks!"

Liz nodded. "Sulphur. The area is plainly volcanic. And those green 'flames' are luminiferous bacteria in a turbulent warm river. Steaming where it meets an ice-cold one. Nothing that can't be explained scientifically if you look carefully at it. I'll bet there is a reason for the 'lamentation' too."

Jerry raised his eyebrows. "And I suppose that the smoking grotto isn't the entry to Hades' Kingdom of Decay either?"

Liz shrugged. "Around here? Who knows? Anything is possible, I suppose. All I do know is I don't much fancy this sacrifice business."

Cruz grunted. "Mac and I have had to carry these goddamned sheep Circe gave us for the last couple of hundred yards. I don't care if they're barbequed or 'sacrificed.' I'm not carrying them back."

Medea smiled pityingly. "I will do the sacrifice. I was the priestess of Hecate, she who is mistress of fertility and of the dead among my people. Come. Dig the trench. A cubit by a cubit."

"Carry the sheep. Dig the trench. Anything else?" muttered McKenna, swinging down a bleating, struggling sheep from his shoulder.

Medea smiled at him. "Yes. You can flay them and burn them when I have cut their throats."

"Gee thanks!" said Mac. "Here, Frenchy. Hold this goddamn sheep."

The plump Frenchman swallowed. "I am not entirely familiar with animal husbandry. Not in the least."

"Just hold it," said McKenna impatiently. Lamont had already taken a firm grip on the black ram Cruz had been carrying.

Lenoir took a tentative hold on the sheep, which bleated indignantly at him.

Watching, Jerry immediately learned Lesson One in the proper procedure of sacrificing sheep. Do not take a tentative hold. Hold *tightly*.

"Hell's teeth, Mac!" shouted Cruz. He left off digging the trench and grabbed the ram from Lamont. "Get after it, you guys. We'll never find another one. We need that sheep! Catch it!"

The rest of them set off in the chase. Even Henri took part, if in a somewhat involuntary fashion. As a result of a slight mishap the barrel-bellied Frenchman actually beat them to the sheep. He lost his footing and rolled down the steep slope, and then landed on the unfortunate animal.

In desperation he grabbed the stunned and winded creature. The others arrived, panting, to find him rolling about embracing a fallen sheep. The creature was bleating plaintively and struggling desperately to regain its freedom.

"*Merde!* She is kicking me in the private parts!" squalled Henri.

Liz took one look and started laughing. "This puts a whole new complexion on my understanding of 'Animal Husbandry'!"

✧   ✧   ✧

Medea, the priestess of Hecate, had offered the libations of honeyed milk, sweet wine, and water. The white barley had been sprinkled. The black ram was ready, held by Cruz and Lamont.

Liz whispered to Jerry. "The ghosts *drink* the blood? Oh, sick!"

His reply was drowned in a chorus of quavering voices . . . "We seek a better sacrifice, mortals. We want the blood of a man. A black man."

"Well, you can forget it!" snapped Jerry. "Come on guys—let's go."

"Yeah. This crap makes me sick anyway," said McKenna, straightening up. "I don't mind killing something for my dinner, but this!" He let go of the ram and gave it a swat. "Get lost, Rambo. It's your lucky day."

With a bleat the ram took off into the mist.

"Wait. Wait!" quavered the voices of the dead. "Give us our blood . . . "

"You might as well let that sheep go," said Cruz. "Come on. That was a path that our Frenchy 'discovered.' Let's go back that way."

With Jim McKenna leading the way, they all began leaving. Behind them, the voices of the dead began wailing. "Wait . . . we must have a blood sacrifice. You'll never get back without us."

A little further on, Cruz came to a sudden halt. Jerry heard a pitiful bleat, and peered around the sergeant's shoulder.

There, lying in the path, was the ram. It should have been a lot more careful about where it ran in the mist.

"Oh jeeze," muttered McKenna. "We'll have to kill it. We can't leave it to suffer."

Medea handed him a small clay flask. "Here. Give the creature this. Force its mouth open and pour it down."

Liz stepped into the breach. "I'll pour, Mac. You hold the mouth open."

The animal stilled. Medea smiled. "Now. I think I have the answer to your problem. This animal is too injured to recover. The poison you have just administered causes sleep, ending in death."

"That's a mercy . . . "

"I am not finished. I am a mistress of illusions. And I *have* been known to deceive people about victims before. After all, I convinced the people of Corinth that a dead pig in a pretty robe was Glauce. Shall we try to deceive the spirits of the dead? Given a piece of the Ethiope's clothing I could indeed make that ram look like him. Thus we may get what you need. But in exchange you must promise to take me to this 'America' place."

Jerry took a deep breath. "We can't promise what we can't guarantee delivery of."

"Yeah. Getting into the States is difficult enough even without being here. Can't make that promise, Medea," said Cruz.

Liz covered her eyes. "I can imagine filling in that work-permit application could be interesting." She obviously spoke from frustrating experience.

"And without it," muttered Jerry, "she'll be an illegal alien." He shrugged ruefully. "Can you imagine putting down *sorceress* as your occupation?"

Cruz frowned. "What about refugee status? Of course, unless we can pass her off as a Cuban, the Immigration and Naturalization Service probably won't accept it." For a moment, his swarthy face was creased by a scowl. "You can always count on *la migra* to be assholes."

He turned back to Medea. "We'll try. But we can't make any guarantees."

Medea smiled at him. "I like your honesty, more than I like glib easily broken promises like Jason's. Swear that you will try your best to take my children and me to this place, and I will help you to the best of my skill and powers."

Cruz nodded. "Sounds fair, hey guys?"

Lenoir sniffed. "*Mademoiselle* can always come to France. It is a far better place than America. And you will not have to claim that Satan is Fidel Castro in disguise to get asylum."

"Enter then the halls of the dead, the realm of dread Hades and august Persephone," quavered the voice. Plainly, Medea's deception had worked.

"This is wrong," protested Jerry. "This *isn't* what happened. That was in later legends."

Lamont shrugged. "Well, maybe it's our break out of here. Come on. We can't just back off . . . "

So down they went. "At least there was none of that blood-drinking stuff," whispered Liz. "But I thought we were underground..."

It was a gloomy enough scene... but those *were* trees...

"We are. This is the vestibule of Persephone, with the black poplars and sterile willows again. The Gate and Cerberus should be next."

The three-headed guard dog of Hades was monstrous. On the elephant side of Great Dane. Black venom drooled from each slobbery mouth. It grinned at them, revealing huge yellowed teeth. Thumped its tail. Then it cried *"Welcome!"* with a voice of brass. Then it stopped paying them any attention at all, in order to scratch.

"So why do I feel that this is one of those dogs that will let you in but not out?" muttered McKenna.

"That's its reputation," said Jerry glumly.

The gates swung silently open. The land beyond was barren and flecked with small white flowers. "Asphodels. Complete in every detail except it's the wrong myth," said Jerry dryly. "Amazing."

"Hic." The tall, slender, dark-haired woman in the gateway swayed slightly. "Are you coming in, or are you going to stand out there all day?"

"Um. We weren't too sure about the dog," said Jerry.

She reached out a long, white, elegant hand to scratch Cerberus. She nearly fell over. "Come on in, do. He's a soppy old thing really, and I do feel like some company. Liven this place up a bit."

Bemused, they went in. The goddess looked them over, with a faintly silly smile on her face. Her eyes fixed on Lamont. "Ooh! *Hello, handsome.* I do *so* like Ethiopes."

She gave a little ladylike burp. "Hermes came with a message that the Ethiopian had to be sacrificed. It seemed such a pity. I'm so glad you've got another." She turned to Medea and whispered hoarsely. "They're so sexy, don't you think, priestess? I like dark colors. It's what I found so attractive about Hades. But Hades is so *staid.*"

Lamont looked as if he hoped the earth would open up and

swallow him . . . and take him to Hades, if he wasn't there already.

She swayed closer. Ran her fingers up Lamont's arm. "I'm Persephone. But *you* can call me Kore."

Cruz sidled up to Medea. *Sotto voce* he asked: "Which 'sweet wine' did you use for those libations to this Persephone?"

"The amphora with the white flowers, and the hunting scene," answered Medea, puzzled.

"Oh lord! That wasn't wine. That was Mac's 'brandy.' That stuff that he distilled. It's a helluva lot stronger than wine."

"I've still got quite a lot left."

Persephone beamed at them. "So why are you all standing around like statues? Let's have some music. Dancing . . . wine, laughter. This place is *so* dead. Hic. I'm so sick of being gloomy and reshpectable. Feel like kicking over the trashes for a bit. 'S been a long time s . . . shince I had a party, and Zeus shays we're all gonna be powerful again. Let's shelebrate!"

Jerry got a sudden look of rapt concentration—what Liz had come to think of as his "terrier-scents-a-rat" look.

"Would you like another drink, Persephone?" he asked.

"Thas goddess Persephone to you, dear, but I'd *love* another drink. Let's *all* have a drink . . . wooee, that last libation really went to my head. Great times are coming again!"

Jerry handed her the amphora with Mac's attempt at "brandy" in it. "Tell us all about it."

Persephone chugged straight from the amphora, spilling the liquor down her chin. "Not supposed to tell any mortals," she said, doing her best to look goddesslike.

She vaguely handed the amphora away and staggered towards Lamont. "I'm always doing doom and gloom and misery. That's Persephone: 'sposed to be 'xempt from the passions that make all the other gods mess 'round. I've got feelingsh too." She threw her arms around Lamont and kissed him with noisy enthusiasm. "I've got to keep you prisoner. Going to enjoy tha'!" And then she slithered down to flop onto the ground. "Damn 'gypitians. Don' *like* pyramids. S'Greek temples not good enough for them?" She began to cry gently.

"Egyptians?"

"Prisoners?"

"Er. I think it is visitors that we have." Henri gestured nervously at the gray host.

The dead clustered round in a great throng. Gray forms of warriors with gaping wounds, young men, women—but all in the garb of classical Greece. Except for the one who pushed his way forward—he looked as if he were a policeman from the early twenty-first century.

"Stavros is the name. Can you tell me what the hell I'm doing here?" asked the shade.

"We were kind of hoping you could tell *us*," said Jerry.

Stavros told his tale . . . and then faded back.

More and more came. The modern visitors got no wiser.

"Let's get the hell out of here," said McKenna. "Before she sobers up."

"The idea is one of remarkable sense," agreed Henri. "This place, how do you say, 'gives me the willy.' "

"Willies," corrected Jerry.

"Ah? You have it too?"

"HRRRRRR." The rumbling that came from Cerberus' throats made mere basso profundo seem like treble. "And where do you lot think you're going?" asked the middle head.

"We thought we would go and take a little of the night air," said Henri. "It is very close in here."

"And very close is where you stay," said the left head.

"And do try that little spear, dark one. Do," pleaded the right.

"We haven't had new souls for a long, long time," snarled the center head.

"Not for ages. Did you know that we are immortal?" said left head. "You can't kill us."

The right head missed his chance to speak because he was nibbling at fleas, the huge fangs champing at coarse fur.

"Lord Hades will return from Olympus soon. He sits in council with his brothers," said the center head.

"Great things are afoot." The left head eyed them hungrily. "Hades will be receiving many new souls."

"These gods-bedamned fleas are driving me demented," said the right hand head, obviously ordering a scratch of the ear.

"So how do we get out of here, Doc?" asked Cruz in an undervoice.

Jerry looked worried. "Honey cakes can distract him."

"Damn. I knew I'd forgotten something. What about half a transformed Hershey bar?" volunteered Liz, digging in her bag.

They broke the sticky honey-scented papyrus-wrapped thing in three.

"Right, guys." McKenna and Cruz and Lamont had been given the task of throwing. "On the count of three . . . "

Four seconds later it was painfully obvious that they'd need a whole crate of mythworld-type Hershey bars.

"Okay, Doc," grumbled McKenna. "Next?"

"Hermes' caduceus and Orpheus' sweet music on the lyre were supposed to soothe him," said Jerry doubtfully.

Liz looked at the big dog. "Well, Hermes seems to be involved with who or whatever is trying to capture or kill us. So I don't think that likely. What about music?"

"How do you feel about Tina Turner, dog?" asked Lamont, grinning.

The music played. The dog appeared no less vigilant. "Don't like singing," said the central head.

"Got anything instrumental?" asked the left head.

"Strings are good. Damn these fleas."

"You got anything else, Lamont?" asked McKenna.

Lamont was staring at the air where the shade of Tina Turner had appeared. "Tina doesn't do it, I don't imagine Donna Summers will either," he mused. Doubtfully: "I could try some Miles Davis . . . "

Cruz looked at the dog, weighing chances. "Doc?"

He shook his head. "I'm fresh out of ideas, Anibal."

Liz cleared her throat loudly. "What about something for those fleas? I happen to be an expert on *fleas*."

She had all three heads' focused attention. "If you can do something about these fleas, you can go," said the central head.

"You personally, that is," said the head on the right.

"More than our job is worth to let all of you go," added the left head, wrinkling its nose.

"Very well," Liz said, calmly. "Fleabane. Some advice and a good long scratch in all those hard to reach spots."

She turned to look in her bag. "You guys make like a banana, while I deal with this," she said in an undervoice.

"What?" asked a puzzled Jerry.

"Make like a banana," she said urgently. "Split. South African idiom. Our canine acquaintance is aurally sensitive but a trifle microcephalic."

"What are you talking about, flea-girl?" demanded Cerberus.

"My friends want to know if I have your promise to let me go," said Liz, without a quaver.

"Promise."

"Swear to the gods."

"By the Styx."

"Oaths sworn on the Styx are binding," said Jerry.

Liz walked forward calmly. "Very well. This will drive the fleas off and kill them on contact. But it is important that you break the life cycle of the flea. Now, I wonder if you know . . . " She continued to speak softly while rubbing the fleabane, wormwood and rue mixture into the huge dog's rough fur.

Cerberus gradually subsided into a catatonic state of bliss, grunting occasionally. "A bit more to the left . . . ooh."

"We must get someone to sweep around here . . . "

"The fleas sound worse than humans, the way they breed."

Liz went right on scratching with both hands while gesturing furiously with her head for the rest of them to *go.*

Halfway back to the ship and they could still hear the angry baying of the tricked Cerberus.

"Mademoiselle. That was *très magnifique.*" Henri made her an elegant Gallic bow, when the panting Liz joined them.

"Yes, *Sir!*" said McKenna. "That was slick."

She beamed. "It was nothing, really. It's just a pity that we didn't succeed in getting home."

"Well, at least we learned something," said Lamont.

"Yes," agreed Jerry forcefully. "We have learned that the gods, or at least Hermes, are out to kill or capture us. That something weird is happening here—wherever 'here' is—involving the myths themselves." He frowned. "As if something long moribund was being brought back to life, but all jumbled up."

"And," said Henri, cheerfully, "I have also some interesting botanical material which will make for a wonderful publication if I can get back to civilization, although I could probably manage in America."

"Jeez, you're an arrogant French prick," snapped McKenna, when this had sunk in.

Henri twitched his mustachios. "At least I have something to be arrogant about."

"I'll—"

"Will you two stop snapping at each other?" snapped Liz. "We want to get back to where we left Odysseus and see if he's abandoned us here."

"And then we can do some thinking about where we should go next," said Lamont in a depressed tone. "I really hoped we'd find some way out of here."

Medea pursed her lips thoughtfully. "Persephone mentioned the land of Egypt. And pyramids. I have been told that those are a feature of that land."

"We're chasing straws," said Jerry in a flat voice. "But we've got to try. Oh, well. If Ody's there we'll go for a quick trip to see the pyramids."

There was something to be said for landing on a full tide. By the time Odysseus and his crew had talked themselves into sneaking away . . . they'd had to wait for the tide to turn, in order to launch. Even if they'd done the long portage to the water, there was still the river bar of the Acheron. So the modern folk returned to find the ship nearly floating.

"We heard you coming, and wished to be ready," said Odysseus. He projected all the integrity at his command. Lamont muttered something about used car salesmen.

Jerry was just too keen to be away and to see the sun again to argue—or to even to tell the ass what he thought of his lies. They just climbed on board and slept in the bow, as the black ship made its way back across the river ocean to the Enchanted Isle.

Odysseus woke them when Aeaea was again in sight.

Jerry shook his head. Oh, for coffee! "Provisions, and then we're away."

"And I must say farewell to my children for a while," said Medea in a subdued tone.

"Where will we sail to next? Will my oath have fulfillment then?" Odysseus enquired.

"Egypt, Odysseus. And maybe."

26

WIND INSTRUMENTS, PERCUSSION AND STRINGS...

Their stay in Aeaea lasted only a day. Just long enough to take on provisions for the voyage to Egypt. On the morning after their departure, Odysseus came forward, wringing his hands.

"Alas, good Americans. If I am to go to Egypt I will need more wind."

"Wind is the one thing you're not short of, Ody," sneered Liz.

Odysseus' face registered protest at misunderstanding. The more-in-sorrow-than-in-anger expression, thought Jerry, was about as convincing as it would have been coming from a wolf.

"We do not have enough food or water for such a journey without favorable winds." Odysseus pointed somewhere in the distance. "But help is at hand. Yonder lies the Isle of Aeolus, keeper of winds. He is a generous man. He will help us."

"I wouldn't trust that son of a bitch to speak my weight," said Liz, looking at the flapping sail. "He's right, though. Without a favorable wind, undertaking that voyage in this tub is a hopeless cause."

"What he's talking about is a visit to the island of Aeolia," explained Jerry. "You can see the sun gleaming on the 'unbroken wall of bronze.' Aeolus is the 'Warden of the Gales' in the Odyssey. He gave Odysseus a fair wind for Ithaca and imprisoned the other winds in a sack. In the gospel according to the ever-truthful Odysseus, his foolish men thought it was treasure and let the winds out, which blew them all over the place. Aeolus crops up again in the Aeneid."

"Lucky old Aeolus," said Liz sourly.

Jerry's snort was every bit as sour. "Lucky, my ass. Nobody's too lucky whenever they run across Odysseus. When Odysseus' fleet visited him, Aeolus was forced to wine and dine them at his expense. He was foolish enough to let ten ships into his harbor and disgorge their crews before getting the measure of the commander. After a month of that, the keeper of the winds handed over the windsack just to see them out of there. And he was careful not to let them disembark when they came back the second time."

It was a superlative natural harbor set in an inlet in the cliff wall that surrounded the island. The island was, however, relatively stark and stony compared to the shores of Thrinicia or Circe's wooded home.

"Good defensive spot," said Cruz, giving it a professional once-over.

"According to the book," said Jerry, "it has Aeolus and his six sons and six daughters on it. That seems a small group to defend an island of this size. But perhaps there were more. It wouldn't have seemed so, because the six sons were married to the six daughters. That kind of counts out too much other available nobility, although peasants and slaves wouldn't have been part of that number."

Liz made a face. "Yuck. *Nice* people. Founts of modern morality."

Lamont grinned at Liz. "You don't know half of it. The ancient Greek gods were always so busy doing something nasty, or screwing around with someone, I'm surprised they had any time for blessing wombs and crops. I was quite shocked by it all."

Jerry chuckled. "True. Not to mention the Heroes. Anything

you can think of from cannibalism to killing their fathers to marry their mothers, eh? But what about this place? Do you think we'll be attacked, or helped?"

Cruz looked thoughtful. "It's a good position for defense. But they're not above the ships. They can't really attack us, but they could hold out for months. Tough to hold with a handful of men though, especially if they rely on some trading. Like—who do you let in?"

Jerry shrugged. "Yeah. And I don't know what sort of welcome we'll get. Odysseus was here with the better part of five hundred men last time." Jerry looked up at the bronze walls. They appeared impenetrable.

Aeolus was there to meet them on the shore. He scowled ferociously at Odysseus. But he studied the modern folk with interest.

"Greetings, newcomers. What is it that you have done to get Zeus so spitting mad at you? Hermes has come to tell me that I am ordered to keep you here. Feed you royally and fill you with strong wine, while Olympus prepares to loose its might against you."

Four young men were staggering down to the stone quay with an enormous leather bag. Aeolus pointed to it. "Stow it carefully and row your way out before the tide changes. I'm not having that damned freebooter inside my walls again," he said, pointing at Odysseus, "and Zeus doesn't have much regard for other people's property when he tosses his thunderbolts. Get you gone. Where do you want a fair wind for?"

"Egypt. Thank you," said Jerry.

Aeolus smiled. "How fortunate. It is my gift to you. Speed you swiftly, and keep all the contrary winds trapped in the bag. I do not like whatever is afoot with Olympus."

"What? I mean, what is happening?"

Aeolus shook his head. "I do not know. But I was once a god . . . I do *not* like this. I will thwart it with my small power. Now go. And take care with that bag."

"I'll look after it for you," offered Odysseus. "I'll see it safely stowed. You can trust me. I'm a prince."

"You're enough of a bag of wind, without adding this one to your responsibilities," snapped Medea. "Typical damned Hellene."

"I'm an Achaean!" protested Odysseus.

Aeolus had provided the wind he'd promised, and had also provided Jerry with further food for thought.

He sat with Lamont, watching over the windsack. "Look. Every step we take we learn a fraction more. We've just got to put the pieces together. Then somehow we can break out of here, I'm sure."

Lamont pulled a face. "And we've got to stay alive. Obviously whatever the thing is, it's manipulating this place and its gods as if they were puppets."

Jerry nodded. "Rather disobedient and inefficient puppets. But still dancing according to strings that something is pulling somewhere."

"So what do we do about it?" asked Lamont.

Jerry ran his fingers through his hair. "Brace ourselves. The next problem's coming. The ancient Greek gods tended to work through intermediaries, but Zeus, for example, was quite capable of tossing thunderbolts. We've got problems, if they've got it in for us."

And problems weren't long in coming. Poseidon's minions found them at about two in the morning. It was a very rude awakening from sweet dreams.

The noise was reminiscent of a hippopotamus being sick into the big end of a tuba, which was, at the same time, being played by a very inept player. Only that description is really too mild. It sat every person on the ship bolt upright. Bolt upright and reaching for weapons in most cases. Which was just as well.

Triton was leading the charge himself, in a chariot drawn by pincer-footed white-foam horses. He was blowing like fury on an enormous trumpetlike shell. His look-alike minions showed that imitation was the sincerest form of flattery. The half-human Triton-genii were very like their master. From the chest up they were human enough. Below this they were scaled and finned, the sinuous sea monster bodies ending in a predator's narrow-forked caudal fin. They carried a variety of tridents and barbed harpoons. Their musical skill carried "bad" to new depths.

Odysseus and his men had other faults, but a lack of courage in a fight for their lives wasn't one of them. The Tritons had expected panic. Instead they were thrust off. Speared. Shot. Attacked by dragons. And all the while Medea calmly walked along the central passage between the rowing benches and anointed the oars with a potion of her own. When she'd finished, she walked up to Odysseus and told him to get the oars into the water.

Medea was a former princess and a person of power. When she told Odysseus to tell the men to get the oars out, he jumped to it.

The Tritons backed off.

"They will not dare to come within twenty cubits of those oars," said Medea calmly.

The men found this comforting. Unfortunately it didn't keep the Tritons out of earshot. The Tritons took it in turns to "accompany" the ship with the blaring of their conches. And by midmorning it was painfully apparent that the Tritons weren't going to give up easily. Beeswax might shut out sirens but, for sheer volume and terrible low-frequency noise that penetrated to the very marrow of their bones, this was unbeatable. Tina Turner in competition just increased their volume.

"*Merde.*" Henri shook a plump fist at the Tritons, who may have included a raspberry in their next arpeggio. "This is worse than German music! I think at least I should attempt to teach them some Ravel."

"How many more days to Egypt?" yelled Liz, having to bellow to make herself heard above the cacophony.

Odysseus simply held up seven fingers. And pointed to an island on the starboard horizon. He shrugged his shoulders and threw up his hands.

Liz nodded. The noise was simply insupportable.

As they came inshore and water shifted from wine-dark to azure the Tritons drew off a bit, but not completely. The water was less than three fathoms deep. Dangerous sailing in uncharted waters. Hell, it wasn't even something you wanted to attempt in waters you were even slightly unfamiliar with, as Aeolus' fair wind for Egypt was moving the ship on at a good clip.

"We'll have to make a landfall and see if they'll go away."

The coastline did not look promising. There were smoke trails from distant hearth fires in the hills. But the verdant coastline, thick with wild vines and stands of poplar and pine, bore the look of a land ravaged by some mighty destructive force—as if a sequence of small cyclones had windrowed through them.

Odysseus was looking about like a cat in a dog pound. "Cyclops country," he said nervously, as they pulled the ship up. The sound of the dreadful conch was now distant enough to make speech plausible.

"Oh, great!" said Liz. "I presume the one-eyed giants *won't* be pleased to see you back."

"We'd better get out there again," said Mac.

Liz pulled a face. "I don't know if a blind one-eyed giant isn't better than that racket. Doesn't it bother you?"

McKenna shrugged. "I guess my ears are toughened. The volume is a bit much, but it reminds me of myself trying to play the bugle. Ma used to make me go and practice at the far side of the south forty. She said I was putting the cows off their milk."

Lamont snorted and nodded in sympathy. "Yeah. I tried the sax for a bit."

"I always wanted to be one of those really wild drummers," said Jerry with a grin. "Of course, I haven't got any sense of rhythm."

Henri looked regretfully at the ground. "It was the wish of my mother that I should become a great violinist." He shrugged. "She ran out of teachers prepared to attempt this labor, and became tired of the complaint about the mistreatment of the cat. I remain devoted to classical music, of course. But alas, I cannot play."

Cruz allowed a slight smile to crack his impassive countenance. He looked at his thick stubby fingers. "Me, I decided I was Carlos Santana's natural heir. Or Jimi Hendrix."

Jerry looked at the thick fingers and wondered how they'd ever managed to press chords. "Well, it's a good thing one of us has got some musical talent."

There was a flash of teeth. "Hey, I said *I* thought I was. Not like anyone else did."

Lamont looked pensive. "Do you think all of us taken are bad musicians?"

"Nah. I think the world has a lot more failed musico-wannabees than anything else," answered Cruz.

Liz stuck her nose in the air and said, in a lofty tone. "Ha. I wasn't about to tell you guys this, but seeing as you're all such musical geniuses, *I* was lead singer for an all-girl group at high school. We called ourselves 'The Supremes.'"

There was a moment of silence. Lamont looked at Jerry. Jerry looked at Lamont.

"And what did everyone else call you?" they asked together.

Liz pursed her lips. Her shoulders were shaking. "'The Substandards.' They said they even preferred my attempt to play the bagpipes."

The laughter was stilled by a running trill of notes, liquid and gentle, yet with enormous depth and power. Goat-footed and shaggy Pan arrived, playing his syrinx. He stepped around the grape-laden wild vines. The still-green grapes darkened and swelled. They were silent as the god continued to play. Haunting and bittersweet . . . then abruptly the music shifted to a quick leaping of notes, and the shaggy Pan began to dance. Then he lowered his pipes. Looked the group over carefully.

"So this is the group which has all Olympus in a tumult." He didn't look as if that displeased him much. Especially after his eyes fell on Liz's voluptuous figure.

Jerry was determined to confront these "gods" with what he saw as the glaring inconsistency. "How come you can speak English?"

Pan looked mischievously at him. "I'm not."

Jerry realized he'd become so used to Medea's translation magic that it had never occurred to him that their latest "divine" visitor might be speaking Classical Greek.

"Okay. So why are we here and how do we get out of being here?"

Pan blew a couple of thoughtful notes on his seven-reed pipes, eyeing Liz all the while. "No wonder you disturb Olympus with your direct questioning. I think you mortals have been called into the realms of heroes and gods because we were fading away. There are things afoot that Pan wants no part of. I am a shepherd god, not a god of blood and pain."

"What is going on that you don't want any part of?"

Pan blew another trill of high wavering notes. He was silent for a while. "I don't know. Zeus, and the earth shaker, and Hermes . . . they've all been very odd. Very odd indeed. And something has been happening. Our histories are being . . . reenacted. I have been chasing the nymph Syrinx. But it felt to me as if I had done that before. And the more I thought, the surer I was, that I had chased her before, and that Ladon had transformed her into a reed. I played the pipes I made from the river reeds . . . and my mouth and hands *knew* how to do this. I don't like it. I don't understand it, but I *do* know you are a thorn in the flesh of whatever is causing this. Therefore I am determined to help you."

He scowled. "Word is out from Olympus that you must be slain. So: how can I help you? I have soothed the terrible man-eating Cyclops to sleep with sweet music. What other help can I offer?"

"Send us home? Even the U.S.A. would do," begged the hopeful Henri, treading American sensibilities like grapes.

Pan knitted his brow. Danced a few steps. Which brought him closer to Liz, Jerry was *not* pleased to notice. The goat-god's reputation for lasciviousness was notorious.

"I would . . . if I could. But I don't even know where your home is. It must be a place that is incredibly far from here. Tell me how you came here?"

Jerry explained. Pan looked puzzled. "Do the herdsmen of your country, those who tend the sheep and the goats in the high and lonely meadows, still worship great Pan?"

Jerry swallowed. "Er. Not much."

Pan trilled his pipes sadly. "You mean 'not at all.' Alas, then I have no presence there, and no influence."

"Well, what about some advice?" asked Lamont. "We were heading for Egypt. Is that worth doing?"

Pan wrinkled his long goaty nose. "I don't know. But in the

realm of Egypt you would at least be beyond the hand of Olympus. Nowhere here would be beyond the Olympians. I would go there. The wind is set fair for the coast of Africa."

"We'd be going just as fast as it would carry us, if it wasn't for the Tritons."

Pan pulled a face. He seemed to like doing that. "Their idea of music is abominable. Unfortunately, sweet music has no charms to drive them off."

"Does bad music?" asked Lamont.

The idea seemed to shock Pan. "It is possible. It would have to be both louder and worse than their cacophony."

Lamont looked at the group of moderns. "I think we've possibly got a really talented group of failed musicians right here. If we had or could make some instruments . . . "

The goaty god jigged. "The making of musical instruments is my attribute. Allow me."

Pan worked with small pieces of metal or wood. He could, by what to Jerry appeared to be principles of cohesion, create larger things. Sprites and spirits of trees and waters danced at his command, hammering out bizarre shapes. The bagpipes and the drums were almost recognizable as such. Bagpipes were after all a shepherd's instrument, and the drum was another familiar concept. The guitar was not too wild an idea, although the device was more like a lute. However the attempts at the magical construction of a violin would have had Stradivari turning in his grave. At about 9000 rpm, at a guess. The brass instruments had totally flummoxed Pan's magical construction skills, until Jerry had mentioned a salpinx, a Greek trumpet.

The work would have gone faster, Jerry noted sourly, if Liz hadn't been there. Pan spent more time ogling her than he did assembling the instruments. It didn't help any that Liz was making no effort to make herself less visible. Rather the opposite, actually. She almost seemed to be displaying herself for the goaty creature, in a demure sort of way.

The extent to which that aroused his jealousy came as a bit of a shock to Jerry. He was even more shocked when Liz came up to him, after Pan was finally done, and chucked him lightly under the chin. "Oh, *relax*," she murmured. "I'm really not attracted to hairy types, Jerry, especially when they smell that much. Just keeping the help happy at their work, that's all."

With a low chuckle, she wandered off. Leaving Jerry simultaneously chagrined, confused—and quite happy.

Pan blocked his ears in horror at the testing phase. Lamont blew a note testing his mysterious and complex brass and reed instrument ... "I think that's a B flat."

"Be flatulence, more like," said Jerry with a grin. "Now what are we going to play, guys?"

Henri lifted a sneering lip. "Parsifal. Or perhaps 'Götter-dämmerung' would be more appropriate."

McKenna looked even more confused than the extra valves had any right to make him. "Huh?"

"Is that one of those old 'Abba' songs, maybe?" asked Liz with a perfectly straight face.

Pan had left them. He was not a sea god, and he was determined to gather a few like minds and try to reason with Zeus. And a brief encounter with Liz's handbag was enough to convince him that naiads were more receptive to his charms.

Besides, he said, the noise was driving him to drink. He had left them with an amplifying spell, and he wanted to be gone before they used it. . . .

In the bow of Odysseus' black ship, the new musical sensation was bickering about the really important stuff. When the gods are out to kill, you might as well be silly. The band needed a name.

Henri's *New York Philharmonic* had been rejected unanimously. So had McKenna's *The Herb Boys*. Argument now was centered on *Non-serious Skews* or *The Gathering Moss*.

The conches sounded. Debate was brought to an end with Cruz leaping to his feet. He hunched over his Pan-made instrument and struck chords. Or something approximately like chords.

"AAAH CAIN'T GET NO-WOOO . . . "

"*Merde!* I do not know how to play this. Is this singing or some kind of fit?"

"It's just a jam session."

The Frenchman looked puzzled.

"Just play as well as you can and try and fit in."

Henri drew the bow across the semi-violin. A shriek of tortured strings erupted from the device. "I will have to have a fit, too. This will be 'raspberry jam' no?"

But you could hardly hear him above the magically amplified shrill wail of the pipes and flatulent chorus of brass. Jerry, in his determination to give them all something to play along with, regardless of what speed they should desire to play at, thrashed away at the drums . . .

The Tritons disappeared, flinging conches.

On the shore, the Cyclops that Pan had lulled to sleep came pouring out of their scattered caves.

The first rock fortunately fell astern and surfing the wave took the black ship out of range.

"Holy Macaroni! I'm used to them throwing eggs and tomatoes. But rocks!" said Cruz.

Jerry smiled beatifically. "I always wanted to be in a rock band!"

The ship wallowed on a swell. Lamont blew a defiant flat note. "Jerry . . . *This* is rock and roll!"

Henri looked triumphant. "I think it was just a question of age. I was simply not ready for the violin. Now I feel it is my natural *métier*. Shall we give them, how do you say, another number?"

Odysseus wrung his hands. "Please. The crew says you can have all of their loot. Just no more music. Please. It is too far to swim for shore."

Cruz was sitting in the bow talking to Medea. She was looking a trifle miserable. "It wouldn't have been safe to bring the children. But I miss them terribly."

"They'll be fine," said the stocky gorilla of a paratrooper, patting her hand gently. "Your aunt and Glauce will take good care of them." He went on polishing the pair of hardwood batons linked with a short section of bespelled chain. Cruz had got the idea for the chain from Pan's altering and "stretching" a cartridge into a trumpet. The chain had once been a few links on Liz's handbag strap, before Medea had got to them.

"I know. But I can't help worrying." She looked at him with a wry smile. "You don't miss your children?"

"I haven't got any," said Cruz, feeling as if he might be stepping into deep water.

Medea shook her head and clicked her tongue sympathetically. "Your marriage is not blessed with children? Fertility magic is one my specialties. I can help you."

"I'll bet." He grinned. "Actually I'm not married. Never have been."

She gave him a skeptical enquiring look. The kind that says: *yeah, tell me another one.*

His copper skin darkened. "No. Honestly. I had a steady girl-friend for a while . . . but it kind of wasn't going anywhere. And she wanted to get married, settle down and have a family. I wasn't ready for that sort of commitment back then. She got married to one of my buddies, about two years back. Funny. That seems like a lifetime ago now."

She smiled devastatingly at him. "So, you don't like children?"

Anibal Cruz knew he was painting himself into a corner. "Erm. No. No, I like kids."

She backed off hurriedly. "You like *goats?*"

The Krim device came from a civilization that had been old and decadent before the mythology it was now exploiting had even conceived gods that were more complex than venerated trees. It possessed within it energies and devices that could turn a continent to slag. But of what value to the Krim was slag? The Krim wanted that which they had all but lost. This meant working in the Ur-Mythworlds. And despite the vast powers contained within the force-shielded pyramid, that meant working within the reality framework of each particular Ur-Mythworld too. It meant you had to hire local labor. And it was so hard to get decent help in those days. Really, you'd have thought the primitive Ur-gods would have been glad of the work. But no. Bone idle and far too independent to make good Krim servants.

But rich in anger. And credulous. Perfect for prukrin manipulation.

27

EMPLOYEES MUST GIVE
TWO WEEKS' NOTICE.

"It's not working." That was the second time Miggy Tremelo had heard that exact statement in the last twenty minutes. The first time had been from the head of the insulation-project team. He'd restrained himself from the desire to kick the idiot downstairs. The woman might be an expert on insulating materials but she had absolutely no common sense and was so deeply involved in her field as to be blind to everything else. *Of course* the polymer spray wouldn't stick to the pyramid surface. If she'd bothered to read the reports or even talk to anyone . . .

Now it was the turn of the representative from the National Security Council who had replaced Harkness. Tremelo took a deep breath. "What isn't working, Mr. Milliken?"

The NSC man ran his hands through his once impeccably ordered hair. "Project Poison Pill. The pyramid just pushes the bombs ahead of itself when it expands. Like a bulldozer."

Tremelo steepled his fingers. "I sometimes wonder why the hell we bother to write reports," he said conversationally. "That bit of information has been available since the first day. Fairly *early* on the first day, in fact—Colonel McNamara tried it right off. Several times."

He sighed heavily, biting off further sarcasm. "Any 'poison pill' will have to go in with the snatched victims. You'll have to get sufficient new material, and hope the pyramid selects one of your 'pill' carriers."

Milliken stared intently at him. "Will that work?"

Tremelo shrugged. "I wish I knew."

"We'll try it!" Milliken rose to his feet. "We'll arrange for new soldiers with heavy weapons. Some of them will be snatched."

"In the meanwhile, I'm going ahead with a project of my own. At least seven of the victims could definitely have been resuscitated if we'd gotten to them fast enough. We're going to saturate the area inside the cordon with medics. If we can get one more survivor in a better mental state than the last one, we can learn a great deal more."

Milliken nodded. "That sounds like an eminently effective plan. Just see that you keep me posted."

Miggy Tremelo stood up, stretching out his lanky frame. "You could try doing that, too. It might save you having to explain more non-working projects," he said dryly. "Now, if you'll excuse me, we've been conducting interviews with the next of kin of all the disappearance victims that have not returned. I'm especially interested in the relatives of that one large group that hasn't come back. We're trying to establish just how the pyramid selects people and how this group have managed, presumably, to stay alive. We've only had two returns from them, and that was within minutes of their being snatched."

When Miggy Tremelo met Marie Jackson, he was a bit surprised. Knowing from the files that Lamont Jackson was in his late forties, he'd assumed his wife would be about the same age. Instead, the woman who came into his office was in her mid-thirties.

She was a very attractive woman. A bit on the short side, with a full figure and an open, pretty face. Her complexion was a lustrous coffee-with-cream, her eyes were light brown, almost hazel, and her short hair had been dyed a faintly red tinge.

Tremelo knew that she worked as a waitress, and she was wearing what he assumed to be her work clothes.

His guess was confirmed by the first words out of Mrs. Jackson's mouth. "I can't stay long," she said curtly. "I got three kids to take care of, you know. Without Lamont's paycheck any more. And my boss said I couldn't take more than two hours off or there'd be hell to pay. And he's just the bastard to ring up the bill, too."

Tremelo was rather charmed by the slight gap between her two front teeth. Despite the woman's surface belligerence, he sensed the friendliness lurking beneath. "We *are* in a state of national emergency," he said mildly. "Or hasn't your boss heard the news yet?"

Marie Jackson snorted. "You think that motherfucker gives a shit? He woulda docked Jesus half a day's pay for taking too long to haul the cross up to Calvary. Sure as hell would have fired him for taking three days comin' back to life."

Miggy was amused by the woman's vulgarity as much as by her sense of humor. He suspected that she was testing him, in the way that a combative lower-class person will sometimes poke the muckety-mucks, just to see how high they'll jump.

He grinned. "Mrs. Jackson, you stay here as long as you need to. If that boss of yours gets nasty about it, you just give me a call."

He made a casual gesture toward the window. The rumble of another Abrams tank turning what was left of Midway Plaisance into mash could be easily heard. "I guarantee I can make him see the light of day. Unless he wants his restaurant inspected by a platoon of paratroopers who don't know anything about the building code and couldn't care less. Just shoot the cockroaches."

Marie's grin was even wider than his own. "Well, *okay* then. What can I do for you?"

The grin faded, replaced by a slight frown. "If you just want to ask me more questions about Lamont, I don't know what I can tell you more than I already told all those—" He could practically see her biting off the profanity "—shrinks."

Miggy waved his hand, dismissing the idea. The hand wave turned into an invitation.

"Coffee?"

Marie peered suspiciously at the coffee pot. The device looked much the worse for wear. "You make that coffee?"

Miggy nodded. Marie rolled her eyes. "Not a chance. But if you've got the makings, I'll brew another pot."

Tremelo laughed aloud. Then, guiding her to the adjoining room where the coffee was kept, he waited in companionable silence while Marie made a fresh pot of coffee. She went about the task with the quick efficiency of long practice.

When the coffee started brewing, he led the way back to his office and invited her to sit in a chair across from his desk. "I really don't want to ask you anything, Mrs. Jackson. I mostly want to see if you can *tell* me something."

"What's that?"

Tremelo leaned back in his chair and steepled his fingers under his chin. "Why is it, out of hundreds of people who have been snatched by that alien *thing*, that your husband is one of only a handful who haven't come back dead? Which leads me to suspect that he might still be alive."

Marie Jackson's eyes teared suddenly. "You really think Lamont's still alive?" she whispered.

Tremelo shrugged. "I wish I could tell you so, with any degree of certainty. But I really can't. On the other hand . . . "

He paused for a moment. "The thing about it, Mrs. Jackson—"

"Call me Marie, please."

"—ah, Marie, is that *none* of the people who were with your husband when he was snatched have come back. Except the two soldiers who seem to have been killed almost immediately. That's completely atypical from the normal pattern. Which leads me to suspect—and don't ask me to explain it logically, because I can't—that he might still be alive. Actually, I think they're *all* still alive."

Marie started crying. She lowered her head and dug into her purse, coming up a moment later with a packet of Kleenex. "Oh, God," she whispered, "I love that man so much."

In the middle of blowing her noise, a little laugh burst through the tissues. "Damn if I don't think you're right, Professor Tremelo!"

"Call me Miggy, please."

She lowered her tissue-clutching hand and beamed happily through still-moist eyes. "Miggy. The thing is, I always *told* that rascal he'd probably live through hellfire. That's part of why I married him, even though lots of people said he was too old for me. But I was no damn fool. I wanted a husband been through the wringer already and come out with some sense."

Marie gurgled laughter. "I even put up with his damned puns! He's such a quick, clever kind of guy, you know. People don't think it, just looking at him, but—"

While Miggy Tremolo listened attentively, Marie Jackson talked about her husband non-stop for two hours. There was nothing of the guarded and carefully phrased description she'd given the government's psychologists. Just the rambling speech of a woman depicting a man with whom she'd shared a life and raised a family since she was nineteen years old.

When she was done, Marie glanced guiltily at her watch. "Oh, shit," she murmured. "My boss is gonna have a conniption."

Tremelo studied her for a moment, weighing a decision. Just listening to Marie's way of thinking, he realized, had done more for him than every official analysis piled up in heaps all over his office. She'd managed to crystallize what Tremelo had begun to suspect.

There was a common thread between those who got snatched, which was missing from those who didn't. What was so unusual about this one group, Miggy was certain, was that most of the members were of the type who would *not* normally have been snatched. Only their accidental physical contact with Salinas had gotten them taken.

Something *different* . . . And it had precious little to do with the psychologists' elaborate "profiles."

He swiveled his chair and stared out the window. Well, that wasn't being quite fair to the shrinks. There *did* seem to be a connection with anger levels and belief patterns. But Miggy thought the key was something else, which was such a practical talent that the psychologists overlooked it. And if there was no polysyllabic psychological term for that talent, there *was* a popular expression which captured the spirit of the thing. *I'm from Missouri. Show me.*

He swiveled the chair back around and gave Marie a quick glance. The woman was not relaxed any longer. She was beginning to fidget, her mind obviously on the firestorm she would face when she returned to work.

Of all that party of snatchees' next of kin, he knew, she was the one who was most hurt. Emotionally and financially. It was within his power to do something about the second part. And he could use an assistant who made decent coffee and—most of all—could help him cut through the habitual "caution waffle" of scientists. He'd bet this woman wouldn't just cut it. She'd slice it to the bone.

Besides, he thought cheerfully, *she intimidates the hell out of the troll. Who knows? Maybe the creature will even keep her voice down, with Marie around. Low enough, anyway, that I don't have to listen to it.*

"Forget him," he said. "How'd you like to come to work for me instead?"

She peered at him quizzically. "For how long? And how much you paying per hour?"

Tremelo laughed. "I've got no idea how long. And as for hourly wages, don't worry about it. The one thing the government has piled on me that I *don't* mind is a budget you wouldn't believe." He snorted sarcastically. "And they're complaining because I'm not spending money fast enough."

Marie was now frowning. "I don't know as how I could be of any real help to you. And I'm not taking charity money, Professor Tremelo." Her return to formality emphasized the point. "That's something Lamont and me both see eye to eye on. Can't raise kids right if you don't set an example yourself."

Tremelo's eyes fell on the paper at the center of his desk. He picked it up and handed it to Marie. "Read that and tell me what you think of it."

Miggy waited patiently while Marie fought her way through the turgid officialese. By the time she was finished, her frown was positively awesome.

"What do you think?"

Marie snorted. "What I can tell, they got a problem on their hands and they figure to solve it by gettin' a bigger hammer. Stupid, you ask me. Lamont always tries to figure out what the problem is in the first place."

Tremelo burst into laughter. "You're hired!"

He leaned forward and picked up the telephone. "You'll be making *consultant's* money, Marie. I can start you at $500 a day plus expenses. With a guaranteed contract for three months' work, minimum."

Marie Jackson had the quickness with arithmetic of every experienced waitress. Her eyes widened, and widened. "*Forty-five thousand dollars? In three months?*" She leaned back her head and barked a laugh. "Hell, Miggy, that's more than I make in two years! You got a deal!"

As soon as Tremelo finished his call to the accounting office and set the phone down—*click*—Marie asked to use it herself. The physicist leaned back in his chair and enjoyed a moment's relaxation and pleasure, just overhearing her side of the ensuing conversation.

Brief conversation.

"That you, fat-ass? I just called to give you the same notice you give everybody you fire. Two seconds. Go fuck yourself. Use the plunger in the women's bathroom. You know—the busted one I been complainin' about for six months."

Click.

PART VI

*All things are taken from us, and become
Portions and parcels of the dreadful Past.*

—Alfred, Lord Tennyson,
"The Lotos-Eaters"

28

❏⌐⌐⌐⌐❏

LOTUS-EATERS.

Jerry glared at the shore. Odysseus, plain to see, was up to his usual tricks.

The sun burned down. Heat reflected off the curving beaches like a whiplash. The wind that had carried the black pentekonter this far was still. Odysseus' vessel lay like a painted ship in a sun-bleached painting. Its artistic merit was enhanced by the two dragons lolling in the water beside it.

All very nice, thought Jerry sourly. The only problem was . . .

Liz put it into words. "The Nile seems to have shrunk, Odysseus," she said sarcastically, looking at the sliver of a stream that split the beach ahead.

Odysseus shrugged. "This is the coastline of Libya, Sorceress. Egypt lies a few days' sailing along it. We have made landfall some distance to the west, that's all. We need fresh water. And it would be good to cook a meal and get some rest on land. The local inhabitants are a peaceful and hospitable people. They will have food for us.

"ʃS'about time we ate," said Smitar, lazily flapping his crest of tasseled crimson spines.

"Yeʃs. What'ʃs for lunch, Lamont?" demanded Bitar, flattening his vermilion and purple crest. The two dragons might be in the service of the sorceress, but their affection, by way of their stomachs, had been usurped by Lamont and Cruz. Besides, Cruz was the only human they'd ever met with enough strength to give a dragon a good scratch with an oar.

Any wariness Jerry had felt about the small aboriginals on the shore had long faded. They'd seen the ship land and come down to it with cheery smiles and broad-leaf trays of sticky yellow sweetmeats, obviously pulp of some plant and gods alone knew what else. Definitely flies. Now what was worrying Jerry was straight morality. There was no doubt that the aboriginals would end up as slaves. Probably after the Achaeans had swiped their sweetmeats. The little guys didn't even seem to be selling the things. They were certainly eating occasional ones themselves. Odysseus made a great show of taking a whole sweetmeat in one bite.

Jerry attempted to refuse. The little guy was hurt. "Is good! Is sweet. Is nice. Eat, traveler, eat." The loincloth-clad man took one himself, and chewed it with obvious gusto.

Heaven knew how many fly feet had walked over this stuff, but Jerry tried to look on the positive side. If he ended up dead, he'd end up home. The yellow-fruit base was not very nice. Even honey did little to hide that. The stuff was resiny.

"Well, I'll be dipped in shit." Cruz grinned, looking at his half-eaten sweetmeat. He sniffed it. "These are hash cookies. No wonder the locals are smiling."

It all clicked into place. Jerry realized instantly that Odysseus was pulling another trick. "Lotophagi!"

The little aboriginal nodded happily. He pointed at the sweetmeats. "Lotus." He pointed at the yellow-fruited trees on the hill slope behind the beach. "Lotus bean. Plenty plenty."

"And the green plants in between them are *Cannabis sativa*," said Henri with a nod.

Maybe it was the half a hash cookie in his empty stomach, but Jerry began to giggle. No wonder the locals encouraged the visitors to eat. Two or three of these cookies and you would probably forget your own name, never mind forget that you had a home to return to. It was indeed a magnificent defense. Raiders would eat first, knowing that they'd have plenty of opportunity to take slaves later. It wasn't poison because the locals ate it too. Only the locals ate quite a lot of it, and were habituated to it. Raiders weren't.

It could very well turn into a case of the raiders being the victims in the end. And Jerry was willing to bet that Odysseus, cunning Odysseus, hadn't actually eaten that sweetmeat.

"Hey, Odysseus!" yelled Jerry. "Prince Odysseus. These sweet-meats are great. You have another. In fact, have two. Sergeant. Help him to some."

Odysseus backed off. "I'd love some. But lotus . . . they give me terrible indigestion. Honestly. You have some more for me. Enjoy."

Jerry laughed. "Ody, you're a slimy bastard." *Man, that hash must be strong!* "But I've read all about you and your whole life. I know what happens in the land of the lotus-eaters. I knew all about the Cyclops. I know about your wife, and Telemachus, and how you survived Circe."

Odysseus looked startled. "I am in a book? Written, as they do for stores tallies?" It took the Achaean some time to come to terms with this. Then he strutted. "You hear that, Eurylochus? I'm famous!"

"For your bad breath, probably," muttered the henchman.

"Ha. Jealousy makes you unpleasant. Tell me which of my great adventures you know about, barbarian. Do you know how I slew twenty Thracians, including their King Rhesus?"

"It was only twelve. And Diomedes killed them, while they were asleep. You just ran off with the horses."

Odysseus gaped. "How . . . " he asked weakly.

"I told you," said Jerry scornfully. "I read about your 'adventures' when I was a child. But I thought you were a hero, not a louse. It was only when I came across Euripides that it even occurred to me you weren't the perfect hero."

Odysseus looked annoyed. Put a hand to his sword. "Who is this 'Euripides'?"

Jerry shrugged. He was definitely feeling the hash. "You rippa dese you buy me a new pair . . . He's either long dead—or if we really are in your time, not yet born. You see, we're from your future. Even our children learn about you and your family."

There was a silence. Then Odysseus asked: "I went to Hades to consult the blind Theban, Teiresias. He told me that my wife Penelope was being courted by over a hundred suitors. Is this true?"

Sympathy welled up in Jerry. "Yes."

Odysseus slapped his fist into his hand. "And their servants too?"

"Yes." Why should that matter?

Odysseus ground his fist into the opposite palm. "I've got to get home! Those wastrels are eating MY food. Feasting at MY expense! They're impoverishing MY kingdom!"

Jerry looked at the man in disgust. "So the fact they're pulling a train with your wife isn't important to you?"

The translation spell dealt with this one somehow. Odysseus looked like he was about to explode. Jerry thought he'd finally gone too far. Finally Odysseus almost spat out, "Without *paying*!?"

The *Odyssey* came to Jerry's rescue. "No, she demanded rich gifts from the suitors." That was true enough anyway, even if the reasons were different.

"Oh. That's good. But I still need to get home. As my friend King Agamemnon says, you can't be too gentle with women or trust them too much. A man can see all the gold he's looted disappear if he stays away too long."

Suddenly, Mac lurched to his feet and grinned broadly. Uneasily, Jerry realized that the young corporal had eaten at least two whole sweetmeats.

"Hey, Jerry!" he boomed. "What was that son of Ody's name? Telemachus, wasn't it?" The corporal swayed a little. "Yeah. He's probably pulling a train with some of those suitors too, Ody. Keeping them off your wife's back."

This didn't seem to worry Odysseus much. In fact, he started mocking McKenna. "Ha! If I was a pretty boy like you, I'd have taken on all hundred every night. Eurylochus says you can hardly cope with three."

McKenna lunged forward and grabbed Odysseus. In a split second, the corporal was thrown to the ground. Hard. The Odysseus of legend was a wrestler of note. And whatever else the Achaean prince might be, he was tough as nails and not at all reaction-slowed by cannabis. Jerry had the sudden realization, as Odysseus landed on the corporal's back, that McKenna might just have gotten himself into a fight where he could get killed.

Odysseus' crew must have been expecting this, Cruz understood immediately. They'd boxed Mac and Odysseus. Shit. The kid was gonna get killed before the sergeant could get there. Cruz pulled the nunchakus from his belt. It had come to this . . .

Then Lamont spoke, loudly and clearly. "Mac, you're an idiot. Telemachus got married in the book. He gave all the goats to the girl he was in love with."

McKenna felt the terrible hold on his throat and the scissors on his ribs slacken slightly. "My *goats*! Never!" Odysseus bellowed, outraged.

"He didn't know that *you* were in love with them," snapped Medea.

"And the pigs too," said Jerry calmly.

"What?! Impossible!" Odysseus had forgotten about throttling Mac, at least temporarily.

Jerry shrugged as Liz stalked closer. "Why? You've never been around to bring the child up properly."

That bag weighed about seventeen pounds. It had reinforced metal corners. Liz gave it a full overhead arc, before it hit Odysseus across the side of the head. And then Cruz was there, with a weapon that the Achaeans had never encountered. Mind you, Odysseus might have been better off being hit by the nunchukus.

It was instantly a battle royal. And it would have been very short and nasty except that Bitar and Smitar had not eaten more than three or four sweetmeats each. Or if the Achaeans had not planned to take them alive.

Mac, having barely gotten to his feet, found himself bowled over. A dragon tail flailed overhead. He had just time to see Jerry duck, allowing two Achaeans to crash headlong.

✧　　✧　　✧

Liz writhed. Those arms holding her from behind were like steel hawsers. She stamped with all the force at her disposal on the sandaled foot.

"Yeeeow!" But the crewman didn't let go. And then a dragon mouth closed over both of them. The gums were toothless but viselike. Her captor let go of her in haste, just as Smitar spat them out. "Phtpt. *f*Sorry, Liz."

There was a smack of wood on flesh and Cruz barreled through, to Lamont's aid. Medea had taken up a position on a washed-up stump and was walloping heads in the melee. Then there was the amazing sight of fat Henri delivering a two-footed flying kick into Eurylochus' abdomen.

"To the ship! To the ship! *Quickly!*" shouted Odysseus.

The reason stood black along the ridgeline. The Lotophagi had been happy enough to make no moves except to peacefully offer hash cookies around. But when it seriously looked as if the merchandise could turn itself into hamburger, they decided to intervene a bit more directly. By sheer numbers alone they'd even overwhelm the dragons. For the moment, the little internecine conflict was forgotten in the scramble to get the black ship launched and to escape a common enemy.

If it hadn't been for the psychological effect of the dragons, they would never have managed it. But the first Lotophagi warrior to advance got the full force of Smitar's tail. He was batted a good twenty feet in the air to land on top of the mob. A couple of those he landed on still had their spears ported.

Mac made a face as he helped to shove the black ship into the waves. "If you're going to land on a spear, I guess you should try and do it headfirst."

"Jump. Up. UP! To oars!" yelled Odysseus.

Soon the only sign of the close encounter was a few Lotophagi spears falling short and dimpling the water.

"Tho*f*se *f*sweetmeats have given me a funny flying feeling," said Bitar.

"Ye*f*s. Did nothing for the hole where my tummy u*f*sed to be, either," grumbled Smitar. The red-tasseled dragon was, if anything, the greedier of the two, although this was a marginal difference. Only Henri really competed in the same league.

"You can start with Odysseus," said Medea grimly.

"We still have our weapons, Sorceress." Odysseus touched his bronze sword meaningfully.

Maybe Jerry was still a bit stoned. Or maybe he was just mad. He certainly had a prize black eye from the little exchange of pleasantries back there on the beach. He stood up and planted himself in front of the Prince of Ithaca. "Showdown time. I'm sick of being nervous about you every time I go to sleep, Odysseus. You and your crew are going to be chained up."

"And how are you going to make us accept chains, little man?" sneered Odysseus.

"Can you swim back to shore from here, Odysseus?" It was a long, long way. The better part of a couple of miles, at least.

"Are *you* going to throw me overboard, weakling?" Odysseus barely suppressed his laughter.

"No." Jerry smiled sweetly. "I'm going to jump. And so are the rest of us. We Americans swim like fish. We'll take our chances dodging Lotophagi. It beats dodging you." Well, they'd all seen Liz and McKenna swimming. They did indeed both swim like fish. "Then Bitar and Smitar can sink this tub of yours and we'll see who has the upper hand."

"You wouldn't! The sea is full of sharks and monsters," sneered Odysseus. But there was no conviction in that sneer.

"Watch me. Compared to you, *cunning* Odysseus, sharks and monsters are pretty decent. Choose. Chains or swimming? We'll let you go once we reach Egypt. Let's say once we're at the pyramids? And remember—*we* have never broken our promises."

"But—"

"Choose. Choose now." Jerry pushed his way into Odysseus' personal space.

"You don't have any chains," said Odysseus sulkily.

"We have a couple of sorceresses," said Jerry with supreme confidence.

✧   ✧   ✧

"Have you been taking an assertiveness course?" asked Liz dryly.

"From you." Jerry held onto the bench so that they wouldn't see how his hands had begun to shake.

She shook her head. "I think the pupil just wiped the floor with his teacher."

"The pupil was stoned and is now into nervous reaction. Let's hope like hell Medea can do her chain trick."

"I've just figured out why Ody is taking this so easily," said Jerry later, very quietly.

Lamont looked across at the Achaeans, ankle-chained and then with two running chains snaking through the rowing benches and ankle chains. Medea had "magicked them up" out of loose odds and ends in the soldiers' rucks and Liz's handbag.

"Why?" he asked.

"Because a hundred and eighty feet of fine iron chain is worth a damn sight more than this ship. He was looking for angles—until Medea started her tricks on the chain. Then suddenly he shut up. He hit Eurylochus just as he started to say something. I thought he just didn't want trouble. Ha. He'd outthought me. They can pull those benches up in two seconds."

Lamont looked at the captive Achaeans. "They'd still have to come at us in single file."

"Three jerks together and they'd snap that bowsprit stave. Or the chain."

Lamont looked at the solid oak bowsprit stave they'd attached one end of the chain to. "Maybe not so easy. But you're right."

"What are you guys gossiping about?" Liz had squatted down next to them. They explained.

Her eyes narrowed as she looked at the chain. "Hmm. Are you sure, Jerry? About the chain being worth an arm and a leg, that is?"

Jerry nodded. "Absolutely certain. Look at the fights and effort that went into recovering any of the 'arms' of a hero in the *Iliad*. We've got no conception of just how valuable wrought metal was, and a piece of work as fine and uniform as that chain . . . "

"Okay, okay. Now I get what you were saying earlier, about

Cruz and Mac carrying a fortune in metal with them." Liz pursed her lips, to stop them twitching into a smile. "I wonder. Do you think this tub has drainage bungs?"

Jerry blinked. She thought like a jackrabbit. "I don't know."

"Hmm. Must have, I guess. Maybe back near the steering oars. I'll take a little swim this evening," she said, with a wicked little chuckle.

29

NOT SO WILY, AFTER ALL.

The black pentekonter had a shallow draft. She wouldn't have far to swim to check out the underside. That was a blessing. It was still as scary as hell, even with the moon bright in a starlit sky, to swim quietly through the dark water, feeling the hull. Presently Liz's exploring fingers were rewarded... with a brass loop.... Just behind the steering oars. Carefully she tied the rope onto it before swimming back.

By the afternoon of the next day even the value of the chains they were planning to steal wasn't enough to stop Odysseus' crew from being on the edge of revolt. They were after all not serfs or slaves. They were all at least minor nobility. And even their prince had been poorly in control of them. Being chained up was bad enough. But being chained up for a day and night at sea, when they were accustomed to landing, was too much—especially in the heat. Well, especially as they were an ill-disciplined pack of minor aristocracy, accustomed to doing things their own way, and not having to take it in turns to urinate over the side.

Then the sea boiled with an immense dragon.

"*ʃ*She's *mine!*" yelled Smitar and Bitar in obvious delight, diving down at the newly appeared dragon in the water.

"Hey gorgeou*ʃ*s, where have you been all my life?" bellowed Smitar.

"Ignore him. He'*ʃ*s a boor. And he'*ʃ*s got no teeth," shouted Bitar.

"Neither have you, *ʃ*silly!"

The bickering, snapping dragons tumbled out of the sky, onto the newcomer. And she disappeared.

"What did you go and frighten her off for?" complained Smitar.

Bitar looked huffy. "*I* didn't! *You* did!"

A tree slowly disappearing into the ocean attracted Smitar's attention. "I *ʃ*say. What'*ʃ*s this carob tree doing here in the water?"

Bitar looked thoughtfully at it. "*ʃ*Sinking," he said, finally.

Smitar snorted in irritation. "I didn't expect it to be doing the brea*ʃ*st-*ʃ*stroke. I meant it wa*ʃ*sn't here a minute ago."

The carob tree, about to disappear forever into the depths, turned into a leaping and dancing flame. This was also a poor choice of shape for the water. In a flicker there was a huge gray seal swimming there, twisting agilely in the wine-dark waves. The Achaeans, who had been on the verge of rebellion moments before, now moaned in fear.

"Who or what is this . . . creature?" asked Henri warily.

"Proteus of Egypt," said Jerry. "Otherwise known as 'the old man of the sea,' who lives at Pharos, an island off the mouth of the Nile. He can change his shape at will. He keeps seals like a shepherd."

"He's welcome to them," snorted Liz. "Smelly, nasty things."

"I always thought seals were kinda neat," Lamont protested, looking at the plump gray seal that was now riding the bow wave.

"You aren't a commercial fisherman. Hell. I shouldn't say that. If you ever get home, with your luck, you could go commercial with a handline, Lamont. But go on, Jerry. Wrack that brain. Is this thing dangerous?"

"He is a renowned seer, but I have not heard ill of him," offered Medea.

Jerry tugged his wispy beard. It had become less wispy over

the last while. "He owes allegiance to Poseidon, like Triton. But he is one of the sons of Oceanus and Tethys."

"Indeed." The seal spoke, its face transforming briefly into that of an old, gray-bearded man. "My father Oceanus sends greetings. He sent word to all his Oceanid sons, to search for you."

"What does the Titan Oceanus want from us?" asked Jerry suspiciously.

"He wishes to cry you a warning, mortals. Poseidon has suddenly left off his banishment of my father to the distant waters of his retirement. Poseidon is seeking you instead. He wishes you drowned or buried beneath the shaking lands."

"And what's this Oceanus guy's beef?" demanded Cruz.

Proteus' fins briefly transformed as he threw out his hands. "My father was lord of the river ocean, until the rule of the Olympians. Then he was retired to distant waters and the oceans passed into the hands of blue-eyed Amphitrite and her consort Poseidon. For many years now our universe has been a fading and passing thing."

The old man of the sea dived and emerged with a fish across his jaws. This he tossed up, caught and swallowed before continuing. "Yet, a short while ago came a force which the Titans, the powers before Olympia, had never felt before. A blossoming of a strange and dark life came to our universe. My father found himself lord of the river ocean again . . . reinstated . . . and now the Olympian Poseidon has come to banish him again. Olympus is mighty. But we Titans would give what aid we could to those who oppose it."

"Help your enemy's enemies." Cruz nodded. "That makes sense."

McKenna looked skeptically at the seal-man. "So what's on offer?"

"Guidance and speed to Pharos. Aye, and even into the heaven-fed waters of the Nile. My oracular skills to see as much of your future as I can. I know you must go to Egypt. I know you must get away from the wrath of Poseidon. The sea will be unsafe for you. It is uncertain what happens in Egypt because you disappear from my vision."

"Maybe we get home!" said Lamont, with longing in his voice.

"Holy cow!" roared Liz. "What have you done to the ship?! She's nearly up on the plane! There are hundreds of seals pushing us! Get that sail DOWN! Get to the back!"

It was strange to sail in still water. To the west and seaward lay Pharos, the isle of the seal herder, Proteus, its sandy shore licked by the rollers. Here in the broad mouth of what must be the Canopic Nile, the rowers had to stroke again. The seals and Proteus had gone. It was already late afternoon, but the sun beat down mercilessly, and had Jerry blessing the northerly breeze. The shoreline was verdant.

The settlement looked small and fairly non-threatening. Jerry was still as nervous as a cat. Not even the sight of other peaceful vessels convinced him this was not yet another unpleasant surprise. The dragons were keeping a high and distant eye over them so as not to frighten the townsfolk into fits. It made sense. It also made them further off and this left Jerry feeling quite uncomfortable.

They slid alongside a simple quay. That was a pleasant surprise. It would make a change not to get wet to the waist hauling the black ship up. The sun was lowering in the western sky, casting long shadows. Ha! Ashore for the night and not having to dry out by the fire before going to sleep! Undreamed of luxury!

"Do we unchain them?" asked Jerry quietly.

"No," said Liz, smiling nastily.

"Well, should some of us stay on board?" Lamont was gathering his possessions.

Liz shook her head. "I gather the sea is going to be a good thing to stay out of, Lamont. If the silly buggers run away we can always hire one of the local boats. They can't be as untrustworthy as our buddy Ody."

"Why don't we just let them go, then?"

"We might want a ride a bit further upstream. Let's first check things out around here," said Cruz.

The locals hadn't exactly rushed up to the Mycenaean raider. Still, they hadn't run away yet either. And some fresh food and a chance to stretch their legs on a surface that didn't move would be good.

✧   ✧   ✧

Odysseus watched them go ashore with satisfaction. The dragons were gone. And the fools hadn't even made them take the
oars out of the leather slings. He slipped the folding boarding
pike out from under the rowing benches. "Pass it down. Cut that
rope and we'll be away from here. It's a pity that they've taken
their bags, but tonight we'll slip in when they think we've gone.
Cut their throats. Best thing to do with sorcerers. Anyway, we
can pick up a few good slaves from among the locals. Also we
have this chain! Did you ever see such a magnificent piece of
workmanship. Worth a king's ransom."

The leather hawser didn't last long. "Right. Push her off quietly. Then churn the water, boys. We'll get free of the chain once
we're well clear."

The splashing made Jerry look back. "Look! Odysseus and his
gang are taking off!"

"How sad," said Medea, looking anything but.

"Oh dear. They're still chained," said Liz cheerfully.

Odysseus smiled triumphantly. "Right, men! All together now.
A-one, a-two, three! I felt it move! Again! A-one, a-two, THREE!"

Odysseus' crew fell over each other as the chain's attachment
came free. The crew cheered.

"Pull it through the leg loops."

"Come on, move it up!"

Odysseus had already climbed onto the stern railings. "Hear
me, you Americans—and you, evil sorceress of Colchis. I, the
wily Odysseus, the son of Laertes, Sacker of Cities, Conqueror
of the Cyclops, the Symplegades, the Sirens, and even the mighty
Tritons, have outwitted you! I have stolen your great chain! I
gloat!"

"Here, Odysseus." Eurylochus handed him the chain end. "Get
it through your legs. We need to set a course to lie up in those
reeds till tonight."

"What's this on the end of the rope?" Odysseus looked at the
large wooden plug with a loop of hammered brass set into it.

Eurylochus shrugged. "Whatever it was tied to. . . . " His eyes went wide. Water was already flooding up between the rowing benches.

He grabbed Odysseus by the throat. "*VERY wily Odysseus!*" he hissed.

From across almost seven hundred yards of water, the party of snatchees heard the taunts of Odysseus. And then saw the black ship being frantically rowed towards a mudbank. It didn't look like the Achaeans were going to make it.

"I think he's just pulled the chain," said Jerry with a straight face.

"Do you think he's feeling flushed with pride?" asked Lamont.

Liz groaned. Still, it had been worth going swimming in the dark.

"It is his own fault. Fancy referring to *me* as 'American.' Pah. He was totally lacking . . . "

As Mac scowled at Henri . . . the view blurred.

It wasn't just the wind escaping from the windsack either.

Egypt! The Thunderer was just so lazy! He was the only one of the gods who had interfered much in Egypt. And that had been in the fight against the Titans. But right now Zeus was more concerned with the unrest in the ranks of the Olympians than in obeying the Krim device's commands. Well, they had put themselves into the geographical sphere of another Ur-Mythworld. Let them go there. The masters had now had word about the place the Krim device had prepared for them to play in.

It needed to eliminate the disruptive element. Let them go to Egypt. Let them rot there. The Ur-Mythworld of ancient Egypt was proving exceptionally difficult. He had Set. He had Sekmet. And he had Sebek. But that little dwarf had told the Krim probe to go fuck itself. It had been a novel idea to the sexless device. Anyway, the whole Ur-universe was only partially reanimated. A few of the primitive aliens taken by the Ur-transfer device had been put there, to help with the reanimation process. The image in their cellular memory helped. But this was all annoying in the extreme. The Krim had not encountered such independence in the Ur-universes of the other species they'd parasitized. Let the problematic unbelievers go and rot there.

30

YOU CAN'T BREAK
WHAT YOU CAN'T TOUCH.

Miggy Tremelo sat in Colonel McNamara's commandeered office. There were still signs of the previous occupant's interest in geology all over the place. McNamara leaned back and fiddled with his pipe. It was a ritual plainly designed to give the man thinking time. Tremelo played along.

"Your idea about using the men who had been on day one of operations worked. We only lost one of them."

"Glad to hear it. The device must be selecting or detecting certain types of victims. That is the first decent step forward we've had all day."

"But the damn thing is still expanding. And the snatch range just gets bigger." The colonel puffed on his pipe. He fiddled with a match. Then he took a deep breath. "I'm not supposed to tell you what I'm doing. Orders from on high. But . . . it appears you'll detect it anyway. And even if not, the NSA will probably tell you about it. We've got a specialist demolitions team coming in this afternoon."

Tremelo nodded. "We advised them to try coned-steel-cutting demolition charges. One of our men will be accompanying them."

225

"Humph. And I'm supposed to keep it a secret! However . . . that wasn't what I wanted to talk to you about. If that fails, we're to pull everybody back to outside a five-mile perimeter. They're starting to talk about using a small tactical nuke."

Tremelo raised his eyes to heaven. "And what do these geniuses think they'll achieve with a nuclear explosion, besides a smaller package to deliver the explosive and some incidental radiation? Every single thing we've thrown at that alien device has bounced off. No, worse—the destructive energy actually seems to help the thing *grow*."

The physicist stared at a rock hammer lying on a nearby bench. Following the direction of his eyes, Colonel McNamara chuckled. "Hey, Miggy, gimme a break. It's not *my* idea, so busting my head won't accomplish anything." He blew out a cloud of smoke. "Truth is, I pretty much agree with you on this subject."

Tremelo smiled. "Look, Frank. I won't let on I heard about this from you, but I'll get onto my contact at the NSC, and if necessary get hold of the President himself. I'll do what I can to head off this tactical nuke scheme. Without knowing what we're doing, that's a recipe for disaster."

McNamara gave him a level gaze. "You know how it works, Miggy. The Powers That Be want *action*. Half the time, at least, they're more worried about their standing in the public opinion polls than they are about anything else."

"I should have stayed in pure research," muttered Tremelo. Then, firmly: "I'll toss them a bone. I'll suggest—as one of several alternatives—that we try a bomb-pumped laser. And you never heard me mention *that* either. Officially, the U.S. doesn't have any neutron devices."

He sighed. "I can't say I like that idea much either, but by comparison the device we don't have is a lot cleaner than a tac nuke. And more likely to be effective, if anything is."

The colonel lit his pipe again. "It's not being able to hit back that's driving everybody nuts."

"I understand that. And I'm aware that the government is under a fair amount of international pressure, too. Being as this is the University of Chicago, there have been a large number of foreign nationals snatched as well as American citizens. But the fact remains that 'hitting back' for the sake of it, when you're swinging blind, is still just stupid."

Colonel McNamara nodded. "No quarrel with that here. Especially since it's my men who have to do the swinging."

Tremelo stood up. "I'll do what I can. Now, you'll have to excuse me, Colonel. I've got to get back to the team doing the analysis of the snatch victims. This information about the men who were within range but not taken yesterday being ignored today could be a real lead."

Marie was serving as Tremelo's unofficial chauffeur as well as everything else, using—for mysterious reasons having to do with the intricacies of "expense accounts"—her own very-far-from-new Buick. On the drive back to his own office, Marie gave Tremelo a questioning glance. The physicist's tight face was answer enough.

"Get a bigger hammer," she muttered.

Marie dropped Miggy off at the front of the building which held his office. Then she drove around to Tremelo's "officially designated" parking space. She was not surprised to see that a Humvee loaded with soldiers was occupying it while they had lunch.

These soldiers knew her, since they were assigned as guards for the building. When she pulled up the car and leaned her head out of the window, they greeted her with grins. Like most veterans of the campaign against the pyramid, they were quite cheerful and relaxed.

Service against the alien device was a unique experience in military history. In the first five hours, casualties were about 10%—all of which seemed random, and almost all of which were fatal. At least, only one of the 87% who had returned had still been alive. No one yet knew what had happened to the other 13% of the snatchees. But thereafter, it was no more dangerous than a traffic jam.

"Gonna have us towed, Marie?" called out one of the soldiers.

She matched the grins with a bigger one of her own. "I wouldn't do that, boys, and you know it. But if you don't move it, I *will* put a dent in that fancy expensive U.S. government *vee-hicle*, and let *you* fill out all the forms. You think I care about this jalopy of mine?"

With Marie, it was never entirely clear when she was joking. The driver of the Humvee pulled it out of the space and made room for her to park the Buick. After she got out and began walking away, one of the soldiers tried a riposte.

"Are you in *that* big a hurry to get back to your Sugar Daddy?"

The other soldiers in the Humvee frowned. That joke was crossing a line none of them much appreciated.

Marie stopped, spun around, and planted her hands on her hips. "You think I'm humping the *Professor*?" she demanded. "A nice married woman like *me*?"

Then, with a laugh: "Shit! I'd kill the old man." She sashayed off, swinging her hips.

The soldier who'd made the wisecrack fumbled for a response. Failed. The other soldiers laughed derisively.

"You wanna trade slams with *that* lady, Hannon," chortled one of them, "you'd better get yourself a bigger hammer."

PART VII

My works are all stamped down into the sultry mud.

—William Butler Yeats, "On a Picture of a
Black Centaur by Edmund Dulac"

31

ᄆ▢ᄆ▢ᄆ▢

I WANT MY MUMMY.

It was the same river. It wasn't the same place.

The village they'd landed at had disappeared. So had Odysseus' struggling crew. The snatchees were in knee-deep water.

Well . . . calf-deep anoxic mud, and the rest water, at the edge of the dense papyrus reeds. Obviously the water dropped off sharply in front of them. Jerry realized that there were tiny fish nibbling at his hand.

He saw a piece of floating gnarled old log move. It opened an eye, which was an unusual thing for a log to do. It was a very big log.

"Keep together. Let's try and get out of the water." Liz's voice had that steely edge of *control* in it. "That is a crocodile. Don't run."

"Çøað Þøø?" asked Medea.

Despite the crocodile, Jerry closed his eyes briefly. Medea's translation spells obviously didn't work here. He'd gotten himself repromoted to chief translator . . .

Damn. While Jerry had studied liturgical Coptic, which was as near as anything came to ancient Egyptian, he was willing to bet it wasn't *that* close. And the vocabulary at his disposal was rather limited.

Herodotus had described the Egyptians as the most religious of men. That made ancient Egypt an interesting hunting ground for a mythographer. It also made it a place you didn't necessarily want to experience firsthand. For starters, it had crocodiles. For seconds . . . lots of gods. If something was taking possession of these gods this could a bad place to be.

They edged back from the water cautiously. The crocodile regarded them with interest. A sudden frantic splashing in the reeds sent them up the slippery muddy bank. It was only a lapwing, but it was enough to have the group forget systematic retreat and fling themselves up the bank.

Medea looked skywards. "Bitar? Smitar?"

Then she dissolved into tears. Cruz, who happened to be nearest, held her and patted her awkwardly.

"What's wrong? She's not that attached to those dragons," said Liz, in an undervoice to Lamont.

"Her children," answered Lamont quietly, understanding perfectly.

There was a path, and at length they came to a small mud-walled village. It reeked of fish. The locals were busy with the tasks of a small fishing village—the men lounging in the pretense of mending a net, while women washed. All the villagers shrieked in unison at the sudden appearance of the strangers. Previously indolent villagers moved with startling rapidity inside the wall. The heavy palm-wood gate thudded shut in the faces of the visitors.

Liz chuckled. "They certainly don't like door-to-door salesmen much."

"I wonder how they feel about telemarketers?" mused Lamont.

Jerry tried out a phrase in his best liturgical Coptic. No response.

"Ask if they'd like to come out and listen to a high-tech stock presentation," suggested Lamont. "Tell them there's a free gift holiday for two on offer."

Jerry snorted. "Right. I was hoping for some dinner and shelter. It'll be dark soon."

Jerry altered his intonations in his next attempt. The result was totally unexpected.

Crabs began to appear. Not by ones and twos, but by the hundreds. Crawling out of every conceivable hole and crevice. The crabs ranged from pea-sized to the size of generous soup plates.

Of course, Henri got nipped. "*Merde!*" He stamped at the crab, splattering it with one of his once-elegant Italian shoes.

The results of that unpremeditated action were even more unexpected. The palm-wood gate was ripped open and the once-frightened villagers began pouring out in a flood. Judging from appearances—the faces transformed into berserk grimaces, the dervish dancing, the howling and shrieking, not to mention the waving clubs—they seemed hell-bent on beating the sacrilegious foreigners to a bloody pulp. . . .

Two things saved Jerry and his companions.

Firstly, the avenging Oxyrhynchites had to, at all costs, avoid hurting the crabs—which were all over the pace. Secondly, there was the fishing net hanging from a series of poles.

Cruz kicked over one pole. The net, probably the village's most precious possession, fell on top of half of the crab worshippers. Mac and Lamont between them picked up an enormous basket of river sardines and flung them at the crowd. Now the locals had the double jeopardy of avoiding standing on their catch and the crabs.

"*Merde alors!*" cursed Henri. "You have me covered in fish slime!"

"Come on! Into this boat!!" yelled Liz. She and Medea had shoved three of the village's papyrus-reed-bundle boats out into the Nile to drift away. They were waiting with the fourth, the last and the largest.

It was a splash and scramble, but the seven of them were soon out on the muddy waters, drifting upstream under a coarse flax sail away from the angry yelling mob on the shore.

"I think this is likely to stay virgin territory in the high-tech industry," said Jerry ruefully.

"God alone knows what they'd have done if you'd offered them the opportunity to invest their precious crabs," grumbled Lamont, feeling his bruises.

"Just what the hell happened back there?" asked Liz.

Lamont held up two fingers. "Well, I'd say we discovered two things. For sure."

Liz raised an eyebrow. "Like what? Besides that they've got a crab problem. And they don't like visitors."

Jerry shook his head. "They might be quite friendly. But we—or at least Henri—committed sacrilegious murder. So . . . one of the things that we found out is that the locals belong to a sect, the Oxyrhynchites, who regard the spider crab as sacred. Ancient Egyptian reverence for various animals was truly amazing. There are whole cemeteries full of mummified cats and crocodiles. They were buried by the hundreds of thousands. I remember reading that the modern Egyptians were actually using the cat cemetery at Beni Hasan for making artificial fertilizer."

It was the kind of information that usually silences cocktail parties. It did pretty well with the muddy-refugees-in-a-reed-bundle-boat party, too. It was a good minute and a half before Liz said: "And what was the second point?"

Lamont glanced at Jerry and snorted. "Those crabs. I think we've got ourselves a new magician. He summoned them."

Jerry winced. "The ancient Egyptian magicians were the ultimate believers in the power of words and names. Magicians could even compel their own gods to do their bidding."

"Holy cow!" Liz looked at him askance. "Do you think you can send us home, O Great Magician?"

There was both embarrassment and exasperation in Jerry's reply. "Look. I tried to get us some shelter and I got us a plague of crabs. If I had enough of a grasp of what I was doing, maybe I could do something. But right now the results are more likely to be terminal."

Liz nodded. "Right. The wind has pushed us upstream. I think we should keep going for a bit and then find a good patch of reed to lie up in for the night. Tomorrow—O Magnificent Sorcerer Lukacs—you're going to have to start systematic experimentation."

Lamont grinned. "Be careful, Liz. He might turn you into a newt in the trial run."

Mac shook his head, scowling. "I vote for turning Lenoir into a frog. That'd hardly take any magic at all."

Lenoir's response was all in French. Fortunately, Jerry was not able to translate.

The night was still . . .

Except for the mosquitoes, who filled the air with *bzzzz*. And the snort of a hippo.

Liz noticed that the moon was full again—as if the full moon on the night she'd swum next to Odysseus' boat hadn't happened two days back. She reminded herself to point out to Jerry the difference in time . . . if the delta mosquitoes didn't drive her mad and get her to fling herself to the crocodiles first. She slapped. She wasn't the only one.

"These things are going to drive me mad," snarled Mac.

"They'll almost certainly give us mythical bloody malaria," said Liz.

"They had malaria?" asked McKenna warily.

Liz snorted. "I'll tell you in ten to fourteen days."

"Why?" asked Lamont

"That's the incubation period."

Henri stood up and shook himself. "I do not think my sanity I will still have in a week, not to speak of ten days. These *moustique* are driving me insane. And the dinner was execrable."

"I wish we could drop him into the Seine," muttered Lamont. "He ate enough of the 'execrable' dinner for a hog, never mind a frog!"

Liz sat up. Slapped again. "Look, why don't we get out into the main stream? Out there, there's a breeze and hopefully we will be away from the mosquitoes. There's a full moon, too. We can navigate this tub okay."

"What about hippopotamus?" asked Henri nervously. "I really do not wish to encounter in the dark a hippopotamus."

Liz shook her head. "They move out of the water at night to feed."

"I'm for it," growled Cruz. "Anything beats listening to all the grousing and whining."

So they pushed the boat out into the open water between the seas of papyrus and raised sail, because they had no anchor, and let the gentle north wind carry them deeper and deeper into the delta. It was cooler on the water. And the mosquitoes were mercifully absent. And somehow all of them on those fish-reeking bundles of papyrus reed . . . they slipped into sleep. Even Liz dozed, at the helm.

And the small vessel sailed on silently, pushed by a divine wind.

There was a gentle shake. Jerry sat up with a start. He hadn't meant to sleep. "*Shht.*" Liz had a hand over his mouth. "Look," she whispered.

The boat had slid onto a mud bank overhung by a huge tree. From its shadows, Jerry could see a stark moon-etched tableau. A figure was stalking toward the water's edge. It was at least twice the size of a man. The snout was thin and cruelly curved. The ears stood up straight and square in the moonlight.

It was the head of no animal on earth. . . .

Jerry shuddered a little. He recognized the figure. It was the typhonian beast. The head of Set, who is the eternal adversary. The Egyptian god that is the soul of drought, desert, and darkness.

Set was carrying a burden. A manlike form, which he began to rip limb from limb and toss into the water.

Jerry stiffened with comprehension. Then, convulsively, he grabbed the spear from McKenna's hand, lurched upright, and flung it as hard as he could.

Alas, Jerry was never going to make the Olympic javelin team. And a stick with a bayonet on the end was a lousy javelin anyway. It struck the mud a few feet from Set and then flipped over to strike the destroyer lightly across the ankles. Set didn't even notice. He tossed the last gruesome piece into the water, turned, and strode away. In seconds, he was gone.

"Quick!" hissed Jerry. "We've got to get those pieces. Particularly the penis! The crabs got that bit the last time."

By now, Jerry's companions had learned to trust his knowledge, even if they didn't understand it. The crew scrambled from the boat and began the grizzly task of hauling piece after piece out of the shallows.

Liz found the vital bit, already being attacked by two of the spider crabs. She had it in hand and was lifting it—triumphantly and daintily at the same time—when—

Cruz shouted. The sound was inarticulate, filled with simultaneous rage and terror. A large form surged out of the water. Liz gasped.

The crocodile nearly took out Cruz. It *would* have taken out any other member of the party, except possibly McKenna. But Cruz had the trained reflexes of a paratrooper and a martial arts devotee. He'd caught sight of the croc at the last moment. As the teeth ripped into his flesh, seizing his leg, the muscular soldier struck the beast's snout with the only weapon he had at his disposal. A severed arm.

Instantly, the crocodile let go. Jerry and Medea hauled Cruz up onto the bank, still clutching a severed mummified arm. His bitten leg was pumping blood. McKenna was there at a run. He applied pressure to the wound.

"Fucking monster let go," said Cruz weakly. "The minute the arm hit its snout, it let go." He seemed more astonished than anything else.

Jerry was no longer surprised that Lamont knew that myth also. "Only the spider crab was prepared to touch the remains of the Osiris," the mechanic said quietly, looking at the mummified arm.

"Do you ever forget *anything*?" Jerry muttered.

"Stop blabbing and get a fire going!" snapped McKenna. "I need to see what I'm doing."

The younger paratrooper's voice was a little high-pitched. Like all of them, Jerry realized, McKenna had come to rely on Cruz's calm good sense and quiet courage. And, like all of them, had found professional respect transmuted into personal friendship. The thought of losing Cruz was well nigh terrifying.

Fortunately, the leg wasn't severed. Badly lacerated, true, and it would need a lot of sewing. Mac was already starting the task.

Jerry sighed. But Cruz wasn't going to be walking anywhere soon. And even if they solved that set of problems with the limited medical care facilities they could offer . . .

He sighed again. The next problem had just arrived.

"Do we *ever* get a break?" complained Lamont.

✧   ✧   ✧

There was no longer any need for a fire, so Lamont left off struggling with it.

There was plenty of light. It streamed from the lunar disk balanced on the ibis head of one visitor. The female figure at his side bore a small throne on her own head. Which would have been odd enough if she had not also had winged arms.

And, just to make things complete, behind them walked a very large man with the head of a jackal.

"Ah, how delightful," muttered Jerry. "Just what we needed. Thoth, Isis and Anubis."

The triad of Egyptian gods did *not* look delighted to discover the bedraggled group of humans, with the fourteen collected pieces of Isis' beloved brother and husband.

In fact, if Jerry understood the hauntingly familiar speech at all, what Isis was saying was: *Grave robbers. Kill them all.*

Hastily, Jerry cleared his throat. It was time for a fast explanation—*very fast*, with a sadly limited vocabulary and, he was quite sure, a truly terrible accent.

"Er. We have just—" *what the hell was the word for 'rescued'?* "—saved these pieces of your husband from the water."

Alas. The large and frightening-looking gods did not look as if they were impressed, or even particularly believing. But at least they had stopped moving forward.

Desperately, Jerry continued searching for the words. "Look, we saw Set . . . ah, pull apart Osiris. We came to save the parts."

Silence.

Jerry tried again, pointing at the grisly remnants. "See! The wrappings are still wet. And we have saved his phallus from the crabs."

Isis seemed simultaneously pleased and angry. She glared at Liz. "Insolent woman! What are you doing with my brother-husband's phallus?"

Jerry didn't bother to translate. The way Isis snatched the thing away from Liz was pretty self-explanatory. Fortunately, the stubborn South African biologist did not argue about it.

Jackal-headed Anubis advanced, growling. "What do you want us to do with these defilers, Isis?"

A part of Jerry's mind said: *How interesting. Graecophone name-forms.* Another part said: *Help! For heaven's sake get someone else who can talk to these monsters.*

Trying a spell under these circumstances was probably not the cleverest thing he'd ever done, but he was pretty well out of other ideas. Short of screaming "run!"—which Cruz wasn't going to be doing for a while.

He tried a phrase.

Nothing happened.

"What are you saying?" whispered Liz.

"It's supposed to be a spell," said Jerry miserably.

"A spell?" She repeated the Coptic words. "For what?"

The sound of her distinctive voice fumbling at the incantation caused Jerry to stiffen, startled and hopeful at the same time. Especially when low-pitched and stressed, Liz's voice was accented. Slightly guttural. And she had a habit of drawling a bit. The pitch and preciseness of wording, Jerry suddenly remembered, were supposed to be nearly as important as the invocation of secret sacred names.

"Er. I think you have the voice for it," he said.

"You've got a rainbow in your mouth! On your tongue!" she exclaimed.

"So have you," said Jerry, embarrassed. "I was trying for the tongue of many peoples. It looks like I got the tongue of many colors . . . "

But at least it had stopped the advancing Anubis. "Wizards!" The jackal-headed god stepped back a pace. "Your business, Thoth."

Thoth eyed them with beady ibis eyes. "*KarrrK?*"

Whatever that meant, it wasn't "welcome home, dearly beloved." Jerry knew that Thoth, the grand vizier to Osiris, was a stickler for absolute precision. He probably didn't approve of their word-mangling.

"My vocabulary is a bit limited," he whispered to Liz. "Try this." He hissed a few words. "And *don't* suppress that accent of yours." He added another phrase full of as many names as he could recall.

Liz took a deep breath and orated.

She was nearly knocked off her feet by the large wooden platter of results. Sliced as well as whole . . .

"Let's guess," she said through clenched teeth. "You got me to ask for the gift of tongues."

"Try this instead." Hurriedly, Jerry rattled off another phrase.

This time the effect was even more startling and unexpected. However, it did enhance communication.

Having baboon barks issue from your mouth doesn't usually do that, true. But Jerry knew that in ancient Egyptian parlance, speaking the tongue of animals was considered a particular virtue. And Thoth was known to assume the form of the wise dog-headed ape.

Being addressed in his native tongue was a good move for Thoth, that most precise of Egyptian gods. He was also known as the master of truth. And as such, addressed in his own language, he was able to ascertain that, far from being villains, the foreigners were actually the heroes of the piece. He soon established that they had indeed rescued Osiris' remains from the water and the crabs. He also found out that having done so was likely to cost Cruz his leg, and possibly his life.

The Egyptian gods offered help, and a form of speech easier on the vocal chords.

"Please!" barked Liz.

"Keep the pressure on. There's some arterial bleeding," said McKenna.

Isis loomed over him. Then pushed him away. "You look too much like Set for you to be trusted."

"At least I have first aid training . . . " began McKenna, anxiety flaring his temper.

Lamont restrained him. "Leave her, Mac. She's kind of famous for gathering up the pieces of her husband, sewing them together and bringing him back to life."

Isis paused in her recital of magical formulae. Already the blood was no longer spurting, but trickling. "Cushite, you say it is famous? But . . . I haven't done that yet . . . have I?"

Thoth stopped his chanting. "To be precise, you have only

begun to do so," he said pedantically. "I, Thoth, the sacred scribe of Osiris, will record the deed." He paused. "I have. It is in the Book of the Pyramids."

"Fix the leg," commanded Anubis. "We don't want to be here if monstrous Set returns."

Isis bent to her sewing and chanting, stitching Cruz's leg back together. Anesthetic was no part of the chanting magic. Cruz held Medea's hand. His teeth were set, but when Medea gave a low moan he realized he was nearly crushing her hand.

"Sorry. Didn't realize I was squeezing so hard," he said.

"You are very strong. You are also very stupid. How dare you nearly get yourself killed by that water dragon? You knew the water here was infested with them." Her voice cracked slightly. And she sniffed, swallowed and continued to chew him out. "And you can be lucky that I am not sewing you up! I would hurt you much more. Much. Idiot American!"

Mac turned to Lamont. "I think he was better off with the croc."

Lamont smiled slightly, but made no reply. The look on Medea's face reminded him of the time Marie had spent sitting by his hospital bed after he'd been in a car accident. The memory was a fond one. And heartbreaking.

God, I miss her. And my kids.

Isis was a fast worker. After she finished, Anubis began to wrap the leg in a linen strip. McKenna began to mutter something about unsterilized bandages, but the glares of his companions shut him up.

Cruz moved his toes experimentally. "I don't believe this. I thought I'd lost that leg."

McKenna grinned widely enough to endanger his ears. "I thought you were going to die on me."

"Indeed, this leg has passed through death," said Isis calmly.

"To be precise, the Sa had departed the leg." Thoth was nothing if not a pedant. "It was necessary to allow the Sa from Isis into the limb."

"What does all that mean, Jerry?" Cruz flexed the leg experimentally.

"Sa is vital fluid. Life-force, for want of a better term. Um. I think you may have an immortal leg."

Thoth nodded his long beak in agreement. "Now that the leg has passed beyond death it cannot be killed again."

"The stuff of Leg-ends," whispered Lamont.

Jerry laughed so much he nearly fell into the water and got himself eaten by the next crocodile.

Their stolen vessel made a good funerary barge. But they didn't row across to the other world. Instead they poled it along winding channels between the tall papyrus, deeper and deeper into the marshes of Buto.

"It is to be hoped we do not . . . how do you say, 'piss these people off,'" said Henri, looking at the endless reeds. "I have no idea in the least where we are."

"Egypt," said Mac, yawning. The stress of dealing with Cruz's injury, and the sudden realization that if the sergeant bought it . . . he'd be left as the only military defense of this bunch, had taken it out of him. For the first time in his twenty-one years, he was realizing a few things about responsibility and mortality.

Henri eyed him in a jaundiced fashion. "It is to be hoped that you can cure yourself of this *gaucherie.* But considering your American origins, that hope is in vain."

Mac yawned again. "Oh, give it a rest. I don't want to toss you overboard. I'd give some poor croc heartburn and cholesterol problems."

Henri moved off, muttering.

"That's the way to deal with him, y'know," said Lamont quietly. "The more you rise to his bait, the more he throws."

Jim McKenna looked at Lamont. The guy must be what . . . Forty? Fifty, even? He'd kind of written him off at that first meeting. He'd been reassessing the man ever since. He'd come to realize that Lamont Jackson was no pushover. He never even mentioned the subject, but the way he fitted into any combat said: *military experience.* If Cruz wasn't around . . . of all the people here, he'd be the one to take over the sergeant's role.

"You were in the service, Lamont?"

Lamont smiled. "I forget. It was a long time ago." Something about the way he said it indicated: *subject closed.*

Jim McKenna was learning to grow up at last. He changed the subject. "Well, you obviously know how to deal with that goddamn anti-American bigot."

Lamont smiled again. "You should try being black for a while. Eventually you learn to fight hard when it's worth fighting for, and to ignore assholes otherwise."

The boat juddered slightly as they brushed another mud bank.

"I hope like hell we don't have to get out and push," said Jerry, nervously looking at the dark water. The moon was down, and sunrise was not yet due. It was actually pretty cold. No time was a good time to go wading around here, but somehow the dark water in the predawn was even less appealing. But Thoth and Anubis thrust them forward with poles instead. And it was apparent that they'd reached their destination. A fire burned on the low island between the acacias.

Well, Henri said that they were acacias. They were thorny enough. That figured.

32

A SEW-SEW JOB.

"What happens now?" Liz asked Jerry.

Jerry tugged his goatee. "Well, according to the myth, Isis will sew the bits together, and Osiris will be reanimated. He will answer Set's accusations and vindicate himself before the tribunal of gods. Then he'll go off to become lord of the dead."

"I meant: what are we going to do? I want to go home, Jerry. Lamont *needs* to go home. Medea also wants to get back to her kids."

"Yeah. Well, I was getting to that. Isis and Thoth both seem to believe that if anyone can help us, it will be Osiris. He's a pretty major ancient Egyptian god. You don't go much higher except for Ra . . . or perhaps Amon, although the two get confused and once again we are dealing with a mishmash mythworld . . . "

Liz stamped her foot. "I wish you'd stop lecturing and just get to the point, Jerry. Do I need to know all this stuff?"

"He only lectures when he gets nervous," said Lamont.

Liz shook her head. "So what's spooking him now?"

Lamont's shoulders shook slightly. "You, at a guess."

Liz raised her eyes to heaven. "Oh, for goodness sake, Jerry.

You can tell Odysseus off, come up with spells under pressure, you even give a surprisingly good account of yourself in a fight. Why should I frighten you?"

Jerry wisely did not answer that all women made him nervous and the more attractive he found them, the more nervous he got. He was fine with Liz most of the time, just so long as he wasn't thinking about it. "Sorry. Habit," was all he said.

"Well, break it!" she snapped.

"How many smokes have you got left in that packet?" asked Lamont dryly.

Liz sighed. "Touché. So you reckon we are stuck here until Isis gets through with sewing up her husband."

Jerry decided that monosyllables couldn't be construed as lecturing. "Yes."

"Then I'm off to help with the sewing," said Liz.

"Bully them, you mean?" Lamont asked.

She smiled. "Something like that."

Jerry found his eyes tracking the sway of her hips as she walked away. He shook his head. "I didn't know I was that obvious. Life's complicated, Lamont."

The older man leaned back against the bank. "And then you die."

The early morning sun sent streamers of mist rising smokelike from the limitless green extent of the marsh. The birds raised a paean to the dawn. Anibal Cruz sat looking out across the limpid water of one of the channels. He felt kind of like singing himself. He'd known last night, when that crocodile had seized his leg, that he was dead. The beast must have been at least fourteen feet long and immensely powerful. It had already begun to pull him into the murky depths when he'd hit out at it, and he'd *known* that blow was totally ineffectual. A severed arm in mummy wrappings is no sort of weapon to fend off a giant reptile.

Or shouldn't be. This place was *weird*. He couldn't accept it. Except . . . that it would also mean not accepting Medea. And that woman was really getting to him. He dug out his poker dice, and began to toss them idly.

A pair of cool hands came to rest on his shoulders. Cruz felt a thrill jolt through his spine.

"How do you feel?" asked Medea.

He smiled up at her. "Just fine. Glad to be able to talk with you again."

She looked down at him, thoughtfully. "I have decided to ask you to teach me to speak American. I might also find myself deprived of my powers when we get there. But I also need to get back to my children."

Cruz sighed. "If Jerry can work out how to get back to the States, he can figure out how to get back to . . . to . . . the place you came from. And I guess learning to speak English could be pretty useful. But with this translation stuff . . . how could you do it?"

Medea shrugged. "We'll just have to take the spells off. I have been learning some of the names and spells of power from Doc Jerry."

Anibal grinned. "Given Jerry's luck with spells so far . . . "

Medea dimpled. "Ah. But I have more practice than he has. He has the knowledge, without an understanding of the rhythms and cadences." She sat on the soft grass next to him. "What is that that you are fiddling with?"

"Poker dice. It's a game."

"Oh? How do you play?" She took the well-worn ivories from his hand.

"Well, I'll show you, but I'm really not too sure of the rules."

"Then we can be two amateurs together," she said, smiling cheerfully.

"Well, this is a straight . . . " He explained, and rapidly began to realize that the girl of his fancy was smart as well as gorgeous. "Here, let me hold your hand and show you how to throw."

The dice landed on the grass, cocked.

"We need somewhere flat. There is a better spot back there in the thicket. Come, I will show you." Medea took Cruz by the arm and led him back into the trees.

It was as secluded as you could get on a relatively small swamp island. There was still a view out over the water, through a gap in the trees, but it was a narrow window onto the world. Flattening a sand ring was easy enough, as the grass was thin and scattered under the spiky trees.

"A pair." She leaned forward. Cruz found concentrating on the pair . . . of dice difficult.

"Now, I throw the other dice again . . . " She threw a trey, and clapped in delight. She tilted her head and lifted her aristocratic nose. "Beat that!"

"I'll do my best." Old habits die hard. "Hmm. Shall we liven this game up with a small bet or two?"

"I don't have any money," she said demurely.

"We could play for other stakes," he said idly, as if it was a totally unimportant suggestion.

She raised an eyebrow. "That sounds interesting. Are you not playing some sort of trick on me?"

"Me?" Butter would not only not have melted in Anibal Cruz's mouth, it might actually have unchurned itself and gone back to being cream. "Never. Now what I suggest is that the loser takes off an item of clothing. Just to keep score."

A small smile teased the edges of her mouth. "Very well. Just to keep score."

The sun shone down through the angular branches onto Anibal's bare back. His face was exceedingly red. And it wasn't only his back that was bare.

He consoled himself with the thought that he'd learned a really valuable lesson: NEVER play strip poker with a sorceress. Even in the wrong universe. So far she'd only taken off her sandals. She had very pretty feet . . .

He was buck-naked.

"This is a fun game!" Medea's smile was extremely wicked, as she examined the discomfited and naked paratrooper. It was not a brief examination. "Why are you so red in the face?" she asked innocently.

"This grass is tickling my bare . . . " choked Cruz.

"Why don't you spread some of those clothes of yours out. Then I could come and sit on them too. It would be a gentlemanly thing to do. Sitting on the grass is terribly undignified for a princess." She was looking a little flushed now, and she pushed away an errant curl from her forehead. "My, but it is hot this morning."

"I've got nothing more to lose," he growled.

"Tch." She fluttered her long eyelashes at him. "Then *I'll* just have to play to lose."

Anibal Cruz choked.

She cocked her head to one side and smiled provocatively. "That is what I was supposed to do, wasn't it?"

Cruz choked again.

Medea, the sorceress of Colchis, twined her fingers through the hair on his chest. Her eyes were soft. "I can tell you're not a Hellene," she said with a small, satisfied, secretive smile.

"Why?" he asked warily. "Did I do something wrong?"

"No. You did everything *right*. But so gentle . . . and you were trying to please me. Jason never bothered to. I know: That is only a small sample of one. But Absyrtus was like that too."

"Absyrtus?"

"My half brother. I killed him."

Cruz swallowed. Medea was nothing if not to the point. But if he understood what she was saying . . . Well, maybe the guy was just lucky Anibal Cruz hadn't gotten to him first. Very lucky.

She nibbled at his jawline. "It's a pity that Isis made the wrong leg immortal."

"Er. I think that some of the magic may have affected that limb too. It's certainly feeling like it may have died anyway."

She looked slightly alarmed. "Have we hurt your leg?"

"No . . . It's the one you were concerned about a few moments ago. The middle one. I'm sure it has died. I can feel rigor mortis setting in."

She rolled on top of him and began punching him in the ribs. Well, that's how it started anyway. Unfortunately, it wasn't that big an island. Fortunately, some of the marsh birds make just that kind of shriek.

It was a good thing that she'd gone to assist with the sewing up, thought Liz. There must be physiological limits on what magic could do. And there were *certainly* limits on Isis' knowledge of basic internal anatomy.

No matter what spells are uttered, a liver is a prerequisite for a decent afterlife and connecting the bile duct to the heart is almost certain to cause problems. Anubis was all for removing the whole lot, and simply substituting jewels or suitable scrolls of papyrus. Or filling the space with bitumen. He'd even brought suitable canopic jars and hooks.

"I can clean out his sinuses properly once and for all," he offered in a gravelly semi-growl. Liz did not take to Anubis. Not that she had anything against jackals. Very useful at waste disposal, scavengers were. Liz just found his drooling a bit off-putting.

Isis' twin sister, Nepthys, was also "helping." She combined being a terrible seamstress, with being Anubis' mother (by Osiris, to boot), and the murderer Set's wife. It seemed like a very complicated arrangement, added to Osiris being both Isis' husband and brother. Incest was one thing, but this!

Talk about keeping it all in the family . . .

Liz felt she had enough to contend with, dealing with the gory sewing-up task. But she also had to listen to the ceaseless lamentations of Isis, Nepthys, and the doleful chanting of Thoth, who ritually cleansed each piece before the sewing team was allowed loose. However, she soon found there was something further required of her. "You must either lament, chant or leave, sorceress," demanded Thoth.

Liz sighed. "Fine! But don't complain . . . "

The island and the reconstruction of Osiris echoed to ancient Egyptian funerary chants. And to: "de-hip-bone, connected-to-de-thigh-bone . . . "

Well, perhaps that too was a powerful spell in this universe. In the end, Osiris went together in more or less the right order, and with all the right bits connected to the right bits.

And then to Liz's alarm . . . he stirred. Liz had done more dissections than most people had had hot breakfasts. She was normally as squeamish as lead, but this was asking a bit much.

Osiris groaned. Liz, stepping back, took a very deep, deep breath and wondered if now was not the perfect time for that second-to-last cigarette.

He sat up. *This,* thought Liz, *is where I get the hell out of here.*

But the small island glade was too full of chanting Egyptian deities to let her just slip away.

"Ohhh. Well, it's a better job than last time." Osiris croaked and felt his groin.

"Thank Ra for that. That desert jackass won't be able to call me 'dickless' again." He massaged his throat. "Isis, my queen, you wouldn't have something to drink, would you?"

"No, my lord brother-husband. We came in haste."

Liz had some of Mac's "brandy" in her bag, in a small wine-skin. It was all that she had, besides river water. "Here, Isis. It's pretty strong."

She passed it over. Osiris struggled with the cork and then gratefully swallowed some.

The mummy-man's greenish pallor flushed. His eyes bulged. He sprayed the liquor out. "Gah! Kehaph!! Eheh!"

Strong, rough hands seized Liz.

And Osiris took another pull at the skin. This time he swallowed it. He shuddered. Then he took a deep breath and smiled beatifically. "By Ra, Nut, Geb and even my brother Set—now *that's* what *I* call embalming fluid! Here, my good vizier! Try this. Make sure that you write down the recipe."

He passed the skin to a doubtful-looking Thoth. "Chug it, old birdbrain!"

The rough hands ceased holding Liz in a grip of iron, as the pedantic grand vizier spluttered but did not die. Indeed, even Osiris was looking remarkably lively for a fairly ripe corpse that had just been sewed up by a bunch that would have been rejected by most sewing circles, never mind med schools.

Osiris turned to Liz. "Tell me, she who brings Sa, that which warms the very cockles of the Ka—who are you? How do you come to the land of the Nile?"

"We were kind of hoping *you* could tell us how we got here. But what we're really interested in is how we could get home."

Osiris shook his head vigorously. It was a good thing, thought Liz, that she and Isis had done most of that section of the sewing. If it had been Nepthys, it could easily have just fallen off again.

✧   ✧   ✧

Liz was the noticing kind. But you could hardly *help* noticing the looks on Cruz and Medea's faces, even if they hadn't been
leaning against each other. She couldn't help feeling a little
envious, if pleased for Medea's sake. The broad sergeant was a
nice guy. Heh. He was looking a bit bemused. That was good.

"Basically," she said, flopping onto the bank, "Osiris has no
trouble remembering that this was a decaying Mythworld. He says
even now things are barely beginning to change. There are large
tracts of upper Egypt where the desert just disappears into
nothingness."

Jerry studied her intently. "He seems very cheerful. If a bit
unsteady on his feet."

She chuckled. "He's dead drunk. Which is not bad seeing that
he was just plain dead, earlier. I think any favors we want to ask
had better be soon and not tomorrow. Still, he and Isis are very
obliged to us right now. He says he can feel the Ka of this
universe being drawn into the naos of a dark force that sucks
out its Sa. Whatever that means."

"Better than it sounds, I hope," said Mac with a grin, looking at Medea and Cruz. "I wonder if it's infectious."

"I'll thump you," growled Cruz, without any signs of a deep
desire to do so. Actually, he was looking very relaxed. Almost
as if, were he to relax any more, he'd be asleep. "So what does
it mean, Doc?"

"Ka is soul, Sa is life-force. Naos is the inner sanctuary of the
temple."

Cruz's expression showed that Jerry's explanation was as clear
as mud. "So . . . can we go home? Or even back to—to—the
Olympians' universe?"

Liz shook her head. "The linkage, from the 'gods' point of view,
seems to be having believers in both universes. Whoever or
whatever is running this show seems to be able to ignore or
override that."

Lamont, as usual, was quick on the uptake. "So. Aren't there
any gods in common?"

Jerry pursed his lips thoughtfully. "In a way, there are. In the
latter days of Egypt, the Greeks identified numerous of the

Egyptian gods as being the same as their own. Bastet was considered to be one with Artemis. Anubis with Hermes, Nepthys with Nike, Osiris with Dionysus or Hades. Isis got identified with Demeter, Hera, Selene and even Aphrodite."

Liz sighed. "Great. So the only two I've taken to, are so confused they don't even know who they are. Anyway, Osiris is off to face the judgment. Then he will be going to preside over the weighing of souls. We have been invited. You can ask as many gods as show their faces in the halls of the dead."

"I just can't wait," said Mac.

Liz gave him a wry smile. "Well, you'll just have to. We must stay here on the floating isle of Chemmis until a ship is sent for us."

"I do not like the sounds of that," said Henri, doubtfully.

Liz shook her head at the Frenchman. "And just how do you propose to go elsewhere?"

It was a good question. They'd been guided there in the dark, through a maze of twisty papyrus channels. Of course they could—in theory—navigate by the sun. Mac looked at the curving channel. The landmarks were occasional tufts of trees. All remarkably similar to each other.

A small Egyptian in a loincloth came up and bowed. "Buto has ordered us to set food for you, foreigners. Barley beer, bread, lentils, onions, cucumber, fish, pigeons and ducks, lotus root and pomegranates. My lady apologizes for the inadequate fare, but supplies have been disjointed of late."

A second servant approached. "Toiletries await: oils, unguents and kohl for the ladies to darken their eyes. Cones of perfumed fat for your heads are prepared. Fresh garments of pleated linen are just being starched. Collars of faïence and coiled gold." He took a long look at the men. Shuddered. "Bronze-bladed razors and tweezers await the lords, for the removal of unwanted facial hair."

"Are you *sure* you don't want that cone of perfumed fat to melt slowly into your hair?" asked Lamont innocently.

"Are you sure you want to live until nightfall?" retorted Liz, her eyes darkened with kohl and her ears adorned with large golden earrings. Around her neck was a fine-woven gold collar.

"And no, I wasn't prepared to shave all my hair off and wear a wig either. Or wear a thing that exposed one breast!"

Jerry swallowed. No point in letting your imagination run away with you. "It's a mishmash. They don't all come from the same era . . ."

His explanation was interrupted by McKenna.

"All right. Out with it! Who told them to do this?" McKenna descended on them snarling. He was wrapped in a shred of linen and still dripping. He was incandescently angry. He was also clean-shaven. Entirely clean-shaven. Well, they'd left his eyelashes. But otherwise not a hair on his head or chin . . . or armpits. "*Who* told them I was a priest? That bastard Henri?"

"*I* am well aware of who my father was," said Henri, tugging his goatee complacently. "My neat beard they thought Pharoic."

Mac seemed on the verge of removing Henri Lenoir from this plane of existence. Cruz stepped forward and wrapped his thick arms around the corporal. "Cool it, Mac. He was already with the flunkies when you went off. He wouldn't have even known you were going."

"*Somebody* told Isis I was a priest!" snarled Mac. "Was this your idea of a practical joke—*Sir*?"

Liz went bright red and slapped him hard enough to make his do-it-yourself loincloth fall off. This revealed that they'd not stopped shaving when they got to his armpits. "If I'm going to abuse you I'll do it firsthand!" she snarled, as Mac groped hastily for the fallen linen.

Jerry cleared his throat. "I think you did it yourself, Mac. You said to Isis that you were trained in 'First Aid.' If you try and translate that, it could come out as knowing the rituals of healing. That was the province of priests. And they were shaved bald."

"You look like a boot, Mac," said Cruz with a grin.

Lamont nodded and chuckled. "But that strip of linen does things for you."

"Seriously," said Jerry, trying to cool things off, "it's a good thing Mac got rid of his hair. It could help us a lot."

McKenna was not mollified. "I don't know anything about being a priest!"

"No, it's your hair and skin color," explained the mythographer.

"Set was supposed to be white-skinned and red-haired. Rough and rude, too. That was one reason Isis was so upset when she saw us with the dismembered pieces of her hubby."

Lamont grinned. "Well, Mac could get a job as a stand-in. Wasn't he supposed to have ears like an ass too?"

Jerry shook his head. "Shut up, Lamont. You're stirring things up just because you were the only one besides Liz who could stand that vile beer."

"Real African beer has lumps in it. Not thin clear stuff like cats wee." Liz was grinning broadly.

Jerry pulled a face. "We were all expecting . . . beer. It was vile, Liz. I don't know how you and Lamont could drink the stuff. But Mac'll be useful as a 'priest.' I'll teach him a few chants. Hmm. We could use some upgrading of our status. If you've seen the numbers of soldiers around here, fighters won't impress them, but an extra sorceress might."

"Medea's learning too damn fast," grunted Cruz. She responded by tickling him.

Jerry grinned at Lamont. "Actually, I was thinking that what we really need is the most powerful and feared of sorceresses. The ones that came from Nubia—or, as it was otherwise known, Cush. Black people."

Lamont blinked. "Me? Aren't you forgetting something?"

"Like what?" asked Jerry, innocently.

Lamont shook his head. "Like I'm the wrong sex."

Jerry clucked his tongue. "Nothing to it, Lamont! Cross-dressing has a well-established precedent in ancient Egypt. Queen Hasheput who was regent for Thutmose III dressed herself as a man." Jerry's grin got more wicked still. "All we need to do is shave your head and put you in a dress. You'll be a winner."

"You're not going to do that to me?" said Lamont, with disbelief.

"Oh yes, we are!" said Mac fiendishly. "If I've got to suffer for a good cause, so do you!"

"There was the wig they tried to give me . . . " said Liz. "And another dress that was way too big."

"The topless one?" asked Medea, getting in on the spirit of

things. "And there is much makeup." She looked at Lamont. "Fortunately."

Liz snorted. "I don't think he's gynecomastic enough for the topless one. And he's probably got hairy boobs."

"I'm not going to do this!" protested Lamont.

"It's all right, Lamont," murmured Medea sweetly. "We'll do it for you."

Jerry managed to wipe off the grin. "Lamont . . . Seriously, Nubian sorceresses were big-time power. And I've got a feeling we may need that desperately. And what do you care what you look like, if it can get us all home?"

"I'm not going to do this." But Lamont sounded less sure about it. His companions arose and advanced upon him.

"Not going to . . . " Mumble, mumble.

By the time the ship arrived to transport them, Lamont had been made into a strapping lass, if not a pretty one. And a very sulky lass, he was.

The vessel was a far cry from the papyrus-bundle boat that they'd used to bear Osiris' remains to the island. The ship was at least a hundred and fifty feet long. It was made of curved cedar wood, with a high pointed prow and stern. It was canopied with spotless linen, with a team of rowers sweating at the long spear-bladed paddles. A harpist played melodiously from under the shaded canopy. "I think we have elevated our status in the world. Now if only they have more of that tilapia scented with cumin and fenugreek . . . " said Henri happily. "And perhaps something to drink other than that terrible beer."

Liz looked at the vessel and shook her head. "It looks like a thin wooden banana. I could make a fortune here as a boat designer."

Lamont struggled to board the ship. "I can't even walk in this stupid tight dress. This is a dumb, dumb idea."

"Are you in Dis-dress, Lamont?" asked Jerry.

Lamont was less than amused. "I should toss you to the crocodiles, Jerry."

"I think he's skirting the issue," offered Liz.

Jerry snorted. "Dressed like that, you never know what it might be. But I'd better say no more. I might get kilt."

Liz groaned. "Why did I ever join in this ridiculous punfest?"

Jerry smiled. "Because you like them?"

Liz shook her head. "Who ever admitted to *liking* puns?"

Liz was far more impressed by the vessel now that she was aboard. "Not one nail. It's amazing. This ship is held together with strips of linen. Like a mummy."

Henri Lenoir shuddered. "*Madame*, I do not think I wish to know this. A few pieces of linen between my person and the crocodiles? Not even the finding of something the locals call 'wine' can adequately comfort me. Although," he said, drinking some from the jar, "I shall do my best to insulate myself from water, both inside me as well as out."

33

HEAVY ON THE SOUL, PLEASE.

Despite his professional interest, Jerry really wasn't all that keen on going to Duat and the land of the justified dead. People who made that trip generally wound up working in the rich fields of Osiris. . . .

Perhaps it was worth doing the trip just for the scenery and the architecture. If you liked massive, blocky architecture. And immense pillars crowned with stone palm leaves, the details picked out in reds, and blues and gold foil. And lots and lots of other *bright* colors.

The white statues of Greece had once been brightly painted, Jerry knew. The paintings and murals to be seen in modern Egypt are magnificent. But they're *old*. These were bright and new. Red and blue pennants fluttered from the temple pillars. The walls gleamed with glass and semiprecious stone murals. There was gold foil on anything that there could be any excuse to put it on. And every flat surface, pillar and lintel was carved and set with murals or hieroglyphs.

The whole thing looked like some immense jeweled insect, against the stark and barren desert cliffs that loomed above the verdant valley.

The colonnaded temple was cool after their brief walk in the blazing sun. Cool and reeking of incense.

They were greeted by Anubis. He grinned toothily at them. "Welcome to the hall of double justice. I have news for you . . . "

Isis had come up behind him. "Ah, here they are. There is a soul that has come to face psychostasia. Osiris has been await-ing your arrival. He is from none of the forty-two nomes. We think he may come from your nome."

"I was not aware that I had a nome," said Henri, with a gen-teel hiccup.

"*I bin through the desert on a horse with no nome . . .*" Lamont had also been dipping deeply. He was much worse off than Henri, as he was normally not much of a drinking man. The French-man had a well-trained liver; Lamont didn't.

In a way, it was Liz's fault that Lamont was reeling drunk. She'd told him that the "beer" was like the African beer of her home-land. Perhaps Lamont had felt it incumbent on him to prove his roots. He'd drunk the stuff—with distaste. Then he'd had some more . . . on the ship he'd topped it off with lots of wine. He hardly noticed that he was dressed in women's clothing anymore.

"*'Cause in the desert you cain't remember your nome . . .*" he sang tunelessly, cheerfully.

"Indeed. You are very right, Lady! I am sorry that I did not realize that you were in disguise when we met beside my husband's body. Come. We will give you a winding sheet. The soul must be questioned. You shall act as one of the judges."

Lamont hiccupped, and veered into another song. "*Show me the way to go nome . . .*"

Osiris' face was a pallid green. Liz blamed it on Mac's "brandy." After all, she'd stopped them attaching the gall bladder to the heart valves. It could also have been the frieze of coiled cobras on the small roof above him. Occasionally they stirred. That would have been enough to make most people green.

In the middle of the hall stood an enormous balance, with burnished brass pans. Lamont, complete with a funerary shroud, was led off to sit among the judges.

❖   ❖   ❖

"Don't stare," hissed Jerry to Henri, whose mustachios were bristling fiercely as he peered at the scale's attendant. Jerry was trying not to stare himself. The goddess Maat, she of truth and justice, was depicted in several papyrus scrolls as having been clad in a garment that started just below the breasts. They'd got it right. . . .

They dragged their attention to what was happening at the doorway. The person there was dressed in the remains of a uniform. Well, his shade was dressed in what would have been a uniform if it had been any more substantial. It wasn't.

He stepped over the threshold. Anubis hauled him back, not bothering to be gentle. Obviously those jackal teeth could still hurt whatever this was. He stood. Anubis pushed him forward. So he stepped into the room. Anubis hauled him back by the scruff of the neck.

"Kiss the threshold," said Jerry in a stage whisper.

The strange ghost looked horrified. "Kiss the *floor*? But that's so unhygienic," he said fastidiously, backing off.

Jerry took a deep breath. "You're dead, in an Egyptian myth. I think worrying about germs is the least of your problems, and it is a bit late to think about health hazards."

The language obviously suddenly registered. "You speak English! Thank God!"

Jerry had an upwelling of sympathy for the shade. "Yes . . . "

"Go *in*, mortal soul. But kiss the threshold," snapped Anubis testily.

"Better do it," said Jerry.

The once-uniformed man staggered in and kissed the doorsill. Then said: "Please, please translate. I've learned about ten words in the construction gang, and they're not getting me very far. 'Stop hitting me' is real useful but doesn't make for communication." He looked closely at Jerry. "Ah. Dr. Lukacs, I believe? You're one of that large party that went missing."

"Yes. We're all here. How do you know? Who are you?"

"Captain Michael Halstrom. I am—ah, *was* part of Professor Tremelo's research team. I'm an Army psychologist detailed to put together profiles of the snatchees. You were a very atypical group. The largest since the pyramid started operating a few days ago."

"*A few days?* We've been here for weeks!"

Anubis shoved Halstrom. "Go on, mortal soul. Greet the judges. You must then answer to each and every one. Then your soul must be weighed against the feather of Maat."

"What did he say?" whined the Army psychologist.

Halstrom had done his rounds of all the judges. Talking to him as he walked, Jerry learned that back in Chicago the pyramid just kept on expanding. It had expanded enormously just after the trial of the neutron device. Halstrom hadn't been supposed to know about it, but the story had leaked out. They were in the process of being evacuated further back when he'd been snatched.

The alien pyramid was still snatching, still growing. So far, to the point where Halstrom found himself among the peasants in the pyramid construction team, pulling huge limestone blocks up a ramp lubricated with fresh Nile mud.

Nearly a thousand people had vanished, in toto. Most of them came back dead within a few hours. The research team had already worked out that the victims had been gone for longer than just the elapsed time.

The last judge hiccupped. "Who won the Super Bowl in 1999?" "she" demanded.

The feather was an enormous one. And it was made of gold. Amemait the devourer—part hippopotamus, part lion, part crocodile—was already licking his lips in anticipation when Halstrom got onto the scale.

Thoth verified the weight. "Hmm. These many hours of playing 'Free Cell' at work, O foreign magician, you say that it is a religious observance? One of great respect to the hierarchical position of the black and the red Kings? Religious observances are permitted during working time. We can give him some credit for that."

"Oh, definitely," said Jerry, hoping that he wouldn't have to answer for his own deeds soon.

Thoth moved the adjustment chain. The two pans balanced.

"Let the deceased depart victorious," intoned Osiris.

"What happens to me now?" asked the justified Captain Halstrom's Ka.

Mac had listened to Jerry's briefing on the journey up the Nile. "Don't worry, Captain Shrink. You'll get to do lots of nice physical outdoor field labor in Osiris' kingdom. Raising crops, digging ditches, good healthy outdoor work. And if you're feeling lazy you can send in the watchamacallems. Doc?"

"Ushabtis," said Jerry.

"Yep. Them." Mac stretched. "You send them out as your substitute. They're like little doll-things that you put a spell on and they do all your work. Sorta like Egyptian afterlife grunts. It'll be a piece of cake. Just think of yourself as an REMF, which oughta come naturally enough."

Halstrom looked confused. "Where do I get them?"

Jerry gave a wry smile. "They're supposed to be buried with you. Egyptian belief is the opposite of 'you can't take it with you when you go.'"

Halstrom looked even more confused. "Er. My body disappeared. The embalmers were a bit taken aback . . ."

Just then Lamont wove his way up to them. He seemed to have sobered up considerably. "Listen, guys. If we can slip out for a minute, Anubis cornered me when I went out. He says he's organized a meeting with Min, or something like that, who is Pan back in Greece. Apparently he can get us back, possibly even home. Travelers are his domain. We're supposed to go and meet him in his temple."

The Army psychologist's shade looked in need of counseling. "Can I come with you? I really don't like an outdoor lifestyle. I've always lived in the city. Don't leave me here," he begged, looking as if he'd start shedding ghostly tears at a moment's notice.

Jerry shrugged. "I've no idea whether that will be allowed. But you're welcome to tag along as far as we're concerned. You've been judged. You're free to go. Of course you may not be popular with Osiris. I gather it's been a while since he's had any new labor."

Liz had come up. "This Min—who is she?"

"He," corrected Jerry. "He's a very ancient god. He was called the 'Lord of Foreign Lands.' And as our 'sorceress from Nubia' just told us, the god of travelers as well as fertility. It sounds hopeful, doesn't it?"

Liz nodded. "So what does *this* one look like? Does he have the head of a goat? Heaven knows how their digestive systems worked. Or is this the head of a politician on a human body?"

Jerry swallowed. "Human. With two tall feathers sticking up from the headdress. And er . . . Well, you'll know him when you see him," he said uncomfortably.

"Well, not being female, he can't be another one of these topless waitresses," said Liz. "It's discrimination, that's what it is."

Jerry blushed. "No, it isn't. He's your equal-opportunity male flasher."

Lamont gave a very unladylike shout of laughter. "He's not the one from gallery three, is he? The one that was removed because of the complaints back in the fifties?"

Jerry nodded. "The same."

Lamont chuckled. "Nearly fifty years later that section of papyrus is legend. They say that most of the complaints came from men who felt pitifully inadequate . . . "

"Ha. That describes most of them," said Liz to Medea. "Come on. My curiosity is killing me. Anyone know where we're going?"

"It's supposed to be pretty unmistakable," said Lamont. "There's a stele with snakes and crocodiles and an ugly sort of dwarf on it, under the portico next to the cliff. Then according to Jackal-face, we just follow the lights." He stumbled. "Damn it! How do you walk in this stupid thing?"

"Take smaller steps," Liz advised the swaying Lamont.

He tried and tripped over his feet. "Why the *hell* did I ever let you get me into this thing?"

McKenna grinned. "Because you didn't have a lot of choice, that's why. Look—that must be the whatsit. Stele. The dwarf is pretty unmistakable. He looks cheerful enough."

Jerry smiled too. "Yeah, he does. That's Bes. The protector. Dwarves and pygmies were very popular in Egyptian history. I guess it's only right that they had one of their own as the buffoon of the gods."

"Are you calling me a buffoon?" The bandy-legged little man

who had stepped out from next to the stele picked Jerry up without any sign of effort. He seemed to find doing so a source of humor. "Who are you, mortal, to be wandering around taking my name in vain?"

Up close and—ah, *active*—Bes' dwarfish stature didn't seem cute any longer. The Egyptian god was a very *robust* dwarf, who almost exuded bestial vigor. His head was big and vaguely lion-shaped, his eyes huge, his cheeks prominent. His chin was hairy. And a truly enormous tongue hung from his wide-open mouth.

"Sorry," squeaked Jerry. "No offense intended!"

The little guy must have found a short leopard somewhere, thought Liz. Otherwise his leopard-skin cloak would have been too long for him. Mind you, he was pretty wide, as if to make up for his lack of stature. He was nearly as wide as he was high, but he didn't look too broad because he had an enormous head. He wore a topknot, with a bunch of ostrich plumes set in it. Most of the ancient Egyptians in this Mythworld were either fastidiously bearded or clean-shaven. Bes was neither of these. A veritable mane of thick, curly hair framed his broad, grinning face.

He set Jerry down. Jerry appeared none the worse for the experience. "Bes. You are Bes, aren't you?"

The dwarf-god cut a little caper, and clumsily executed a cartwheel. "That is my name, yes."

"Well, sorry to disturb you, Bes," said Jerry. "We were just told to look for this stele, and I was telling the others about you. Sorry about that. Here's our passage, guys."

"Are you going down there?" asked Bes.

"Yes. We need to see someone."

"Ah. I'll come along for the walk," said Bes.

The party wound its way through the narrow corridors, down flight after flight of stairs. There were various branches but only one set of corridors was lit. Little calcite lamps burned in regularly spaced embrasures. It was still dim between the painted walls, which were covered in hieroglyphs and murals. Rather unpleasant murals. Not what you'd have thought a fertility and travelers' god would have liked, but then, Jerry didn't want to stop and try and read the hieroglyphic story.

"Did Anubis tell you we could blasted *walk* home this way?" demanded Liz.

"Indeed," grumbled Henri, "my feet they are quite worn out."

Mac spoke quietly. "Have you noticed the lamps behind us are going out?"

Liz scowled. "We'll never find our way out without lights."

"Damn," muttered Lamont. "I forgot my handy little Maglite in my other trousers." He pressed a hand to his forehead. "Ooh. My head hurts."

"You expect us to believe that?" said Jerry.

"What? That my head hurts?"

"No. That you have other trousers . . ."

They stepped through a blocky stone lintel-and-post threshold and into a dim chamber. Scattered lamps still burned in sconces. But it was downright gloomy. Jerry wasn't even that surprised to hear the huge stone slab grate into place behind them, blocking off the passage. Something moved in the shadows on the far side of the chamber. Something big. No, wrong word—something immense. Amemait. Amemait the devourer.

The monster opened its gray-green, scaly crocodile snout, full of evil yellow snaggled teeth.

Halstrom's Ka gave a panicky squeak and ran. The crocodile jaws of the devourer snatched it . . . And bit air several times. "Where did it go?" growled Amemait. "It just disappeared. You lot had better be more substantial."

"Or what are you going to do about it, fishbreath?" Bes stalked forward, his hands on his hips.

"Bes!" Amemait spat. "What are *you* doing here? They were supposed to be alone."

"I saw these innocents walking into your lair. So I came along for the fight." Too late, Jerry understood the significance of the protective stele including the arch-defender against dangerous wild beasts at the entrance. It wasn't a signpost. It was supposed to prevent Amemait from wandering.

"I'll eat you too, dwarf." Amemait's voice was chill. From the corner of his eye, Jerry saw Liz start fumbling hastily in her bag.

Bes chuckled. "I daresay you'll try."

"Ha. The New Order doesn't want you. Your time is over, Bes! I will devour soul after soul after soul in the new rule. Already Sekmet readies herself to drink the blood of men. The Krim does not want that feeble do-gooder Osiris and that empty-headed wife of his. I've been promised Maat for my pleasure too."

Bes shrugged. "I should have known you'd accept the lures of that thing. But you've still got me to deal with, snaggletooth."

"That will be easy enough, midget." Amemait opened his huge crocodile jaw and began to advance. But it was obvious that, despite the big talk, the devourer was more than a little wary of the small, potbellied, bandy dwarf.

Jerry whispered to Liz: "Try this . . ."

Hastily Liz repeated the cantrip.

"*Amon cause thy nostrils to clog,*

"*By Bichon, Suramp and the god of the North.*

"*By Net, thy throat be dry.*

"*The serpent Apep coil and roil in that stomach*

"*Whose secret name is gastroenteritis*

"*Hapi and his servants Ecoli, Streptococcus and . . .*"

Amemait snorted, belched, and retreated. Bes peered into the darkness after him. "He'll be back, loaded with amulets of protection against spells. Well, foreigners. We will have to act together. The greatest danger lies in the jaws and that tail."

"I've got a bit of practical experience with this," said Liz. "If Amemait's is a typical crocodile jaw, the opening muscles are weak. The strength lies in the muscles that close. Prizing the jaws open is nearly impossible. But I've held a small croc's mouth shut with one hand. If we can get it closed, we should be able to keep it closed."

Bes changed his grin to a wry one, briefly. "There are the lion's claws and the strength of the hippopotamus too. His hide is too thick for spears, or for my dagger. His eyes and the inside of his mouth are the only vulnerable spots."

"I think I can blind him." Liz held up what she'd apparently been rummaging for: an atomizer. "At least temporarily. The base

of my cologne seems to have stayed as high-proof alcohol. It's
not stuff you want to get in your eyes."

Cruz raised his nunchaku. "How thick is its skull? If I can get
close enough . . . "

Bes grinned broadly. "A man after my own heart! You shall
have your try. I will seize the mouth as this fine bully woman
sprays its eyes. The rest of you must seize the legs. You can pound
its brain with that flail of yours. *Hist*. Here the monster comes!"

It was a miracle that the monster could move at all. The legs
clanked with amulets. There must have been a hundred to each
leg. The coarse mane now billowed onto a collar of strips of
faïence, emerald and turquoise which would have stopped a spear
thrust, never mind a spell. The slit-pupil eyes gleamed golden . . .
Until Liz sprayed alcohol-based perfume into them. Amemait gave
a furious spitting roar and clawed at his eyes. Bes, choosing his
moment, grabbed the snout. Flung himself around it, arms and
legs.

Jerry nearly missed his dive at the amulet-behung foreleg. Then
he thanked heaven for the brass bracelets, for providing hand-
holds. Amemait was incredibly strong. Mac clung to the hind
leg along with Medea. Henri made a slightly more substantial
anchor on the other foreleg and Liz had joined Lamont on the
other hindleg. Jerry knew he was the weak link. He just wasn't
heavy enough. He barely managed to restrain the claws from Bes,
wrapped like a grinning monkey around the jaw. The sound of
Cruz's hammer blows with the nunchaku was like thunder. But
Amemait with pure hippo strength was managing to head for
the wall. The monster obviously intended to rub them off, like
ticks against a branch.

The one stave of the nunchaku splintered with the blow. *Fuck!*
Stupid thing worked better in theory than in practice. Wouldn't
the monster go down? He was going to be trapped against the
wall in a minute. Out of the corner of his eye Anibal saw a leg,
with Doc clinging like a leech, rake backward and brush a claw
tip across Medea. He dropped the splintered nunchaku and seized
an enormous calcite lamp from a wall sconce. It must have

weighed easily a hundred and fifty pounds. Adrenaline-loaded, he snatched it cleanly above his head and brought it down, pointed corner first, on Amemait's skull.

Even a hippo-thickness braincase was not proof against that. Amemait's head dropped. "Get out from under!" yelled Cruz, trying to suit the action to the word. The monster fell against the wall, trapping and crushing him along with several of the others.

Then Cruz got to see just how strong the dwarf really was. Bes had leaped clear, and now hauled the monster away from the wall. Actually the wall had undoubtedly saved Henri, Lamont and Liz's lives. If Amemait had simply fallen on them, they would have been squashed. As it was, they had time to squirm clear. Just.

"Phew." Cruz felt his ribs, after carefully inspecting the claw slash on Medea. "Thanks . . . mister. What did you say your name was? Bes. I wouldn't want to wrassle with you."

Bes grinned his wide red-mouthed grin. "Fun!" He chuckled. "I like to fight. I don't like what . . . "

A chanting was coming down the passage from whence Amemait had come. Bes stood, as if turned to stone. His eyes burned.

A column of bald-headed priests in their white robes came down the passage. Behind them came more spearmen. The long passage was full of them.

"Greetings, foreigners. We have come to rescue you."

"You're a bit late," said Jerry weakly. And he saw Mac fall over. Too late, Jerry realized he was falling also. He should have picked up on the spell-chant earlier.

They were bound and gagged and carried out, leaving Bes standing stonelike, staring angrily.

They were loaded like so many sacks of potatoes onto the waiting donkeys, and carried away into the twilight. Away, and out across the desert. One of the guards mentioned a name in low-voiced conversation with the others. *Sebek*. Then there was silence for a long time except for the clop of hooves and the distant howling of a jackal.

34

OLD CROCS NEVER DIE.
THEY JUST SMELL THAT WAY.

The lake lay like a sheet of silver in the predawn. Not a whisper of a breeze dared to ripple the glassy water. On the far side, Jerry could make out the dark square bulk of the temple of Sebek.

Crocodilopolis, the Greeks had called it. The domain of Sebek, the crocodile-headed god. Jerry's mind worked overtime all of that long night, coming up with new and highly innovative spells to use on the crocodile-god and his followers, particularly the ones who had trussed him up like this. He set aside an especially nasty one for the donkeys.

But the gagging was singularly effective. And all the spells needed to be spoken.

He soon had some more curses for the bald-shaved son of a bitch that tipped him off the donkey into the mud, and then dragged him to the small felucca and tossed him facedown onto the ribs of the boat.

At least on the other side they were carried. Before being tossed into a stone cell.

✧   ✧   ✧

271

For her part, Liz spent all night determinedly chewing away at the foul-tasting rag. By the time the three of them were tossed into the stone-doored cell, the linen was nearly ready to call it quits. It was too dim here to see who'd been tossed in with her, but the high-slit window would give more light later. In the meanwhile, she chewed.

One of the others—Medea, as it turned out—rolled in a clumsy fashion across the floor to her. The third bound figure just groaned. Medea spat out her gag. She'd obviously spent the night chewing too. The sorceress squirmed her way down to the thick, coarse ropes that bound Liz. Medea was going to take a lot of stopping. Liz chewed on determinedly. Eventually the linen strip gave in.

Pah. By the taste she guessed at old mummy wrappings.

"Let's go and see who else they put in here," said Liz, as soon as she could talk.

The third prisoner was Lamont. Even in the dim light it was obvious he'd been beaten, as well as trussed up.

"Shit. Why did they hit him?" Liz was furious.

"They said *she* was a Cushite sorceress," replied Medea.

Liz strained at her bonds. "We need to get our hands free and give him some first aid. Do you think he's okay?"

Lamont nodded weakly.

"Well, he's responding to us anyway," said Liz with relief. "Come on, tug at my knots."

Medea cursed. "Damn them. I wish I could use my magic."

Liz took a deep breath. "Well. Let me try. If we had Henri here, he could tell us what the fiber was, perhaps. But I don't know. So I'll have to use animals . . .

"*By the Hathors I command thee,*

"*By the scarab,*

"*By the pincers of Selket.*

"*By the secret name Arachnida.*

"*I summon thee to devour and destroy this rope.*

"*By Horus of horizon, I command make it writhe away*

"*Like the holy uraeus . . .*"

"EEEK!"

The only reason that Lamont didn't join in Medea's shriek was that he still had the gag in his mouth. He did a pretty good shriek despite of it.

Scorpions came crawling by the hundreds out of the smallest cracks . . .

Belatedly, Liz remembered Jerry telling her that Selket was a scorpion goddess, particularly charged with the preservation of the entrails of the dead. Probably, as Lamont said later, because they'd been emptied out so nicely.

"Just lie still!" snapped Liz. "I thought we'd just get one or two. Not thousands." Liz spoke as calmly as she could, as more and more tiny clawed feet made their way down her arms to the ropes.

Which were writhing . . .

Lamont leapt to his feet kicking frantically, his fear of the scorpions totally submerged by his very urgent need to get rid of the rope that had become a uraeus. The knotted cobra that had been a rope hit the wall with an angry hiss. Nobody knows their own strength and sheer determination until they find their ropes turning to cobras. Ten seconds later they were all on their feet in a corner, stamping scorpions and frantically shaking them off their clothes, while three very large, angry Egyptian cobras hissed like about-to-explode kettles in the far corner. Liz untied Lamont's gag. It was bloody. He'd lost a tooth.

"For god's sake, Liz! I am really, really, really scared of snakes. And I ain't too fond of scorpions, neither." Lamont's voice was slightly shaky and definitely high-pitched. "We're just lucky we didn't get bitten!"

Liz looked a bit crestfallen. "I'm sorry. I don't really understand this magic stuff too well."

Lamont raised his eyes to heaven. "Well, why don't you leave it to somebody who does understand it? Like Medea."

Medea's reaction was quite different. She was staring at the cobras and scorpions with admiration. "You *must* teach me that spell, darling Liz."

Liz glared at Lamont. "Quit grousing! *You're* the Cushite sorceress. *You're* the one who's supposed to be doing the spells."

Lamont felt his jaw. "And I've got the lumps and bruises to prove it. Damn Jerry and his crazy ideas!" he said thickly. "I've got a hangover on top of it all."

"Shhh. Somebody's at the door," whispered Liz.

Indeed, outside the cell they could hear a heavy bar being raised. The stone slab door on the far side of the cell swung open to reveal three soldiers, with spears at the ready.

Ready for three *prisoners*. Less than ready for an equal number of angry Egyptian cobras. The door had just missed one. The three snakes swayed in unison, hoods flared. Which might still have been okay if a scorpion hadn't marched up the one fellow's sandal and set off further upward, exploring cheerfully. The guard's eyes, already the size of golf balls, got wider.

"Kill it, Bedety! Kill it!" The guard's teeth were clenched. He stood as if flash-frozen.

His companion was about to calmly flick it off with a spear point . . . when a scorpion walked onto *his* foot. The spear point jabbed as he stamped and danced clear.

"Yeow!" yelled the stab victim, as the spear point jabbed him on the inner thigh. Of course the stab missed the scorpion. The alarmed creature scuttled higher, aiming for the safety of the kilt.

"Horus' Eye! The floor is alive with these scorpions!" The third soldier was backing off, his voice shaky.

The scorpion, for which the stab victim was frantically searching under his kilt, must have reacted as frightened scorpions do. The poor man shrieked and flung his spear away. He missed a cobra by a hairsbreadth and nearly took out Liz's toes. The angry cobras struck at the guards. . . .

Up the passages they could still hear the panic-stricken yells as the guards ran. The words *"Cushite sorceress!"* were the most frequently repeated. Liz used the abandoned spear to persuade the cobras to let them pass, and the trio walked off into the passages, away from the yelling.

Hearing the sound of panicky female voices added to those of the guards, Liz paused for a moment to study the ornamentation of the hallway.

"Congratulations, Lamont," she chuckled. "I think you've achieved every man's fantasy. We're locked into the Harem."

✦　　✦　　✦

The eunuchs guarding the Harem might be lackadaisical in their attitude to prisoners. But as Jerry, Cruz, Mac and Henri had learned, the regular soldiers of Sebek's army were *not*. Merely being trussed and tossed into a cell would have been the height of luxury for the "official" men of the party. Instead they'd been hung on the ends of offertory poles. Their gags had been refreshed. The poles were long and pivotable, rather like those used for a shaduf. A weight at one end counterbalanced the dangling humans, who were then swung out over the lake. Glancing from side to side, Jerry thought they looked for all the world like a row of fishing poles with baits about to drop into the water.

In the limpid water below, the crocodiles were beginning to gather.

At least they weren't hanging upside-down. On the other hand, that would have meant the crocodiles got the head-end first. Once you'd lost your head, at least your troubles were over. This way it would last longer—although, to judge by the gaping maws, not *much* longer.

Jerry had been thinking about what was required for Egyptian magic. It was unusual in that mere mortals could, given the correct words and intonation and use of secret names, compel even gods to serve them. All that was required of a magician was that he should be an "appropriately constituted authority."

And he *did* have a Ph.D., after all. Now if only he had the ability to speak.

The women in the colonnaded room that Lamont, Liz and Medea had entered were proving that they certainly had the ability to shriek. Their weaving abandoned in a chaos of scattered skeins, they huddled together in the far corner of the room and attempted to deafen their "attackers"—or, at the very least, lift the roof.

"Don't kill us, Sorceress," begged the elderly nineteen-year-old matron of the crowd, who was a veritable Methuselah compared to the others.

"If you don't scream again," said Liz, brandishing the spear.

She might as well have been waving a stick of limp celery for all the attention the scantily clad damsels paid to her. "*Eeee!!!!*" they shrieked.

"Oh—shut up!" snarled Lamont, clutching his head. "I'm still feeling a bit fragile." He said it in rather a gruff voice.

There was a silence. A long jelly-like silence.

"She's a *man*," whispered a girl with a particularly ornate hairdo. Her expression went from one of fear to one of predatory interest. "*A man!*"

Lamont instantly realized two things, which had taken Faust far more time to understand. Firstly, fantasies are more fun as fantasies than as realities. Secondly, no matter what trouble you're in, it can almost always get worse. A minute later, he had his dress hitched up around his thighs and he was sprinting away with Liz and Medea behind him, and a pack of young women behind them.

"Why did you run?" panted Liz.

Lamont risked a hasty glance back. "There must have been forty women in there. They'd have torn me to shreds. Quick. Up here."

Behind them, Sebek's Harem echoed to the sounds of two packs of relentless hunters. One of the groups of pursuers, the eunuchs, was so heavily laden with jangling charms and amulets that a fast shuffle was all they could manage. The other ranged from scantily clad on down, and were making very good time.

Among the crocodile-god's faults, plainly enough, was neglect of his Harem. Maybe he was cold-blooded. Maybe he preferred lady crocodiles. Or maybe several dozen young women chosen for their attractiveness and high libido were simply too much for one old croc.

Whatever the reason, they were lighter and more effective in their pursuit. And in their effort to elude these faster pursuers, Liz, Medea and Lamont found themselves eventually boxed in. Cornered by both groups, when they finally fled out onto the flat roof.

They backed into the far corner. Only the bickering between the two groups had so far prevented either side's success. Now Lamont, Liz and Medea faced stark choices. Up. Down. Or capture . . .

Short of flapping their arms very, very fast, "up" was a

nonavailable course. "Capture" was, as far as Lamont was concerned, no option either. The pursuing houris had betrayed Lamont's sex to the amulet-laden eunuchs. The Harem guards, clearly enough, were planning to recruit him to their ranks.

That left *down*. Into the lake. Well, it wasn't more than thirty-five feet. Which is awfully high, until you are faced with such choices.

A drum throbbed in the distance. The sun beat down on the rooftop.

The eunuch guards made no attempt to cut them off from the wall. Nobody would ever dream of leaping over that low balustrade and down into the lake of crocodiles. The eunuchs and the houris watched incredulously as the three hopped up onto the wall.

Medea looked down into the clear water. "I can't swim," she said quietly.

Liz took a firm grip on Medea's tunic. "You concentrate on holding your breath when you hit the water, and *don't panic.* I'll do the rest."

"Come down from there, you fool fake sorceress!" bellowed the porky chief eunuch-guard. "Before you kill yourself!"

"Why shouldn't I beat you to it?" Lamont swayed on the narrow wall. "I am not a fake sorcerer! Beware lest I call a rain of scorpions and nightsoil on your head. I call on my protective genii Malarky and Prostaglandin to smite you down. May..." he needed some names, desperately. He only picked them up to pun with... "May Tauret trample your entrails. I summons Bes, may he tear your head off, and push it up your posterior. May Apep spit in your eye..."

The porky guard poked his spear at him. The watching houris squealed as Lamont flailed wildly and toppled with a yell off the wall.

"Let's go!" barked Liz. "I don't know how well Lamont swims in a dress."

Being fed to the crocodiles was bad enough, thought Jerry, but did they have to turn them all into raisins first? It was hot and windless. His head was throbbing.

It seemed unreasonable to die with a headache. Wasn't being eaten alive bad enough? Jerry realized that he was somewhat lightheaded. He was at the stage of feeling as if this life belonged to someone else. Then he realized that the throbbing wasn't actually inside his head. It was someone playing a drum. Slowly and steadily. The offertory poles were being lowered towards the water. The crocodiles were nearly solid under them.

It's at times like these that most brains go on strike. Jerry's brain simply got angry. It wasn't prepared to have its vehicle eaten just yet. There were things it still wanted to think about. It spat out an order: *Subvocalize. They're gods, dammit.*

Jerry did his best. The gag peeled away.

"*I call on the Bes, the defender against noxious creatures.*

"*I banish you, Creatures of Sebek, by your true name Crocodylus niloticus.*"

He hoped that was right. He'd gotten it from Liz, the day before, as they'd made their way up the Myth-Nile. It was as close to a "true name" as anyone could come up with.

"*Begone! Thrice I tell you.*

"*Begone. Begone. Begone.*

"*By Harmakhis, I call on the genii of the east to lambaste and lithify you.*

"*I call on the genii of the south to pulverize*

"*and send down plagues of pyretic pustules . . .*"

A team of priests was furiously swinging the offertory pole inward. A flung javelin narrowly missed his cheek. Jerry looked down. No crocs . . .

"*I call on Osiris, by the names Bennu, Djed, Mendes and Onuphis.*

"*Make this rope as frail as corn before the sickle.*

"*Seker, corrupt and rot these bindings—*"

"Shit! Doc—NO!" yelled Cruz, as he spat the gag bindings off.

But it was too late by then. They dropped like overripe fruit into the water.

Cruz had thought that it was all over. He'd been trying to work out whether he could flex his legs enough to kick the first croc on the snout when he'd caught sight of something in the periphery of his vision. It was Lamont, Medea and Liz, on the top of the one wing of the huge temple. Then Doc had suddenly started to spout. Then Lamont had fallen, followed by Liz and Medea jumping. To his horror, he saw crocodiles streaming like arrows towards the three of them, who were threshing their way towards the reedy shore.

In a way, the Doc's incantation had worked. The crocs had left them to seek prey that was already in the water. Then, just as he was able to speak, the ropes parted.

Liz lost her grip on Medea as they hit the water. Medea having gone rigid, went straight down. Liz took a deep breath and duck-dived after her. She nearly met her head-on coming up. She grabbed the struggling Medea lifesaving style, just as the woman was going down again. The clinging dress was a menace. You couldn't possibly do a scissors kick in it. She grabbed it and ripped. Time enough to worry about appearances if they survived. Those were javelins hitting the water. And not that far away either.

She looked around for Lamont, saw him a few yards off doing a determined doggy-paddle crawl. She looked at Medea, who had stopped struggling but had suddenly given a little moan of fear. Liz saw the cause of Medea's cry. There was a V of crocodiles coming for them, led by a monster. A crocodile at least twenty-four feet long. More like a ship than a croc. It had a golden collar, and golden rings through the eye-ridges. And that switching tail drove it through the water like an oversized outboard motor.

Then she saw the others about a hundred yards off, splashing down into the water.

The crocodiles were closing in. They swam faster than the three of them could. They'd get Lamont first. Liz wanted to close her eyes. She just didn't know what she could do. For one of the few times in her life, Elizabeth Maria De Beer was at a total loss. She wanted to scream.

Water erupted around Lamont.

Liz screamed.

35

⊡⊐⊐⊐⊐⊐⊡

TO GET TO THE OTHER SIDE,
FOR SOME FOWL REASON.

It rose like Leviathan. Water streamed from the gray expanse. Liz saw Lamont, facing the tail end, cling desperately to the broadness of a giant hippopotamus' back. It threw back its massive head, exposing huge teeth, and gave that peculiar groaning bellow which is a hippo's warning cry.

Liz was too frightened to speak. She was nearly too frightened to swim. Hippos kill far more people every year in Africa than crocodiles do. They're curious, territorial, dangerous, enormous and fast.

This one seemed to have an aversion to crocodiles. Normally, hippos treat crocodiles with contempt and occasionally to a spot of abuse. Normally, hippos work cooperatively in herds to make this possible. But this one, having bellowed its challenge, was heading for the shore along with its clinging and wild-eyed passenger.

Jerry realized, too late, that the crocodiles hadn't "begone" very far. That they were likely to reach the others before they could gain the shore—and then he plunged into the lake himself. The

281

sacrificial victims had a far, far longer swim ahead of them than Lamont, Medea and Liz.

He went down like a stone, and then rose to the surface, spluttering. The water was prickled with javelins. And then something knocked stones flying from the temple wall. The huge squared blocks could have killed him, but they'd missed. And at least the javelins had stopped.

A gruff voice spoke from the water beside him. "Well, foreigner. You do like to lead an exciting life, don't you?"

It was Bes. Somehow, sharing crocodile-infested water with the protector was a lot more comforting.

"We must . . . " A wave hit him in the face. He choked and spluttered. "Help the others, Bes! Crocodiles!"

Bes chuckled, treading water. "Between Tauret and the sphinxes, the crocodiles haven't got a holy Shu's chance in a furnace. A pity. I feel like knocking old Petesuchos, the king crocodile, about a bit. Establishes a decent respect."

Jerry realized he'd swallowed an awful lot of water. Then he saw a winged monster snatch Cruz from the water.

"She'll be back for you, in a minute or two," said Bes.

"But that's the Greek sphinx! What's she doing here? And isn't she just going to eat him?"

"Not if he can answer her riddle." Bes grinned even more broadly. "And that one was old when Nun the first god was a boy." In a hoarse singsong: "*What walks with four legs . . .* "

A short while later, Jerry found himself transported to shore, some distance from the temple. Henri and Cruz were already there. So were Liz, Medea and a pale gray Lamont. There was also an enormous woman with a gray hippo head, which was beaded with pink sweat. And the gigantic Egyptian sphinx. With his nose still attached. It had, after all, only been hacked off by a Muslim zealot in the fifteenth century. Squatting alongside the Greek sphinx, the Egyptian one made even that monster seemed small.

"Well, Jerry," said Lamont in a shaky voice. "You know, for a moment there I thought I saw Chicago again. It was so real!"

Jerry swallowed. His entire stomach seemed to be a bag of water. "For a moment you were nearly dead then," he said quietly.

The Egyptian sphinx was colored red, blue and yellow, which the Pharaoh Thutmose IV had had it painted. Jerry leaned his head against the huge forepaw and was thoroughly sick. Fortunately for him, the giant sphinx seemed more bemused by the episode than anything else. Even, perhaps, a little apprehensive.

"Is it something I said?" rumbled the avalanche voice.

"I thought about your offer," said the Greek sphinx to Lamont. "And I'll take you up on it. Another riddle for my help."

Lamont sat upright. He'd been cradling his head in his hands, feeling sorry for himself. "All right. But no eating anyone you've been introduced to. What do you think, Jerry?"

Jerry sat upright, from where he'd flopped against the big stone-but-alive Egyptian sphinx's legs. "Hell. What do you mean, Lamont? You want a riddle? I dunno. 'Why does the chicken cross the road?'"

Lamont gave a wry grin. "That'll do. Why does the chicken cross the road, sphinx?"

"I don't know. Tell me," demanded the Greek sphinx.

"Not until I introduce you to everyone," said Lamont dryly.

The sphinx smiled. "I could get to like you, Ethiope. But why will this riddle be any different from the last one? You humans gossip so. Pretty soon everyone will know this one and I'll be back where I started. Hungry all of the time."

Lamont shook his head. "There are two answers."

"So?"

Lamont folded his arms on his chest. Smiled. "So . . . *you* decide which is the right one."

The Greek sphinx mulled over this. And slowly began to smile toothily. "That makes the answer given always wrong, if I say so. *How nice.* How tasty! What's your name, Ethiope? You can call me Throttler."

"Lamont Jackson."

Bes, hands on his hips, grinned at Throttler. "I don't think I'll tell you my name. You want to make something of it?"

"As if everyone and everything hasn't heard of you, Bes," snorted the hippopotamus-headed Tauret, summoned by Lamont's curse. "Anyway, I must be off. Work to do. Babies to catch."

✧   ✧   ✧

Cruz looked up from his important task of comforting Medea, across at Crocodilopolis. The stone-like Egyptian sphinx must have walked across the temple on his way here, smashing it up good. And plainly some of the other curses had come to rest on it. But a party of priests, their shaven heads gleaming in the sun, were heading out of the temple. Behind them came a huge mob of soldiers.

"I'm Cruz, this is Medea, that's Liz and Mac, Henri and Doc. Now we're all introduced, can we get the hell out of here?"

Henri looked up from where he was gloomily inspecting his ruined shoes, and saw the group advancing out of Crocodilopolis. "*Merde*. Let the big sphinx go and walk on them."

Cruz shook his head. "There is one thing you've gotta learn, Frenchy. About as dumb as you can get is to think you've always got the upper hand 'cause you're bigger than the other guy. I'll bet the locals have got an 'equalizer' or they wouldn't be coming after us."

Mac looked up at the sphinx. Even reclining it was about sixty feet tall. "Self-propelled howitzers?"

"In local terms, spells," said Jerry. His voice was faint, but he sounded like he was feeling better.

Mac slapped him on the back. "Well, we've got our own magician."

"Yes. And we have our own Cushite sorceress," said Medea.

The "Cushite sorceress" looked at the advancing mob. "I think it's time to run like hell. There are some eunuchs in that bunch."

Traveling on sphinx-back had numerous disadvantages and extreme discomforts. There was absolutely no give in Harmakhis. Stone surfaces, even living stone, are just plain hard. But there was one huge advantage. Distance. They'd outpaced the pursuing chariots in minutes. Now, sitting in a bleak desert valley, they were as safe as possible in the Mythworlds. Needless to say, among the pleasures of life that they didn't have were food and water. Still, they were all alive and intact, which had seemed unlikely earlier.

They sat in the shade of Harmakhis and compared notes. Jerry peered at the Greek sphinx, who was fanning herself with her wings. "There's just one thing I'd like to know, Throttler. What are you doing here? This is a world of Egyptian myth. You're a Greek sphinx."

Throttler shrugged. Having wings really helps you to do that expressively. "I can go anywhere that has those that believe in the sphinx. Almost all sphinxes are linked in origin. Once we were desert genii. Some of those powers remain wherever there is a sphinx statue. I wasn't sure that I'd find you here, but with those two dragons making so much fuss about Egypt, I thought it worth trying."

"Not me," Harmakhis rumbled. "I can't go outside of Egypt, I don't think."

Bes chortled. "I can! I can go to Punt, where I came from. Or anywhere within the Phoenician world. Carthage too. But it's a dump."

Jerry sighed. "I'm just trying to work out what's going on. We got whisked from our lives into a world or . . . or . . . a universe or something, which only exists in hoary old legends back home."

The dwarf wasn't grinning for once. Instead he was looking intent. "And just how did this happen?"

How did you explain space-time-travel to a primitive god? Simple: by skipping most of it. "This pyramid appeared. And it started snatching people."

Bes' eyes narrowed. "A five-sided pyramid?"

That much Jerry had learned from Halstrom. "Yes. Five sides."

Bes nodded. "The same device is corrupting the gods. It has come promising a new and powerful time in what it calls our 'Ur-universe.' It has come to prepare the way for its masters, the Krim. As soon as there are enough new believers, it will begin the great revival. At present only parts of Ur-Egypt are existent. Old legends are being reenacted with these new ones."

Throttler shook his head. "Whatever you do, don't go along with it. This Krim-master has arrived in the universe of the Hellenes. Things are going back to the bad old days of human sacrifice and cannibalism. War is raging. Ares rides out in his chariot spreading devastation. I have seen just such a pyramid on a pendant around his neck."

"Your warning is too late," Bes growled sourly. "Set, and some of the others, like Sekmet, have already gone in with this pyramid scheme. They say it will make them rich and powerful. Ha. Each of them gives a small portion of their powers and self-control to this Krim device. I'll bet who or whatever is at the head of it will become the new power, not the old gods. They're a lot of fools... even if the old places *were* falling apart."

"Throttler. This war. It has not raged across Aeaea, has it?" asked Medea in a small voice.

Throttler gave her a smile. "Your children are safe, Medea of Colchis. I was there looking for you not two days ago. The wars ravage Thrace and Boeotia. You 'Americans' even have some of your own loyalists sitting in Asia Minor, in Mytilene on Lesbos. They're a sorry lot. All the real warrior gods and goddesses have gone in with the pyramid scheme."

Jerry took a deep breath. "You say the—'Krim,' is it?—are actually there in Myth-Greece? I suppose we should call it Ur-Greece. Anyway, they're present in Ur-Greece—but whatever is here in Egypt is merely some sort of servant. Well, I hate to say this because I've actually learned to do some 'spells' here and I've got some degree of power, but I think we should go back to Ur-Greece and take on the masters not the servant. If we can."

Throttler shrugged her enormous wings. "I can take you back. I'd have to do a couple of trips, mind you. I'm strong but I can't manage all of you at once."

"And me, little cousin?" Harmakhis rumbled tectonically. The huge sphinx sounded as if it found the idea quite funny.

Throttler shrugged. "I'm afraid you'd have to walk."

"It's all right, little cousin," said the huge living-stone sphinx. "I was only teasing because you were boastful of your strength. I think I'll stay here, and organize resistance against this pyramid. It has too many sides. We should rather buy Egyptian."

The Greek sphinx muttered something. But she muttered it very quietly.

Jerry turned to the others. "Well? What do we do? I'm for returning to ancient Greece."

Medea looked at him curiously, as if really seeing him properly for the first time. "I, of course, wish to go home to my children. Back to Ur-Greece. But you, Doc Jerry, are the proof that appearances lead to deceive. You are the slightest of all of these Americans, yet you are the one who is most ready for battle. A battle against Olympus itself."

"What about me, then?" demanded Bes, sticking his tongue out at her. "I'm smaller than him and I'm even more ready for a fight."

Medea stuck her own tongue out at the aggressive bandy-legged dwarf. Knowing her children were reasonably safe had eased some of the small lines of tension about her face. Knowing that she could return to them had made her near radiant. Anibal Cruz was staring at her with the intensity of a man who has just moved from an infatuation to love. "I'm with Medea," he said gruffly. He was rewarded with a hug.

But the sorceress was in a chaffing mood. "Bes, you would fight the tide! Anibal, you are a warrior. But that's not the point. Bes loves to fight. Doc Jerry does not. But he will. Even though it means surrendering his power as a magician. Here he is very powerful. In my—what did you call it, Ur-universe—he is a man, who is not a warrior, going to challenge the might of Olympus. Here in Egypt the might of the mind and the words is great. Greater than the sword. Where he is going, the sword has far more power."

Jerry looked excessively uncomfortable. "I know a lot about the myths. I can probably work things out. And somebody's got to try and stop this thing. They don't seem to be having much luck with stopping it in Chicago. Maybe, just maybe, we can do something from the inside. I may not manage it, but I'll give it a try."

Liz laughed. "Yes. Lamont wants to talk to you about a few of the things you worked out and tried. Anyway, count me in."

Jerry gave her a shy thumbs-up. "It's a pity that we can't count on that lethal shoulder bag of yours anymore."

Liz shrugged. "The only one who didn't lose nearly everything was Cruz. I don't know why Bes should find his rucksack and yet not discover the 'lethal weapon.' Lamont lost that precious boombox of his, too."

McKenna rubbed his itching scalp. A thin red fuzz was sprouting. "He's got room to complain. The guy's born lucky. He got to be the only man in a harem, while the rest of us got fed to the crocs. I'd have thought I'd died and gone to heaven."

Lamont snorted. "Mac, you might have found there were a few 'short cuts' to take on the way to your heaven." He clutched himself reflexively, and then, embarrassed, thrust his hands behind his back. "Those eunuchs wanted to give me a job—after they punched my ticket, so to speak. I'd have swapped places with you in a heartbeat. Anyway, Jerry, I'm in. I've got a wife and children I want to get back to. But I think we're looking at the thin end of the wedge here. Not only are more people like us going to end up in this mess . . . "

"What? In torn women's clothing?" teased Mac.

Lamont quelled him with a look and continued as if he hadn't been interrupted. "But I figure there are men, women and children as real as Medea in trouble. Sometimes, brother, you've got to lend a hand. If we can stop this thing, let's do it."

"You've got me convinced, Lamont," said Cruz. "Not that I see quite what we are going to do. Only two of us are soldiers."

Lamont shrugged. "Jerry will come up with some ideas. Or Liz will bully them out of him. But I draw the line at wearing a tight dress again."

Jerry smiled. "No. Next time it's a g-string and nipple caps. Look Mac, I don't want to argue with you but . . . well, modern history shows that soldiers win fights, even battles, but to win major wars you've got have the support of the people. You've got to convince everyone. Once ordinary people are ready to fight—yes, and get killed too—they're a force to be reckoned with. Soldiers without public support will eventually lose."

Lamont and Liz both nodded.

Mac shrugged. He plainly wasn't convinced.

Jerry turned to the Frenchman, who was admiring the Greek sphinx's frontage. "And you, Lenoir? I can organize things here so that you get reasonably well looked after."

The botanist bristled. "I did not speak because it was not necessary! For the honor of France I cannot allow you Americans to claim all the glory. And the food here is *horrifique*—it has given me 'the run.'"

"You watch who you call an American, *Skatlam*," said Liz. "And I think you mean the 'the runs.'"

"Ah. You are also afflicted?"

36

RADIO-ACTIVE CAR-PARK.

Tremelo shook his head. "That's insanity. Look, we just don't know enough about it yet. We have only the one survivor—"

Milliken shrugged. "Unfortunately, he's still in the intensive care unit, and it appears that his mental state is . . . precarious. He certainly can't tell us much." The NSC man squared his shoulders. "The United States Government can't be perceived as just sitting on its hands while the lightning strikes, Professor Tremelo. Steps must be seen to be taken."

Tremelo steepled his fingers and glanced at Marie Jackson. His new assistant had been bringing two cups of coffee into his office and had heard Milliken's last remark. Seeing her eyes roll sarcastically, Miggy fought down a laugh.

"Mister Milliken. Steps seen to be taken, *which fail or backfire,* are far worse for our prestige. News about the effect of the bomb-pumped laser leaked. We've stopped that leak. But the fact is, we gave it our best shot, and the result was that the pyramid *grew* by twenty-three percent and increased its snatch radius to over two miles."

Marie set the coffee cups down in front of Tremelo and Milliken. Tremelo nodded his head in thanks. As Marie walked

289

back toward her own little office, now behind Milliken's back, she began making vigorous motions with her arms. As if she were swinging a sledgehammer. Miggy *really* had to struggle not to laugh this time.

The sight of Milliken's expression—Official Set Upon Upholding The Party Line—quelled his amusement. Tremelo leaned forward and spoke forcefully. "It is *not* true, for starters, that we have 'not progressed at all.' We've so far made three important discoveries."

He began ticking off on his fingers. "First, that the alien artifact absorbs all the energy we put into trying to penetrate or destroy it. The energy taken in is directly proportional to its growth. Second, it grows in size and increases its snatch range by a small but measurable amount for each victim. Third—and most important, in my opinion—we've established that if you've been inside the perimeter for at least five hours, and not been snatched—you appear to be safe."

Milliken shrugged. "That's all very well, Professor. But the White House wants action that the world can see, not mere information. I quite understand your viewpoint as a *scientist*, but—"

Tremelo ground his teeth. "Look. The action proposed would, let's see ... at a rough estimate ... "

He did some quick calculations in his head. "If the tactical nuclear device fails to destroy the pyramid—and I see no reason whatsoever to think that it will succeed—it will increase the pyramid size to plus-or-minus thirty times the size it is now. It would increase the snatch radius to one hundred fifty miles. Damn near from here to Detroit. An area over three hundred miles across would become a no-go area, except for the people the pyramid has refused to take. The pyramid appears to select one person in ten. Mr. Milliken, do you have any idea of how many victims we'd have if there was a sudden increase like that? Or are you proposing that scale of evacuation? We lost sixty-seven people in the last sudden expansion. That also goes into pyramid growth, remember."

"Detroit!" This NSC man was considerably more intelligent than Harkness had been. Despite his "official certitude," he was badly shaken.

"Yes," said Tremelo. "Victim numbers in the hundreds of

thousands—to be conservative. *Now* do you understand why I said it was the stupidest idea I'd ever heard of? And that's not all. We've established that the thing is moving. Satellite imaging shows us the apex of the pyramid has shifted about five meters since landing, to the northwest. Extrapolating on a straight line, the thing is headed directly toward the spot which was formerly occupied by the west stands of Staggs Field."

That item of information clearly meant nothing to Milliken. Tremelo explained: "That is *exactly* where the first controlled nuclear fission reaction took place, back during World War II."

Milliken's face was still blank with incomprehension. Tremelo was unable to completely suppress his anger. "*Think, damn it!* What drew that alien device to Earth in the first place? What signaled our existence to it? What was it homing on?"

Milliken wasn't actually stupid. His eyes began to widen.

Miggy nodded. "That's right. *Nuclear power.* I'm now almost certain that thing is an unmanned probe, guided by artificial intelligence." His lips quirked. "Un-*aliened* probe, I should say. But if I'm right, it means it's programmed to hit a certain target, and is now making the final adjustment. It was the fact that we developed a nuclear capability which attracted alien attention in the first place. Which, in turn, tells me that this thing they sent isn't in the *least* bit worried about a nuclear counterstrike."

Miggy frowned. "Almost the opposite, actually—I'm seriously beginning to think it's trying to provoke us into using one."

Milliken took a deep breath. "I'll make this very clear to the NSC, Professor. But we need to do *something*."

Tremelo stared at him. " 'Do something,' " he mimicked savagely. "When you don't know what you're doing, Milliken, 'doing something' can be as stupid as removing an appendix with a chain saw."

"The government's *got* to do *something*," repeated Milliken. "It'll look bad if we don't."

The Krim device waited. Only twice in the nearly 300 civilizations that the Krim had parasitized had the massive nuclear energy boost it required failed to materialize. Once that threshold was crossed the prukrin dynamic was irreversible.

PART VIII

There may be in the cup
A spider steep'd, and one may drink, depart,
And yet partake no venom . . .

—William Shakespeare,
The Winter's Tale

37

SITTING ON A TUFFET.

The sphinx literally moved between sphinx images or statues. The molding on the temple in Asia Minor owed more to the Persian period of Phoenician history than it did to ancient Greek settlements in Asia Minor. But that didn't seem to worry Throttler.

High above in the clear sky were two gleaming tasseled bronze arrows, diving inwards. Medea's dragons had been waiting.

Bitar and Smitar were beside themselves. They squirmed, bounced and fawned around Lamont, as if he'd just returned from the dead.

"ʃStarving! We haven't had a bite . . . juʃst thoʃse ʃseamen. Nothing. ʃSince you left uʃs!" Smitar's accusing, soup-plate-sized slanty eyes were full of misery.

Bitar nodded. "Yeʃs. And they were *much* too ʃsalty."

"We need ʃsome chewy food. We're teething." Smitar proudly displayed tiny flecks of white in his pink gums.

"ʃSome ʃsquid would be niʃce." Biter showed his gums too. And then the sphinx turned up with Cruz. Liz's assessment of the bio-dynamics of a flying creature the size of the sphinx was not inaccurate. Only with effort could Throttler carry more than one adult human.

Still. The "gap" between Ur-Egypt and a sphinx in Ur-Greece seemed to be a narrow one. She was able to ferry them "through" quite fast. The dragons left Lamont to cavort around Cruz.

"How old are they?" Lamont asked.

Medea shrugged. "Quite young, I think. My grandfather stole the eggs from the mountain eyrie. About sixty years old, I suppose. They're very slow growing. And quite rare. Apparently they do not breed until they are at least half a century old. And they lay very few eggs."

Liz, standing nearby, began to understand why the species might have become extinct.

The small coastal town, with its sphinx-guarded temple, was abandoned. Understandably, as the dragons had been hanging around for a few days.

Looking at the nets hung out to dry, Jerry cleared his throat. "Look, this is what I suggest. Let's feed Bitar and Smitar . . . "

"Good idea!" Bitar caressed him affectionately with a long forked snaky tongue. At least Jerry hoped it was a caress. Snakes tasted with their tongues, didn't they?

"Yefs! Ecfthallent!" agreed Smitar, sticking a snaky tongue-point into Jerry's ear.

"Shut up. Let him finish," said Medea. "Go on, Doc Jerry."

"Um, as I was saying, get them full of gas. Then hook up one of those nets . . . "

"Can we use it to catch fsome fsquid firfst?"

"Shut up, Bitar. Or I won't scratch you any more," said Cruz.

"Hook the net between the two of them and get Throttler to tow it. That should be much lighter for the dragons than a chariot, and much faster than their 'swimming' through the air."

"One of you dragons wouldn't like a fight, would you? I haven't fought anything like you before," said the small bowlegged man, clad only in a loincloth and his short leopard-skin cloak.

"Bes! What the hell are you doing here?" demanded Liz.

Bes scratched his topknot so that the ostrich plumes danced. "Told you. I came for the fighting. My sort of fight, against the odds. Besides, I'm the Protector. I've got a feeling you might need me. Oy! Leave off with the hugging!"

✧   ✧   ✧

The concept worked remarkably well. Of course, in practice it meant you only had some flax cord from a fishing net between you and a long fall. The sphinx needed to take advantage of thermals to fly any real distance. That meant getting up really high. A long way above that wrinkled landscape.

Looking across the water from a height, they could see a dark pall to the west. "Greece. It is burning," said Throttler grimly.

Jerry clung to the netting. The four layers of net seemed pretty fragile from up here. But he was doing better than Henri, who had been sick several times. The Frenchman was gray and sweating, and rather blue around the lips.

Still, by the time the sun was sinking and the thermals were getting harder to find, they'd covered many miles.

They landed in an open meadow, in the late afternoon. The sphinx and the dragons were tired. Besides, the dragons needed regassing. The rest of the party, glad to be on terra firma, set off for a small village they'd seen from the air. It looked like there were about six little buildings, surrounded by a patchwork of fields and gray-green olive groves on a little plateau above the blue Aegean. It hardly seemed a threat, and it beat hunting for food. They could trade some metal, and everyone would be happy. Bitar and Smitar didn't understand why they could not come along.

"Phtt! Why do you want to trade for food when we can frighten them all off and just help ourfselvefs?" hissed Smitar.

"Yefs, and maybe there'll be some maidenfs." Bitar was ever hopeful. "I fstill want to tafste maidenfs cooked American-fstyle."

Cruz raised his eyes to heaven. "Just stay here, willya? Please."

The dragons were putty in his hands. "All right, Cruz."

"You promifse to bring back fsomething nifce?"

"Do our best. Promise," he said, giving them each a farewell pat with the butt of his spear.

The seven of them set out, leaving Henri, who still did not look well, to recover from the flight with the resting sphinx and dragons.

✧   ✧   ✧

The path led down into a little valley. In the olive groves, between the twisted and pitted gray trunks, they suddenly discovered just what a mistake leaving the dragons behind had been.

Liz was the first to hear it. "There is something in the bushes . . . "

And there was also something between the trees. Webs.

Cruz stepped forward to break the web. The looted spear was no substitute for the steel of his bayonet, lost back when the priests of Sebek had captured them. But the solid spear shaft would make short work of a spider web.

"No, Cruz." McKenna grabbed his arm, and held him back from smashing the web.

The burly sergeant looked puzzled. "It's just a spider web, Mac. And it's between us and the village."

"Yeah, but you don't have to break it," said McKenna. "Or at least let me take the spider out before you do."

He leaned forward and let the spider walk up onto his arm.

Cruz gaped. "You crazy, Mac? It'll bite you, man!"

McKenna shook his head. "Not unless I scare it or try to squash it. Here, spidey. Climb onto this bush. You'll be safe there."

Cruz shook his head. "It's just a goddamn spider, Mac."

McKenna shrugged. "They're good little critters. Never do any harm and they eat lots of pests."

The myrtle bushes shuddered. "You are a very wise man," said someone with a voice like the tinkling of chimes. The webs and bushes were suddenly alive with spiders. Myriads of them. Enough to swarm over a small army, never mind a handful of travelers.

Medea clung to Cruz.

"What the hell . . . " muttered Lamont.

The spiders moved aside to allow passage to a giant among their kind. The spider coming forward was huge . . . for a spider. At the same time she was delicate. And she was definitely a she. She had a very feminine head. Feminine and human, with beautiful, luminous dark eyes, framed by long lashes. Her cascading tresses were pinned with a fine silver comb. A few strands fell back onto her long spider body.

Jerry cleared his throat. "Arachne, the daughter of Idomon of Colophon, I presume."

"You're very cool for a man who is moments away from death." The spiderwoman's voice was very musical.

McKenna had gone down on his haunches. "Your voice is nearly as lovely as your face."

"You have a very smooth tongue." She didn't sound displeased about it. "Now, explain. Why do armed men come creeping down on my father's estate by the back trail?"

"We were just passing through," said Cruz, in as calm a voice as possible. "We were hoping to buy some food."

"Buy? With spears? And traveling across the mountains! A likely story," she tinkled scathingly.

Cruz threw out his hands. Nearly dropped his spear. "For God's sake! We left the dragons and the sphinx behind, so that we didn't frighten anyone."

"Appealing to me in the name of the gods is unlikely to get you any sympathy," snapped Arachne.

"Does the fact that we're trying to attack Olympus alter that?" asked Jerry.

"Attack Olympus?" Again, the tinkling scoff. "*Another* likely story!"

Jerry sighed. "Sounds crazy, doesn't it? And, to be honest, I've got no inkling of an idea just how we are going to set about doing it."

"But we're tired of being victims, lady-spider," said Lamont. "We're going to take the fight back to them. Somehow."

Arachne seemed to relax slightly. "You are plainly mad. Not that I don't agree with you. But not even one of my spider-sisters can scale the cold heights of Olympus. And when it comes to power, not even the great Titans could overthrow the Olympians."

Lamont spoke up. "Hey, Jerry. How's about if we enlisted the Titan Prometheus?"

"Hmm . . . " Jerry pursed his lips, considering the idea. "It's a thought, now that you raise it. He *should* be chained up to Mount Caucasus."

One thing at a time, he reminded himself. He turned back to Arachne. "Honest, ma'am. We're just passing through. Apparently there are a few others gathered on Lesbos. Ares is ravaging mainland Greece."

"My spider-sisters say that half of Thrace is burning. And there are cruel sacrifices being demanded in the other half. But whatever the Olympians are doing, it is yet confined to the area around the mountain. We are prepared here, however. The Olympian gods are capricious and cruel. They and their servants will not leave Lydia in peace for long. You stumbled into one of the traps we have prepared for their reivers."

"Well, can we stumble out?" asked Jerry, carefully suppressing any arachnophobic thoughts. "All we want to do is to buy some food, and then we'll be on our way. You can even keep the rest of us here. Mac can go and dicker about some food, and then we'll leave."

The spiderwoman nodded. "My sisters confirm: there are two dragons, a sphinx and a man resting in the high pasture. Come, follow me."

"Listen, Doc," said McKenna quietly as they walked along. "You obviously know who she is. How come she's a spider?"

Jerry grimaced. "For the same reason I never really liked working on ancient Greek mythology. She was a skilled human weaver. She dared to challenge Athena to a weaving competition. There are variations to the story, but basically she chose as a subject the philandering of the gods of Olympus. And she *did* weave better than Athena. Either for her disrespectful choice of subject or because she was a better weaver, Athena turned her into a spider, doomed to weave eternally, and to spin her own thread from her body. There is another version, which has Athena destroying her work in a rage and the girl committing suicide and being changed into a spider out of pity. It seems that here, anyway, you can guess the former story to be the true one."

McKenna ground his teeth. "You mean she was human and some so-called goddess did this to her 'cause she just couldn't cut it in competition with a human?"

Jerry pulled a wry face. "That about sizes it up, yes."

McKenna's eyes narrowed. His normally cheerful face was hard. Jerry was just glad not to be on the wrong side of the man when he looked this serious. "Look Doc, I admit I don't know one hell of a lot about this mythology stuff. But I thought

Athena was one of the good guys. This is a bit petty and childish for a so-called goddess."

Jerry shrugged. "The ancient Greek gods were prone to pettiness, to be honest. And they weren't what you'd call a particularly ethical bunch, either. Zeus, for instance, had affairs by the score. Jealousy and revenge were an intrinsic part of the mythology. A *lot* of it was petty. In this case, it was also a message reinforcing the social order of the day. Athena was just explaining to anyone else who got uppity that it wasn't what you could do, it was who you were. If I remember right, Colophon was a bit of a maverick society anyway."

"Any way you can turn this Athena into a cockroach? Or help Arachne?" asked McKenna.

Jerry shook his head. "Mac, Egyptian mythology and magic were different. Firstly, power there is vested in words. I could manage those. Here, it is in the commanding of the 'spirits' of what we'd regard as inanimate things—you know, wood, rocks, rivers—all controlled by a hierarchy of gods. Medea draws much of her strength as a sorceress because of the powers over these 'spirits' given to her because she was a high priestess of Hecate and granddaughter of Helios. I don't have any skills here. Secondly, a mortal could make even the Egyptian gods do his bidding, with magic. The ancient Greek pantheon were there for supplication, and are pretty much beyond mortal command. Ask Medea if she can do anything, but Athena was one of the most powerful of the ancient Greek pantheon. I doubt if she can help."

The red-headed corporal nodded determinedly. "I'll ask her."

Lamont, coming up behind them, put a hand on Mac's shoulder. "One thing I'd like to know is how come you like spiders so much?"

McKenna smiled. "They're useful critters. Like bees, Lamont. Bees don't hassle you, do they?"

Lamont looked at McKenna and shook his head. "I'll tell you straight. I'm not crazy about either spiders or bees. Spiders make cobwebs and bite you, and bees sting you."

"My Ma would give you what-for, Lamont Jackson. Spiders eat bugs. Bees make honey. And neither bees nor spiders will ever attack you on purpose."

"I don't think we're going to agree about this," said Lamont, looking at the army of spiders accompanying them.

Olives, sun-dried, black and wrinkled; pastries bulging with delicacies; five different cheeses; cyclamen-pink wine, with a bouquet of honey and old roses, and the strength of a lion; barley bannocks crusty and slightly flavored by wood ash; chopped cucumber and yogurt; pomegranates; skewers of cumin-scented lamb; roasted kid with garlic and lavender. And eight-legged allies . . . was all they could bring back from their expedition. True, those were a lot of allies.

Everybody liked the food. And it was entirely due to McKenna getting on well with spiders. Opinion was divided as to what the quality of the allies was—depending on how much you liked spiders.

As far as Lamont, Cruz, Medea, Throttler and Bes were concerned, that was not at all. Jerry and the dragons were ambivalent; Liz, Henri (when he could muster breath) and Mac enthusiastic.

And Pan, when he arrived from Lesbos a few hours later, was downright miserable and depressed about everything, never mind allies.

"Orpheus is dead." Pan burst into tears.

38

THE PARTING OF WAYS.

"They hit us in the morning while we were yet at our rest. We were woken by the terrible rumble of the bronze-tired chariots of the gods of Olympus and the thunder of the hooves of their great horses. War was joined, and we were all unprepared. Apollo, Athena and Ares scythed through our camp. Our heroes fell like corn before the reapers, before their cruel stabbing spears and arrows with heads of wrought iron. But Orpheus took up his lyre and played. The magic of his music would have stilled the wolves of battle—as he soothed even the terrible sirens. But then Apollo cast his bright spear. It struck Orpheus between the shoulder blades and pierced him through."

Pan burst into tears again. Gradually the story emerged. The army at Lesbos, small, and still arguing about what course to take against Olympus, was no more. And with the death of Orpheus, Pan had no more heart for the fight.

Cruz took a deep breath. "Well. We'll have to raise another army. One that understands 'sentries.'"

"I don't think that's worth doing," said Jerry with a sigh. "We're not going to beat the Olympian gods at a straight slugging match."

303

"So what do you want to do now, Doc?" demanded McKenna hotly. "Give up? Run away?"

The sneering undertone made Liz snap. "Mac, you better hope for bloody cold weather so that your head can contract and the two brain cells in there can make contact with each other. What Jerry is saying is that a dumb-ox-brute-force solution isn't going to work. We've got to out-think the bastards."

"Well, I wouldn't have put it quite like that . . . " said Jerry, pacifically.

Liz snorted. "No, you're too polite, except when you've eaten lotus-cookies."

Jerry winced, acknowledging a hit. "But in a nutshell, that's right. We've got to either out-think or out-*modern* them. Look . . . "

"So all we need now are a couple of Blackhawks," said Mac, sarcastically. "*Brilliant,* Doc. *Brilliant—Sir.* Only we've lost most of our gear and the only things that work are primitive stuff."

Lamont stood up. "That's enough, Mac. Liz, settle down. There's no point in fighting each other. Let's think of things and ways they didn't have in ancient Greece. Mac, you came up with that brandy. That was a winner and it didn't take stuff we haven't got."

"He's right," said Cruz.

Jerry nodded. "In a way, Mac's right too. We're still going to have to do some fighting. But mano-a-mano against an Olympian we're going to lose. So I think we need to look at two things. Allies. And something Olympus won't have heard of. Or, at least, something they think they've got the monopoly on."

Jerry smiled at Cruz and McKenna. "Your field of expertise, not mine. Airborne assault."

McKenna scratched his head. "I suppose, even without 'chutes we could use the sphinx and the dragons. But, well, how many of these gods are there?"

"Many, and they're enormous, and immortal," Jerry said quietly.

Cruz tensed his massive forearm. "Yeah. Look, I'm not washing the idea out, but what advantage does it give us to attack them? If we take the fight to them, and let it be on their home ground, we're *worse* off, Doc."

Jerry smiled. "I want to get some allies. Or at least one. A big one."

Liz chuckled. "Besides, we've already got a lot of allies. Expert parachutists, too. Spiders."

Cruz shrugged. "Liz, I suppose the spiders can bite a few of these gods . . . but they're supposed to be immortals. Gonna take more than spider bites."

Liz smiled. "Even immortals got taken captive, didn't they? Arachne. Show him just how strong spider silk is."

Arachne smiled sweetly. "I just have. Try to free your legs."

Cruz hadn't even noticed the silken strands going round his legs. Try as he might he couldn't pull them apart.

"Let me try," said Bes.

He snapped the web like a rotten carrot. "Strong."

Cruz took a deep breath and said to McKenna: "Remind me not to wrestle with that guy, Mac."

Liz shrugged and Arachne looked totally taken aback. "Oh well. So much for that idea," she said, looking regretful.

"But it *is* very strong," said Bes with a chuckle.

"So is he," said Medea.

"That's the point. If Bes can break free, then indeed, the Olympians can," said Jerry.

Liz looked at the three-foot-six hell-raiser. "You've just acquired a job in destructive testing of materials, Bes."

The dwarf looked suspicious. "What does that mean?"

She smiled at him. "It means you get to try and break things, Bes dear."

He grinned broadly back at her. "Oh, good. Fun."

Jerry grinned. Bes was infectious. Even Pan was looking a little less down in the mouth. "Test them quickly," said Jerry. "I want to go and break some unbreakable chains, and I reckon you're the Bes't breaker around. I think it's time we went to free Prometheus."

"Who *is* this Prometheus guy, anyway?" asked McKenna.

"A Titan. He's called 'the friend of mankind.' He took the side of man against Olympus. I'm hoping he's still inclined that way, even though it got him in trouble. How do you feel about visiting Colchis again, Medea?"

Cruz had more of a grasp of the geography than anyone else there. "Doc. That's about a thousand miles away."

Jerry took a deep breath. "Yes. It's going to take some time. And I want us to split up. Some of us have to stay here and prepare some kind of glider. Something we can pack ourselves, a Titan, and about a million spiders into, to tow behind Throttler. Or am I asking the impossible?"

There was a silence. "Build a *plane*? I don't think so," said Mac, shaking his head.

Liz narrowed her eyes. "What about a hot-air balloon?"

Mac nodded. "Yeah, could do. But what can we use for material?"

"Talk to your spider girlfriend about silk," said Liz.

Arachne looked startled. Whether it was at the idea of her providing silk, or of the girlfriend comment, was uncertain.

Medea sighed. "My father Aeëtes will *not* be glad to see me back. In fact, he will do his best to kill you. He is a magician of note. He draws his powers from Helios. My own, as high priestess of Hecate, are small by comparison."

Lamont snorted. "Back down to magic. Pan, you don't feel like endowing me with some powers over your secondary sprites, do you?"

Pan looked up. "No. *You* are already in the service of another. But I will place my blessing on one of you."

Liz shook her head. "Better be you, Doc. I don't understand this stuff."

Lamont snorted again. "You can say that again."

"Anyway the magic of Pan-Priapus sits ill with a female votary," said Goat-features.

Jerry hastily changed the subject. "Where is Throttler, by the way?"

"She said she was just nipping out for a quick riddling," said Bes cheerfully. The dwarf was striking up quite a warm relationship with the sphinx.

Jerry looked alarmed. Throttler seemed quite content, indeed pleased, to eat cooked food with them. Her dietary history hadn't worried him. "But she said she was stuffed."

Bes shrugged. "She wanted to test her riddling. Even when she can't eat them, she likes to practice. Catch and release, she calls it."

Sitting on the high gray-white stone outcrop beneath whispering pines, Jerry listened to Pan play his pipes, bittersweet and full of mourning. Jerry spent the better part of the night being introduced to the mysteries. More precisely, the names of the myriad sprites and lesser genii that owed fealty to Pan. His hand ached. He'd written as phonetically as possible, but why the hell did it have to be by moonlight? The moon was nearly down, but Pan was finished.

Well. It was magic of a sort. If Jerry ever got back, he'd be able to make a fortune out of curing erectile dysfunction for starters. And then he could make himself a fortune as a trophy-hunter guide . . . if that was his scene. Not to mention the stuff about sheep. And sudden and illogical alarums. And it was great for musical instruments, and employing the principles of contagion and sympathy . . . Which were not infectious diseases and grapes and cards for the poor victims.

Contagion meant things which were once in contact remained in contact and could be drawn together again. Sympathy meant that like produced like.

He looked at the list. Well, at a guess he'd have five or six days' flying time to the Caucasus in which to memorize all this stuff.

Mac smiled, with a confidence he was far from feeling. "You worry too much, Doc. I'll be fine. And I won't lose it with Henri. The guy is sick."

It was true. Henri had developed a hacking cough, either from the water inhaled in the lake of Sebek or the high flying. He was pale and even turning down food—a sure sign of extreme unwellness for the French gourmand.

Arachne produced a small, golden, silken parcel. "Do you think this will do?"

It was a perfect miniature balloon, complete to the basket underneath, woven from grass stems. "It flies," said McKenna proudly. "We tested it."

"Well done," said Jerry. "If I recall correctly, the silk used to be varnished."

"What is 'varnished'?" asked Arachne.

"Hey, Lamont! What goes into varnish?" asked Jerry.

"Spirit varnish is resin and spirits," replied that repository of miscellaneous information.

Arachne looked a little puzzled. "Spirits? A magical compound?"

Mac chuckled. "No. Alcohol. I can do a bit of distilling and we'll cook some up. If you've got resin?"

Arachne looked a trifle put out. "Colophon is famous for it. Our Colophonium is known throughout the Hellenic world. Which barbarian land do you hail from, that you have not heard of Colophon's resin?"

Medea raised her aristocratic nose. "They come from the distant island of America. It is a wondrous place. The men there all cook and wait on the women." She sniffed. "Although I notice that lately the local habits are starting to infect them."

The diminished party drifted on a fine following wind across the Anatolian Plateau. The comfort of the net-nest of the twin-dragon dirigible was somewhat enhanced with some fine woven blankets and two light struts with padded ends, to keep the dragons apart. The few support ropes also meant that they didn't all end up lying on top of each other as they used to.

The dragons complained about it. "It makeſs uſs look like beaſstſs of burden," muttered Smitar.

"Yeſs. Beaſstſs," agreed Bitar.

They were also laden with the gastronomic delights that Colophon had been famed for. But the dragons didn't moan about that at all.

Medea stretched. In-flight movies consisted of the occasional bird going by. There was nothing to do but relax and enjoy the view. And talk. But learning Cruz's language was more fun with privacy and tickling. She felt the fabric of the garment that Cruz had traded for with Arachne. The spiderwoman had a peasant's interests in money. She, Medea, loved fine things. But this money-grubbing was all a little sordid. She sighed. Her princess upbringing had not couched her in habits of economy. She'd tried with Jason, when they'd lived at Ephyra. But he'd been more spendthrift than she was, and had found it even more irksome than she had. The metal Anibal carried suggested that he was a wealthy man. But he didn't behave like one. . . .

She sighed again. She was getting used to the way he behaved. It was different but nice. Actually, very nice. He cared about her . . . first. Maybe that was worth more than all the rich estates he must have.

"What's up, beautiful?" he asked, smiling at her.

"Just thinking about the future. How big are your estates and how many serfs are there to call you master back on your America?"

Cruz swallowed. She was a damn princess, according to the Doc. She obviously put him fairly high up the ladder. Well, given the way she misinterpreted the U.S. that wasn't really surprising. But what princess would want anything to do with a lifer with years to go? Shit. Best to tell the truth, even if he wanted to lie, really badly. But he got the feeling Medea had been lied to quite enough.

"I don't have any estates," he said abruptly. "And there are no serfs in the U.S. Not officially, anyway."

Medea looked dumbfounded. "But—you carry arms. You are a warrior."

"I'm a soldier, yes." He floundered, mostly at the hurt in her eyes.

"But . . . but . . . all the cunningly wrought metal, the fine-woven cloth . . . "

"Belong to Uncle Sam," said Cruz, determined to leave no stone unturned in his attempt to bury himself.

Medea smiled dazzlingly. Cruz felt himself melt. She twined her fingers in his. "Ah. Then we will kill this wicked uncle together. He must have usurped your lands and even your throne, no?"

Anibal Cruz began to realize that being eaten by crocodiles might just have been the soft option compared to taking Medea back home. "No. It, um . . . doesn't quite work like that."

39

⌐┐┌┐┌┐┌┐┌┐┌

BESIDA SPIDA.

The catamaran dragon balloon drifted off towards the horizon. McKenna sighed. He'd hoped that Lamont would stay. But the sphinx had made it very clear that her pact was with Lamont Jackson. Where he went, she did too. And while the sphinx did little more than steer, when the wind was helping the twin-dragon dirigibles along, they'd need more help if the wind turned against them. Mac found it scary to be on his own, except for Henri. And the Frenchman sounded like he might be leaving this world by coffin soon.

"Well," he said to Arachne. "We'd better get down and get to work."

"And what work do you intend to do?" Her voice was curiously neutral.

"Whatever needs doing," McKenna grinned. "I can turn my hand to anything. Hey, I mean back at Circe's castle I ended up being chief helper to the cooks. Otherwise I'm real good for heavy lifting. I want to make a still, to sort this varnish out. But you tell me ... I do it."

"You're a very odd sort of aristocrat," Arachne said, sounding impressed. "Or is this the way of the princes and nobles of this America?"

"Well," said McKenna dryly. "There aren't any princes and nobles in the U.S. of A."

Arachne stopped dead. "Your home is a Timocracy, too?"

"Er. We're a democracy," he said.

"What's that? Rule by the people?" She seemed amused by the concept.

McKenna was mildly offended. "Yeah. Pretty much. Look, it originated here in ancient Greece."

She shook her head. "Well, I never heard of it!"

What was it that Doc had said—democracy was about the fifth century B.C.?

"What year is this?" he asked.

Her answer simply confused him further. "Look. I think the reason you haven't heard about it, is, well, it may not have happened yet. Doc said that Odysseus was long before democracy. You see . . . we're sort of from your future," he said, expecting more bemusement.

She was silent for a while. And then she truly amazed him. "Well, well, well . . . that has a lot of commercial possibilities. You and I could become very rich. I know how things do work here now and you know what things will work. Like this balloon. I wondered where the idea had come from. It's got a lot of possibilities for the Timocracy of Colophon."

"What's a Timocracy then? Rule by the timid?" he asked with a grin.

The spiderwoman raised an eyebrow and dimpled. "Close. We're traders. Not warriors. Fair Colophon is ruled by those who have wealth."

McKenna shook his head. "That doesn't sound right or fair to me."

"Elsewhere it is rule by the nobility. In Colophon we don't have to claim to be descended from the by-blows of philandering gods. And the result is that Colophon is rich. You must have read of us in your history?" she asked, obviously proud of her city.

McKenna was embarrassed. And also in an awkward spot. If he hadn't heard about it, chances were the place hadn't made much of a mark or had been wiped out. "Uh. No, but the Doc has heard of you. But it sounds like you Colophon guys would get on just fine in the States. It's not who you are born as, but how you use your head and how hard you work."

Arachne raised an eyebrow. "This 'states' you talk about. Is it several islands like this America you hail from, each state following this 'democracy'?"

McKenna grinned. "Well, I dunno where Medea got this 'America is an island' story. 'The States' is short for 'The United States of America.' It's a goddamn sight bigger than Greece. Got two hundred fifty million people." He sighed. "I'd love to get *back* there. Anyway. Let's get on with making balloons and varnish."

"Yes. You can tell me more while we work. It sounds quite unbelievable," she said curiously.

McKenna tramped back up the hill to the mountain meadow where the teams of spiders were weaving. He was glad to be alone with his thoughts for a bit. That was quite a kid. A real go-getter. She hadn't let being turned into half a spider stop her. Also, well, she was having an interesting effect on him. Normally his mind was more on any pretty woman's body, than on what she said.

Only Arachne's body . . . well, it didn't exactly turn him on. She had nice legs. Eight of them. But she was just at his wavelength. He could talk to her so easily. Sort of "natural." He'd joined up to get off the farm, do a short hitch and go to college. Only he wasn't sure what he'd do in college when he got there. So he'd ended up telling a half spider/half woman about it. They'd talked, just talked, into the small hours. Jim McKenna couldn't remember ever doing that with any girl, ever. Maybe if Arachne had as pretty a body as she had a face, he'd never have done it with her either. But he was really glad he had. What a nice kid! If he ever met this Athena bitch . . .

Arachne was already in the field. "Hey, Mac!" There was pleasure in her voice. "I've got a joke for you. How many gods does it take to change a lampwick?"

After he'd finally gone to bed, so had Arachne. But sleep had been a long time coming. And finally she'd cried herself to sleep. It was the first time in a long time that another human had treated her just as if she were human. He was a bit weak in the head about business, but there was nothing that solid female sense couldn't see him through. And he had to look like Ganymede, too! If only she'd still been the favored daughter of the great dye-master. She.*wanted* the American. Cursed gods! She wanted him so badly her spiracles hurt. But he wouldn't even look at her in that way. And she was revolted by the idea that, like some of her spider-sisters, she might want to eat him afterwards. She determined to avoid him henceforth as much as possible.

But when he came whistling up to the meadow the next day, she called to him with that silly joke, a joke that was old when Zeus was a boy.

He laughed. It was like daggers stabbing her heart.

"How is Henri this morning?" he asked.

She shook her head. "Still coughing, poor man. He is not looking any better. The potion Medea left for him does not seem to be helping him a great deal. He still has no real interest in food."

McKenna pulled a wry face. "He needs a course of antibiotics. I wouldn't be surprised if he had a dicey ticker too. Fat. Unfit. That sort of age."

"A ticker? What is that?" she asked.

Mac put his hand on his chest. "Heart."

"Ah. I wish I knew more about the healing of them," said Arachne quietly.

Mac nodded. "Yeah. But I think it is pretty well out of reach of the medicine of this time. Listen, I've got some of that varnish I'd like to try. Although it seems a waste of good brandy."

She made a face. "Pah. I do not see how you can describe that terrible firewater as 'good' for anything. But you say it is a good solvent. That I can believe. I thought it would dissolve away my innards."

Several hundred miles away, Jerry was called away from memorizing Pan's minions to deal with another misunderstanding across the ages.

"Jerry. Please tell Medea I'm not just being squeamish," said Cruz. "That she simply doesn't understand."

"What's the problem?" asked Jerry sympathetically.

The humor of it had finally gotten through to Cruz. "Medea wants me to kill off our wicked Uncle Sam so that I can get back the estates and serfs which are rightly mine, and become king. I showed her my pictures of Vegas, and she thinks it's my palace with all my serfs."

Jerry took a deep breath. You either start at the beginning— or take the direct route. Cut to the chase. "Medea. Jason left you to try and gain a throne. What would you rather have? Someone who wanted power and position or someone who wanted you?"

Medea was looking flushed and quite angry. But Jerry's reminders had obviously struck a chord. "Someone who wanted me, of course. But we've got to live somewhere, Doc Jerry, and on something. Is it within your gift, as a Doc, to grant us estates?"

Jerry shook his head. "Medea, one of the things you're just going to have to accept is that the life where we come from is just unimaginably different from here. Believe me, by the standards of your time, Anibal can support you in the lap of luxury. Liz, help me here. How many dresses and skirts do you own?"

Liz looked up from where she was gazing out over the hills. "I'm a bit of a pack rat, Jerry. I can't bear to throw anything away. I boxed up most of my stuff when I came over to the States. I don't know. Seventy or eighty outfits, I suppose?"

Medea gaped. In a time when every garment was handmade, all the way from spinning the thread, that was more than a queen would have owned.

"And no, we don't have serfs and servants, but we have . . . sort of Golem-servants. Machines," said Jerry, hoping he had kept a straight face. "There is 'dishwasher' that cleans and scours kitchen utensils, 'vacuum cleaner' that with a mighty roaring wind clears dirt, and 'automatic washing machine' that washes clothes."

Medea was silent for a bit. "And cook?" she asked.

"Ah!" said Cruz. "Microwave and TV dinners!"

"Are they as good as you, Anibal?" Medea asked.

"Um. Not really," he said cautiously.

She smiled at him again. "Well, you will just have to teach them, dear. But I am not so sure about living in a country with no nobility. How does anyone know where he or she stands? Who do you look up to?"

Bes swung himself in from the dragon's neck. "Stand on your feet. And look up to those you can't knock down. Stop worrying, woman."

Lamont clapped. "Bes, you'd fit right in."

The dwarf grinned widely. "Why? Have you got a lot of dangerous pests for me to fight?"

"Oh, lots!" Lamont rubbed his hands. "Let's start with the Internal Revenue Service . . . "

Two minutes into Lamont's explanation, Bes was growling ferociously. Three minutes later, after Lamont started in on telemarketers, the dwarf god was shaking his fists at the heavens and bellowing with fury.

Henri was looking old. His moustache and pointed little beard were as neat as ever, but his face was slightly gray instead of its normal florid hue. He'd barely nibbled on some pastries and that was all that he'd eaten. In eight days he'd lost weight, and gained years. And most alarming of all he seemed too exhausted to needle McKenna. Mac found himself tiptoeing around the man, on his visits to the sickroom at the farm. But the Frenchman's mind was still strong. He was curious. Two of the men from the farm had helped him, largely carried him, up to the meadow.

"How are you doing, Henri?" asked McKenna, more solicitously than he would have ever thought possible.

"I am afraid that I am not so well." Henri sighed, and summoned a grimace of a smile. "I always wished to die in France, with an empty bottle of Chateau Lafitte in my hand. Ideally, of course, with an angry husband in hot pursuit also. But I would settle for the empty bottle."

He sighed again. "Not likely now, I fear. But if I die . . . well, I have spent the last few days writing down as much as I can remember of our gallant band's adventures. I have them here." He patted his breast pocket. "Maybe they will read of our deeds, at least."

Mac was rather taken aback by the Frenchman's morbid assessment of his health. "Well, you're on your feet, anyway. Look, maybe we'll all get back alive."

Henri smiled weakly. "You Americans are incurable optimists.

It is very irritating." He sighed again. "How is the balloon going, Mac?"

McKenna was just pointing to the half-inflated trial balloon when he caught sight of the chariots in the sun.

"*Quick, into the bushes!*" McKenna shoved the Frenchman into the cover of the evergreens.

40

THE RAGE OF OLYMPUS.

The gods must have gotten wind of what was happening here in Lydia. The concept of a preemptive strike was obviously not a new one.

After what had happened on Lesbos, those who opposed Olympus had been forewarned. "Scatter and take cover!" yelled Mac.

He and Cruz had talked this over with Jerry before the rest had left. The baseline answer was that the immortal ancient Greek gods could be hurt, but not killed—by mortals anyway. So—make time. Let everyone get away, scatter and regroup.

The chariots of the gods were two-wheeled affairs, looking like they came out of a low-budget remake of *Ben Hur*. They had all the aerodynamics of bricks. Their godly riders clung to the slow and bucketing vehicles. In the lead was unmistakably Zeus, deep-browed, his noble head surrounded by windswept dark ringlets. His robes of majesty streamed in the wind. In one hand he clutched a thunderbolt—in the other the chariot and reins. His noble expression reminded Mac of a kid heading for the dentist. The next chariot had two occupants, both female. One of them wore a suitably hammered breastplate . . .

Must be that bitch Athena, he thought. The goddess riding beside her, judging from her expression, was having a bad hair day. Maybe that was Hera. The chariot behind had some guy in armor and another god, stark naked, admiring his reflection in his sword blade . . . Ares and Apollo.

The first of the "time-makers" was about to get a test run. The meadow was a long, narrow one, with the rocky ridge on one side and a small, tree-fringed stream on the other. To land their huge and heavy chariots, the gods would be obliged to come in down the length of the meadow. Which, as the half-inflated balloon was at one end, meant coming in from the south. The first of the chariots skimmed in to a bouncy landing, to Mac's dismay. The second touched down just a bit further back. Its progress was more pleasing to McKenna, if a lot less pleasing to the horses and charioteer.

The trench had been well hidden with a layer of sods on top of thick strands of cobweb. The horses, galloping like fury, simply kicked aside the sods and made the far bank, hooves scrabbling. Mac was glad of that. He was quite fond of horses. The chariot didn't make the ditch. It went down into the angled stakes. The next chariot tried to avoid the ditch. The horses did better on the cornering than the chariot. They dragged it off, on its side, sans occupants. Then the lead chariot hit defense two. A rope at neck height. A spider-silk rope half an inch in diameter. Only Mac had miscalculated on Zeus' height. The rope hit the mighty arm holding the chariot rail.

Then he realized just how strong Zeus the thunderer really was. The rope was tied to two medium-sized oak trees—that were just ripped out by their roots. The entire rail and the front half of the chariot split off in a shriek of tearing bronze. The once peaceful glade was full of the screaming of horses and the fury of gods.

Right. A little bit of smoke and fire and it was asses-and-elbows time. The catapults weren't much to write home about. Bent-over limbs with small pottery vessels for missiles. But they didn't have to deliver the mixture of rosin, alcohol, green grass and fire very far.

As the first one arced into a column of smoky fire, McKenna saw something that made his blood run cold.

Arachne. She'd been on the top of the balloon doing some last-minute sewing when the raid had begun. She was now lying sprawled in the middle of the grass in front of the balloon. Just then, she sat up groggily, much to Mac's relief. At a flat-out sprint he ran towards her.

One of Zeus' thunderbolts exploded at his heels. He still had a good eighty yards to go. Thirty to Arachne, fifty to the shelter of the stream. He wasn't going to make it.

"HEY, YOU! *YOU* WITH THE UGLY BEARD!" Henri Lenoir stepped out of the bushes twenty-five yards down from where McKenna had begun his run.

McKenna didn't pause to watch. He just snatched up Arachne, and kept running. He heard the thunderbolt, though.

"Ya! Missed. Cowardly pig!" yelled Henri. "Come over here and fight like a man, if it is that you dare!"

They dove over the lip. McKenna couldn't resist peering back to see if the old Frog had managed to get away. If they both did, he, Jim McKenna, was going to have to eat some crow. The Frenchman had done this simply to save their lives.

But Henri had not bolted. Apparently, the sick Frenchman had decided he had no chance of evading Zeus anyway. So he just stood there, rigid as any statue, his arms folded on his chest and a sneer on his face as the livid Zeus stalked down on him. Even from here Mac could see a black, five-sided pyramid on the pendant that hung among the god's tangle of dark-golden chest hair. Henri twitched his mustachios arrogantly.

Then the Frenchman sniffed and languidly waved his nose. "You have a bouquet of the most terrible. Why is it that you stink so? Have your bowels turned to water at the thought of a real fight?"

McKenna scrambled to his feet. "I've got to help the crazy bastard . . . "

Just then Henri answered Zeus' incoherent bellow of rage with a splendid Gallic gesture which transcended all language barriers.

Zeus was so angry with this mere mortal that the lightning bolt missed. Barely. Three yards behind Henri, the earth leapt and exploded. Zeus drew back his arm to fling his great spear instead.

But Henri had disappeared. All that remained was one, once-beautiful, Italian leather shoe.

Mac wished like hell he could have given the guy his bottle of wine, too.

"We must go!" Arachne tugged him by the shoulder. "Quickly!"

"Yeah. But what a guy! What a guy!"

She nodded. "We can hide under those roots."

A willow tree had been somewhat undercut. The roots formed a roof overhead with a few inches' clearance between them and the water. From this bank they would be nearly invisible. The water was cold and clear. Nice for drinking. Lousy to hide in.

Only, by the sounds of it, the anger of the gods wasn't confined to this bank. Being discovered was clearly going to be terminal. Slowly terminal.

"We'll have to hide in the bottom of the pool," whispered Arachne.

Mac looked doubtful. "How long can you stay down?"

"My spider body needs little air," she said quietly. "But come. I will arrange it so that you can breathe. Trust me."

He did. They went under. The bank they were sheltering under was deep. McKenna followed the wall, pulling himself down by the roots. The whole thing curved inwards away from the light. There, in a dim nest of roots, Arachne had already spread a net of web. She was brushing bubbles off the hairs on her back and legs into it. She pushed him towards it.

She obviously had delusions about how much air a human needed.

It looked like the last woman to come down here had the same delusions. Only this woman looked like she'd been happy about it. She was smiling, even if she was very obviously drowned. Well, wide-eyed naked women with their mouths open, fifteen feet down in the willow roots are *dead*. Sharing the water with a drowned body was suddenly too much for Mac. He grabbed for the roots.

And she grabbed him.

41

᠊᠊᠊᠊᠊᠊

GETTING FLEECED.

The two-dragon craft crossed the corner of the Black Sea and began to drift towards the snow-topped mountains.

They set down in the stony mountainside, above the tree line. Before them towered a sequence of mountains whose tops seemed to almost prick the sky. They'd set down because the unpredictable gusts and eddies of wind in the high valley had nearly splattered them on the rocks below.

Jerry shivered. It was bitterly cold up here, on a high spur looking down on a cascading river far below. In the shade, icicles still clung.

Liz, as was often the case, seemed able to ignore physical discomfort by thinking about biology. As they undid the net and pole arrangement, she asked: "If dragons are reptiles, then how come they live in the mountains?"

"Caufse it'fs easier to launch," said Smitar.

"Launch for lunch," agreed Bitar . . . "And what'fs for lunch?"

"They're pretty warm," said Lamont, battling with numb fingers to untie a knot. "I think that warm-blooded dinosaur theory is right on the money, myself."

Liz looked at him open-mouthed. "Where do you get all this stuff from, Lamont?"

The mechanic grinned. "Somebody at the Institute leaves their copies of *Nature* in the john."

Jerry chuckled. "Great mysteries of the world finally solved. Now we finally know who the hell steals my copy!"

They met the locals about three miles up the trail. The local bandits, anyway. They'd had a profitable session. A herd of fat-tailed sheep and several ponyloads of fleeces. And about half a dozen stumbling, miserable and terrified captives. Two women and several young boys.

Both parties took the other by surprise. "Brands!" yelled the bandit leader, a villainous-looking fellow wearing a greasy sheep-skin coat and a helmet with rams' horns on it. Rams'-horn helmets were obviously quite the fashion around here, but his was the biggest.

Several of the bandits were carrying spears with bundles on the ends. In a trice, these were flaming bundles. This was dragon country and plainly the locals knew how to keep methane-farting dragons at bay. Several of the other bandits had already drawn bows.

"Get behind the dragons!" yelled Cruz. An arrow splintered against Smitar's scales.

They were in trouble. The bandits couldn't shoot them—yet—unless they tried with drop shots, but as soon as they had their sheep out of the way, they could use the flaming brands to drive off the dragons. And they outnumbered the snatchees by five to one.

Jerry's mind raced frantically, trying to think if there was some spell he'd obtained from Pan which could deal with the problem. Unfortunately, the goat-god's magical powers tended to be highly specialized. True, Jerry *could* give the bandits instantaneous sexual arousal . . . but somehow he felt that that might just be worse for Liz and Medea.

Rams'-horn helmet bellowed out another order. And into Jerry's mind an idea came.

"I've got to hand it to you, Jerry," said an awed Lamont. "It's not every day that you see a bunch of thugs taken out by rampaging, sex-mad sheep."

One minute a group of thirty grinning and very evil-looking bandits had been pushing their way through the sheep. The next moment a strange, hungry and wild-eyed look had come into those sheepish eyes. Perhaps seven of the thugs had not been wearing rams'-horn-bedecked helmets.

There must have been at least three hundred desperately unsatiated sheep in that herd.

Maaadness had overtaken them. It had also overtaken most of the bandits. Jerry could still see one man. He had made the safety of the cliff. He hadn't made it very far up, unfortunately for him. He was clinging to a ledge about eight feet off the ground, just above the bleating pack. Two of the shepherd boys were amusing themselves by pelting him with dung.

Several of the other bandits had gotten lucky and had managed to run over the cliff, before the sheep reached them.

The bandit chief had fared the worst. The patriarch ram of the flock didn't like competition from upstart humans with big horns.

Jerry shuddered. What the sharp hooves hadn't managed, the two once-captive women had done. Jerry looked at the spear he'd acquired from Arachne. The bronze edge was bloody. He shuddered again.

Well, one of the bandits without a rams'-horn helmet had chosen Jerry as a soft target, rather than Bes. Just because you're a murderous bandit doesn't mean you have to be stupid.

Jerry had simply reacted. Right now he couldn't say exactly how it had happened, but someway or another he'd skewered the man.

Cruz put a hand on his shoulder. "I see you're one of the guys that don't freeze up."

Jerry looked at the blood. For once it was his turn to be mystified. "Huh?"

The sergeant gave a half smile. "In contacts most men just don't react. They freeze up. We put a lot of time and effort into training that outa guys. It looks like you're one of the few that don't need training. It was him or you, Doc."

Jerry still found the blood . . . *bloody.*

✧   ✧   ✧

The two women who had been captives looked fearfully at the newcomers, and cowered nervously against each other. "We're not going to hurt you. We promise. You're free," said Jerry soothingly.

They clung to each other.

"What is wrong with you?" snapped Medea. "You've just been rescued. Be grateful."

"They're going to rape us," said the younger woman, who was barely more than a girl. She looked terrified and on the verge of tears.

Medea laughed slightly. "I promise you they will not," she said in a gentle voice. "The men are all foreigners from a place called America. They have weird customs, but I think it's a nice change myself."

"What are you going to do with us, then?" asked the older woman, plucking up her courage. She was not more than thirty, but already her face was lined from hard living and hard work.

"Nothing," said Jerry. "You're free to go. The boys can gather the sheep. I suppose that's all your stuff. Collect it and go home."

The two women goggled at him. The younger woman shook her head. "This America place. It must be very, very strange. *You* kill them and *we* get the loot? It is not usually done that way, here."

"Sorry. But that's the way we do things. Now, can we get past the ponies? We've got a Titan to free."

The smallest shepherd boy tugged at the older woman's sleeve. "Why is that man so dark, Mama? When all the others are white and blue?"

It was an accurate enough observation. "It's my natural color, son," answered Lamont. "And the blue on the rest of them is just because they're cold."

The woman smiled and clapped. "Aha! Cold! Timotar. You and the other boys collect the clothes from the bodies of Cholkar's band. Come on. Jump to it."

Jerry looked at the heavy sheepskin jacket the boy was handing him. He'd live through the blood on it. The shepherd boy had done his best to wipe it away. And Jerry'd become a lot less squeamish since coming to the Krim Ur-universes. But the black line of migrants pouring out of it . . .

Whether freezing to death wasn't better than being parasitized to death was a moot point, at least while the two, brightly dressed, Colchian tribeswomen had such a nice fire going. Looking at Liz he saw a similar expression on her face. Her eyes narrowed as they always did when she was thinking.

"I say, Jerry. Those wild animal spells—do you think the size of the animals matters?"

Lamont looked at the line of hungry lice. He shuddered. "Believe me, Jerry. Those critters look really wild to me. We'd probably be better off with tigers. At least they'd just eat you alive and not eat you alive and give you diseases as well."

"Then let us try some game-driving spells . . . "

The jacket, overtrousers, scarf, fur hat and even the boots fit reasonably well; the leg wrappings that did duty as socks were now at least vermin-free, if not clean. The warmth seeping into his bones from being insulated from the wind outside was delightful. And so was the hot, spicy soup.

The Colchian tribeswomen had long since passed from fear into a state of bemused amazement. Lice were things you lived with . . . A life without them was unimaginable. Looting, rape, murder and servitude were facts of life. People who captured a pack train of stolen fleeces and a herd of sheep, and then told you to help yourself, were a totally unheard of experience. The women and their children weren't at all sure about what they were seeing here.

The older woman asked in a carefully artless voice. "And just whereabouts is this 'America'?"

Cruz gestured vaguely. "It's quite a long way to the west."

Half an hour later they set off up the mountain, warmly dressed and certain they were heading in the right direction. That much the Colchian hill people could tell them. The Titan was up there. Up where no man ever went, but the snow lay eternal.

An errant snatch of wind brought voices up the mountain.

"And where will we go now, Mama?"

"First back to your Uncle Sebatia, Timmi. Then we are going west."

Cruz halted. Looked guilty and all set to turn back downhill. "I didn't mean it like that . . . "

"Leave it," said Lamont. "I don't think you can explain—or that she'll believe you."

Liz gave a wry grin. "And in the long run you might just have planted the seed for a place not unlike the U.S."

Cruz shook his head. "They'll never reach America."

Jerry shrugged. "America the continent probably doesn't even exist in this Ur-universe. But what they may get to is a place where the rule of brute force isn't all that there is. And if not, they'll make one of their own. They know it is possible now. The dream exists."

Lamont pulled a face. "And they might find the U.S. a bit of a letdown, compared to the dream."

"Compared to *this*? I mean, I'm not saying the U.S. is perfect . . . " Which, coming from Liz, was a bit rich. It would have been even funnier from Henri.

"Well, at least they have much wealth now," said Medea.

Lamont chuckled. "A herd of killer sheep and some ponies?"

"No, the golden fleeces," said Medea.

"They looked like bundles of sheepskins to me," said Cruz.

She frowned. "They *are* sheepskins. They peg them into stream beds to gather the heavy grains of gold."

"That's what a golden fleece is?" asked Jerry, fascinated.

Medea looked at him as if he were a slightly mentally deficient child. "Of course. What else?"

Cruz, with thoughts about having to support a princess and her two children, looked at Lamont. Lamont, with thoughts of the constant battle to pay rent, never mind the bills, looked at Cruz. "Oh, Lord. Gold. No wonder they thought we were crazy!"

The golden subject returned to democracy, a concept that puzzled both Bes and Medea severely, as they continued up the mountain.

Jerry finally realized the truly amazing thing about it all. He was actually talking while walking up a thirty-five-degree slope. Either Pan's spells had some kind of bio-enhancement effect, or he was getting fit.

42

LA MORT DU FRANCAIS.

The three medics in the patrol had had four partially and brutally dismembered bodies that morning so far. The guy with the goatee and singed moustache was at least still in one piece, even if some of his clothing was on fire. The medics had rolled him, smothered the flames and started with cardiac massage and mouth-to-mouth within ten seconds. The third one was already sprinting for the nearest outpost. A chopper pilot with scant regard for his personal safety saw to it that Henri Lenoir received his second massive electrical shock for the day, within four minutes. This one started the heart beating erratically instead of stopping it.

It was only later when the nurses in intensive care were removing Henri's clothes, something he would have far preferred to be conscious for, that someone found the notes in his top pocket.

When Miggy Tremelo arrived fifteen minutes later, he found out, in precise longhand, just what the largest group of survivors had been up to.

Milliken stared at the copies. "It can't be genuine. It simply can't."

Miggy Tremelo pursed his lips. "It may be hallucinations, but it certainly *is* a genuine recital of what he experienced. There is categoric proof. Lenoir was nowhere near the large group when he was snatched. Prior to that he cannot even have seen the paratroopers. He mentions them each by name, and describes them with remarkable clarity."

The phone rang. The hospital had, true to its word, called the moment Lenoir became conscious.

Henri Lenoir was sitting propped up against the pillows, being fussed over by three nurses in crisp whites. By the gleam in the Frenchman's eye he was already engaging in thoughts not at all in congruence with the ECG monitoring equipment, the IV drip, and oxygen mask.

"He's very weak," snapped the doctor. "His heartbeat is erratic. Try and keep it as brief as possible." She plainly had no intention of leaving the room of her celebrity patient. Doctors are allowed to be curious too.

Henri patted his doctor's hand avuncularly. She just happened to be titian-haired and more than slightly attractive. "Ah, Madeleine, my dear. Just a peck on the cheek from you, and my heart would beat more strongly. It would give an old man a reason to live."

Well, thought Tremelo, the guy certainly appeared to have his wits. "Dr. Lenoir—"

"Call me Henri. I have to your American familiarity become so accustomed in the last while."

He took a couple of panting breaths and continued. "I suppose you want to know about what happens within the pyramid. I will tell you. But first you must bring to me a bottle of Chateau Lafitte. From one of the great years." He went off in a paroxysm of coughing.

The doctor shook her head, angrily. "I utterly forbid it."

But Lenoir was determined. "One small taste will do me no harm, Madeleine, *petit*. Just one small taste, please."

Milliken, who had also come to the hospital, was a man of decision. He turned to one of his men. "Johnson. Get it for us, please."

Miggy thrust his hands into his pockets. "Do you think this is wise, Mr. Milliken? The doctor has advised against it."

"Professor Tremelo, I know the type. You'll get nothing out of him unless you go along with him. And this guy has definitely got all his marbles. We need that story out of him."

Henri chuckled weakly.

The doctor shooed them out.

Henri Lenoir held the glass with its perfect ruby liquid in one unsteady hand. He pulled aside the oxygen mask and straightened his goatee and mustachios with a practiced if shaky gesture. He pushed aside the attempt to put the mask back. "To nose this," he panted, "will do me more good than any oxygen. This is the bouquet of the very lifeblood of *la belle France*. Ah! *Magnifique!*"

It did indeed seem to do him good. His voice sounded stronger when he spoke again. "I am afraid, good gentlemen, that I have— how do you say it?—'pulled you on a fast one.'" He smiled. "The story you already have. She is exactly as I have written it down." He put the glass to his lips with a beatific expression on his pale face.

Henri Lenoir died for the second time. But the glass that fell to the floor was empty.

PART IX

... there to dwell,
In adamantine chains and penal fire,
Who durst defy the Omnipotent to arms.

—John Milton,
Paradise Lost, First Book

43

⊡⊡⊡⊡⊡⊡⊡

PROMETHEUS BOUND.

The bleak mountain crest was full of a craggy Titan. Looking at him, Jerry knew that whatever went into Titan construction it wasn't ordinary flesh and blood. Jerry was glad to see the guy. It hadn't been rock-climbing—not exactly—but the last section of the mountain, up bleak rocky slopes and icy gullies had been steep, treacherous and exhausting. Without the sphinx and the dragons, it would have been impossible. But now it was already well into the afternoon. They'd have to get off this peak before dark. With or without the big guy.

The eagle pecking at his liver hadn't even seen them. Or heard them coming, either, as Prometheus had been bellowing in pain.

Jerry looked at it worriedly. He'd forgotten about the creature. "How do we deal with Zeus' eagle?"

Cruz held up a bow, retrieved from the sheep-savaged bandits. "I can try. I'm a pretty terrible shot so far."

Jerry had been part of the practice team back at the cave where they'd stayed the night. Cruz was by far the best shot, but hitting an eagle on the wing might be a challenge beyond most experienced archers.

"The point is I'd rather not have the bird carrying word back to Zeus. We would like as much of a break as possible from foes that could be sent against us. The same goes for the dragons and Throttler. Eagles are fast and maneuverable."

Medea produced a small bottle. "I have a potion here that will silence that eagle forever."

Everyone stared at her. The woman from Colchis had become so much a part of the group that they tended to forget that she was a mistress of poisons.

Cruz nodded. "But how do we get it into the eagle?"

"I'll sort it out," said Bes easily. "I'll sneak up and get it down his gullet before he realizes it."

They also tended to forget how quietly the rambunctious dwarf-god could move when he wanted to. They watched from behind a small spur as Bes ghosted forward. Then, when he was just next to the Titan, he stood up and yelled. "Here, birdy, birdy, birdy. Here, birdy, birdy, dinner. Dinner!"

The huge eagle, startled from its gory feasting, looked up and spotted Bes. With a squawk it dived onto the small piece of new prey.

"Bloody lunatic!" yelled Liz. She broke from cover along with the rest of them, sprinting toward the wild flurry of wings, claws and flying feathers.

By the time they got there, Bes was sitting astride the eagle with the bird flat on its back. Bes' feet were holding the wings down, with the bird's talons immobilized with one hand while he wrestled with the beak with the other. "Ah. Glad you came. I can't work out how to get the stopper out of this bottle, and I haven't got another hand to pour with."

"You're a maniac," growled Cruz, cutting the eagle's throat hastily.

Bes shook his leonine head. "What's the point of doing that, Cruz? Not worth giving it poison now."

And Prometheus laughed. "Well done, mortals! Well done indeed. I have watched long for your coming." His voice was like low thunder.

Jerry had had several vague ideas about how to defeat the chain that bound Prometheus to that pinnacle. Unfortunately, he'd failed to consider the size of the Titan or the quality of the chains.

The Titan stood at least forty feet high and the chains that bound him were welded around each wrist and ankle, and then around the basalt plug. If the chains couldn't be broken, then the plug would have to be moved—and it was a pillar at least twice as big as the Titan. It had to weigh at least ten or twelve hundred tons.

Prometheus' head stood just below the top of the rock plug. Jerry thought frantically about the limited magic powers at his disposal. "If we made your chains longer, could we get them up and over the top?"

Prometheus wrinkled his shaggy frosted brow. "You could try," he said.

So Jerry and Medea got to work. They started on the chain between his arms, climbing up a pile of ice-shattered rocks to where they could reach it. The chain grew without becoming broken. Soon Prometheus could move his arms.

"Bless you, mortals! Do you know how good that feels? Just to be able to move my arms. Ah, that was a fine job you did on that eagle, but I wish I could have done it myself."

Next they climbed to the top of the rock pillar and stood on the very summit, hauling on the spiderweave rope. It took all of them, sphinx, dragons and Bes too, to haul the chain up, and over. Dropping it over the other side, they nearly brained Prometheus.

The Titan bellowed his delight at his new freedom of movement.

"The legs will be worse," said Jerry grimly.

"Why?" asked Cruz.

"For starters, there are several tons of rocks on top of the chain from that rockfall. Then, to get it over the top, we'll have to make it *much* longer. And I don't know if you worked out that we were changing the size of the links to get the chain bigger. They'll have to be bigger and heavier by far, to get them over the top of the pinnacle."

"Forget it then," said Cruz brusquely. "It's a no-can-do."

Jerry blinked. "We've got to try something."

"Then try something *else*, Doc. That one's not gonna work."

Liz looked intently at the chain. "Jerry. You can't break it. But can you change it? Pan always worked from scraps when he was making those instruments."

His eyes gleamed. "You're a *genius*, Liz!"

She gave a wry grin. "Yeah, and beautiful into the bargain."

"Well, *I* think so," said Jerry, leaving her blushing and himself amazed.

A triangle is the simplest of musical instruments. It also has an open corner.

Ten minutes later, Prometheus was free.

His triumphant laughter rang across the Caucasus. "Well, mortals. My thanks! I have been amply repaid for being the friend of mankind."

Prometheus was large. Jerry was relieved to discover that he also seemed good-natured, despite the wound in his side.

"Who do you keep calling 'mortal,' you big oaf!" bellowed Bes.

The Titan peered at the dwarf, a smile creasing into familiar lines on his gigantic face. "I see I am mistaken. But I do not know you. You are not one of the Olympians, nor yet one of the Titans. Are you perhaps one of the giants?"

"You come down here and say that and I'll punch your big nose for you! I'm a dwarf, I am, and I'm proud of it. And I'm from the land of Punt, and certainly not one of your foppish Olympians."

"I can see I'm going to like you," chuckled Prometheus. Then he grew . . . to at least three times the size he had been. "I am free of your binding, Zeus! Your chains are gone, and I am come into my powers again. Now, good rescuers, let us get off this mountain. I'd like to try the view from very nearly anywhere else. Can I give any of you a lift?"

44

▢◲◲◲◲◨

NYMPHOMANIA.

Mac screamed. This is never wise when you are underwater. He fought too, with all the berserk strength that panic and fear could lend.

She was unbelievably strong. He struggled for a full five minutes before realizing that if he was going to drown, he would have done so already. And if she was a drowned woman, she wasn't into decay. And that Arachne was tapping him on the shoulder. Smiling worriedly at him. But smiling. Exhausted, he let the woman pull him down to her bower in a grotto beneath the willow roots.

Down there, she let him go. Lungs full of water, he didn't float away. He didn't *feel* dead—or he didn't think he felt dead. He certainly hadn't gone back to the U.S. How come he was breathing water?

Arachne busied herself with tending to his foot. That bolt from Zeus must have come closer and been hotter than he'd realized. His footwear had been one of the big advantages on this trip. That certainly wasn't true any more. Still, the ruined boot had saved him from having a cremated foot. The underwater-woman gave Arachne some green salve for it, and now Arachne was bandaging it.

Mac didn't know what happened next, because, somehow, relaxing down there in the stream bed . . . he fell asleep, or passed out. Drowning—even when you don't end up dead—takes it out of you.

He awoke to find himself on a bed of soft rootlets, canopied with drifts of algae. Sticking a hand out he realized that the water-woman had spared no effort to make it a comfortable resting spot. Warm water from somewhere played over the bed. The canopy of algae wasn't just decorative. It served to keep the bed at least five degrees warmer than the stream. He was still cold.

A greenish hand with long, manicured fingernails pulled aside the curtain of algae. It was his hostess. And Arachne. He tried speaking. Some form of sound did issue from his mouth. Vocal chords designed to work on air found this fluid medium rather different. Pitch and volume were going to have to be learned anew.

His hostess was obviously accustomed to it . . . or perhaps designed for it. "Greetings, mortal. Do you want some help to remove all those ugly clothes?" she said archly.

From off to the side of her, Arachne shook her head franti-cally. Obviously, the movement caught the eye of the naked water-woman. "Go away, little spider," she hissed. "I kept him alive and he's mine now. He looks quite strong for a mortal. I think I'll keep him a while."

Arachne was obviously protesting and indignant. It didn't look as if she was going to prevail, however.

"I said go, spiderlet! Or shall I summons my fish to eat you?" The water-woman showed her teeth.

Arachne went, shaking a foot defiantly, as she moved up the roots towards sunlight and air.

McKenna was left very alone with a water creature with only one thing on her mind. She produced an amphora of wine. Drinking underwater from a rigid container means you'd bet-ter like your drink watered. Mac managed not to drink very much.

Normally, Mac would have thought that getting drunk and being seduced by a naked naiad sounded like a pretty good deal. And the nymph called Neiradne definitely came under the head-ing of "well built."

Now, he just wanted to get out of there. Neiradne made it instantly clear that wasn't an option. And she was unbelievably powerful, as he had found on his only attempt. So Mac had to bide his time. Her fingers worked at his buttons, or trailed over him. Which might have been fun if he wasn't just about at the uncontrollable shivering phase of being cold. And besides, he was anxious to see how many of the balloon-makers had survived.

He couldn't believe that Arachne had just left him like that....

He noticed the change in the pressure first. Then he saw that it was definitely brighter under the roots. Whatever was happening he hoped that it would become warmer. Neiradne was trying to feed him pieces of raw fish . . . when she suddenly noticed the changes.

"My stream! What's happening to my stream?" She shrieked and shot out of the grotto in a trail of bubbles.

As soon as she was out, Mac knew the time had come to bolt, if he was ever going to. His limbs were nearly numb and totally clumsy. But he forced himself to paddle—all he could manage— for the surface. It seemed like a long way.

Arachne was suddenly there, looping a rope over his shoulders, and he found himself being hastily dragged to the surface. When he'd gone into it, the hole must have been twenty feet deep. Somehow the water level had dropped. He crawled up the willow root-mass trying to get a grip with his numb fingers. Arachne and several thousand ordinary spiders hauled him up.

"You must get the magic water out of your lungs!" said Arachne urgently. They dragged him up the steep slope as the water streamed out of his nose and lungs. Gasping and spluttering, he managed to draw breath. There was still a lot of the liquid inside him, but whatever it had done to his lungs, it wasn't ordinary water in there.

Coughing and retching, he managed to breathe again. Of course, he was also shivering uncontrollably. But there was sunlight on his back. And Arachne was clinging to him with all of her spider legs.

"I thought I'd never see you again," he said weakly.

The spidergirl kissed his cheek. "We must get you warm."

They carried him to a cave, as Arachne informed him that the farm's houses were destroyed. He was amazed to be greeted by enthusiastic clapping and cheering from the assembled people. His wet clothes were stripped off without any attention to decorum; he was wrapped in a warm blanket and put in a prime position in front of the fire. Somebody thrust a goblet of hot mulled wine, full of honey and herbs, into his shaking hand.

"Arachne," he said, as soon as he could speak, "thank you. I didn't know how cold I was. I guess I'd just been getting slowly colder." He still felt cold. He vaguely remembered the lectures on exposure. Once your core temperature starts dropping, then it is lassitude down into death. He hadn't quite been there yet, but insidiously it had been creeping up on him. You can die in cold water just as easily as you can in minus-zero air. It just takes much, much longer.

"We were as quick as we could be. We had to dam the stream higher up. We knew it was the only way. No one can defeat a naiad in her own stream."

He managed a smile "I'm just glad that you managed to save me."

She dimpled. "I said 'trust me.' I just didn't expect the naiad to want to keep you. I was very angry with her."

He took another sip. "Why does everyone look so happy?"

She dimpled again. "Because nearly everyone is alive. And because we poked the gods of Olympus in the eye. And we are alive to laugh about it."

"But . . . the balloon is in shreds," said McKenna. He'd seen the remains on the way to the cave. "Your farm has been destroyed."

She shrugged, which is very expressive in a spider. "We have Hera's chariot. The iron axletree alone is worth three farms. The gold on it would buy another two!"

Arachne was full of good cheer and great satisfaction. "And the balloon, we can make again. But the prestige of the gods is in tatters. Mere mortals whipped their asses and taunted them— and got away with it! It's *never* happened before. *Never.*"

She pranced about gleefully. "The tale—indeed, every word!— of Henri's taunting of Zeus is spreading across Lydia like wildfire.

The story will be repeated a thousand times, getting bigger every time."

McKenna digested this. "I never thought about it that way. I guess I'm glad the Frog got to be a hero. He deserved it. I kinda misread the guy."

She patted his knee with a gentle pedipalp. "You are a hero, too. My hero. And you do not understand what this will mean to the people. The Olympian gods are feared. Now it will be known that they can be thwarted."

"Yeah," McKenna nodded. "It's doing it the first time that's the hardest."

Arachne smiled. "That's what my mother said, too." And then with no explanation at all she burst into tears.

Mac did his clumsy best to comfort her. The more he tried, the more she cried.

She had suddenly taken a deep sniff, gotten control over herself and gone away. To effect repairs, judging by the refreshed facade when she reappeared some ten minutes later. She was bright and cheery with just an undertone of brittleness. Mac, more to try and get her away from whatever subject was upsetting her, asked her what she thought he should do when he'd finished his hitch in the army. It seemed as far removed as possible a subject from the destroyed farm, which he thought must be what was upsetting her.

"You are not going to return to the farm?" she asked in surprise. "You said you had grown up on a farm."

McKenna shook his head. "No. I enjoy the farm. No two ways about that, but I like the bright lights, too."

She cocked her head. "The bright lights?"

"The city." McKenna wished that he had one of those photos-turned-pictures from Cruz's Vegas trip to show her. A picture could explain so much. "You know, lots of people, things to do."

Arachne sighed. "Oh, I understand perfectly! I miss Colophon, for just those reasons. Father sent me out to the estate for my safety after . . . Athena did this to me. I used to wish I'd been born a man. I would have become the richest man in Colophon!" She smiled. "Sorry. I gather that wealth is not so important in your homeland."

McKenna laughed. "You're wrong there. There are no kings and stuff back in the U.S., but money is really how most people work out who counts."

"It sounds very like Colophon," she said.

McKenna nodded. "Yeah. It's amazing, really. Everywhere else has been so different. Except it sounds like women still got a raw deal in your city."

"What do you mean?" Arachne was slightly affronted.

"Well, like you were saying, that you wished you were a man so you could get rich. Can't women get rich?"

She thought about it. "Yes. It is more difficult. It must be done through male intermediaries, and when a woman marries, her wealth passes to her husband."

"Well, in the U.S.A. there are plenty of women who are pretty damn successful and rich. I'm not saying they don't complain about men getting it easy, but they can get rich there. And you don't have to get married to do it, and even if you do, you can get to keep what's yours. Well, that's the idea, anyway . . . "

"I wish I could have been born there." Her tinkling voice was full of yearning.

"Come back with me." It was said on the spur of the moment. But when he said it, Mac knew that he meant it.

"Oh, I wish I could." A tiny tear started in the corner of her eye. She brushed it away. "But I'm half a spider, Mac."

"I don't think you'd be any worse off there than you are here. And I'd look out for you. We could go into business together. We could give a whole new meaning to 'the worldwide web.' Soon we would get to be so rich that everybody would treat you with respect." He spoke with a conviction he didn't really feel.

She sniffed. "I wish I wasn't a half-spider. You're quite the nicest person I've ever met."

He sighed. "According to Cruz, I'm a no-brain plankhead. But I certainly think that you're the bravest and nicest kid I ever met. Not many girls could even start to deal with being turned into half a spider."

Her eyes were misty. "I still wish I was just a woman."

McKenna agreed, but he left the words unspoken. Instead, he concentrated on the commercial possibilities for spider silk.

✧   ✧   ✧

It was a bright morning. Mac was feeling much recovered today. Even the thunderbolt-torn field had no power to depress him. "The doc was right! The way to beat these gods is by outthinking them. The next time they come here, there'll be so many booby traps they won't even get to throwing thunderbolts."

Arachne shook her head. "Next time they will come in disguise, or send spies first."

"So we need to work on disinformation."

He didn't even have to explain the concept to her. One thing about Arachne, she was as sharp as a tack.

"They're back! They're back!" yelled the lookout.

Mac anxiously surveyed the horizon. And then, breathed a deep sigh of relief. The lookout was perfectly correct. Of course, he should have said who "they" were.

The huge golden balloon was unmistakably Arachne's handiwork. It was just very much bigger. It had to be, to carry dragons, a sphinx and humans, all towed by a striding Titan.

45

SPIES, LIES AND DELUSIONS.

Council was held in a tent full of song. The tent had been, until very recently, a balloon.

It was all Prometheus' idea. "Planning later!" he bellowed, so that the hills shook. "First we party! Song, drink, dancing! I have a fancy for a roast bird or fifty! Send your people to shoot some birds. I don't care if they are pheasants, eagles or owls, bring them. Pluck them and roast them! I have a grudge against all birds."

This was said with a wink. There was a hasty flapping in the trees.

The Titan shrank. True, he was still twice the size of a man but no longer so visible . . . or so loud. He seized the deflating balloon. "Let us make a tent for our party." He attempted to pull the fabric apart. Veins stood out on his forehead as he strained. "Gnnnnn. What *is* this stuff? It is as strong as the very chains of Hesperus!"

"Spider silk," said Arachne with great satisfaction. "It can be cut."

So, out of half of the balloon they fashioned a tent, in which several relatively inept musicians were playing their hearts out.

Well, they were all inept except for one fellow. He was good . . . and Prometheus grabbed him by the ear. "Out! Until you can learn to keep a tune!" he bellowed. He followed it up with a kick in the nether end. "Here, Bes. I name you bouncer. Toss this tuneless bum out."

Bes grabbed the angry and struggling lyre player and tossed him out of the doorway. Bes could really toss someone hard and far. There was the sound of breaking branches and then a splash.

"I thought Mikalos was playing far better than he usually does," commented Arachne.

"That wasn't Mikalos," chuckled Prometheus.

Jerry's eye's narrowed. " . . . lest ye entertain gods unawares!"

"Indeed." Prometheus grinned. "They love pretending to be musicians or seers. But they can never bring themselves to do it badly, the snobs. Such vanity! Now, we've hopefully got rid of Artemis' owl. And I think that was Hermes. So let us plan quickly. The music will make it difficult to eavesdrop."

McKenna nodded. "Then afterwards we can go for a little walk under the trees and repeat a few things."

"What?" Prometheus asked, a smile teasing his face.

"What we *want* them to hear, of course."

Prometheus gave a shout of laughter that almost brought the tent down. "Ha! Not only has he got hair my color, but brains like mine too! I like it."

"Somebody has to," said Liz dryly.

"Now. What do we have for allies? My brother Titans are lost in the void. Only Oceanus was not sent there. And Typhoeus is trapped beneath the smoking mountain."

"Oceanus seemed well disposed," said Jerry. "He sent Proteus to help us."

Prometheus smiled. "Excellent. I need a river—or even a stream. The Naiads, Limnaids and Potamids owe allegiance to the river gods, the sons of Oceanus and Tethys."

Mac shuddered. "There's a naiad in the stream."

Prometheus clapped. "I will stick my head in and talk to her. I think we will get Zeus to call Poseidon home to Olympus, if he's worried enough."

McKenna shook his head. "That naiad was quite keen on

keeping me. Arachne managed to save me. I wouldn't trust her as far as I could throw her."

The Titan chuckled. "Her kind are tricky in their own stream. But they owe me. It's time to call the favor due. I need word taken to Oceanus."

Two hours later, somewhat drunk, or at least apparently so, the Titan, Bes, and the snatchees held an impromptu council of war under the edge of the trees. "Well, with any luck they'll attack us again," Bes chuckled wickedly. "Have we ever got some nasty little surprises for them from Egypt. Destroy those pyramid-Krim utterly and turn these gods to minced meat."

"They're not likely to be that stupid, surely?" Jerry spoke with excessively dramatic artlessness, having spotted the large owl in the tree.

"If they won't come to us, then we will go to them!" replied Liz loudly. Her own thespian "talents" were every bit as over-done as Jerry's. She even shook her fist at the sky.

"But if they see the balloon, surely Zeus will just blow it out of the sky with one of his thunderbolts?" asked Medea, clapping one hand to her forehead and throwing out the other in a gesture of despair.

The method school of acting was now in full retreat. Cruz turned retreat into rout.

"I'm sure he would—except there won't just be one balloon! *Ha ha!* The Olympians did us a favor and saved us time by shredding the balloon. *The fools!* Each shred can be reanimated by the magic of contagion into another balloon."

His own fist-shaking was prolonged, even by the standards of professional wrestling. "We'll launch tens of thousands of bal-loons! *Ha ha!* Which one will we be in? *Who knows? Who knows?* They can't destroy them all!"

He began a little war dance. Well, not so little. "Olympus will be destroyed! *Ha ha!*"

Cruz's description of the ruin of the gods went on and on and on . . .

And on and on and on . . .

"I didn't realize he was a Wagner fan," muttered Jerry.

✧　　✧　　✧

The real final discussion was held over bits of paper.

"It's insane, Mac!" Cruz looked at the diagram with disbelief.

McKenna nodded. "Yeah. Liz thought of it."

"Does it work?"

"On the scale that we've been able to test it . . . yes." McKenna didn't explain what that scale had been.

"It's crazy, Mac!"

"Point is, it's something they do naturally." McKenna spoke with a confidence he was far from feeling.

"And the 'chutes?" asked Cruz dryly.

"Stake my life on them, Sarge!" McKenna crossed his fingers behind his back.

"It's not you staking yours that bothers me," grumbled Cruz. "It's me staking mine." He tossed the diagram into the fire. "Oh, well."

In the small hours of the morning, as soon as the moon was down, Prometheus set off. No ship could bear his great weight, even when he drew his body into its smallest volume. He would have to cross over to the Greek mainland across the Hellespont by himself.

Liz was dying to cut him up, stick him under a microscope and see how he worked. . . .

She shook off the idle thought. She had to see to a sea party. With an escort from Oceanus, they would be sneaking across from island to island to mainland Greece, heading for the ancient halls of the Titans on Mt. Ortherys. With a crew of spiders, and a cargo of balloon fragments.

When their ship arrived, they found that Greece was a place of smoking devastation. On the march up to Ortherys they passed through the remains of a town.

In the colonnaded and painted temple, the altar still dripped red. Yet not even the bloody sacrifice of their children had saved the people. Devastation and fire had been their reward. Liz stopped to be sick. Medea comforted her. But the sorceress' eyes were hard. "There will be a reckoning," she said quietly. That quietness carried more force than any shouting or anger.

Lamont stood there, his hands flexing, but his face impassive.

Jerry stared at the grim scene, fixing it in his mind. Fixing it in his determination. "Yes," he said quietly. "There will be a reckoning for the Krim."

46

AS YE SEW, SO SHALL YE REAP.

The cavernous halls of the Titans on Mt. Ortherys must once have been magnificent. Now they were dusty—and crawling with spiders. Carefully, Prometheus shooed a number away before he sat on the stone seat.

"We can talk here," he said. "Not even the powers of Olympus can spy in this place."

"Besides, they're probably scared of spiders," said Cruz grumpily. Jerry realized that the sergeant hadn't had much private time together with Medea lately. And Medea's mind was on her children again.

Prometheus smiled briefly. "Now, I have asked great Oceanus to try to free Typhoeus. He is a terrible monster but the only one who has ever defeated Zeus. But we cannot rely on this. We must proceed as if we had no expectations of help. And the Olympians will not wait for us on Olympus. Soon they will sally out on Lydia, and find that we aren't there. We must act soon or not at all. . . . Why are you twisting your pretty hair like that, my dear?"

"I'm worried about my children," said Medea. The scene in that temple was still obviously upsetting her.

Prometheus smiled widely this time. "I have sent Throttler to fetch them."

"But—"

"I am called foresight, my dear," explained Prometheus. "She is much faster than the dragons and the children are light."

Medea swallowed. "But won't Throttler *eat* them?"

"Lamont has threatened to tell the entire world both answers if he does that," said Prometheus soothingly. "Besides, Throttler is at least half human, and female herself. She likes children."

"Right. Fried," said Jerry, but he said it very quietly.

Prometheus gestured at the shadowy halls. "They will be safe here. Or safer than anywhere else in Greece."

Cruz stretched. "Well done, Prometheus. Thank you. But do you want to know what piece of foresight I've got for you?"

Prometheus grinned. Jerry could not help but like the Titan. He was reminded of what Hesiod had said about the reign of the Titans. *In those days, men and gods took food together.* The Titan was not the toplofty sort.

Well, he didn't really need to be. "Tell me, Cruz. Then I will tell everyone I thought of it."

Cruz took a pull from his goblet of wine. "In any damn military operation, anything that can go wrong, will. The more complicated, the more likely to screw up. So keep it simple, and have lots of backup."

Prometheus nodded. "Wisdom, indeed! So what do you suggest?"

Cruz was rather taken aback. "I'll think about it. I'll come and talk to you in about half an hour."

"Try to leave this to the military as much as possible," said Cruz in their later private council. "Mac and I have got the experience. If need be, we can train soldiers."

Prometheus steepled his fingers. "Firstly, we cannot wait and train. The Olympians will not wait. A straightforward military assault on Olympus with two soldiers, no matter how skilled, has no chance of success. The Olympians defeated the Titans who were their equal in strength, but not in skill at war. They defeated the Giants who were both skilled at war and great in strength.

As yet, the only way anyone has got the better of them has been by guile. By strength or even force of arms you will fail."

His eyes grew distant. "So: we are obliged to resort to guile. Let us look at the forces at your command. There is myself. I shall come as fast as I can, on foot from the north. But on my own I can only hope to defeat perhaps two of the Olympians. Oceanus will not come up from his watery kingdom. Remember too that the Olympians cannot be killed, although they can be hurt. Therefore they must be imprisoned. Can you think of any better way to do it than with the spiders? If Bes and I together cannot break this new weave, it will bind any of them, except perhaps Zeus."

Cruz muttered something about amateurs. Then, he sighed. "I don't see any way out of using the spiders, I give you that."

"What *I'd* like to do is see a way to prevent Arachne going up there," said McKenna. "Yeah. I know, Cruz. She's some kind of freak to you, but she's a nineteen-year-old girl to me. That's what she *is*, dammit! Not what that bitch Athena made her into."

Cruz shrugged. "I guess I'm just not crazy about spiders. But she's the only one who can control them. We need her right on the scene."

"And we need to transport about a million spiders up there. Warm. Can you think of any other way but the tube?" asked McKenna patiently.

Cruz frowned. "No."

McKenna threw out his hands. "Right. That leaves the others. Let's start with Doc. The little guy is the only one of us that really knows much about these Greek gods—except for Prometheus and Medea. Not to mention that the guy's 'magic' has saved our asses more than once. And when you think about it, he's gotten a lot tougher, too. He started this trip looking like any stiff breeze would blow him over. He looks more like whipcord now."

Cruz shrugged. "Yeah. I don't have a problem with the Doc. He reminds me of that Lagrange kid in B company. You know: the small, wiry little runt who took a lot of crap at first because the guys all figured that he'd be the one to flake out on the physical stuff. Then he turned out to be an Olympic-class gymnast."

McKenna snorted. "I was there for the sit-ups competition. So, we need the Doc. That leaves Liz, Lamont, Medea, and Bes, if you don't include the dragons and Throttler, that you want to count out. Well, *you* try telling 'Sir' that she's not going. Or Bes."

"Or Medea," said Cruz quietly, with a wry face. "She gets kinda determined. And that temple really upset her."

"So that leaves Lamont. He's the guy—next to you, Anibal— that I'd most like to have with me in a fight." McKenna rubbed his jaw. "I'm *sure* he was in the service, even if he won't talk about it. And no REMF either."

Cruz sighed. "So what else can go wrong? Besides the whole fucking plan?"

McKenna took a deep breath. "Well, to be honest, there are the parachutes."

Cruz put a hand over his eyes. "Yeah. I just *love* the idea of jumping using something made by a spider."

"Well, let's give it a test run," suggested McKenna.

"With a big rock. Get your girlfriend to sew us a bag."

McKenna didn't even attempt to argue over the definition of Arachne. "Okay. Then we can go on with that crossbow project."

"And what do you want me to do?" asked Prometheus with a smile.

The two paratroopers stared up at him. *Way* up. McKenna grinned. Cruz even managed a smile.

Liz was in a pensive mood. She sighed as she wandered through what must once have been the armory of the Titans. No wonder these guys had been outclassed by the Olympians. Their spears and arrows still had flint tips.

"What's wrong?" came a quiet voice.

She hadn't even seen Jerry there. "Hi. I was just thinking. Wondering about things."

"Nickel for your thoughts," he murmured, while fiddling with a bow three sizes too big for him.

"I reckon you'd think you'd been cheated." She smiled all the same.

"I'll take that chance."

She shrugged. "It was just that I was, well, almost enjoying this. Then I saw that town. Those children. And then, when we were talking about the assault, I realized that we could all get killed. That all this was really totally crazy. That maybe we should be out there trying to find the populace, arm them, train them. Persuade them to at least fight back. Fight an ordinary war, instead of this crazy, commando-style raid."

Jerry took a deep breath. "It's not as simple as all that. That's in part what this Krim-monster depends on: That people here at least accept the 'rightness' and the power of the gods. They *won't* fight. Besides, to be honest, even if we got every human in Ur-Greece, armed them, trained them, and sent them on a frontal assault on Mount Olympus . . . we would probably still lose."

"So why are you doing this, Jerry? Why are you taking part in this?"

He paused. Bit his knuckle. Then said, seriously: "For the same reason you are. Because somebody has to do it. And if I won't, how the hell can I expect Cruz and Mac to do it for me?"

She nodded. "You know, I've realized throughout this jaunt how easy it is to misjudge people. I thought you were one of these little academic arts types. Faint at the sight of blood. Ineffectual. Chicken."

Jerry grinned. "That's a pretty fair description. You just forgot about the 'scared of girls' part."

She lowered her lashes. "Even me?"

His eyes fell away. But only for a moment. "You more than the others. You're rather like my dream girl. A . . . beau ideal woman."

They stood for a few moments in silence.

"I guess I shouldn't have said that." Jerry flushed a little with embarrassment.

Liz smiled broadly. "Actually, it's pretty delightful being told you're somebody's beau ideal. Especially when you've spent your life thinking you're just a big ox and not very feminine."

Jerry smiled shyly. "Well, you got it wrong."

She stuck her tongue out. "My mother told me so. And it's like your assessment of yourself. Way out."

Jerry put his nose up in the air. "*I* have thirty-six years of experience with my subject matter. How dare you tell me I'm wrong?"

She smiled. "You're an idiot."

"Ah! Now I happen to agree with you about that."

Silence returned. Jerry cleared his throat. Cleared it again.

Liz laughed. "Sure, Jerry. If we get out of this alive, and ever get back to our own world—it's a date."

47

⬚⬚⬚⬚⬚⬚⬚

SPIDERWEBS AND MOONSHINE.

Before dawn, Prometheus had transported the balloon fragments and all his companions across to the southeastern flank
of Mount Ossa. A sea mist lay heavy across the Aegean, rolling
off the sea and onto the mountain itself, cold and clammy.

Prometheus smiled. "Oceanus and his Oceanids have done their
work well, Liz. Knowledge is a powerful tool."

"It's just upwelling," said Liz dismissively. "Deep cold water
meets warm moist air."

Prometheus shook his head. "I will say it again. Knowledge
is a powerful weapon. And out of the mist will come the balloons. To the Olympians they will rise out of the mist. They could
just as easily have come across the sea from Lydia as from the
slopes of Mount Ossa. Oceanus has sent his sons to fetch Aeolus,
lord of the winds, to direct them. Now. To work, Magicians. To
work! We have long hours ahead of us."

With the dawn, the first balloon rose out of the rose-tinted
pearlescent mist. Halfway across the vale of Tempe, a thunderbolt from the high ramparts of Olympus struck it and it fell,
burning.

But the next two were already on their way. All day long the thunder and destruction continued, until the red sun hung in the west like a balloon itself. . . .

"I don't know what the gods feel like, but I'm exhausted. Totally and utterly exhausted," said Liz.

Prometheus laughed. "Believe me. They feel far worse. Come. We will go back to the halls of the Titans. I will give you the draught of the Titans. Unlike ambrosia, it does not confer immortal life. But it does restore and refresh. Ambrosia makes the gods drunk."

Cruz was dirty, sweaty and tired. His face was covered in sooty smudges. "I could use the ambrosia myself," he muttered, wiping his hands on his trousers.

But the draught of the Titans was indeed refreshing. It reminded Jerry of coffee. The effect was similar, only more like espresso. Double espresso. Make that treble espresso. Actually, just-leave-out-the-water espresso. Jerry felt as if he might have to prop his eyelids shut if he ever wanted to sleep again.

By the time Cruz and McKenna reappeared, their hands and faces blackened, clothed in the darkest items they could find, Jerry was feeling as if he'd been transformed into a very wide-awake superball. He was ready to bounce off walls, never mind take on a mere frontal assault of Olympus.

Liz arrived, her face similarly blackened. She was carrying a short, bronze-bladed stabbing spear.

"What's the get-up for, Liz? We've still got to get everything across to the vale of Parnassus." Jerry was carefully tying bundles to the huge spider-silk-reinforced basket.

"I'm going in with the parachute party," she said calmly.

Cruz looked up from where he was coiling what looked like miles of fine line. "You can't come along with us, Liz!"

"Why not?"

"Because *we're* paratroopers. You're not."

Liz glared at him. "I have a parachute too, thanks to Arachne. I've jumped before. I even went for a test jump yesterday. Which, according to Smitar, is more than you two have done. Tossing rocks off a poor dragon."

Mac looked at Cruz. Anibal raised his eyes to heaven. "Look, Liz. This isn't a yuppie thrill-trip. It's a goddamn night jump! And when we get down we've got do the stuff we're *trained* to do."

"Stow it, Anibal," said Liz scornfully. "I stalk better than either of you. Our job is to get a line down into the vale of Parnassus so that the others, particularly the spiders, can get up there. Any 'commando' stuff, and the mission is history anyway. Because neither one of you is any more able to deal with gods than I am. And anyway, I promised Medea I'd look after you. Otherwise she won't let the dragons go."

"You're both crazy!" yelled Cruz angrily. "Listen to me, for God's sake. This is *not* a game for amateur skydivers."

Liz stayed calm. "It's a BASE jump, Anibal. From a stationary surface, not a plane. How many have you done?"

McKenna looked at Cruz. "We're not gonna win, you know. Arachne told me she wouldn't do the spider stuff either unless we took a minder. I tried telling her we'd be lot safer without, but she wouldn't accept that. She says . . . " He fell silent.

"Actually, guys," said Liz, "you can't stop me. One of the dragons will take me, whether you like it or not. So I don't see how you can stop me, short of tying me up, and I had a few words with Prometheus. You'd have to tie him up first. Seems someone said to him 'have lots of backup.' "

Anibal ground his teeth audibly. "Is anyone else going to jump? I thought the idea was to keep our drop as quiet as possible. Doesn't the loud lunatic dwarf want to come along too?"

Prometheus smiled. "Bes and Throttler have already gone. Throttler will drop Bes to the north. From that direction he can walk in to Olympus. It will be the most heavily guarded, of course. But Bes says he can move very stealthily."

Cruz groaned. "Like he does for eagles."

Jerry stared at Liz, biting his lip in frustration. *Damn it. If he'd had a bit more time to think he'd have found a way to stop her.*

Medea bustled in. She carried a large bowl, in which a mint-reeking salve lurked, and made occasional threatening gestures. She put it down on the table. "Here. Coat your weapons in this. It should make monsters, nymphs, and maybe even the gods sleep."

Jerry walked up to it, his heart doing trip-hammer imitations. He carefully coated his blade. "It doesn't hurt people, does it?" he asked calmly.

Medea shook her head. "No. It is harmless to those who are not of the blood of Cronus."

Liz had walked up with her short spear. As she bent forward over the bowl . . . Jerry pricked her forearm.

A droplet of blood welled up. Liz looked at it and then at him. "What the hell did you do that for?"

"Sorry."

Then her eyes narrowed. "Oho! You're a sneaky bastard! Does this stuff work on me, Medea?"

Medea shook her head. "No. I said so."

Liz grinned nastily at Jerry. "Nice try though, Jerry."

He shrugged. "I had to give it a go."

"Well, don't even *think* of trying it again!" she snapped. But her voice seemed very warm.

Jerry watched as they mounted the two dragons and rose in a slow spiral towards the moon. Scudding cloud obscured it and the parachute "brigade" was lost in the darkness. He felt his cheek. She'd given him a peck in parting. Forgiveness for his attempt to stop her going, as she said, and in case something went wrong. He shrugged. He wished like hell that he was a big handsome he-man. He wished he'd tried skydiving.

He turned to go back to the preparations for the frontal assault. The problem was a simple one. The icy, bleak heights of the mythological world's Olympus were too cold for the spiders. Yet Prometheus, who had been to the top, assured them that the dwelling place of the gods was not more than pleasantly cool. Somehow they had to get huge numbers of spiders up to the city of the gods.

Jerry was extremely glad he was not a spider. The basket would be bad enough.

Up in the silent darkness clinging to the harness on Smitar's back, Liz felt her bravado drain away. Still, it was too late now.

They continued the long slow spiral upwards. Her mouth was

dry. It was going to be like doing a BASE jump in total darkness, and you'd have to be damn sure you hadn't tangled the
risers. And there was no reserve chute . . . maybe she should have
encouraged Jerry a bit more. He was a nice guy. The sort that
wouldn't make a move without an invitation in triplicate. And
she'd been brought up not to issue invitations.

Then below them in the darkness were the lights of Olympus.
And the blessing of moonlight reflecting off the scudding clouds.
She began carefully arranging her 'chute on the broad dragon
back. Cruz and Mac could take it in turns to jump. The lights
looked a long way down against the bulk of the mountain.

"Cruz *f*say*f*s to wait for the cloud. Rendevou*f*s near the
*f*southea*f*stern light*f*s."

The cloud came. Taking that deep shaky breath, Liz jumped.
The spider-web 'chute spiraled. She jerked frantically at the risers.
Felt the 'chute bite air. She nearly broke a leg on the bruising
landing. The only way out of the harness was slow, or cut. She
cut.

Now she was loose, free at the top of Olympus in the pitch
dark. She couldn't see the lights. She had no idea in which
direction they lay. She'd been too busy anticipating the landing
to pay attention to her bearings. Maybe there was something to
all this military professionalism after all. Oh well. *When in doubt,
don't scream and shout, pick a direction and move out. . . .*

It was easier said than done. The top of Olympus was rocky
and confusing. And the moon remained obstinately cloud-hidden.
Eventually she had the bright idea of climbing the highest rock.
And then of course the moon came out from behind the clouds.

What Liz saw nearly made her sick. There must have been more
wind than she had anticipated. She was right on the edge. If she'd
chosen a different bearing, she'd have taken a shortcut down to
the bottom of the mountain. And another few yards of wind
speed and she'd have been parachuting down to the others. Maybe
there was more to this than she'd opened her big yap about. The
lights were back there.

Then she realized that she had made yet another mistake. Cruz
and McKenna were each carrying at least a thousand yards of
light spider-line. She wasn't. She was in a good position to get

the line down, but she had no line. And maybe the other two had had similar problems. Maybe they'd gone over the edge. Maybe they'd landed in among the rocks. Broken legs or necks. Maybe their 'chutes had failed. Maybe . . . Liz felt very alone and very scared as she made her way towards the lights.

Fortunately Argus of the hundred eyes, the last watchman of the access to heaven, coughed. Otherwise he'd have seen her before she saw him. He was standing at the rendezvous. If the others were not on this side of him . . . They'd have to get past him somehow. And short of major rock-climbing there didn't seem to be a way.

Liz was not normally prey to indecision. She was now. Could she get close enough to stab, or should she try to throw that assegai, or—?

In the shelter of the rocks, Cruz took a careful bead. The sights on the half-assed crossbow were nearly as half-assed as the crossbow itself. It was just a bow set in a plank, really. With a groove to give the arrow a reasonably straight run, and a sort of curved fork at the end to provide a string-holder trigger. Even so, from this range he shouldn't miss.

He missed.

McKenna was already running in, his Gerber in his hand. Argus lunged forward. Liz's spear hit him in the shoulder instead of the spine. She, at least, had the sense to throw herself at his head and to grab his mouth. Cruz flung himself into the fray too. But Argus was a giant, and if he was of the blood of Cronus, he seemed immune to Medea's potions. And even three to one, with Cruz choking and being choked, it could have no happy ending. Liz, clinging to his head, was knocked off against a rock. The Giant got McKenna by one leg and Cruz by both arms with the other immense hand.

"Ha. Now you die," growled Argus. He was going to dash McKenna's brains out against the wall.

Then Bes arrived. The little hooligan ran straight up the giant as if he were a staircase, grabbed him by the ears and head-butted him. Mac fell free. Then Bes wrapped those bandy legs of his around the giant's throat. Argus wasn't going to be screaming for a while. Then, just when Bes had hauled out that evil-looking dagger of his, Argus stumbled. Nearly squashed the dwarf as he fell. He gave a bubbling snore, all hundred eyes closed.

McKenna picked himself up. "I'm gonna have to talk to that girlfriend of yours about how long it takes for her potions to work," he said quietly, flexing a bruised shoulder.

Bes grinned. "I don't approve of all these potions. Sport and drugs don't mix. Why did you start the fighting without me?"

Cruz took a deep breath. "Because we didn't know you were there. Come on. Let's get this big goon out of sight, and tied up, in case this shit wears off."

Spotting the target for the drop was easy. One tiny fire burned down in the folds of Olympus. Getting the cord down was less so. It was extremely light, and it had to be weighted. The weight kept getting stuck on ledges, and, by the sound of it, causing minor avalanches. But eventually there came a tug. It was a good thing Prometheus had said to secure the cord and themselves first. Only the Titan could have tugged that hard. After a minute they began to haul.

It was also a good thing there were four of them, and that Bes was one of those four. Spider-line is very light. But that was nearly nine hundred feet's worth. Liz was soon blessing the gloves she'd been given by the Colchian shepherds. The cord was run through the big wooden pulley and clipped by one of Mac's heavy iron (once steel) snap links, as a guide to the line that was coming up. Eventually, that reached the bottom and then obviously the Titan began to pull. Thicker line came up. And more. And then the pulley began to squeak as a real load came onto it. Cruz, swearing, muffled it as best he could. There was a lookout on the far pinnacle. Presumably the watcher was keeping an eye out for balloons, and it was three hundred yards away . . . and the rope line was in a groove out of his line of sight . . . but still.

The waiting had been the worst part. Jerry had never thought he'd be so grateful for a rock that nearly brained him. They all retreated hastily. It soon became obvious that the cord was not getting all the way down. Eventually, Throttler flew up and fetched it, from a good four hundred feet up.

"Anything that can go wrong, will," murmured Prometheus. Then he turned to the assembled group. "Who is in the basket first?"

"Me," said Jerry stepping forward.

"And me," said Arachne and Medea together.

"I must secure the tunnel," said Arachne.

"Right. Jerry and Arachne first," said Prometheus. "You see that you keep warm, Arachne."

They went up, unwinding the huge spool of spider-web tube. Every hundred feet or so Prometheus paused to allow Arachne to secure the tube with sticky threads. It was a sickening, bumpy process, as the basket dragged against the cliff wall. It all nearly ended in disaster, too.

They could see the summit. And the basket hooked. And Prometheus just kept on pulling. Somehow, as the basket tipped, Jerry managed to grab the remains of the spool while clinging to the handle. Then the basket sprang free, leaping on rope stretched at least twenty feet. Jerry lost his grip on the handle. And fell.

He landed back in the bouncing basket, with a pulse rate of about two hundred.

But there was worse to come. When they finally arrived at the top, there was Bes. McKenna. Cruz.

No Liz. Jerry's heart nearly stopped. "Wh—where's Liz?" he stammered out, his voice high-pitched.

"She's having a scout around," said Cruz. "Just back that way. Be careful. Bes found this interesting hole. We nearly lost him down it."

Jerry set off hastily and found Liz some thirty yards off. She was on hands and knees, peering at Bes' "interesting hole." Jerry restrained a strong and irrational inclination to kick her down it for frightening him so.

She looked up and smiled. He forgave her instantly. "I've solved the mystery of Olympus' pleasant climate. Feel the air coming out of there. It's a geothermal vent."

"They always say necessity is the mother of in*vent*ion," he said cheerily, his heart full of lightness.

She groaned. "Jerry, I could kill you. Punning at this stage."

"Well, it was that or give you a hug," he said bravely.

"That's what I call unfair persuasion," she said, giving him the hug instead. "I must stink. Can't be nice to be near."

Jerry grinned. "The joys of civilization. Cigarettes, coffee and deodorant."

Liz grinned back. "I could use the last two. But do you know it's been nearly two whole weeks since I had a smoke?"

Bes wandered over. "The first spiders have come up."

Prometheus, he who had stolen fire from the gods and taught man its use, tended this fire with great care. It must produce an even, steady heat. Enough to inflate a long, tubular and insulated chimney. The little spider parachutists entered it in a steady stream higher up. Then with silken thread parachutes they drifted up to the heights of Olympus. The tube had been designed to retain heat. It was still a long, long way. And the balance between too much heat and too little was tricky. There were several million spiders to do the trip.

Up on the plateau the spiders, under Arachne's direction, began to weave silken coverlets for Athena. This particular piece of weaving showed in magnificent detail the ill doings, debaucheries and philanderings of the gods.

Athena wouldn't be tearing this one up in a hurry, though.

Throughout the marble halls of the gods, covers were spun. Soft as down. Strong as steel. It was all going according to plan . . .

Except for Hermes. The rest of Olympus might be sleeping off their labors against the balloon fleet, but Hermes was occupied in taking advantage of Poseidon's wife, Amphitrite. Free, those two could wreak havoc. Hermes was definitely part of the pyramid's schemes. And they were pursuing their pastime with godlike vigor and stamina, showing no sign of giving it a rest.

"We need to do something!" whispered Liz to Jerry.

"Uh. Film it and make a fortune in the porno industry. I didn't think that position was possible!" Jerry couldn't help staring.

She suppressed a snort. "I meant to capture them. Voyeur."

Jerry looked thoughtful. "Hmm. Arachne. Could your spiders

sew a sort of bag or trap at the window? I could scare them into it."

Liz chuckled. "What? By saying boo?"

"More or less," he said. "Can you do it, Arachne?"

"My spider-sisters are already busy, Doc." She'd picked up her manner of address from McKenna.

"Right. Tell me when you're ready."

They didn't have long to wait. When it was ready Jerry started giving orders. "Cruz. You've got the deepest voice here. That's blue-eyed Amphitrite, wife of Poseidon, on the job there with Hermes. Poseidon is infamous for his bad temper. I want you to bellow 'Amphitrite' at the door."

"That'll never work, Doc!" protested Cruz.

"It will when I add Pan's panic spell to it," said Jerry calmly. "Just you watch."

Cruz shrugged. "All right. I wish like hell Prometheus was here. But he's got to deal with the guards on the way up."

"I did that!" growled Bes, in an injured tone.

"Great! So why did we risk our necks on spider-web parachutes?" demanded Mac.

The dwarf shrugged in his turn. "Well, Prometheus and I thought it was crazy. But you seemed so set on it that we didn't have the heart to stop you." Bes' tone was apologetic. "Anyway, Prometheus said something about you being 'backup.'"

"Here, dear. My sisters have brought Poseidon's trident. When Cruz calls out, stick that in through the doorway."

"Okay, on the count of three."

"One, two, three . . . *AMPHITRITE!!!*"

The result of Cruz's shout, coupled with Pan's spell, fulfilled all of Jerry's hopes.

Poseidon's reputation was particularly foul. Amphitrite shrieked. Hermes, assisted by panic, was *not* going to be caught. Clutching Amphitrite, he dove through the window. Into the spider-web bag. The *sticky* spider-web bag. Soon the two were safely bundled up.

Just then Prometheus arrived, slightly out of breath.

"Not having any trouble, are we? Everything gone according to plan?" He turned, pointing. "I brought us some company. This is Gaea's last child, Typhoeus."

Everyone tried not to flinch. Typhoeus made Medea's dragons look like earthworms. He had three heads and at least a hundred ever-working hands. Vipers sprouted from his back.

"'Ullo," he croaked. "Seen that little bastard Zeus anywhere?"

"He's back there." Lamont pointed. "But don't you think you'd better deal with the watchman on the pinnacle? Sooner or later he'll come down. Spider webs can be cut, y'know."

Prometheus chuckled. "Very well. Will you guide us then, Lamont?"

Liz sighed. "Well . . . we should be able to get home. Did you see that Hermes was also wearing a pyramid pendant?"

"No. I didn't notice," admitted Jerry.

"Distracted, were you?" Liz teased.

"Um. The light was bad."

Liz pointed at the sky. "Well, it'll be morning soon. The moon is nearly down."

Something about that troubled Jerry. "It's a beautiful moon," he said.

"Don't you mean—*romantic?*" asked Liz mischievously.

Jerry slapped his forehead. "Selene!"

"Selene?"

"The moon goddess! She's out at night!"

And so she was, just touching down with her moon-bearing mule. Any moment now there was going to be trouble—as soon as she'd tied up her mule.

They watched in horror as Selene tied the mule to a post and then began walking towards the mansions of the gods.

"Get Prometheus! I'll distract her!" Liz darted forward. She pulled the huge white mule's reins free and leapt up onto its pannier, and thence its back. She dug her heels in, hard. "Giddyup!!!" she yelled.

The mule took off into the night sky like a venturi-less rocket.

Selene turned and shrieked, and took off through the sky after her mule and its clinging rider. The moon goddess normally flew across the sky, leading her mule. But even with her divine powers, Selene wasn't catching up with the wildly bucking animal.

Liz clung desperately to the saddle panniers. She could ride well. But there were no stirrups, and the mule paid no attention to her frantic hauling at the reins. It alternated between bucking and twisting with wild headlong gallops. They were also moving at a phenomenal speed. It felt as if the mule was doing its best to make up for the lack of a Concorde in this Ur-universe.

48

PICKING UP FALLEN WOMEN.

Jerry Lukacs' entire life experience on horseback consisted of one ride on a led pony at a children's petting farm. He thrust that idle thought aside and ran for Throttler. He jumped onto her back.

"Follow that moon!" he yelled. He was vaguely aware of someone jumping up behind him.

Lamont, returning with Prometheus and Typhoeus from watching a guard give a highly instructive lesson in how not to fly down the face of Mount Olympus, saw the moon, Selene, Jerry and Throttler race up into the night sky.

"What's that?" he shouted.

"I don't know, but let's get to Zeus fast," said Prometheus grimly. Typhoeus was already racing towards the sleeping place of the master of the Olympians.

Lamont met up with Cruz and McKenna, who had come in hasty search.

"*What happened?*"

Cruz looked grim. "Some goddess arrived with the moon, on that gigantic donkey thing."

"It's a mule," interjected McKenna.

Cruz shrugged. "Whatever. Anyway, Liz stole her mule to distract her. It worked all right, but the animal is out of control. Mac and I both got arrows into the goddess. They've got Medea's dope on them. But the stuff takes quite some time to work."

"And Liz?" asked Lamont.

"Jerry and Bes have gone after her on Throttler. But look at how fast that damn thing is going!"

"I think 'Sir' has bitten off more than she can chew this time," scowled Mac.

There were shouts from the resting place of Zeus. "Come on, Mac," said Cruz. "Let's get Medea and go and prick all these guys with the dope. Lamont, you know the most about these gods except for Jerry. It sounds like Typhoeus is having some trouble with Zeus. Go and check it out. Take the dragons."

Zeus was indeed the most powerful of the Olympians. He'd somehow managed to start a tear in the spider-web coverlet. Incandescently angry, he'd half sat up . . . to find that Typhoeus, who had once defeated and imprisoned him, was wrapping dragonish coils around him.

Prometheus seized his arms. That would have been folly for the Titan but for the monstrous strength of Typhoeus. Lamont arrived just in time to see the Titan being flung across the room. And Typhoeus slapping an enormous coil around Zeus' chest. Typhoeus snatched the thunderbolt hand in one of his mouths.

Another set of Typhoeus' teeth took Zeus through the nose. "Behave!" said the third head. "Mother is very cross with you."

Liz knew that she was in dire trouble. Extremely dire trouble. Trouble that could only end in falling. Only the panniers had saved her so far. Whatever drove the tides of the Ur-Mythworld, it wasn't the gravitational influence of the moon. That must be negligible. And the moon must be reachable here, as it was not very big. It must actually travel quite close to the earth to be seen. But, from the way things were shaping up, it didn't travel as close to the earth as she was soon going to be.

✧　　✧　　✧

Jerry leaned over Throttler's neck. "GO FASTER!"

"I can't!" shouted the sphinx.

"Use the power to move between sphinx images to get closer!"

"At this speed?! Hold tight. Asia Minor here we come!"

There was a zipping of air.

"We're ahead," growled Bes. "If the damned thing doesn't change direction!"

Jerry just had time to see Liz, with her eyes shut and hair streaming back, when Selene's mule did just that. She nearly fell. They were losing ground again when the sphinx did her *zip* trick.

This time the mule saw them and gave an extra spurt of speed. The chase went on.

"I'm tiring," said Throttler.

"One more jump. Please?" begged Jerry. "Let's try and get well ahead and above them."

"That will take us to the delta," said Throttler. "There is a shortage of sphinx images around here."

"That seems to be the way the beast is going, anyway. Let's try it."

So they did. Below lay the Nile delta. Throttler struggled to gain height. The moon, Liz and Selene's mule were still coming towards them.

Lamont pointed to the pyramid on the table. "I want some answers."

"I am a god, mortal," snarled Zeus. "Not answerable to you or anyone. You cannot make me do anything!"

Lamont snarled right back. "How would you like to *become* a mortal, shithead?"

"No one can kill me! Eventually, I will be free, and then you are going to die. Very slowly."

Typhoeus squeezed. "Mother said to teach you some manners."

Zeus squealed.

Lamont leaned into the god's personal space. "How would you like a trip to Egypt, Zeus? Ur-Egypt. Using the sphinx, we transported an Egyptian god here. He isn't capable of godlike powers *here*. So we can take you *there*. And we've got quite some skills at Egyptian magic. With that we can even compel their gods. *You'll* be a pushover."

Zeus' eyes bulged. Then he wilted. The threat obviously cowed him. "What do you want from me?" The voice changed. There was a certain atonal quality to it.

"Some answers about a certain pyramid you were wearing around your neck. Where did it come from? And some answers about how we can get home."

Zeus tried to shake his head. "Wormhole travel, from thousands of light-years away. A probe—what you call Artificial Intelligence. You are in a collapsing Ur-universe, the remnants of which we have revived. You can travel to other Ur-universes that share elements of common belief, but there is no way of escaping from the Ur-universe, except for a cessation of meme-carrier function. You have to die."

"I think you're lying, but I'll come back to that. So, tell me who you are," said Lamont, almost conversationally.

"I am Zeus, Lord of the Olympians, mortal. Quail . . . "

"Bullshit. Egypt, here we come! You're something to do with that pyramid that appeared in Chicago. Like this one, but bigger." Lamont held the pyramid pendant from the table in front of Zeus' face.

Silence.

"Talk, punk. Or it's trouble time." The very matter-of-factness of Lamont's statement made it hard to doubt.

The captive god was red in the face. Almost puce.

Typhoeus nodded. "Mother said something was going on. That the little monster wasn't himself. Mother is always right."

The horrible-looking creature gave Zeus a good shake. "What's gotten into you, anyway? You always were a poisonous little creep, sure, bullying mortals just to prove you were the boss. But Mother says you've gone crazy. Killing everything. And hurting everything. Mother says the whole place is full of pain-feelings. She doesn't like it. You'd better listen. She's getting mad."

"Your threats do not cow me!" said Zeus with bravado.

"They'd better," said Typhoeus grimly. "When Mother gets mad, she's likely to make your going to Egypt the easy option."

"I am beyond Gaea's control. I am Krim. We are the lords of the universe!" yelled Zeus, straining to get free.

Lamont snorted. "You're about to be the ex-lord. Why are you snatching people, Krim? Talk!"

"My servant collects local gullible sentients with high anger quotients for us. We need them. We need lots of them. It breathes new life into the Ur-universe. We come to take the reins of power once all is prepared. As soon as there is sufficient energy, we come . . . "

"What for?" demanded Lamont.

Zeus-Krim looked puzzled. "Because we are Krim. We find intelligent species and do this. We always have."

Typhoeus loosened a coil slightly. "They like power. Like little Zeus. That's probably why the toad got involved with this Krim stuff in the first place. Only these ones like pain and misery even more than Zeus did."

Typhoeus had slackened his grip on Zeus' hand for an instant. And Zeus-Krim ripped his hand through the teeth, tearing through the flesh, regardless of the damage. He did not fling thunderbolts. Instead he snatched up the pyramid.

"You cannot hold the Krim!" he shrieked.

There was a brief purple discharge. The Krim device in the god's hand suddenly disappeared. The change in Zeus was immediately apparent.

Zeus seemed to crumple. He looked older. Looser in flesh and possessed of bloodshot eyes streaming tears.

"Thank you," he said weakly. "I was disappearing into it. It's terrible! It feeds on pain. And it loved having a body. That's what those Krim are doing here. It's their main form of entertainment."

Typhoeus looked at Zeus. "You are in dire trouble with Mother Gaea."

Zeus began to sob again. "I just wanted to have fun!"

Liz was exhausted. What was worse, her mount was showing no sign of exhaustion. And they must have traveled hundreds of miles in the huge bounds and at the terrific speeds they were doing.

Weird. She could have sworn that she had caught sight of Jerry and that sphinx earlier. She was going to fall. And she was going to die. It was a pity she'd not have a chance to see what might happen with Jerry. It could—just maybe—have worked out better than her past choices.

But it was too late to think about that now. Her hands just couldn't hold on much longer.

"Physical contact seems to work," said Bes. "If we can touch it and you jump from this Egypt in Ur-Greece to Ur-Egypt itself— then I can have my true godlike powers. And the mule will no longer have *his*. So use your hunting spells, Jerry. And try to touch her when we dive."

Throttler folded her wings and dove down to the mule. As they came near, Jerry called to the spirits of the hunt for aid. He leaned out and grabbed with all his strength. As his hand closed on Liz's hair there was the sudden *zip* of sphinx transposition. And then the mule, Liz, sphinx and Jerry were falling, tangled together. Bes wasn't. Jerry saw him deliberately dive off the sphinx's back.

"Bes! Protector!" Jerry's shriek was overridden by the bray of a giant mule that has suddenly found that it is falling.

Jerry managed to transfer his hand from Liz's hair to her arm. He tried to pull her onto the sphinx. A mule hoof, fortunately at the end of its travel, nearly sent him spinning. It did send the mule spinning. Jerry clung desperately to Liz. She clung weakly to him. But a last mule kick ripped her out of his gasp. She was falling.

Jerry did the craziest thing he'd ever done in his life. He dived after her.

It was only when he was also falling that he realized how insane that was. Looking down he realized they were still at least a hundred feet above the ground. And there, clear in the moonlight for an instant, was Bes. The dwarf had somehow landed safely and was waving his arms as if trying to catch their attention.

"BEEEESSSS!" yelled Jerry.

He tried to reach for Liz. The moon was darkened by a diving sphinx. A claw closed on his jacket, which mercifully ripped as it was about to throttle him and pull his arms off at the same time.

Impact.
Soft impact.

After a few seconds Jerry sat up. Or tried to. He was alive. Somehow he was alive. Alive and lying in some soft stuff. Which was getting up his nose...

He sneezed. Somebody groaned.

Something akin to a small hurricane pulled the soft stuff aside. "I wish you'd stayed on the sphinx," grumbled Bes. "Do you know what trouble I had moving this stuff around to catch you both?"

"Liz?" called Jerry.

"Unggh."

Jerry beat Bes pushing through the reed blossom and lotus petal mass. Liz had not had the benefit of sphinx-assisted braking. She'd gone all the way down to the soft deltaic mud underneath. Jerry hauled her upright.

"*Auuuh!*" The mud-and-petal-covered woman caught her breath. "Gently. I think that arm is broken."

Then Throttler came down and covered them all in lotus-blossom petals again. After he burrowed them out, Jerry half-carried Liz to the small tree-covered islet.

He bit his lip. Snapped two branches. Ripped the remains of his shirt into shreds. "I'm going to have to hurt you, Liz. I'm really sorry. I've got to splint that arm."

She looked at him, her eyes moist in the moonlight. "You crazy fool. It hurts like hell but I'm still alive, thanks to you. Do your worst."

"Crazy fool are the right words," snorted Throttler incredulously, "but not strong enough. He jumped after you. Did you know that?"

Liz nodded. "I saw. I'd call him 'my hero' except"—her cheeks dimpled, despite the pain—"he is. *Ow!*"

A while later, after the strapping had been done, Jerry asked, "How come *you* aren't dead, Bes?"

The dwarf grinned. "In Ur-Egypt?" He looked around. "It's nice to be back, but I really fancy this world of yours. Cruz was telling me that they have these dwarf-tossing contests . . . "

"Well," said Liz, her good arm over Jerry's shoulder. "I hate to say it, but I think we must get back to Olympus. They may need us, and I certainly could use some of Mac's so-called brandy."

PART X

In Xanadu did Kubla Khan
A stately pleasure-dome decree . . .

—Samuel Taylor Coleridge,
"Kubla Khan"

49

PUT NO FAITH IN PROMISES.
CASH ONLY.

By the time the sphinx had ferried them back to Olympus, rosy-fingered dawn was already painting the mountain. Their return was eagerly awaited.

"I thought you'd bought a farm that time, Liz!" said Mac. Then, grinning: "Sir."

Liz smiled weakly, pointing to her arm. "Close. But they wanted an arm and a leg for the farm. Jerry would only let them have one arm."

She reached out with the other hand and took Jerry by the arm and pulled him closer. "Our Jerry's something of a hero. If you can call saving me being heroic, that is. Between him, Throttler and Bes, they kept me alive."

"And you got rid of Selene so all of us stayed alive," said Jerry quietly, but firmly. "Now, Mac, come and look at this arm. I did my best, but I'd appreciate it if you checked it out."

Mac's grin widened. "So long as you don't want me to shave all over first."

✧   ✧   ✧

The gods and goddesses of Olympus woke to a new regime. One that didn't want to be there. Prometheus had dragged the beds of the Olympians into the central square.

Oh. And also a net bag with two very unhappy occupants.

The sight of the Olympians sweating away in the bright sunlight greeted Medea's two children, when they arrived from Ortherys. With all the kindness and generosity of youth, they started bouncing on the beds and their occupants. It's a very effective antisoporific.

Prometheus quelled the groanings and querulous "what's-going-ons?" with a bellow. "*Quiet!*"

There was silence, except from the net bag. "Throw a bucket of cold water over them," said Medea to her older son.

Typhoeus allowed Zeus to sit upright. Prometheus cleared his throat. "All right, all of you. Zeus has some explaining to do."

"And Mother is very displeased with all of you," growled Typhoeus. "Very displeased indeed. Especially with *you*, Hera. As Zeus' wife, Mother expects you to keep him on the straight and narrow."

"He beats me if I try," Hera whined.

Typhoeus snorted. "I'm staying on here. Mother says I'm to sort him out."

"I foresee a new silver age for Olympus," said Jerry to Liz, *sotto voce.*

"What's that?"

"According to Hesiod, a time when men obeyed their mothers all their lives. It is interpreted by scholars as an age of matriarchal rule." Jerry grinned. "I think they got it wrong. I think it was a time when Typhoeus said: *Mommy says.*"

Lamont grinned. "The monster's not Egyptian, is he?"

Bes shook his head. "Nope. I wonder whether he'd like a wrestling match?"

Bit by bit the story of how the Krim had misled the Olympians came out. Promises of power and glory, which had ended up with the Krim enjoying all the power and all the joys of the flesh, in their chosen representatives, while these became little more than prisoners in their own bodies. Finally an oath was sworn, on the

Styx and by Gaea, by each and every Olympian that the Krim and its servants were to be hunted and harried hence.

"Hatchoo!" The net bag shook.

"This is all your fault!" hissed Amphitrite, her voice vibrant with anger.

"The Krim bade be do it," whined Hermes. "I don't even *like* you. And I'b caught a coad."

A meaty slap rang out from inside the bag.

"Egypt is a wise choice, my friends," said Prometheus. "Zeus has sworn not to harm or hinder you. Hera and Typhoeus will try to see that he keeps his promises. But I distrust him."

"Yeah, I think getting out of here before he's free is a smart move," said Lamont. "And we can do more with Egyptian myth-magic. Maybe even figure out a way home."

Prometheus smiled. "Good luck."

The former maintenance man and now part-time Greek-god repressor shook hands with the Titan. "You too. You're going to need it."

"You're sure that we can't somehow get Athena to transform Arachne back?" demanded Mac.

Prometheus sucked air through his tombstone-sized teeth. "We've tried. You saw how we tried. But she is vicious and vengeful. Even if we could kill her, she's not going to give way. Perhaps with Egyptian magic it may be possible."

Mac scowled ferociously. He'd advocated torturing Athena, earlier, but had been overruled. "Well, we've taken away her armor and spear. If she wants them back she'd better come to terms with us."

Prometheus shook his head sadly. "I doubt it. But at least it will stop her committing too many more military atrocities."

Their farewells said, the snatchees mounted one of the chariots of the gods, accompanied by Bes, Arachne, Medea, and the children. These chariots flew with more ease than Medea's and were also large enough for a garden party. The dragons were hitched up.

"I wa*f*s thinking," mused Smitar, "what about Olympian *f*stew?"

"Eternal *f*stew," said Bitar.

There was a moment's silence. "I ʃsuppose it could maybe give you eternal runʃs," said Smitar doubtfully.

"Eternal heartburn," added Bitar.

"Eternal ʃsquirtʃs," shuddered Smitar.

Cruz took the reins. "Right. Mount Ortherys and then Egypt."

"Not flying all the way to Egypt again!" protested Bitar.

"Yeʃs," complained Smitar. "Not again. ʃSailorʃs don't even taʃste niʃce!"

"The sphinx thinks that if we're all in contact, we can all go sphinx-to-sphinx-image travel," comforted Jerry.

Jerry looked back at the mountain. He wasn't instantly turned into a pillar of salt—but it was close.

"We're being chased!" he yelled.

Behind them, but gaining fast, were chariots bearing Ares, Apollo and Athena.

"So *that's* how Zeus keeps his promises," hissed Lamont.

"Yeah—to the letter. But not the spirit. He's not following us. Not himself."

"I'll jump before I let Athena catch me!" said Arachne, with grim determination.

"I'm going to put a doped arrow into the bitch first," snapped Mac.

Medea shook her head regretfully. "It won't work twice."

"Throttler!" yelled Jerry. "We need to all make contact and get to a sphinx image!"

Cruz grabbed his arm. "Does it work with any sphinx image?"

"Yes. Anywhere there was belief."

"I'm an idiot!" snarled Cruz. He grubbed frantically in his rucksack, scattering his belongings everywhere. Then, he hauled out a 5" x 3" painting which had once been a photograph.

"In Vegas you can always find somebody who believes in anything you could think of! Especially money! Here, Throttler. *This is the sphinx statue we want to go to!*"

Throttler nodded. "All link up. Athena is gaining fast. One of you dragons will have to take my tail in your mouth. Don't chew."

✧   ✧   ✧

Athena closed with incredible rapidity. Dragons were not that fast at sky swimming. Hands and bodies were just linked, when she threw herself out of her higher chariot at them. "*Got youuu!*" she yelled in triumph.

The *zip* feeling was long drawn out. Something was clutching Jerry's shoulder as tightly as he held onto Liz's hand.

50

⊡⊓⊔⊓⊔⊡

DWARVES UNTOSSED.

They flashed out of the bright Mediterranean morning sunshine into an even brighter desert day. They were heading straight for a black pyramid. For a horrible moment, Jerry thought it was the Krim pyramid. Then, looking more closely, he saw that the pyramid had four sides instead of five, with a glass apex. And the giant sphinx in front of it was painted blue and yellow.

Cruz cleared up the mystery. "That's it!" the paratrooper shouted triumphantly. "*Las Vegas! The Luxor casino!*"

Athena's yell of triumph turned into a shriek of confusion. The goddess, still clutching Jerry's shoulder, was the only one who wasn't bellowing in glee as they bounced to a rough landing on the small plaza right in front of the Luxor, barely missing the obelisk perched on its south side.

Jerry took a deep breath as he looked around. The traffic on the Strip was already screeching to a halt. Even for Las Vegas, he realized, the sudden apparition of a real sphinx, two dragons and a huge chariot was . . . unusual. A traffic stopper.

Then he caught sight of McKenna. He had a gorgeous girl with the face of Arachne in his arms. Apparently, the transfer to the

389

real world had eradicated the effects of Athena's curse. Of course, since the spider hadn't been wearing clothes, neither was the young woman in Mac's arms. But the sight of a nude woman, he supposed, was only a minor distraction in Las Vegas.

"Talk about luck," muttered Lamont.

Jerry turned on him. "That's *just* it! LUCK. You've got Tyche's blessing, Lamont! No wonder you never got seriously hurt. No wonder we got home."

Lamont opened his mouth. "And the rest of you?"

"Since we were with you, we shared your luck. I guess."

Jerry took a long look at the shrunken Athena huddled in the bottom of the chariot. Her face and body had obviously benefited from Olympian magic-style plastic surgery. The magic hadn't transferred to their own world. "Athena's spells don't work here. So Arachne is human again."

Lamont grinned. "So I guess Mac's about to get lucky too. I suppose that means my run of luck is over. Pity. I enjoyed fishing."

Jerry Lukacs grinned back and Lamont chuckled. Now that they were back in their own world, the transformation of Jerry Lukacs was more striking than anyone's. This was a very different man from the weedy academic who had been snatched from the Oriental Institute. It wasn't just the tanned face, the ragged clothes or the sinewy brown arms that protruded from the rolled-up tunic sleeves. It was his posture. It hadn't seemed so noticeable back in the Mythworld. But here, back in the U.S.A., the difference was startlingly obvious to Lamont.

"I don't see why," Jerry said cheerfully. "Lady Luck has got to be the *one* goddess that is still very much in favor. Especially around this part of the world. You could say she still has a fair number of temples and devotees."

Cruz pulled out his dice. "Bet you ten bucks you can't beat me." He threw a straight. Lamont shrugged. Picked up the dice. Tossed a royal flush.

"He's still got it!" Cruz picked up Lamont by the elbows and practically tossed him out of the chariot. "We're going to make a fortune!"

Lamont took a deep breath. "I haven't got any money."

Cruz grinned. He rummaged around in his tattered rucksack. Pulled out a card, miraculously restored from fine-painted ivory to plastic. "I've got a bank card and I'll stake you. And with your luck, it'll still work despite what it's been through."

Lamont nodded determinedly. "Why not? It's not really gambling, when you think about it. And I've got a family to support again." The relief that last thought brought him was almost blinding. "But first I've got to call Marie and let her know I'm back."

By now, a large crowd was gathering and beginning to spill onto Las Vegas Boulevard. Through the mob two policemen pushed their way to the fore, and not far behind them came half a dozen men wearing some kind of uniform. The Luxor's security force, Jerry supposed.

Bes was unhitching the dragons. Medea clung to Cruz's arm. "What king can afford such palaces?"

Jerry was startled to hear Medea speaking in perfect English. Without, even, any accent.

Athena groaned. "Where am I?"

She, too, was speaking English. Somehow, Jerry realized, Medea's language magic was still working. But he didn't have time to figure out how, because the situation began rapidly deteriorating.

"Where am I?" repeated Athena. The goddess' voice was becoming shrill.

Mac, his arms around Arachne, grinned nastily. "You're in trouble. That's where you are, you vindictive bitch. In trouble and a looong way from home. Enjoy!"

The first policeman was now at the side of the chariot. Before he could utter a word, Mac grabbed Athena by the scruff of her tunic and practically tossed her into the cops' arms. "Arrest her, officers! She's a kidnapper!"

The uncertainty of the policemen was immediately dispelled by Athena, who began shrieking like a lunatic and scratching at their faces. Cursing under his breath, one cop subdued her while his partner handcuffed the goddess. Former goddess, rather. Still-practicing deities don't have their Miranda Rights read to them. . . .

Jerry looked around and realized that they were on the verge of pure chaos. And worse.

Even now, Throttler was eagerly advancing on a group of tourists, licking her chops. "*Why did the chicken cross the road?*" she roared.

"To get to the other side," squeaked several of the tourists, edging back in near panic. One young lad, a brash fellow, snorted and exclaimed: "Oh, bullshit! *For a fowl reason!*"

Throttler's eager expression changed to a hurt one. She looked reproachfully back at the Americans.

McKenna chuckled. "Everybody here knows *that* one, Throttler. Try your old standard!" The young paratrooper scanned the crowd cheerfully. "Not too many classical scholars in *this* bunch, I'm willing to—"

"You idiot!" hissed Cruz. "She'll *eat* anybody who blows it!"

McKenna looked chagrinned. Hastily, Jerry hopped off the chariot and hurried over to Throttler. "You can't eat people here!" he shouted.

Throttler's scowl was truly frightening. "I'm *hungry*," she roared.

"*fSo are we!*" bellowed Bitar and Smitar. The two dragons gave the mob their own hungry look. Bitar's eyes fell on a very good-looking young woman at the forefront, dressed in a halter top and tight shorts.

"I*fs* thi*fs* a maiden?" he demanded.

The girl giggled. "In *Las Vegas*? You want Kansas, you big snake!"

The tourists packed at the front of the crowd tried to edge back further. But it was impossible. The press was becoming incredible from the streams of onlookers racing toward the scene from every direction. The traffic on the Strip was now locked solid. People were clambering out of their cars to get a better look.

Jerry was desperately trying to think of some way to forestall an impromptu slaughter when he caught sight of a burly man in an expensive-looking suit forcing his way to the front. The fellow was balding, middle-aged, and accompanied by several security guards. He had "boss" written all over him.

"Are you in charge here?" Jerry yelled.

The man more or less burst out of the crowd and came up to him. "Hank Flanders. I'm the general manager of the Luxor." He stuck out his hand and gave Jerry a firm handshake.

Firm and very brief. The general manager's eyes were shrewd and knowing. "I'm willing to bet you guys are that one big group of alien abductees that never came back dead. Your photographs have been all over the papers. Although—" The knowing eyes flitted rapidly over the party, spending no more time on the nude figure of Arachne than anyone else. "They didn't do you justice."

Jerry nodded mutely. But Flanders' shrewd gaze was already riveted on the sphinx and the two dragons. "Can we figure you're their agent?" he asked. "I'll give all three of them a top contract. Work starts immediately, and for as long as the monsters are willing to sign for."

Jerry gaped. Flanders eyed him speculatively.

Fortunately, Lamont was more quick-witted. "Everything they can eat," he said immediately. "Starting *now.*"

Flanders started bellowing orders. In the chaos and confusion, logic began to return. A number of the Luxor's employees starting racing back to the casino.

"Okay," said Flanders. "That's that. What else?"

Lamont's knowledge of Las Vegas contract negotiations had clearly reached its limit. He stared at Jerry. Jerry shook his head, trying to clear away his own confusion.

"Mr. Flanders, could we continue this inside? And later?" Jerry took Liz by the uninjured arm. "We need to get her to a doctor right away. And I'd better tell Uncle Sam that we're home."

"No sweat." Flanders started hustling him and Liz and Lamont toward the entrance. A squad of security guards cleared a path. "You've *all* got contracts, you want 'em. Top billing every night, for six months running. *How we escaped the alien menace.* I can get half a dozen top singers and comedians—easy—to warm up the crowd."

Jerry goggled at him. Liz burst into laughter. Lamont grinned and said: "First, Mr. Flanders, I intend to clean you out of several million dollars. I'm feeling *very* lucky."

The Luxor's general manager grinned back. "If you can do it, without cheating, more power to you. And if it's pure luck you're counting on, the fastest way to make money is with baccarat. Or the hundred-dollar progressive slots. But I'll give you fair warning—those games can gobble up your own money faster than anything, too."

The rest of the party had caught up with them by now. Cruz, hearing Flanders' last remark, smiled evilly and fingered his credit card. "The rest of you guys want in on this? I'll front you the stake."

The fact that everyone nodded like puppets didn't seem to faze Flanders in the least. After a moment's careful assessment of them, he cocked his head toward one of his assistants. "Andy, better get a press release ready. I have a feeling we'll be announcing some big new winners."

Another of his assistants looked worried. "Uh, Hank . . . You remember that time MGM Grand had an entire quarter's profits taken *in one night* by a guy at the baccarat table?"

Flanders nodded. "Fifteen million bucks. And we lost almost two million not so long ago at the progressive slots. So what?" He jerked his head to the north. The great blue edifice of the MGM Grand was easily visible. "They're still there, aren't they? Making money hand over fist."

And that was apparently as much argument as the Luxor's general manager was willing to accept. "Do it, Andy," he growled. "The publicity'll be fantastic. By tomorrow morning, the Luxor's going to be the most famous casino in the whole world."

Jerry caught side of Throttler and the two dragons, still in the plaza. For such huge and fearsome creatures, they looked amazingly like abandoned puppies. The reproach in their eyes, watching their human companions leave, was almost heartbreaking.

"Hang tight!" Jerry shouted. "We'll be back! And there's food on the way!"

That seemed to mollify them. A little boy edged his way closer to Throttler, holding out a little bag. "You like peanuts?"

The sphinx stared at the bag. "What are 'peanuts'?"

Seconds later, Throttler was beaming. "These are great!" she announced to Smitar and Bitar. "You should try some!"

A moment later, the sphinx and the dragons were being mobbed by tourists offering peanuts and candy bars.

"Gonna ruin their appetite," muttered Lamont. "Thank God."

Flanders seemed like a human bulldog. Before they knew it, he had them halfway up a curving ramp leading toward the casino itself. To their left, a huge replica of Harmakhis loomed overhead, fronting onto the Strip.

"The color scheme's off, y'know," commented Liz. From the pinched look on her face, Jerry thought she was trying to hold off the pain with whimsy. He put his arm around her waist and squeezed gently.

"She's right," he said, more to keep her mind off the pain than because he cared. "Close, but . . . the real Harmakhis is painted red, too."

Flanders was bellowing to yet another assistant before Jerry finished the sentence. "Kenny! Get me some painting contractors!"

"Does *anything* make you pause?" demanded Liz.

Flanders' grin seemed an immovable part of his face by now. "That's why I get paid the big bucks, ma'am."

"Tell 'em to give you a raise," she snorted.

"I intend to. Unless they fire me." Needless to say, the last remark was said without the slightest pause.

Once they were inside the casino, Jerry's eyes had to make an adjustment. The interior combined dim lighting with, off a bit in the distance, the flashing colors and cheerful sounds of the slot machines and gambling tables. As Flanders hustled them past the long reception desk slanting along the right side of the huge and cavernous space, Jerry got only glimpses of the Egyptian decor. The only thing that registered were two statues of hieracosphinxes.

Then he spotted a bank of phones, next to a coffee bar. The words "International Grounds" registered on his eyes, but not his mind.

"Stop! I've got to make some calls!"

Flanders chortled and shook his head. He guided all of them

into a railed-off area in front of the coffee bar. A moment later, all of them were sitting at some round black tables.

"Use my cell phone," he offered, pulling the instrument out of his suit pocket. Then, to Liz: "I'll get you a doctor right away."

Flanders gave some quick orders to yet another assistant. By now, he seemed to have a little mob of them surrounding him, along with at least a dozen security guards. His eyes fell on Arachne, huddled in McKenna's sheltering arms. Now that the excitement of the moment was over, the Greek girl was clearly abashed by her nudity.

The general manager jerked his thumb at a nearby boutique. Luxor Logo Shop, it was called. "Get her a bathrobe, Linda," he ordered. "Now. Comp it. Then go over to the boutique in the Galleria and get her something fancier."

The female assistant's eyes gave Arachne's body a quick and expert size measurement and she was on her way. Not *quite* running.

"Run!" bellowed Flanders.

He didn't wait to see if she obeyed. He was hauling a large cigar out of one jacket pocket and a Zippo out of another. "Been saving this for a special occasion." A moment later, Flander's still-grinning face was shrouded with blue smoke.

"Best day I've ever had," he announced cheerfully. He eyed Lamont and Cruz, and pointed the cigar toward the gaming tables. "Thattaway, gentlemen. Let's see if you can make good your boast."

Lamont looked at Jerry uncertainly. Jerry paused from punching numbers into the cell phone and smiled. "Go ahead, Lamont. It'll take me a while to get through to somebody, anyway. I'll see the word gets passed to Marie. You might as well take care of your retirement."

Lamont rose from the chair, almost giggling. "No more rusted bolts for me!" A moment later, he and Cruz were gone. Medea began to rise, about to follow her new man. Then she relaxed into her chair and hugged her two children close.

"See?" she demanded. "A good provider! Not like that worthless father of yours!"

From the cloud of blue smoke, Flanders' booming voice

issued. "Pedro! Get this lady a divorce lawyer. Best one in town. Comp it."

Perched on his own chair, looking a bit like a squat, lion-headed kid, Bes' voice boomed even louder.

"Where are these dwarf-tossing contests I heard about?"

"Alice!" boomed Flanders. "You heard him—*book the act.*"

Jerry had finally gotten through to the Oriental Institute. But all he got was a message: *this number is no longer in service.* So he overheard the exchange between Bes and Flanders, which caused him to go slightly pale.

"Uh, Mr. Flanders . . . that's likely to be a little tough on the dwarf tossers. *Would-be* tossers, I should say." He eyed Bes uncertainly. "Unless he's lost his powers."

Bes stood up and transformed his wrought-iron chair into a modernistic sculpture. In three seconds.

"Guess not," muttered Jerry.

"Better yet!" boomed Flanders. "Rita! Get hold of the World Wrestling Federation! Book half a dozen top figures. Villain types, you hear? *The Little Guy's Revenge,* we'll call it."

A doctor came rushing up. "Thank god," murmured Liz, holding out her arm. "*Something* in this place isn't showbiz."

"Wendy!" boomed Flanders. "Get the best illustrator in town! I want this lady's cast to be a piece of art!"

From the direction of the gambling area, a loud and excited murmur was beginning to arise. As if someone was beginning to win *big.*

"Freddie!" boomed the voice out of the blue clouds. "Tell Andy to *get moving* on that press release!"

All the numbers Jerry tried to dial seemed out of service. He suddenly remembered that the phones involved had been close to the Krim pyramid. He turned toward Flanders and started to speak. "How much has that thing grown since we were snatched?"

Flanders didn't answer the question directly. "Forget the phone! You're about to go on national TV. Everybody'll get your message."

Sure enough. A TV news crew was hustling forward through the mob in the casino, their way being cleared for them by security guards and policemen.

51

NOT HIRING OR TAKING APPLICATIONS.

Miggy Tremelo sat at his desk staring at the pages of Henri's "diary of events," desperately trying to find *something* that could convince the Powers That Be to cancel the use of the tactical nuke which was scheduled to take place in—

He glanced at his watch. *Nine hours.* The scowl on Miggy's face deepened. They'd have to evacuate the area themselves before much longer. Granted, the bomb was the nuclear equivalent of a shaped charge. Nor did Miggy doubt the claims of the nuclear technicians that the device would create minimal destruction everywhere except the target. "Minimal," at least, by nuke standards.

But he was even more certain that the effect on the alien intruder would be catastrophic. Every time energy had been applied to the black pyramid in the hopes of destroying it, the thing had simply *grown*—and in direct proportion to the energy involved. Tremelo saw no reason to assume that the tac nuke would cross some magic threshold. He expected the pyramid to expand enormously, which, among other things, would engulf his own office in the snatch radius. He wasn't worried about that from his own point of view, but there was no way he was going to risk Marie being snatched. With Lamont already gone, the Jackson kids would be orphans.

"*Idiots!*" he hissed.

One of Miggy's technicians burst into Tremelo's office without stopping to knock. He hardly stopped to open the door. "The alien object has just reduced in size!" he squeaked. "Registered on all our instruments!"

Tremelo's eyes narrowed. "I wonder if someone just got away . . . "

Marie burst into the cluttered office through another door. "*They're back! It just came on the news!*"

A moment later, Miggy and Marie were part of the small crowd standing in front of the little television in the nearby lunch room. The man being interviewed on the screen bore a startling resemblance to Indiana Jones. Except he seemed smaller, dirtier, more disheveled, and a lot smarter.

" . . . *not* try to attack the thing," he was saying. "I repeat— DO NOT launch any kind of attack on the Krim device. The material element involved in its construction is minute and essentially impervious to damage. The Krim device is a probe, essentially. I don't know how it works, because the science involved is way beyond our knowledge. But I do know that the thing survived passage through an interstellar wormhole. Check with any reputable astrophysicist and I'm sure they'll tell you that the energies and stresses involved in such a wormhole passage far exceed anything we're capable of creating."

"Get Milliken on the phone," growled Tremelo to Marie. "No— to hell with Milliken! Get me the damned President!"

Marie nodded, but made no move to comply. Her face seemed almost pale with strain. Belatedly, Miggy realized that the man on the TV screen—Professor Lukacs, obviously, even if he didn't look much like his photographs—had so far said nothing about the survivors.

"Not right now, Marie," he murmured, putting a comforting arm around her shoulders. "It'll keep for a while."

Lukacs was blithering on about the Krim device. For all his own desperate desire to learn as much as he could, Tremelo felt a sudden flash of anger at the mythologist. *Damn all absent-minded professors, anyway! What about Marie's husband? Is he still alive, you—you jerk!*

" . . . only thing we can do is quarantine the pyramid. Evacuate everybody far enough away that its powers—the Krim call it *prukrin*, which seems to refer to some kind of psychic energies, which bears some similarities, as near as I can determine, to Jung's notions concerning the collective unconscious although—"

Blither, blither—damn all scholars, anyway!

" . . . hasten to add that I'm just speculating. But what I *do* know is that it relies on psychic input from the people it snatches. And it can only snatch people within a certain range. So evacuation—quarantine—is an effective way—"

Tremelo saw Liz De Beer come up behind Jerry, cradling her arm. She was scowling at him. The expression held an odd mixture of fondness and exasperation, almost like that of a wife dealing with one of her husband's foibles.

"Stop lecturing, Jerry!" she said firmly. "You're supposed to tell Lamont's wife about him, remember? And if you blather all day you'll blow our date." She planted a kiss on his neck and moved away from the camera.

The scientist on the TV screen jerked to a sudden halt in his logorrhea. A look of surprise and chagrin crossed Lukacs' face.

"Oh. Sorry. Forgot." Lukacs leaned forward and peered intently into the camera. "Mrs. Jackson, are you there?"

Marie stiffened. Her hand covered her mouth.

Jerry Lukacs' face broke into a smile. "Well, I hope so. Anyway, I just wanted to tell you that Lamont's fine. He's back with the rest of us and in perfect health. In fact—"

Marie sobbed, once. Then, her eyes leaking tears of joy, she pressed her face into Tremelo's shoulder and began hugging the elderly physicist. He returned the hug with his own, stroking her hair, while he continued to watch Lukacs.

The disheveled, scholarly tough-looking face on the screen turned away for a moment. There seemed to be a lot of noise in the background.

"In fact, I'd say he's having a run of luck at the casino's tables. Big run of luck, from the sound of it."

A balding, shrewd-eyed, managerial face thrust itself into the camera, puffing on a huge cigar. "Made over a million bucks so far. Remember, folks—this is all happening at the Luxor casino. *The Luxor.* Best casino in the world!"

The face pulled away and Jerry's visage reappeared from the fading cloud of blue smoke. "Yeah, he's fine. And as you can see"— his face colored a bit—"Dr. Elizabeth De Beer made it back also, in good shape except for a broken arm. And so did Sergeant Anibal Cruz and Corporal Jim McKenna. Even got new girlfriends."

The camera panned sideways, catching Liz, Cruz and McKenna sitting at nearby tables. Liz was ignoring the camera altogether, while she practically swigged a large cup of coffee. Corporal McKenna couldn't really be seen properly, because he was fiercely kissing a young woman perched on his lap wearing nothing but a bathrobe.

Sergeant Cruz, on the other hand, was grinning at the camera. His arm was around a beautiful woman sitting on a chair right next to him. Both he and the woman had children perched on their laps.

"Yeah, that's right," he announced. "I'd like to introduce everybody to my new family. The kids are called Priones and Neoptolmeus. My old lady's name is Medea. That's *the* 'Medea,' by the way, so if *la migra*'s got any wild ideas about deporting them 'cause they don't got papers, think again."

A new voice intruded. "*Who is this La Migra?*" it demanded, booming. A dwarf stepped into the camera's field of vision and stood by Cruz's side. For all its short stature, there seemed something enormously powerful about the figure. The fact that the lion-looking face was scowling ferociously added to the effect.

"Someone threatens you, friend Cruz?" the leonine dwarf demanded.

The sergeant shrugged. "Immigration and Naturalization Service. We swarthy types just call it *la migra.*" Cruz looked back at the camera, grinning widely, and jerked his head at the dwarf. "Let me introduce Bes, also. He's an Egyptian god."

Then, to Bes: "*La migra* are pretty much the world's champion dwarf tossers."

The camera seemed to shake a bit and move backward, as if the cameraman was staggered by the incredible roar of fury which erupted from Bes. A moment later, still a bit shakily, the camera followed the dwarf god's progress as Bes bounded over to a nearby statue of a hieracosphinx and proceeded to . . .

"He's *demolishing* that thing," whispered one of the technicians in the room. "Crushing a *statue* with his bare hands."

Tremelo gave Marie a last little squeeze. "You okay, now?" He felt her head nod, and heard the happy little gurgle. "Better get me the President, Marie. I can see we're going to need him to grant some people political asylum, too. Before those idiots at the INS get it into their heads to pull a raid."

The image on the TV switched to an outside view, from a different camera. Two giant winged snakes—dragons?—were being fed by a line of hotel employees bearing platters. A huge sphinx was practically mobbed with tourists, tossing the monster candy bars when they failed to answer its riddles properly.

"Quick, Marie!" hissed Tremelo. "The President'll have to invoke the Endangered Species Act, too."

Marie was watching the screen now. Her little gurgle of happiness turned into a riotous laugh.

"Yeah—but which species is being endangered?"

After she left, Tremelo shook his head. "Damned if I know. Oh, brave new world, that hath such people in it."

One of Miggy's assistants was staring at him. "What're we going to do, Professor?" He pointed at the TV screen, which was now filled again with the face of Jerry Lukacs, resuming his lecture. "If that guy's right, we can't *touch* that damned pyramid."

Tremelo shrugged. "Do about it? Get us all on a priority flight to Nellis Air Force Base, for starters. We can talk about it on our way to Las Vegas."

He burst into laughter himself, now. "What the hell? We'll live with it, I imagine. Just another illegal alien, that's all."

Miggy grinned at the TV, which was now showing an image of the Krim pyramid. "No, that's politically incorrect! Let's call it the undocumented interstellar probe. Frustrated because it can't find a job."

ACKNOWLEDGEMENTS

First and foremost this book owes its existence to my wife, Barbara—proofreader, idea test-pilot and authorial panic tolerator extraordinaire. Between her, Kathy Holton, proofreader of infinite patience, and Eric, whose idea all of this was in the first place, they guided my vague and wandering steps through this mythological mazurka. . . . As usual, Eric and I worked closely and argued mightily about this book. The erudite bits are Eric's. The weird and silly bits are mine.

For her sin of choosing to take her honours in classical Latin and Greek, my sister Helen was endlessly plagued about everything from mythology to pronunciation. And on the rare occasions my odd questions were too bizarre for her or she'd managed to sneak away from a telephone, there was Pam (Pogo) Poggiani, the Baen author's fantastic reference system.

My thanks to Judith Lasker and Ron Kohut for their wine help, and Judith for the photographs of Las Vegas, which inspired the final solution and scene.

I must also thank Fred Geisler, Andy Mendes, Buz Ozburn, John Ringo and Mike Spehar for their attempts to explain the U.S. military to me. I'm still confused, alas. The errors remain mine, the accuracy theirs. Mike, an expert on the subject, provided us with a draft of the HASTY RECEIVER EXECUTE ORDER which appears in Chapter 14.

Eric has also asked me to acknowledge several institutions

which figure in the novel, for their cooperation. The characters who appear in the novel are all fictitious, of course, but the depiction of the physical setting is as accurate as we could make it. We especially want to thank:

The Oriental Institute, particularly Tim Cashion and Emily Napolitano, respectively the Director of Development and the Membership Coordinator. Tim gave Eric a guided tour of the Institute, and suggested the air handler room as the logical place for Lamont Jackson to begin his part of the story. The Oriental Institute's Museum, for those not familiar with it, is one of the world's great museums for the art and archaeology of the ancient Near East. The gigantic Assyrian Bull, before which Jerry Lukacs and Lamont meet in Part I, is worth the price of admission alone. And, over the years, Eric has purchased for his wife Lucille any number of fine items of jewelry from the Institute's excellent gift shop, the Suq.

The Regenstein Library, especially its Entry Control Supervisor Mark Davis, who very kindly provided Eric with a day pass so that he could study the exact location where the Krim pyramid materializes.

Lieutenant James F. Stasik, watch commander for the University of Chicago Police Department, who took the time from a busy day to explain their procedures to Eric.

Various departments at the University of Chicago, including the Department of Ecology and Evolution, High Energy Physics, Astronomy and Astrophysics Center, Enrico Fermi Institute and the Laboratory for Astrophysics and Space Research. Special thanks are due to Professor Nien-chu C. Yang.

Finally, the management of the Luxor hotel and casino, especially their publicist Paul Speirs. When Eric visited Las Vegas and the Luxor, in order to get a good picture of the setting at the end of the novel, Paul was very friendly and helpful.

On the subject of nuclear devices and science in general, Conrad Chu once again came to this poor biologist's rescue. He also crystallized into words an opinion I have long held, which forms an intrinsic part of this book. I quote: "In the face of an unknown, governments have been known to act irrationally. If this unknown scares them, then the government's reactions have tended to be even more irrational and often uncharacteristically destructive without regard for the consequences. As long as the people in charge have little respect for science, scientists or engineers, I can image all sorts of stupidity, including the use of nuclear weapons and even biological attacks under the guise of 'trying to accomplish something.' "

Scary, but in my opinion very true.

Dave Freer
Eshowe
KwaZulu-Natal
South Africa

APPENDIX

Note: Mythology is by its very nature a vague and contentious subject. This book is no way intended to be a serious study of it. Myths often appear in various guises and opinions differ widely. Actually, even spellings differ widely. Those myths or mythological characters described in this appendix are simply the versions used in what was intended to be a lighthearted adventure novel. This is by no means an exhaustive or detailed listing, and we have often simply taken one form of an enormous number of myths.

Hellenic and Pre-Hellenic:

Aeëtes: Medea's father. A magician and king of Colchis, son of Helios.

Aeolus: The Ruler of the Winds. He gave Odysseus the windsack in which all the inclement winds were contained. Supposedly, Odysseus' men opened the bag because they were curious at the contents which they supposed to be rich treasures. So, at least, Odysseus later claimed—as always, blaming others for his misfortunes. (See Odysseus, below.)

Apollo: Greek god. Young, handsome and "insanely arrogant" (Homeric hymn).

Arachne: Daughter of Idmon of Colophon (a city in Lydia), a weaver of great renown, who had a run-in with Athena.

409

In the weaving competition between them, Arachne wove as her theme the philandering and sordid tricks of the gods. Her weaving was flawless. Athena—with the justice, generosity, and nobility of spirit which was characteristic of the Olympians—tore the work in shreds, destroyed the loom and turned Arachne into a spider, doomed to weave forever and draw her thread from her own body.

Argonautica: The quest for the golden fleece in which Jason meets and later marries Medea. See Medea.

Ares: The god of war.

Athena: Warrior goddess, and perhaps the champion sore loser in all of mythology. She took the side of the Achaeans against the Trojans because she lost a beauty contest. As usual with the Hellenic deities, a mortal took the blame for the ensuing carnage—Helen. In much the same manner, Arachne was turned into a spider because Athena lost the weaving contest. She was particularly disgruntled, according to some versions of the legend, because Arachne's weaving was not only superior in form but in content: the insolent girl had the nerve to accurately depict the sins of the gods—which were legion.

Circe: The sorceress from the *Odyssey.* The daughter of Helios and sister to Aeëtes, and aunt to Medea. She lived on the island of Aeaea, attended by four nymphs, in a house or castle of well-built stone. In the glades around the castle roamed wild beasts: boar, wolves, leopards and lions— all apparently tame. She turned the first greedy group of Odysseus' sailors into swine. But because of the intervention of Hermes, who gave Odysseus the protective herb "moly" (possibly garlic), she failed to transform him as well.

Gaea: "Deep-breasted Gaea" was the Earth herself.

Hades: Hades was the king of the netherworld, often also referred to as Hades. The underworld was not the equivalent of Hell for the punishment of sinners, nor was its ruler the devil.

Hecate: While the name has become associated with witch-crones, originally Hecate was an earth-goddess from Asia Minor.

Hesiod makes her one of the Titans, who sided with
Olympus against the giants. She was associated with the
moon, spells and the dead. Through her role as an earth-
goddess, she later became the goddess of spells and
charms.

Helios: The sun-god—a charioteer who drove the sun across the
sky.

Hera: The sister and wife of Zeus. Possibly an original matriarchal goddess who was absorbed by the invaders from
the north and married off to Zeus. Saddled with an
unfaithful husband, and children for whom she seems to
have had no affection, it seems to have been the original miserable marriage. She plainly resented Zeus' endless sexual adventures, and spent a great deal of time being
spitefully cruel to her "rivals" and their children. Zeus,
a charming fellow in his own right, beat her (and her lame
son Hephaestus, when he tried to aid her) and chained
her up when she tried to punish him. So she confined
herself to acts of vengeance against the objects of Zeus'
amorous adventures, many of whom were outright rape
victims.

Hermes: Envoy, herald and messenger of Zeus. Not above deception and treachery. Has winged sandals and a winged
helmet.

Jason: The husband of Medea, who put her aside in order to
marry Glauce, daughter of King Creon of Corinth. As
Medea was not a Hellene, his oaths were not considered
binding.

Lotus-eaters: People encountered by Odysseus on the coast of
Libya. The lotus-fruit or cakes were reputed to have the
property of making one stop remembering the past or
caring about one's home, or future, and remain content
to stay and browse on the lotus forever.

Medea: One of the most villainous characters described in Greek
Mythology. Medea the sorceress was a princess and priestess of Hecate, living in the kingdom of Colchis (on the
Black Sea, present day Georgia). She fell in love with Jason,
leader of the Argonauts, and it was only with her help

that Jason was able to accomplish the "impossible" tasks set by her father Aeëtes and gain the golden fleece. In return, Jason promised to marry her. According to legend, in their flight from Colchis, Medea and Jason were trapped by Absyrtus, Medea's half brother. Under the flag of truce Medea and Jason murdered Absyrtus, and subsequently delayed Aeëtes by casting the pieces behind them for the king to gather up for burial. On their route back to Hellas, Medea and Jason stopped at Aeaea, the isle of the enchantress Circe, who was Medea's aunt and sister to King Aeëtes. Circe gave them forgiveness for the blood-debt. On their return, Medea is supposed to have contrived the murder of King Pelias by his daughters (by convincing them that the aging king could be restored to youth by chopping him up and boiling him with certain herbs). After living for some time with Jason at Ephyra, and bearing him two children, Jason told her he was going to set her aside and marry Glauce, the daughter of the king of Corinth. This was perfectly permissible as she was a non-Hellene and had no rights. Medea is then supposed to have contrived the death of Glauce (with a dress of gold cloth and a coronet), accidentally killing her father too. Medea is then supposed to have killed her children and fled Corinth in a winged chariot drawn by dragons.

In short, Medea is both the all-time Wicked Woman as well as the all-time Wronged Wife. Given that the surviving legends are Hellenic in origin, and obviously self-serving, we cheerfully decided that Medea must have been slandered and set the story straight.

Oceanus: The Titan Oceanus married his sister Tethys. Father of the Oceanids and all the rivers, ruler of the waters, Homer regards him as inferior to none but Zeus. Nonetheless, the Olympians established their empire over the water under Poseidon, and Oceanus was banished to a distant retirement.

Odysseus: Known as "cunning Odysseus," the prince of Ithaca. Odysseus is frequently lauded for his resourcefulness, strength and courage—and by no one more than himself. Less well focused on, but nonetheless clearly shown in the text, is the fact that Odysseus was in poor control of his men. His ability to captain them at all is called into question firstly on a freebooting pirate raid against the Cicones, then in his men's behavior with the windsack, and finally with the killing of Helios' cattle on Thrinicia, in direct defiance of orders. Odysseus' boastfulness after his blinding of the Cyclops incurred the wrath of Poseidon. His rare captaincy insured that covering a distance of less than 500 miles took ten years; and that, of the 600 original voyagers, only one survived.

Not surprisingly, this one was the captain, who also recounted the stories in which he appears as a hero. Everything that went wrong was entirely due to his men's folly. The year spent on Aeaea wining and dining and enjoying the sexual favors of Circe was, of course, a necessary break after spending ten years away in Troy.

Later Greek and Roman authors, perhaps working on material no longer available to us, paint a far less flattering picture, showing Odysseus as a ruthless and self-serving politician. Even within the *Odyssey*, much is made of the need for Odysseus to return home. This is not because the kingdom requires his wise governance, or because he has been away from his wife and child for twenty years. No. It is because the suitors for his wife's hand are consuming his wealth.

Odyssey: An epic poem ascribed to Homer dealing with the return of Odysseus from the fall of Troy to his native Ithaca.

Olympians: The Olympian pantheon, a hierarchy under Zeus, comprised the twelve great gods and goddesses: Zeus himself, Poseidon, Hephaestus, Hermes, Ares, Apollo, Hera, Athena, Artemis, Hestia, Demeter and Aphrodite. Gods, though prone to all the moral weaknesses of the flesh (to put it mildly), had none of the physical problems. Their blood was replaced by a more fluid substance, ichor, which kept their bodies imperishable and incorruptible. Wounds—no matter how serious—would heal, and they stayed forever young. All in all, they are perhaps the perfect example of the old saw: *there ain't no justice.*

Pan: An ancient goaty god associated with goatherds, shepherds and flocks . . . panics and musical instruments. The Pan of Mysia in Asia Minor was Priapus . . . a phallic gentleman.

Persephone: The wife of Hades, king of the underworld. She created winter. Also called Kore, when she wasn't being wintery.

Poseidon: The Olympian sea god who replaced the Titan Oceanus. Poseidon was brother of Zeus and Hades. As well as the sea, he also had responsibility for earthquakes. He was married to blue-eyed Amphitrite, but this didn't stop his sexual adventures with other men and women for an instant. He was a vengeful, spiteful piece of work.

Prometheus: A Titan. Possibly the most attractive of Greek mythological figures, he was called variously the friend of mankind and the champion of mankind. Prometheus means "foresight." The Titan made something of a habit of getting the better of Zeus, for mankind's benefit. Zeus did not take kindly to his thefts, trickery, and raising of mankind above the animals. First, he had Pandora made and sent her to try to seduce the Titan. Prometheus refused her, but his brother Epimentheus took her in. She carried with her a gift from the gods—a vase full of all the woes of mankind. Once again bent on godlike behavior, Zeus sent a great flood to kill off mankind. Prometheus, however, had had his children construct an ark. Zeus then had the Titan chained to a pillar on Mount Caucasus, and sent his eagle to feed on Prometheus' liver every day. The Titan endured for thirty thousand years before he was freed—in the original legends, by Hercules.

Proteus: The old man of the sea. A son of Oceanus and Tethys, he lived on the island of Pharos off the Egyptian coast. The seal-shepherd had the gift of prophecy and the ability to change his shape at will.

Scylla and Charybdis: Charybdis was a terrible whirlpool which swallowed ships. Scylla was a monster with six long necks and six awful heads each with triple rows of teeth. Ships passing through the strait between them were doomed either to be swallowed by the whirlpool or lose six rowers.

Selene: Moon goddess. Various representations show her with a chariot, horse, white mule or bull. The mule transported the moon.

Sirens: One of the perils faced by Odysseus was passing the Sirens, who lured sailors to their deaths with their sweet singing. Odysseus and his companions survived this, by them tying him to the mast and having their ears stopped with wax. The early descriptions are of half bird/half women, sitting in a green field piled with human bones.

Sphinx: The Greek sphinx was depicted with the head and chest of a woman, enormous eagle wings and the body of a lion. Associated with combat and death. The most famous Greek sphinx was the Theban sphinx, renowned for her riddling and eating of travelers.

Tempe: The valley between Mt. Ossa and Mt. Olympus.

Thrinicia: An island on which the sun-god Helios kept his cattle. After surviving Scylla and Charybdis, Odysseus and his crew made landfall here. Despite warnings from Circe and Teiresias, when they were trapped there by stormy weather his crew slaughtered some of the cattle of Helios. As a punishment the black ship was sunk and all but Odysseus lost their lives.

Throttler: The name of the Theban sphinx.

Teiresias: The blind seer of Thebes, whose spirit Odysseus went to consult in Hades.

Titans: The children of Uranus and Gaea who held sway before the Olympians. Godlike, there is no record of them being worshiped. To the contrary, they seem to have encouraged egalitarian behavior. The Titans took up arms against the Olympians, but were defeated and banished with few exceptions.

Triton: Son of Poseidon and Amphitrite, he had the head, shoulders and arms of a man and the scales and fins of a fish. He rode a chariot pulled by crayfish-clawed horses. He was renowned for frightening giants with the sounds he made by blowing his conch—a shell adapted to be a very crude and noisy trumpet. Also marine genii of similar appearance.

Tyche: The goddess of chance. Her attribute is abundance, and she is the daughter of Oceanus and Tethys. One is prompted to wonder if this is why fishing and luck should go hand in hand.

Typhoeus: The last child of Gaea. Sent by Gaea to avenge the defeat of the Titans, he succeeded for a time in imprisoning Zeus. He was eventually trapped under Mt. Etna.

Zeus: Supreme god of the Olympians. A flinger of thunderbolts. Obviously the ancient Greek powers-that-be had their priests shape the pantheon to reinforce the strict aristocratic and hierarchical forms of their society. Zeus was the boss, and tolerated none of the Titan egalitarianism. His rule did evoke some ire from his grandmother, Gaea (who had seen to his upbringing), who sent Typhoeus to put him in his place. Eventually Zeus was victorious. The lord of all seems to have spent a great deal of time beating up rival claimants to Olympus, such as the Titans and the Giants, behaving just as a model aristocrat should. Married to Hera, Zeus' pastime of infidelities, seduction and outright rape would take far too long to list here.

Egyptian:

Amemait: The devourer. A monster with a crocodile snout, part lion, part hippopotamus, all nasty, the devourer of unjustified souls.

Anubis: Jackal-headed Anubis. The son of Nephthys, by Osiris. Usher in the hall of judgment and inventor of embalming techniques.

Bes: A dwarf-god, the protector of man against evil spirits and dangerous beasts. He is always portrayed grinning and bearded, with a topknot adorned with ostrich plumes and a leopard-skin cloak. Fond of fighting and

dancing, his symbol was used to protect against dangerous beasts, and evil spirits that haunted dreams. He
presided over marriages, and the makeup and adornment
of women, as well as protecting pregnant mothers. Revered
in Punt (Ethiopia) and Carthage as well as Egypt, the little
hell-raiser was definitely one of the most attractive figures in ancient mythology.

Harmakhis: The correct name of the huge stone sphinx of Gizeh.

Isis: Moon goddess, sorceress, sister-wife of Osiris. It was she who
gathered up the pieces of the dismembered Osiris (except
for his phallus—which had been eaten by the crabs) and
sewed him back together again.

Min: An ancient god, always represented with his phallus erect.
The protector of travelers and fertility.

Nephthys: The personification of the desert margin, arid but
sometimes fertile. Sister to Isis, married to her brother
Set, by whom she had no children. She got Osiris (also
her brother, and husband to her sister Isis) drunk, and
took advantage of him to conceive Anubis. She abandoned
the child at birth. She helped with the embalming of
Osiris, despite the fact that he was murdered by her
husband. It's all very complicated. . . .

Osiris: A vegetation god, personifying harvest and rebirth of
seedlings (perhaps this explained his greenish skin). He
was married to Isis. Osiris was the enemy of violence and
the bringer of civilization. He was murdered and later
dismembered by Set. Sewed together and reanimated by
Isis, he then went on to become ruler of the kingdom
of the dead. He presided over the weighing of souls.

Sebek: A crocodile-headed divinity, who shared Set's evil reputation. His principal sanctuary had a lake with a real
crocodile, Petesuchos.

Sekhmet: The lioness-headed goddess of war. Bloodthirsty and
merciless.

Set: Red-haired and pale-skinned, rough and rude, with the head
of the typhonean beast (a curved snout with square-cut
ears). Set is the eternal adversary, the destroyer, the desert.

Sphinx: Egyptian. A lion-bodied, human-headed creature. Some authorities think they may have had their origins as protective desert genii. The sphinxes from Egypt, Asia Minor and Greece share common origins.

Tauret: Hippopotamus goddess. Childbirth and protection.

Thoth: Ibis-headed Thoth (also sometimes represented as the dog-headed ape). The herald and scribe of the gods, the keeper of records, and the first magician. A pedant of note.